UNTOUCHED

UNTOUCHED

JAYME BEAN

This novel is a work of fiction. Names, characters, businesses, places, events, and incidents are either products of the author's imagination or used in a fictitious manner. Any resemblances to actual persons, living or dead, or actual events is purely coincidental.

To request permissions, contact the author at Author@JaymeBeanAuthor.com

Hardcover: 978-1-7365329-0-4
Paperback: 978-1-7365329-2-8
Ebook: 978-7365329-1-1

First edition

Edited by Charlie Knight (CKnightWrites.com)
Cover art by Juan Padron (JuanJPadron.com)
Index card artwork by DaysCreativeDesigns (Dayscreativedesign.com)
Interior artwork by Gordon Johnson via Pixabay.com

CONTENT WARNING

This book contains strong themes and depictions of panic and anxiety.

To Wesley,
May you always keep your heart open to the next great adventure

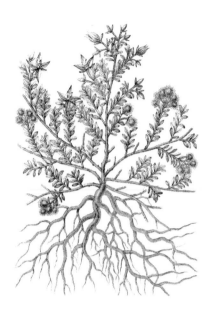

"Many plant pathogens act like 'silent thieves' who want to steal money locked inside of a bank vault. These thieves use specialized tools designed to disable the bank's security system and unlock the vault without being detected. In a similar way, many pathogens establish intimate connections with their hosts in order to suppress plant defenses and promote the release of nutrients."

An Overview of Plant Defenses against Pathogens and Herbivores
-Brian C. Freeman and Gwyn A. Beattie

"And into the forest I go, to lose my mind and find my soul"
-John Muir

1

Raindrops fell lightly and steadily on the tattered tarp covering of the motocar—not uncommon in the tropics of Peru. It rained several times a day, every day. The tires kicked water into the stands on the sidewalks, splattering fresh bananas, fish, and various meats for sale. Despite the weather, the driver steered effortlessly in between the other vehicles and pedestrians on the dampened bustling streets of Iquitos. The sweet but putrid smell of fruit and trash filled the tight alleyways as they passed.

Dr. Julia Morrow pointed out key locations of the city to the two graduate students accompanying her. Botany student Marisol Lugo excitedly looked from all angles of the motocar as she took in the city. Her father made sure she knew that she was the pride of her family back home in Miami. She was the first of her family to go to college, not to mention being chosen from a competitive pool for the opportunity to travel abroad for her doctorate. Marisol held onto the edge of the seat as the cars cut in and around them, wincing when they drifted too close. She was no stranger to hectic traffic, but cruising down the streets on a motorcycle-turned-makeshift taxi was a new experience for her. Iquitos was just the beginning. They would soon be traveling up the Amazon and into the jungle to complete their research.

With his head in his textbook, David Harris didn't care for the atmosphere of the filthy and overcrowded city. He missed his iPhone, his apartment, and, most of all, *air conditioning*. If he didn't require this research trip to support his thesis, he would be sitting at a five-star restaurant enjoying a steak...and a real steak, not the sad excuse for meat served out of the carts on the street. David often wondered why he chose tropical biology as his field of study. He detested being outdoors. Even as a child, he preferred to be inside with his nose in a book. Enticed by works such as *Tarzan of the Apes* and *Around the World in Eighty Days*, his interest quickly shifted toward the rainforest, which was right where he was headed now.

The motocar swerved tightly around a corner, almost toppling the book from David's hands, causing him to grip the sidebars for balance. Cursing, he closed his book and resigned it to his backpack, making sure to keep his neatly filed research papers dry. Dr. Morrow raised her voice over the drum of the engine as she explained the route they were taking. They were to cross through the center of the city where they would stop for a quick bite to eat before heading to the docks to catch their boat.

Primitive speed boat is more like it, thought David as he tried to listen. Even though he was agitated, he admired the professor. He enjoyed listening to her speak, which was one of the initial reasons he took several of her courses. David liked how she tried to suppress her southern accent and how it expressed itself when she was excited. It was easy to see how everyone on campus considered her their secret crush. *Or not so secret*. Every online rating for her had a flame reaction next to her name, as though the headshot on her profile wasn't indication enough. Out in the field, she hardly had the same attraction for him. Her long strawberry blonde hair was all tied up and tucked under a wide-brimmed safari hat. Not only did the hat hold her hair, but it also covered her slim, freckled face and green eyes. David didn't like it. He glanced away and tried to picture her back in the lecture hall in a tight skirt and button-up blouse. That was his favorite.

"Where will we be stopping to eat?" asked Marisol as they bounced along the cobblestones.

"There's this one place on the Plaza de Armas that serves American food as well as a full regional menu. Although, I highly suggest getting something local as we certainly will *not* be having any American luxuries once we head upriver. It's a common tourist place, as so many here are, but it's a decent local hangout, too."

Without much warning, the motocar screeched to a stop, spraying mud out from the wheels.

"And out we go kids! Aca está su propina, muchas gracias." Dr. Morrow ushered the two college students off the motocar while handing the driver a few soles.

Dr. Morrow had made sure that everyone in her party understood the currency and what was socially acceptable before any travel arrangements had been made. She had learned through experience that "winging it," like she did when she was younger didn't always work out for the best. She wanted them to know it wasn't uncommon to be hustled as Americans, especially without being fluent. But for now, at least the two were listening, even if the stuck-up Harris kid had been grumbling incessantly since they got off the twin-engine at the airport. The look on his face when he realized that "taxi" meant a tarp-covered steel frame attached to an old motorcycle was priceless. Dr. Morrow knew it would be a long three months but that they would walk away better people for it. She certainly had.

She joined Marisol and David around the corner, huddled together under a tin roof. Rolling her eyes, she pulled them out from cover and pointed to a large sign that boldly stated *Ari's Burger*.

"Sure sounds like an American place," said David.

"You'd be surprised what you can find here. True, this is probably one of the most American places you can eat, but their selection is amazing." Dr. Morrow motioned to one of the tables.

"Grab a seat and a menu. I recommend the juices as a drink. They are to die for."

The three sat at a bright red table with equally bright red chairs. The walls had lighted pictures of the menu items above the kitchen, similar to a Chinese restaurant or fast-food joint. Marisol twisted in her seat as she looked at the illuminated photos. Small amounts of saliva pooled under her tongue as she contemplated the menu.

"I know you said go for local, but I'm having a good old-fashioned cheeseburger and fries," stated David. "And a Coke. I could definitely go for a nice, cold Coke."

A dark, petite woman came over to the table and began speaking in Spanish. She wore a white and red apron over a white tee shirt and brown shorts.

"Jugo de camu camu, una ensalada de palmito, y una cesta de patatas fritas para mí," Dr. Morrow rattled off to the waitress.

"También tendré la causa y un jugo de camu camu, por favor," followed Marisol.

"Cheeseburger and a fry basket. Um, and a Coca Cola please," finished David, kicking himself for never choosing to learn Spanish. "What did you order, Dr. Morrow? I didn't realize you were so fluent."

"Despite my southern twang, Mr. Harris," she smirked, "I speak very fluent Spanish and quite a good bit of the local dialects. I got a palm heart salad, something you won't ever find served in the States, at least not like this. And a simple basket of fries. Gotta have an appetite when you can't bring snacks aboard."

"Wait. We can't bring food on the boat?"

"Well, considering it's a five-hour trip up the Amazon and its tributaries, I would suggest *not* bringing any food that would attract wildlife or other dangers."

"Other dangers like what?"

Dr. Morrow chuckled to herself at his stunning lack of research on traveling in an unknown place. "There are pirates, authorities that aren't too keen on researchers like ourselves, and

I'm sure we'll come across villages who will be none too pleased to see us bringing foreign trash to their pristine wilderness. But those are just some hypothetical occurrences."

"South America isn't quite like your Hamptons upbringing, is it, Dave?" Marisol teased as she eyed the plates of food arriving at the table.

"It's *David*. You don't see me calling you Mary, do you? And I certainly didn't expect a lounge chair and poolside cocktail on this trip, but I also didn't expect *pirates*."

"You'll see soon enough how great 'the wild' is," Dr. Morrow chuckled, waving air quotes with a fry tucked between her fingers. She popped the fry into her mouth and let out a small grumble of pleasure. "Now eat up; we have a boat to catch!"

The three quickly worked their way through their meals, eager both from hunger and pressures of time. They would have to catch another motocar to take them further down the docks to meet their boat. As they laid their money on the table and gathered their things, a loud snap of thunder shook the building. Everyone jumped, including the waitress gathering the coins. Dr. Morrow meandered to the front and stuck her head out of the open door as the sky opened up yet again. Torrents of rain clashed onto the tin roofs of the city center. She looked back at her students and let out a heavy sigh. She knew this would delay their trip. No boater would be willing to head out on the river in this weather. This would surely cut into the first crucial stages of their project.

"Guess we'll have to find a place to hoof it tonight," she said, looking over at David and Marisol. They had come up behind her while she was deep in thought about their next steps. She grinned as David inched further back as to not be splashed by the hard rain. "Let's find a hotel and get to a phone. We'll have to reschedule our boat for the morning." With that, she strode confidently out into the rain with her hand in the air to flag down a taxi.

Not a minute later, a motocar came screeching to a halt, kicking water up at the sidewalk. As the three squeezed inside, the gears churned back up, and the taxi was off again, speeding down the street and weaving in between cars. There was no escaping the downpour once they were on the road. Not only were the side flaps on the motocar open, but the splashback from the other bikes and cars inevitably found its way onto the passengers. David struggled to keep his backpack on his lap while also trying to hold on to the bars and avoid sliding into Marisol, who was held tight in the middle. As soon as he was settled, the driver pulled down around a sharp corner, jostling everyone into each other. David quickly grabbed up his bag and clutched it tight against his chest.

"What are you so protective about with your bag anyways?" Marisol said. "It's not like we're carrying anything breakable. All of our equipment is already waiting for us at the base."

Ignoring her remarks, David turned away and slid further up against the sidebars. He couldn't count down to the end of this trip fast enough. *Why didn't I just study architecture and go on that trip to Rome...or Paris...or anywhere else?* David sighed and let his mind wander far away from the humid air, Marisol, and her constantly judgy prodding.

The motocar jolted to a stop against the sidewalk as the rain continued to pour off the roof and into the large puddles pooling in the street. Dr. Morrow hopped out and started collecting her bags from the back, pulling them free from the bungees that strapped them to the motocar cover. David and Marisol hesitantly looked around at what appeared to be a simple storefront. As they glanced back at the professor, she simply gave them a sideways up-nod, signaling them to get up and out. Shrugging at each other, they scooped up their packs and hopped out on to the curb. After she paid the driver, Dr. Morrow ushered the two students to a small door in the brick face.

"Welcome to our refuge! This is where we'll be spending the

night…or at least hunkering down until this storm settles. Hopefully, we'll be able to get in touch with the lodge and let them know that we won't be right on schedule." She smiled as a soft laugh escaped her. "Kind of ironic that we sent all of our satellite phones in the bags, huh?"

Despite the rugged exterior, the lobby was brightly colored and had several couches and finely carved tables. David and Marisol fell into a pair of plush armchairs while Dr. Morrow spoke to the desk clerk. Marisol reached into her duffle bag and pulled out a towel, quickly tossing it into David's lap. Before he could offer any retort, she was up and headed over to the front desk.

David never understood her. She was loud and brash and always had something to say. They had shared several classes at the university and yet they never spoke more than two words to each other until being selected for this trip. *Not that we'd be in the same group anyway*, he thought as he let his mind drift again. Cold water dripped onto his nose, calling attention back to the fact that he was drenched and cold. He took the towel and ran it through his hair, trying to soak up at least some of the excess water dripping down onto his face.

As he looked back up, Marisol and Dr. Morrow were approaching with large keys in hand. "Alright then…David, here you go," Dr. Morrow offered while extending a set of room keys. "You'll be sharing a suite with Marisol." David's eyes darted up to Marisol, but her gaze was focused elsewhere. "I'll be down the hall in the last room. It's still early, so I say we clean up, get changed, and I can give you a little tour of Iquitos."

David tossed his backpack onto the bed and let out a heavy sigh before collapsing backwards onto the mattress.

A trip around town? Great…just another set of clothes to get wet again. I'd kill to just have the night alone. I could read. I could sleep. I could...I don't know, just be. *I can't imagine this tiny-ass city has anything worth exploring.*

Feeling his still-damp clothes pressing against his skin, he let out another long sigh and pulled himself back up. "Stop daydreaming and get up," he said into the air. He was used to living in his own head, always talking to himself, daydreaming, reliving scenarios and how he could have changed them. It was normal for him to mumble aloud when he was alone, and heaven knows he didn't have any friends to worry about teasing him if someone overheard. His family therapist used to tell him it was because his parents were always busy working, and that he had to make his own company.

"Most kids make imaginary friends, Davie, you just like being your own friend," she used to say. That was never any help. The kids in school made fun of him. They called him weird and a loser. He never got invited over after school...not that his parents would have been around to give him permission. His dad, Dr. James Harris III, was always on a business trip somewhere. Usually Europe. Or Asia.

David would always ask if he could go on his dad's adventures with him, but his father never entertained that nonsense. "Back to your studies!" or "When you make something of yourself you can create your own adventures," were usually the responses. At nine years old, those words were soul-crushing. So, he delved into his books. He had mountains of them in his room at any given time. His mother would always yell at him for leaving them "strewn about," but she wasn't home enough to make a difference either. So, David left a book in its place as soon as he was finished, usually somewhere in the sitting room.

Some of the only memories of his mother at home, outside of lecturing him about his piles of books, were in between parties and charity events. As a self-proclaimed socialite, even Christmas wasn't off-limits. "Christmas is the biggest event of the year, Davie. Think of all the children who don't have presents and families to go home to." Who was he to argue? He got presents, and they *did* have a Christmas morning. It was usually only an hour once he woke up, and generally she was the only one home to celebrate. By mid-morning, she was off getting her hair and nails done, and by noon, she was out the door in full gala wardrobe.

He'd spend the rest of the day reading, staring out at the snow from the comfort of the sitting room or the sunroom. At least in the sunroom, he had some sense of being outside. His favorite days in there were at the cusp of fall. The leaves were changing, the air was crisp, and the temperature was perfect. He loved curling up in the hammock with a cup of hot cocoa and a book about the wilds of the world.

Now he was definitely in the wilds of the world...or at least would be soon. *This is your chance for an adventure. Buck up.* Peeling off his wet shirt, David headed to the bathroom to take a hot shower before Professor Morrow's *Tour de Iquitos*. He threw his shirt on the chair in the corner of his room and hung his cargo pants off the closet door to help them dry. They were told to only bring a week's worth of clothes to preserve bag space and that they would be hand-washing in the river as they went. "One down, six to go," he mumbled.

As David pulled open the bathroom door, he was met with a towel thrown straight at his face.

"Hey! Don't you knock? It's a suite, remember?" David pulled the soggy towel off his face to see Marisol pulling a tank top on. "Unless you're trying to sneak a peek." She shimmied her shoulders towards him while a smirk danced on her lips.

David rolled his eyes in response. "Wow, really? Think I'm good, thanks."

"Well, at least I'll have something to look at once we're out in the woods," she said, her eyebrows bouncing up and down. "Who knew you had anything going on under those preppy polos? Good for you."

"Oh my God, stop." His hands instinctively folded around his stomach as he turned and headed back into his room, swinging the door closed behind him.

9

As soon as it latched shut, it swung open again, this time with Marisol playfully striding into his room.

"What are you doing? Get out!" David snipped back at her as he unzipped his backpack, scrambling for his clothes.

"Chill out, man. You know we're going to be camping in tents and bathing in rivers, right? I think seeing you in your little boxer briefs is the least of my worries about how much I have to see of you."

"Can you please just get out?" His voice cracked slightly at the end, the words barely escaping him.

Marisol sidled up next to him and reached into his bag amid his hurried hands and pulled out a shirt and handed it to him. "Here. I wasn't trying to upset you." Her voice softened. "If it helps, I grew up with three brothers. There's not much I haven't seen, so it's really not a big deal."

"Maybe to you," he said under his breath. "Are you at least done in the bathroom? I was hoping to take a quick shower," he added with more confidence.

"Yeah, I'll be in the lobby." Marisol sighed as she turned and walked back out through their shared space. "And by the way, it's still raining outside. I'd save a shower before we turn in. Up to you, though."

With that, David found himself alone again. He sat down on the bed and rested his head in his hands. With a heavy sigh, he grabbed a pair of khakis and slipped a leg in. *This is going to be the longest trip ever.*

2

B ack in her room, Marisol collapsed on her bed, a giant puff of air escaping her chest.

"This is going to be the longest trip, ever," she groaned into the air.

A few months ago, when she was told she would be going on a dream trip with her favorite professor, she pictured Dr. Morrow and one of maybe three contenders—none of which were David Harris. It wasn't as if he was a bad student. Quite the contrary, in fact. He didn't seem the type to even try to apply for a grad trip, unless it was to some fancy resort town to study which plants the elite class preferred in their hotel lobbies. They never exchanged more than a glance here and there. One time, they were next to each other for a lab practical. Now they had to spend three months together, in close quarters, *and* work cooperatively on their research.

Although the idea of working with David had her already climbing the walls, she was eager to get going and dive in headfirst. This was her chance to make her mark on the world, to launch her career. No one was going to ruin that for her.

When Dr. Morrow opened up two spots on this year's research trip, Marisol applied without thinking twice. She knew of the professor's work in the Amazon and was ecstatic for the chance to be a part of it. The competition was tight, but she was confident that her grades, work, and doctoral thesis would give her a competitive edge. Although Dr. Morrow went abroad every year for her research, it was seldom opened up for new students to join. This was her last chance to be a part of something great.

Marisol had been working on her thesis for the past year and a half but had known what she wanted to study since she was little. Ever since her father took her and her brothers on a trip to the Everglades when she was ten, she knew she wanted to study the outdoors. In school, she learned about photosynthesis and how plants acted in different environments. She was instantly obsessed. Every day after school, Marisol and her brothers were brought to her father's scrap metal warehouse. While her brothers played ninjas with the different pieces of steel, Marisol was always around back cataloging the different plants.

"Get out of the weeds!" her father would yell from the shop. "There are fire ants, snakes, God knows what in there!"

"Yes, Papa," she would always say while continuing to sketch and list each little flower and blade of grass.

All her brothers went into the family business—Lugo Steelworks and Recycling. Her family owned the largest steel recycling plant in all of Florida. It went back two generations and had always been family run and operated. When Marisol listened to her father and stopped playing with her nose in the grass, she was learning how the operations worked. Her older brothers, Ricardo and Sebastian, enjoyed learning how to weld and spent most of their time competing for who could make the coolest sculptures out of the excess scrap metal. Her twin, Mateo, was more business-minded. He spent his after-school time learning the books and how to run the shop. He was always voted most likely to take over the warehouse in the family debates on inheritance that occurred every few weeks—not that their father was going anywhere soon. As much as she valued family, Marisol knew her place was outside of Lugo Steelworks.

She had big dreams and was excited to be the first in her family to go to college and leave Miami.

It had been hard to go off on her own across the country, but now she was headed out to the Amazon. She couldn't wait to study new botany samples and round out her doctoral project. Her thesis, *I'm Triggered! Idioblasts, Trichomes, and Chemical Signaling – Triggering Stress Responses from Biotic Involvements,* was made for studying with South American plants. From her environmental classes, she learned that over 80,000 plant species called the Amazon home, the most biodiverse part of the world. The rainforest was infinitely better than the arboretum back at the UC Berkley campus. It was Marisol's dream research location, and she couldn't get started fast enough. She just needed to figure out how to do it with her not-so-enthused traveling companion.

Marisol headed down the stairs towards the small lobby, tying up her long curls in a low and loose ponytail. She cursed the humidity as she pulled her hair back, trying to tame the frizz. She usually wore it down, letting it fall below her shoulders. Working in greenhouses and labs meant she had to keep her hair up and out of her face, so when she had the opportunity for downtime, the hair-tie was the first to go.

"Hey, your room look good?" Dr. Morrow asked as she stood up from the sofa in the lobby.

"Yep! More than enough for a single night. I'm happy we're able to see a little bit of the city before we have to leave."

"It's definitely a happy accident. Did you see David? Once he comes down, we'll head out."

Marisol hesitated and raised her eyebrows at the professor, the corner of her lip raising into a small smile. "You sure we can't just leave without him?"

Dr. Morrow chuckled softly. "I know this isn't up his alley, but he'll get there. You both should get to know each other a bit more. I'm sure you have more in common than you think."

"I'd like to think so, but I have a feeling he'll be a tough nut to crack."

"David! Glad you could join us. All settled then?" Dr. Morrow asked as David meandered into the lobby.

"Yeah, sorry, wanted to get changed. What's the plan? Is it still raining?"

"A steady drizzle, but it's probably almost over. I was thinking we could walk back to the Plaza de Armas, where we had lunch, and enjoy some of the atmosphere. There's a lovely boardwalk area along the river."

"How long of a walk is that, Dr. Morrow?" David asked.

"Maybe 10 minutes or so; everything here is fairly close together. It's about five o'clock now, but the plaza doesn't get really busy until around six or seven. And you both can call me Julia. The formality is going to drive me nuts out here."

"That's not going to be weird or anything," Marisol snorted. "I can't promise I won't still call you Dr. Morrow."

"I'll give you a grace period," she laughed. "Now if you're both ready, let's get a move-on. We can talk about what the next couple of days will entail while we walk."

Dr. Morrow walked at a brisk pace down the wet sidewalk. "… and that is one of the reasons why Iquitos is considered a hub for travel to the Amazon River *and* why it's going to be a long boat ride upriver."

"So, do you think there's a diminished chance of invasive species coming from Iquitos given that it's only accessible by boat or plane?" David asked.

"I think that's a good question to address within your final project. Depending on the context, it could almost be considered a closed circuit, but there's still a heavy black market for so many species…even here," Dr. Morrow answered.

"I would be more interested in parasites or bacterium crossing water-logged boat cavities from village to village," Marisol added. "Plant-wise, I think it would decrease the spread since it would be hard to keep them in a healthy enough state during prolonged travel. What's your project on again, David?"

"My dissertation is on the relationship between invasive species and the sustainability of affected ecosystems. I keep toying with the idea of addressing pristine wildernesses, but there are almost no unexplored ecosystems left."

"And that's why you're a perfect candidate for this research!" Dr. Morrow exclaimed. "We're heading into grids that have never been explored before. The Tamshiyacu-Tahuayo region holds the largest diversity for flora and fauna in South America. I would imagine it's as pristine as you could find."

Music filled the air as they approached the plaza. Bass beats thumped from all directions, creating a unique rhythm that bounced in and between the buildings. People gathered in groups in front of street artists and musicians, some painting elaborate scenes with spray paint and others serenading the crowd with guitars.

"Wow! This place is completely different at night," Marisol said as she spun around, taking it all in.

Dr. Morrow smiled as she turned to Marisol. "The nightlife is pretty busy here to say the very least. Why don't we head down to the river, and we can find a place to get some dinner?"

A large set of stairs led down to a walkway bordering the murky brown river. White, Romanesque pillars used as a guard rail lined the edge of the sidewalk before dropping down to the water below. David walked up and set his elbows on the railing, looking out over the open water. There were boats dotted about, bobbing up and down with the slow coursing of the river. Dr. Morrow stopped and strolled over, leaning on the railing next to him.

"I know it doesn't seem impressive," she said, knocking her shoulder against his, "but wait until we get further out. It's like something out of a movie."

David sighed and offered a small smile. "It's honestly already overwhelming. What if I'm not cut out for it?"

"You'll do fine. It's definitely going to be hard, don't get me wrong, but sometimes it's good to do something that scares us and makes us a little uncomfortable." She patted him on the arm, straightened, and headed back to Marisol, who had continued wandering down the boulevard.

David let out one more heavy sigh before shoving his hands in his pockets and following suit. They approached a building with large white archways with yellow, square tiles plastering the façade. The style was almost Moroccan, but hardly out of place. It seemed as if every building they passed called forth some variant of architectural influence. Tables lined the front of the building with more seating offered inside. Dr. Morrow sat at one of the outside tables, followed by the two students. A waiter stopped by almost immediately and placed three glasses of water on the table. The clear glass was already covered in heavy condensation from the humid night air. Dr. Morrow ordered dinner for everyone without having to even look at the menu.

"So tomorrow, our boat leaves at 10 am. It'll be about 5 hours of driving, depending on the current, but then we'll stop off at the research lodge. We'll be spending the night there before gathering our supplies and guides. After that, we'll head out to the next site," Dr. Morrow explained as the waiter returned and placed their food on the table. She looked over at Marisol and then to David, who was staring down at his plate, gently pushing his food around. "Anyway, we're going to be spending a good amount of time together in close quarters. Why don't we take dinner to get to know each other a little better?"

David looked up, catching Marisol's eyes, before tucking his head back down toward his plate. *Great…gotta love ice breakers.*

"I'll go first then," Dr. Morrow continued. "How about a favorite memory? One of mine from growing up is when my older brother took me to a place called Cat's Den Cave when I was probably around 12 years old. I was *obsessed* with being a spelunker back then. There are barely any caves in Mississippi, but he found that one and brought me along. It was one of the best days I've had, hands down."

"A spelunker, huh?" said Marisol. "I could see that."

"I thought exploring deep caves and climbing mountains was my calling," laughed Dr. Morrow. "But that day, I saw an entirely different ecosystem in that cave. I was hooked on the science of it."

"I love that: 'Hooked on the science of it.' I think one of my best memories was when we took an airboat through the Everglades. I know that seems very stereotypically Florida, but it was so cool at the time. There was something about it being so untamed and *wild*. But I think the best part about that trip was watching my brother, Mateo, freak out over an alligator that we were watching. I think he thought it was going to jump in the boat or something. We still tease him about that." Marisol giggled to herself as she sipped on her water. "What about you? Any fun stories of young David?"

"Uh, not really...no," David said. "We didn't really do family things growing up, and I'm an only child, so no sibling stories."

"Oh, come on! Surely there's some kind of fun memory. What kind of things did you do as a kid?" Marisol asked. "You come from a fancy family. Let me guess...horseback riding? Water polo?"

"Yeah, nothing like that. I was mainly on my own, I guess."

"What do you mean on your own?" asked Dr. Morrow.

"Well, my dad was always traveling for work, and my mom kind of did her own thing. I had a nanny for a while...until I was about twelve, maybe. Then it was kind of just *me*. I started at a boarding school in 9th grade, so then I was home for holidays and breaks, but that's about it. I would've liked to have gone on family trips." He paused, taking a sip of his water. "I'm not trying to be a downer. Sorry."

"Sounds like you need to have some more fun," Marisol said. Her chair scraped the concrete as she got up from the table and headed inside the bistro.

David's eyes followed her as she disappeared around a large

staircase. Once out of sight, he found his gaze turning toward Dr. Morrow. Her lips curved upward into a kind smile as she raised her eyebrows at him.

"I appreciate you trying to make this less awkward," David said, giving a slight shrug of his shoulders.

"Worth a shot?"

"To be determined."

"The never-ending conflict between extrovert and introvert." She laid a hand on his arm. "Believe it or not, I'm an introvert, too. I've had to learn how to be a lot more outgoing over the years. Uh, not that you're not outgoing…"

David smiled and let out a soft laugh. "I'm *not* outgoing."

The sound of clinking glass caught his attention. He looked up to see two glistening beer bottles being placed in the middle of the table.

"Alright! Here you go. Drink up!" Marisol said. "I can go get you one, Dr. Morrow. I didn't want to be too presumptuous."

*Right…*that's *what would be too presumptuous,* David thought.

"*Julia,* Marisol, but thank you. I'm probably going to head back to the hotel and do some prep work. You both should stay and enjoy some of the nightlife. We're going to be away from literally everything for a good while; you may as well enjoy a night on the town. And before you say no, David," Dr. Morrow added, "here's the stipend we had for the night." She pulled out a money clip from her purse and placed it on the table. "I always ask for more than we need. I guess it's my way of sticking it to the university funding…or lack thereof." She stood and pushed her chair in. "Anyway, I'll see you two in the morning. Go experience the city."

"Looks like you'll get to have a little fun after all!" Marisol said, flashing David her biggest smile. She sat down and pulled her chair in, snatching the money clip from the table. "So, what's your deal?"

David sighed and squinted at her. "My deal?"

"Yeah, no offense, but this whole quiet and reserved thing is going to get old quick when you're the only one to talk to."

"I get you don't like me, and that's fine, but you don't have to be a jerk about it."

Marisol bristled, opening her mouth to quip back, but softened. "I'm not trying to be a jerk. I'm sorry. I'm used to a lot of ribbing back and forth with my family, and my friends usually dish it back. I'm not really used to sensitive people."

"Hey, I'm not sensitive. I-I'm not. I'm *used* to being on the outskirts of everything. Stuff like this doesn't come easy for me."

"All the more reason to cut loose a little bit! Let's go have fun! We're in an amazing city, we're going on a kickass trip up the freaking *Amazon*, and it's not very gentlemanly to leave me alone to celebrate."

David bit down on his lip and shook his head. "Fine." He grabbed his glass and took a swig, a small grin starting to break through. "Where to?"

Blue and red lights flashed across the sea of bobbing heads on the dancefloor of La Vida Disco. Strips of billowing white fabric draped across the ceiling, spanning the room. Smoke and music filled the club as crowds of people danced and shared drinks. Marisol led the charge, pulling David by the sleeve. She let go when they reached the bar, leaving him standing behind her.

Hovering at a little over six feet, David was taller than almost everyone else in the room. He could barely hear Marisol talking to the bartender over the thumps of the bass. He scanned the room but was blinded by the lights shining back at his eye level. He turned to the bar as Marisol spun around toward him.

"Here!" Marisol shouted. She thrust a shot glass into his hand and tapped it with her matching drink.

"I don't do shots!" David yelled back.

"You do tonight!"

Groaning, David upended the glass. He winced and scrunched his face as the liquid burnt his throat. "What the hell is this? It's awful!"

"Yeah, I don't know! I asked for their cheapest stuff! I'll get us another!"

"No, don't!" David barely had the words out before Marisol had turned back and was hailing the bartender. He leaned over her to place his hand on the counter. Bending down further to talk into her ear, he said, "If we're *drinking* drinking, I am *not* drinking that."

"Alright, then we split the cash. You can get whatever you want, but I already ordered another, so you're having at least one more." Two more shot glasses filled to the brim clanked on the counter in front of them. "Cheers! Let's dance!"

"I don't dance!" David yelled over the music as she grabbed his shirt and pulled him into the crowd.

Marisol's grip on his shirt loosened as they made their way toward the middle of the dancefloor. He watched the top of her head inch away from his shoulder as she let go, easily disappearing into the moving mass. David found himself surrounded as the lights flashed over him in rhythm with the DJ's beats. He scanned the room, looking for Marisol while attempting to swim through the crowd, getting jostled by the jumping and dancing bodies. *This is impossible. I need another drink.*

He pushed his way back out of the crowd and toward the bar. "Hey! Can I get a whiskey on the rocks?"

"Qué?"

"A whiskey? Um…Jack Daniels?" David tried. The bartender turned away and pulled a rocks glass from the shelf. When he returned, David's eyes widened as a glass filled to the rim was placed in front of him.

"Ciento doce."

"Uh, I'm sorry, what was that?"

"Ciento doce," the bartender said louder.

"One hundred and twelve soles, ciento doce," a voice chimed in from beside him.

David, relieved, turned towards the voice and saw a petite woman wearing a low-cut crop top leaning in next to him. "Thank you!" He reached into his wallet and pulled out some of the bills Marisol had given him and handed them to the man behind the bar. "Do you tip here?" he asked the woman.

"Sorry, I don't know much of English," she replied. "I'm Benita."

Maybe this night won't turn out so badly after all. "Thanks for your help."

Marisol was lost in the music. She always loved dancing, and this seemed like the perfect opportunity to let her hair down. It wasn't until the music slowed that she realized how dry her mouth was. She looked around for David, hoping to see his head above the crowd. She had lost track of when she had seen him last.

"He better not have left me here," Marisol grumbled to herself. She looked down at her watch and pushed the button to turn the backlight on. "Shit," she cursed, seeing that she had been dancing for almost two hours. Her heart raced as she frantically looked for any sign of David. She wove her way through the crowd and headed toward the bar. Managing her way to the front, she flagged down the bartender. This time, a woman approached from the other side of the counter.

"Que le puedo traer para tomar?"

"No gracias. Nothing to drink. I'm looking for a tall guy, blond? Alto y rubio?" The bartender looked at her blankly. "American?"

"Si, por alla," she said, pointing to the end of the bar along the back wall.

Marisol headed to the far end of the club and could make out David's blond head above the crowd. She stopped in her tracks as she pushed her way closer. The reserved David she knew from two hours ago was bent over, his tongue halfway down the throat of a young woman in a black crop top. Marisol wasn't sure if she was angry or surprised with him. Deciding on a healthy balance between the two, she walked up to him and tapped him stiffly on the shoulder.

David straightened and turned, immediately reaching out to the table for balance. "Marisol, hey!"

"I thought you left me!" she yelled over the music.

"Me leave you? *You* left *me*...in the middle of the dancefloor," he replied as his words slurred into one another. "I couldn't find you, so I came to get a drink."

"I can see that. And exactly how much have you had to drink?"

"I don't know. A few of these." David made a sweeping gesture with his hand to a high-top table covered in glasses. "This is Betina. Bertina. Berina? She ordered them for me." He turned to introduce the woman from the bar, but she had already begun to walk away back toward the front of the club. He frowned as he watched her sidle up next to another man at the bar.

"Wow," said Marisol, looking him up and down. "I think maybe we should get you back to the hotel." She wrapped her arm around his waist and began walking him to the door.

"We're leaving?" David asked. "It's not even that late."

"It's like midnight."

"Really? That went by fast."

"I'm sure that's what your little fling said."

"Oh, you're funny," David said. "You told me to have fun."

Marisol laughed. "Well I didn't mean get wasted and go make out with a stranger in a foreign club."

"Nothing I do is going to be the right thing is it...whoa!" David tripped on the edge of the sidewalk and dropped into the street.

"Okay, we're switching places. I'm not going to be responsible if you get hit by a car. Also, and this is a long shot given all of this, but do you remember the name of the hotel?"

David closed his eyes and put a hand out to balance himself on a nearby street lamp. "No...you?"

"Alright, well I guess we're walking back then. Let's hope no one tries to mug or assault me because you certainly won't be any help."

"I wouldn't let you get hurt," David stated, his words still melting together. "You should try to be less pretty, though. Less of a target."

Marisol smiled. "You think I'm pretty?"

"Of course I think you're pretty."

Still smiling, Marisol grabbed David, stood him up, and started walking back to the hotel.

"...so that's basically my thought process with my distertation, uh, dissertation," said David as they rounded the corner toward the hotel.

"Gotcha. I didn't realize you were so passionate about it."

"What do you mean?"

"Well, you've been talking about it nonstop since we started walking. It's kind of a lot," she laughed.

"When you take into account all the factors involved in conservation..."

"You realize how important the research is. So I've heard at least three times. Alright, this is us." Marisol helped David through the front doors. "Now to get you up the stairs."

"I'm fine. I can walk. I'm not a child."

"Can you? I'm pretty sure you'd fall flat on your ass right now."

David ascended the stairs slowly, catching his foot slightly on one of the stairs. He gripped the handrail and steadied himself as he wobbled in place.

"Can I help you yet?"

"Fine," he groaned. "I'd have this if the whole room wasn't spinning."

Marisol walked him up the rest of the stairs and down the hall. She fished his room key out of his pocket and unlocked the door to his side of the suite. Flicking the light switch on, she moved over to his bed to clear off his backpack. She broke out in a fit of laughter as she turned to get him. He was standing in the open doorway, leaning against the frame with three buttons of his shirt undone and was working on his belt.

"Okay, let's just get you in the room before we do that." She pulled him past the threshold, closed the door behind them, and walked him over to the bed. She finished taking off his shirt, folded it, and placed it on his bag. "I'm leaving you with everything else. You want me to leave the light on or off?"

David moaned in response before crawling onto the bed and burying his face in a stack of pillows. Marisol slipped off his shoes and put them by his nightstand before quietly turning off the light and heading to her room.

She plopped her bag on the bed and unzipped it, carefully searching for her toiletries; she pulled out a small picture frame, instead. Smiling, she sat on the edge of the bed and traced the frame with her fingers. Mateo sent the frame and enclosed photo to her the day after she called home to tell him about her trip. He was the first person she called. He was *always* the first person she called. Having a twin bond was something Marisol never took for granted. Mateo was her best friend, there whenever she needed him. Leaving him to go to school in California was one of the hardest moments in her life. They took this picture of the whole family the day she flew out to start at Berkeley. Her father had taken her and her brothers out to her favorite restaurant to celebrate. That morning was filled with laughs and tears and everything in between.

She ran her hand along the frame one more time, pausing to appreciate the gaudiness of the bright Puerto Rican colors that made up the border. The letter that came with the photo read:

Sunny,

Thought you could use this so you don't forget about us while you're out being a total badass explorer. Dad insisted on buying this frame so you can show everyone where you come from. I tried to stop him. Feel free to chuck it and save the photo...promise I won't tell. I miss you, be safe, and try not to work too hard (I know that's impossible).

Love you —Matty

She tucked the photo back into her bag, making sure it was snugly set between some clothes. Yawning, she stood up to check the lock on her door before slipping off her shoes and turning the faucet on for the shower. Stepping under the hot water, she let out a huge breath and tried to focus on relaxing her shoulders. Marisol knew that this would be the last hot shower in months, and she planned to savor every second. She closed her eyes and let the water run over her, saturating her hair, and rinsing off all the sweat and fun from a night of dancing.

Marisol took another deep breath when a loud slam beside her made her heart catch. She shot her head around the curtain to see David, in his underwear, crouching next to the shower with his head in the toilet.

"Yikes, you okay?"

David groaned as he reached up and tugged on the lever, flushing the toilet. He lifted his head up, resting it in his hands while still leaning over the bowl.

"Fun fact." He moaned into the palms of his hands. "So, I don't really drink. I mean, not really."

"What? What do you mean you don't drink?"

"I just don't. Maybe a glass of wine now'n again. I didn't want you to keep thinking I was boring. I wanted—" He dropped his head back down to vomit again.

Marisol crouched down, holding the shower curtain around her, and placed a hand on his back. "Shit. I'm sorry."

Resting his head on his arm, he looked up at her and smiled

weakly. "It's okay, nothing you did. I think that girl was trying to scam me anyway. It's my own fault."

"Are you gonna be okay? I still have to wash my hair and everything, but I can stay down here with you."

"Yeah, I'll be fine. I think I'm going to puke a few more times and go to bed…and then never drink again." He hung his head and ran a hand along the back of his neck.

Marisol chuckled. "Okay. Well, make sure to drink some water." She patted his back gently before standing back up. She slid the curtain closed behind her as David heaved into the toilet again.

Several minutes passed before she heard rustling by the vanity followed a few minutes later by the faucet running and the door closing shortly thereafter. Shaking her head, Marisol took the time for some more deep breaths in the humid bathroom.

She'd discovered breathing exercises through a meditation club on campus. While she never understood the visualization of meditation, she did enjoy the controlled breathing. It made her feel loose and relaxed, like everything was going to be okay.

She rinsed her hair, turned off the water, and wrapped a towel around her head and chest before stepping out of the shower and back to her room.

"Jesus!" she swore, jumping and clutching her towel as she stepped inside.

She looked over to her bed to see David, still in his underwear, facedown and passed out on top of her comforter. His legs were askew and his arms were curled up under the pillow. Tiptoeing, she moved closer, realizing he wasn't laying on her pillow but was curled up on her backpack.

"My clothes," she whined quietly. She reached under David's head to try and slide her bag out. He grumbled in response and buried his head further. "Just great." Sighing, she grabbed her watch from her nightstand, strapped it on her wrist, and headed back through the bathroom and into David's room.

Marisol woke up to the sound of cars and motorcycles whizzing by in the streets below. She checked her watch. *8 am*. She lazily rolled out of bed and looked around for something to put on outside of the towel from her shower last night. She pulled a t-shirt from David's bag and threw it on. His shirt fell almost to her knees, reminding her of how short she was next to him. Marisol ran her fingers through her hair, catching some snags where the curls had dried as she headed to the bathroom. As she approached the door, she heard the shower running. She brought her hand to the door and knocked.

"Yeah?"

She cracked the door open slowly, peeking her head inside. "Hey, morning. I was hoping to get back into my room if you're done with it."

"Oh, of course. Hey…" David paused, finding his words. "I'm really sorry about last night. I didn't mean—"

"Don't worry about it," Marisol said, stepping into the bathroom. "How are you feeling? I thought I'd end up having to wake you up to avoid missing the boat."

"I've been better. Killer headache, though. Thanks for getting us back here. I'd love to say I remember it, but…" He laughed.

"Well, it was either coming back with me or going home with that pretty girl at the club."

"Yeah, about that…she was definitely a hustler."

"What? You don't think you have game?" she teased.

"Oh, I *know* I don't. But, no, she kept offering to get me more drinks, and I would keep giving her money to get them for me. I'm pretty sure she was conning me. At the very least, I'm blaming this all on her."

Marisol laughed, stepping in further and closing the door behind her. She unzipped her toiletry bag and noticed the hotel soaps mixed in with her things. "Does this mean you want me to bring the bars of soap with us into the jungle? Not the most eco-friendly move."

"Oh, shit, no, I'm sorry. I knocked your bag over last night and tried to put it all back the way it was. I was clearly not in the best state of mind. But I promise I didn't snoop."

"I had a feeling my stuff was going to get caught in the crossfire somewhere. You were a mess." Marisol smiled as she set the hotel toiletries back onto the vanity. "Do you mind if I get ready since I'm already in here?"

"Have at it. Can you hand me a towel?"

Marisol grabbed a towel off the hook on the wall and stuck it around the shower curtain. David stepped out a minute later with it wrapped around his waist. His blond hair dripped water down the sides of his head and onto his shoulders.

"What happened to Mr. Modesty?" Marisol said with her toothbrush half-hanging from her mouth.

"Well, you did spend last night watching me puke my guts out. I figure I've hit peak embarrassment after that. Not really an experience I wanted to share if we're being honest. And speaking of sharing...is that my shirt?"

Marisol looked at herself in the mirror and shrugged. She leaned over and spit out a mouthful of toothpaste. "You literally fell asleep on all of my clothes." She could feel David staring at her as she rinsed her toothbrush. She looked up at his reflection and smiled. "I promise I didn't snoop either."

David returned her smile but redirected his eyes to the vanity lights. Marisol watched him tug on the edge of his towel, pulling it tighter around his waist while fiddling with a loose string around the hem. She leaned over and put her toothbrush back in her toiletry bag.

"Can I be completely honest with you?" David blurted out.

Marisol raised an eyebrow and waved her hand out in front of her, welcoming the break in the tension.

"I'm insanely uncomfortable standing here like this. In my towel. Like nothing is weird about it."

Marisol chuckled and intentionally looked him up and down. "Then why are you? Though, for the record, there *isn't* anything weird about it."

"Maybe to you. I don't know. You make me, like, super nervous. You're crazy intimidating, and I'm really doing my best to play it cool, but I just want to completely disappear and wipe this entire interaction from your memory…and mine."

"Wow. Seems a little extreme, even for you." She noticed redness spreading across his skin. It crept up from his chest, through his neck, and was now flushing through his face.

"It's just…I'm still so embarrassed from last night…*and* this morning." David tilted his head up at the ceiling to avoid looking at the two of them in the mirror. "I swear it took me no less than five minutes to even realize I wasn't even in my own room."

"If it helps, I'm only wearing your shirt. That's it. Same thing. I'm not exactly comfortable either."

"Yeah, except for girls like you, it's sexy. For me…it's *blech*," he said, shaking his head in minor disgust.

Marisol turned to face him, trying to catch his eye. "One: this shirt is *not* sexy. It's like you went to REI and picked up the first thing you saw. Two: you know you shouldn't be that hard on yourself." David looked down at her, his face almost completely crimson. "I mean, yeah, you don't have a six-pack or anything, but…"

David's chest deflated and threw his hands around his waist.

"I'm kidding!" she laughed. "Look, you don't have anything to worry about, okay? We're cool." Marisol punched his shoulder softly and grabbed her bag before turning to walk into her room.

David watched as the door closed behind her. He leaned his hands on the vanity, studying himself in the mirror. *You need to stop being so fucking awkward.* He pushed himself up and ran both hands down his face, trying to push the redness away. A creak pulled his attention to the door.

"So you can finish packing," Marisol said, tossing his shirt towards him. "And you better get going. We're going to be late."

"Thanks!" he said, feeling like he had said it too cheerfully. He looked back in the mirror, ran a hand through his damp hair and mumbled at his reflection, "I can't wait to spend five hours on a boat with this hangover."

3

The boat engine clicked off, silencing the cacophony of grinding and whirring that had encompassed the group during their travel upriver. Gliding solely on the current, the driver steered effortlessly down the narrow tributary, avoiding fallen trees and low-hanging branches. Without the steady background noise of the engine churning up water, Marisol could finally hear herself think.

She glanced over at David; his head lolled off to the side while his sunglasses hung sloppily over his ears. He had fallen asleep almost instantly once they took off from Iquitos. Marisol figured it was probably for the best, given how green he already looked by mid-morning.

The trip so far had been smooth. They stopped briefly at a local village to trade out supplies but stayed on the boat while the crew loaded the back row of seats. Marisol spent the majority of the ride watching the water. Occasionally another boat would whiz by, making them slow down to avoid the waves given off by the passerby.

Once they went a few hours up the Amazon, she realized just how remote they were going to be. They passed small villages off the river here and there. Small children bathed at the river's edge as they passed, the mothers dipping their clothes and linens in the water as they watched over the young ones. The villages themselves were crude and comprised of large timber logs. All of them stood on stilts. Dr. Morrow had explained how the Amazon gets its water, and why all the buildings needed to be elevated.

"Once the snowcaps from the Andes melt, the water comes down and floods the Amazon basin. We're here during the middle of the dry season. Shortly after we leave, almost all of our camp will likely be underwater. If you look at the building supports as we go by, you can see the water line from the flood-waters." Dr. Morrow pointed up as they drifted by the last village on their route. "During the wet season, they will get around mainly by boat. It's really amazing to see. Unfortunately, we rely on the dry season to get most of our research done."

"So, what do you do during the wet season?"

"I actually have a former student who wanted to stay behind after our trip and keep the research going year-round. We'll be meeting him at the most interior site in a few days. He's in charge of the equipment and keeping the camps accessible. He makes sure the paths are clear and bunks at the research lodge during the wet season. Last year, he took a canoe out just to see how far he could get without having to walk." Laughing, Dr. Morrow continued, "Let's just say he didn't make it very far. If he's one thing, he's ambitious."

"He wanted to stay? Just like that? That's strange."

"That's definitely Ben," Dr. Morrow said. "He fell head-over-heels with the jungle. He's wicked smart, and to be honest, he's been an incredible asset. We've cataloged more samples with him here than in my last two trips combined. When he's not at the site, he helps out as a guide to visitors at the lodge. The eco-tourism helps to fund the research projects, but Ben never needs an excuse to keep exploring."

"Geez. He seems intense," Marisol said. A smirk crossed her face as she raised an eyebrow. "Is he single?"

Dr. Morrow let out a barking laugh. "Yes. He is. And only because he and his boyfriend broke up when he decided not to come back to the states." She turned and reached behind her to shake David's knee, jostling him awake. "We're about five minutes out. Rise and shine."

David blinked his eyes open, looking out the side of the covered boat. Tall trees loomed over the brackish water of the river, creating a green border that hugged the bank and followed its every curve. The water sloshed up against the metal siding of the boat as it slowly skirted the surface.

"Wow," David breathed as a group of small, colorful birds congregated on the branches of a nearby bush.

"Wire-tailed manakins," said Dr. Morrow, pointing.

He glanced up, studying the sounds of birds chirping. The trees on either side of them were dripping with bromeliads, dotting the endless greenery with splashes of pinks, oranges, and purples. They rounded a bend as a series of both large and small huts, mounted up on stilts, came into view. The driver steered the boat seamlessly between tethered canoes and pulled up next to a small, wooden dock. Small fish darted in and out of view in the shallow riverbank. A short man jogged barefooted down the set of steps leading to the dock.

"Julia! It's about time!" the man yelled with a thick Spanish accent as he approached the boat.

"Claudio, hi! We got held up by some rain, but we made okay time, though. It's good to see—"

"Yes, yes," he said, cutting her off. He leaned in and lowered his voice. "I need to talk to you about Ben. We have a situation." He reached and grabbed Dr. Morrow's hand, helping her out of the boat.

"Guys, I'll be back in a few," she said, her smile dropping. "I'll have Paul, the biologist here, show you where to go. David, would you mind grabbing my bags?"

"Sure thing, Dr. Morrow," David replied.

She sped up the steps alongside Claudio, their hushed but harried voices growing quiet as they climbed the stairs and out of sight. David's eyes followed her, his eyebrows pinching in concern at her quick change in demeanor. He grabbed his bag and lifted Dr. Morrow's backpack and suitcases out of the boat and onto the dock. Marisol handed him her bags before taking his hand, steadying herself as she climbed out of the rocking boat.

"Do you know what they're talking about?" David whispered to Marisol.

"Dr. Morrow said that she has an old student here who's kept the research active while she's back teaching. Hopefully everything's okay."

"It's going to take me at least two trips to get all these bags. Why don't you head up and I'll bring everything up behind you?"

"Well, that's very gentlemanly of you," she said, giving an exaggerated curtsey before heading up the wooden stairs towards the main stilted hut.

Dr. Morrow stood with her arms crossed at her chest as she stared at the lodge director pacing in front of her. She glanced around the circular room, empty outside of the hammocks strung up every couple of feet, attached to the support beams. The lodge was quiet with most of the visitors out on guided hikes or fishing trips in the late afternoon. Dr. Morrow narrowed her eyes onto Claudio and stepped toward him.

"What do you mean you haven't heard from him?" she asked, a sense of urgency floating through her tone. "How long?"

"He missed the last check-in. He's gone radio silent. We've been trying to reach him for the last three weeks."

"And you haven't sent anyone out to the site to look for him? Why wasn't I notified?"

"We *did* send a couple of guides. They reached the second camp and wouldn't go any further."

"What do you mean they wouldn't go any further, Claudio?" Dr. Morrow asked through gritted teeth.

"They said that they had to turn back. Th-they were scared, Julia. They called it *tierra maldita*."

"...Cursed Earth?"

"I haven't heard it said before out here, but you know all of our guides are from local villages. There are a lot of superstitions."

"Enough superstitions to leave Ben missing?"

"I know, I know," he said, holding his hands up between them. "I have two guides, Andy and Nelly, ready to accompany you tomorrow at dawn. But they said they'll go only as far as the second site. They won't go deeper."

Dr. Morrow bit the inside of her lip as she shook her head, her eyes never leaving Claudio's. "Okay. First thing tomorrow we head out." She turned and left the hammock room, the door swinging shut behind her. "I hope to God he's okay," she whispered to herself as she walked back toward the main cabin.

David pushed through the front door of the main cabin, hauling three suitcases and a backpack, which he promptly set in the middle of the room with the other luggage. Wiping the sweat from his forehead, he crumpled into one of the wooden lounge chairs to catch his breath.

"I think that's everything," he panted.

He jumped up to his feet as one of the doors creaked loudly and swung open. Dr. Morrow and a man donned in an oversized soccer jersey and khaki pants walked into the room. Dr. Morrow looked distracted, a sharp contrast to her normal, cheerful demeanor.

"David, Marisol, this is Paul. He's the staff biologist and a guide here. He's helped with a lot of our work. He grew up in Iquitos, but don't let him fool you...he's an expert in the area."

"I figured that you both might like to go on a bit of a small hike. Introduce you to the area?" Paul said.

"And to show you how to use the proper tools and equipment," Dr. Morrow added. "You'll each be carrying a machete as well as some rope and multi-tools. It looks like we'll be progressing without guides after we hit our second camp."

"A machete?" Marisol asked.

"For what?" David added.

Paul grinned at their apparent nervousness. "For cutting through the vines and branches. Don't worry. Most of the really dangerous things come out at night." He winked quickly before breaking out into a raucous laugh. "Come, I'll show you the cabin you're in for the night."

Paul pushed the door open and walked through, leading them down an elevated plank walkway. Small palm-thatched cabins lined both sides, many with muddied shoes and clothes strung up by the doors. The walkway and cabins were situated about twenty feet off the ground, raised by large timber poles. Each cabin was made of the same timber and every window was covered by a thick screen.

Looking beyond the cabins, the river flowed not more than a couple of hundred feet away. Small, jet-black birds with bright orange beaks flitted from railing to railing. High-pitched chirps escaped their beaks, creating a staccato din on top of the loud and constant screeches from a flock of caciques roosting in the nearby trees. The atmosphere itself sang, creating a boisterous backdrop to the serene landscape.

"This one is yours," Paul said, opening a thick, wooden door to the second to last cabin.

David and Marisol stepped inside. Two twin beds made neatly with white linens and separated by a nightstand lined one wall of the small room. Two empty, wooden bookshelves sat opposite the beds. David quietly set his backpack on the far bed, surveying the room.

"Is there no bathroom?" he asked.

"The bathroom is at the end of the walkway. Showers, too. The left side is the men's, and women's is on the right. The water is brought up from the river, so all of it is cold. If you're going to shower, I recommend doing it sooner than later, while it's been warmed by the sun," Paul explained. "If you go back out past the main hall, you'll end up in the hammock room. It's what it sounds like. Most of our guests enjoy relaxing in the hammocks in their downtime. We have a full house right now, so that's why you're sharing a room. Dinner is served at five and breakfast at seven, although our cooks will be preparing an early breakfast for you tomorrow."

"Earlier than seven?" Marisol asked.

"You, Julia, and your guides will be leaving at sunrise to make the most of your time. I'm sure she'll fill you in more once she's settled in. In the meantime, get comfortable, explore the area. Our hike and your quick training will start in about an hour. I'll meet you in the main hall."

The hour sped by as David and Marisol walked the lodge and took in the rainforest. Paul stood in the open hall, now donning knee-high rubber boots. Two additional pairs sat next to him. He waved to David and Marisol as they approached from the cabins.

"Grab a pair and toss them on. We don't like to introduce foreign bacteria to the grid, if possible," he said. He walked over to a nearby cabinet and returned with two machetes, handing them off. "Let's get to work!"

Paul quickly took off down the stairs toward the edge of the trees. A crude and muddy trail led into the jungle. They made it fifty feet in before they became completely immersed in the rainforest. The air was thicker, unable to fully circulate in the dense wood. Sinewy vines crept down, brushing against them as they made their way forward. David swatted at his neck, grabbing at the leaves and pulling them away. Thick roots jutted up out of the earth like hands waiting to grab an unsuspecting adventurer. Paul chopped at bending branches, blazing a walkable path along the ill-defined trail.

Marisol gasped as she pitched forward, throwing her arms in

front of her. There was a tightness around her shoulders as she stopped, half-bent forward. She looked back over her shoulder to see David gripping her backpack. He pulled at it, righting her.

"You okay?" he asked.

"Yeah, thank you," she said as she adjusted her bag. "Must have snagged my foot on something."

"You both coming?" Paul yelled from several yards ahead.

"Yep! We're coming!" David shouted back. He motioned to Marisol. "After you, if you're good." She moved forward, stepping over the exposed roots while peeling wet leaves from her hair. David pulled his foot out of the mud and trudged onward behind her.

After forty minutes, they approached a small, shallow pond. The area nearby was mostly cleared. A slight breeze wafted over them in the clearing, giving relief for a moment from the oppressive humidity. Giant lilies spotted the surface of the water. Tropical cormorants sunbathed on top of the green pads, stretching their wings to soak up the last of the sun's rays.

"You'll need to be confident in your skills once you venture out past the lodge. Your machete should never leave your side. Clearings last a few days at most before the new growth takes over. You can practice on these vines and twigs. You'll have your equipment with you, but basic necessities will be up to you to find."

Paul pointed to the base of the palm trees on either side of them. "These palms have edible nuts. More importantly, these ripe and fallen nuts are eaten by palm weevils. He bent down and grabbed a large, black orb from the detritus. With the nut pressed up against the tree, he swung his machete, slicing into the shell. The nut cracked open. Paul shook it over the palm of his hand, and a fatty, white grub wiggled out. He held up it up between his fingers and quickly popped it into his mouth. "These grubs are the perfect jungle snack. Lots of protein, can be eaten raw, cooked, or used for bait for fishing."

David stared, mouth agape. Marisol bent down and grabbed a

palm nut, held it to the tree, and hit it with her machete. She yipped as the nut fell to the ground. As she picked it up, she peeled back the shell to see a grub inside. She made wary eye contact with David before shrugging and tossing the bug into her mouth.

"Huh," she said, chewing. "Tastes like coconut."

"*Like coconut*? Seriously? You're not just trying to trick me into eating that?" David asked.

"I swear!"

David swallowed, mimicked Paul and Marisol, and dislodged a thick grub from the fallen palm nut. He stood, staring at the bug in his hand. *Here goes nothing*. He raised his palm to his mouth and bit down. The larvae squished between his teeth. It reminded him of Gushers, one of the many junk foods his mother would never let him eat growing up. Surprisingly, it did taste like coconut.

"These palms grow everywhere. I recommend collecting the ripe nuts as you go. Most fish will eat the grubs too, so they're helpful for catching meals. It's important to eat and drink enough while you're away. Julia's latest research site is about a four-day hike, so you won't have access to much."

"Other than these bugs," David interrupted, "what are we supposed to eat?"

"You'll have some packets of dehydrated food, but Julia will show you how to fish, if you don't already know how. You can eat almost anything you catch here. Most likely, you'll catch piranha, catfish, or sabalo. Julia is also well-versed in hunting undulated tinamou. Claudio affectionately calls them jungle chickens," Paul said.

"And we're camping in tents, right?" Marisol asked.

"Small tents, yes. There are also larger and more complex tents at each site, to house the research equipment and logs. You'll bathe in whatever water you come across, but make sure you do not go in or around the water at dusk or later. That's when the caiman become active." Paul turned to David. "And I recommend keeping your underwear on when bathing. Piranha think anything is bait. Then there's cañero, which swim up, you know..."

"What?" David gulped, his eyes widening. "Are you serious?"

"Very. It's dangerous out here, and the nearest medical center is over an hour away from the lodge, let alone being almost a week's hike deep in the jungle. Now...let's get practicing with those machetes!"

The three hikers returned to the lodge as the sun was disappearing behind the trees. Small lights flickered in the occasional elevated cabin. A steady noise of dishes clacking and lively conversations emanated from the main hall. David and Marisol passed by on the way to their room. A large buffet table filled with heaping plates and bowls stood off to the side. Long, wooden tables with benches filled the main floor. Several small groups of people gathered at the tables, laughing, and passing cameras back and forth. The smell of freshly cooked fish wafted out onto the raised walkway as they continued by.

David stopped at the entrance to their room. "You can get changed first if you want. I can wait out here," he said.

Marisol offered a quick smile as she skirted around him and into the cabin. David slapped at mosquitos that landed on and around his neck and face as he waited. He stopped short, cocking his head to the side. Marisol swung the door open, almost hitting him.

"What are you doing?" she asked.

David threw up a hand. "Shhh! Do you hear that?"

They stood silently as the seconds ticked by. The only sound was the clatter from the dining hall.

"We done? I'm starving. You can stay here and do whatever it is you're doing. I'm going to have dinner."

David stood a few minutes more, listening intently. *I could have sworn I heard something.* Looking around the thatched roof and seeing nothing but the occasional spider, he resigned himself to the cabin to put on some clean clothes.

Cooked fish, rice, and fresh fruits spilled over David's plate as he walked over to sit with Dr. Morrow and Marisol at a long table. Claudio and Paul sat nearby with two younger Peruvian guides. The four of them slid down the bench to join the group once David found his seat next to Marisol.

"Guys, this is Nelly and Andy," Dr. Morrow said, motioning to their new company. "They're going to be helping us for a few days while we push through to the third site."

The two guides exchanged a nervous look. Their eyes darted to Claudio, who gave a curt shake of his head. David could tell something was off with them. He hoped it wasn't that they were inexperienced. He didn't want to be responsible for remembering everything Paul taught them earlier.

He set his silverware down and looked across the table to Dr. Morrow. "Paul was saying we were traveling alone after the second research site. Why go all that way and not keep going? Isn't it more work to backtrack?"

Nelly turned to him and began speaking in Spanish. Her voice wavered and her tone became manic. Claudio reached over, placing his hand on her arm. She immediately quieted, looking over at him and shaking.

"I didn't mean to say anything offensive," David said, holding his hands up. "Did I say something wrong?"

"No," Dr. Morrow said. "Apparently, there are some deep superstitions about the area. Just folklore."

"Tierra maldita," Nelly spat. She waved her hand over her chest, making the sign of the cross.

Marisol looked at Nelly, her eyes widening. "Dr. Morrow, what's going on? She's saying it's...*cursed*?"

Dr. Morrow let out a frustrated breath, resting her forehead in her hand. "Let me say first that there is nothing to be worried about.

Claudio informed me when we arrived that my researcher, Ben, has been out of contact for three weeks. The guides are refusing to go further into the jungle to go find him because of these *superstitions.*"

"What does that mean, 'out of contact?'" David asked.

"He is supposed to come back here and check in during the first week of the month to refill supplies, drop off new plant pressings or field notes, or to mark his progress. When he didn't come back, they tried to get him on his satellite phone, but there's been no response. That's why we're leaving so early tomorrow." She stopped and looked at Claudio. "It looks like we're the only ones that are willing to go that far in to find him."

They finished the rest of their dinner in silence, slowly filtering back out to their rooms for the evening. Marisol couldn't get Nelly's reaction out of her head. The idea of curses made her skin crawl. She went to the showers to try and wash away the tension she could feel growing in her neck and shoulders.

She tiptoed back into the cabin, wrapped in her towel. The light on the nightstand cast harsh shadows across the walls. Marisol's hair stood on end. She couldn't shake the apprehensive feeling from dinner. She looked over to the far bed to see David sleeping, a book left open in his hand. Marisol grabbed a sports bra and a pair of sweatpants from her bag. As she adjusted the waistband, her stomach dropped. She froze.

She shuffled over to David and shook his shoulder, whispering fiercely. "David! Get up!"

David lifted his head from the pillow with a groan. "What?"

"Do you hear that?"

A slow and faint scratching came from the other side of the door, like bark peeling away from a tree. David shot up. "I knew I heard something earlier. I told you!" he hissed.

"Go check it out!"

He could tell she was scared, something he hadn't seen from her normal tough-girl persona. *I am literally the last person that should be doing this.* "Alright," he whispered, unclipping a penlight from his bag, "stay here."

David crept out to the walkway, following the sound. He directed the light up to the rafters of the thatched roofing. As his light shone over the dried palm leaves, the noise immediately stopped. He scanned the beams for movement, swallowing hard with each pass of his flashlight. He tilted his head from side to side, trying to listen harder. The hair on the back of his neck raised as he heard a scraping noise close behind him. The sound got louder, dragging along like a broom brushing over a concrete sidewalk.

Turn around. Be brave. Turn around. Just turn around, goddammit!

With his hands shaking, he shifted his feet, slowly turning towards the noise. "Whoa…"

The cabin door eked open as Marisol stuck her head around the frame. David held out a hand toward her and waved her forward. She squeezed through the thin gap of the open door and started to walk up to him. He put a hand on her arm as she got closer, stopping her from moving. She looked from David to the railing in front of him, her mouth dropping open.

Perched in front of him, stood a small creature, about the size of a cat. It rocked back and forth slowly, its black and white quills rustling up against one another and standing out at odd angles.

"It's a prehensile-tailed porcupine," David whispered, letting go of her arm. "He just climbed down this pole."

"How do you know that?" Marisol said.

At her voice, the porcupine let out a soft hiss and stood up on its hind legs, rocking back and forth more fervently.

"Shhhh…it's okay. You're okay," David whispered to their evening visitor. "You scared him. When they get defensive, they stretch their skin out—it has kind of an elastic quality—and it erects their quills. He's trying to make himself more threatening.

But look at that giant nose, you aren't that scary are you, buddy?"

Marisol looked at David, stunned. "Who *are* you?" she half-whispered.

David let out a soft laugh, but kept his eyes trained on the porcupine. "I double majored in integrative biology with a focus on zoology. Almost went for that PhD, too."

"I would never have taken you for an animal person. Hey! Don't get so close! Can't it shoot its quills at you?"

"What? No." David shook his head. "These guys do have a cool adaptation, though. New World porcupines have tiny little barbs at the end of their quills. The Old World porcupines, like the African Crested, just have straight quills, like the end of a bird feather. Both defend the same way. They can't shoot them because quills are only keratin, modified hair. Instead, their quills stick out like this and then they back up or charge you, sticking you with them. You ever watch *Homeward Bound* when you were little? Remember Chance ran into a porcupine? Well, that's what happened. The quills come out easily from the porcupine's skin, sticking into the target. But when they're barbed, like on this little guy, they can't just fall out once they've stuck in you. It's like a tiny little fishhook embedded in your skin. When you do yank them out, it takes a chunk of skin with it. It's amazing."

David inched closer, crouching down to see the porcupine at eye level. The quills angled down toward him as it continued to sway and hiss. He brought his flashlight up and moved the light over the porcupine's back, investigating it. Completely entranced, he followed as it began to climb up the pole and to the crossbeams of the roof.

Marisol was more focused on David than the porcupine. She didn't even recognize him. She watched his face light up as he observed the animal navigate from beam to beam before it disappeared around the neighboring cabin.

David turned around, a giant smile plastered on his face. "That was incredible."

"Definitely neat," Marisol replied with a hint of sarcasm on her tongue. She shook her head as they walked back into the cabin. "Double major, huh? Did you minor in porcupines specifically, or?"

"Haha. Very funny. I guess I always thought they were cool. If you haven't picked up on it yet, I'm a *bit* of a nerd. I think I've read every zoology book on campus."

"That does seem like something you would do," Marisol said, getting into bed. "Thanks for going to check."

David slid under the covers and flipped the switch to the small lamp between them. He stared up at the dark ceiling, thinking about what other things he could see here. *I'm finally doing it. A real adventure.* Soft whispering from the other side of the room snapped him out of his daydreaming. He strained his ears, listening closer. Marisol was praying.

"Hey," he said softly. "Don't let what that girl said freak you out. There's no such thing as curses."

The whispering stopped, leaving them entrenched in nothing but the sound of cicadas and crickets singing in the dark. David rolled over to try and see Marisol, but she was facing away from him. *There's no such thing as curses*, he repeated in his mind as his eyes closed and he drifted off to sleep.

4

L oud squawking echoed overhead as a flock of blue and green macaws passed above the trees. Their vibrant colors were barely noticeable between the small gaps in the leaves above. Macaws had been a frequent find throughout their trek, making themselves known by their brash and incessant calls. David pulled out a small notepad and pencil and made a hash-mark on one of the pages before shoving it back into his pocket. He adjusted the straps on his shoulders, shifting the weight from the additional camping bag he was now carrying.

Upon departure from the lodge, each of them had to carry extra bags. The backpacks contained packages of dehydrated food, extra water bladders, a sleeping bag, and their personal tents. Each person was also equipped with a satellite, or SAT, phone. The phones themselves ran on solar power, so they could be charged during the day in the case of an emergency.

Carrying the extra weight from the backpacks had initially slowed their walking speed. Dr. Morrow insisted on pressing forward at a faster pace and led the way for a short while. The dense trees and shrubs required them to remain single file. They took turns dropping to the back of the line when breaks were needed. The group had stopped once for a brief lunch, but that had been hours ago.

David glanced down at his watch. They had been walking for ten hours. A mixture of sweat and dew from the surrounding plants soaked through his shirt. He pulled at the fabric as it clung to him, looking ahead to see Marisol hiking her backpacks up higher on her shoulders while she ducked under a large, woody vine. It was clear that there was a trail hacked through the brush at some point, but fresh growth obscured most of the path. There were several places where thick, fallen branches blocked the way, causing them to divert through heavy weeds and bushes. David was relieved the guides knew their way and were proficient at recalculating the path, as they somehow always ended up back on the trail. He couldn't help but wonder how they were going to manage once they were left to continue on alone.

As they worked their way deeper into the rainforest, the environment became more formidable with each passing hour. Almost every plant, including the larger trees, had some kind of thorn or spine protecting it. Marisol pricked herself more than once while maneuvering through the dense foliage. They used their machetes to chip away at the long spines, being careful not to brush up against them. Dr. Morrow explained that there were several different ecosystems within the reserve. The area they were traveling through now was mostly Igapó rainforest. She described this blackwater-flooded ecosystem as one of the harshest environments in the area.

"I always like to describe it as something from a horror movie. It's nothing but sharp edges and thorns. It's hostile… nightmarish," Dr. Morrow said during a brief rest. "In this part of the grid, there are no floodwaters from the Andes. Instead, the water builds up in the interior from the swamps. Because of this, the plants leach compounds into the ground, essentially poisoning the groundwater."

"So, these are harsh plants born from a harsh environment?" Marisol asked.

"In a way," she continued. "The seasonal flooding and leaching of compounds give the water a high acidity."

"Most waters are alkaline, though, right? These are all adaptations from having to survive in an almost toxic environment," David said.

"Precisely. And it's one of the reasons this area is so ripe for new study. It's essentially uninhabitable. Not even indigenous peoples live in here. Paul once told me that it's 'inhospitable for anything other than the creatures that exist in the swamps.' A little dramatic, but I will say it's definitely not pleasant. It's manageable in the short term, though." Dr. Morrow quieted, staring off into the trees.

"I'm sure Ben's okay," Marisol offered gently. "We'll find him."

"We should keep going. We should be close to the first camp. Probably just another hour or so," Dr. Morrow said, standing and pulling her bags onto her back.

Andy blazed the trail ahead of the rest of the group, hacking his machete into a thick branch and slicing it in half before tossing it aside. He paused and held up a hand, signaling to the rest of the group. He moved forward, slicing smaller branches out of the way, then stopped at a thin tree and bent down. Tied to the tree with vinyl twine was the bottom half of a soda bottle. Water pooled at the bottom of the algae-covered plastic. David, second in line, squeezed next to him.

"Surrogate bromeliad," Andy said. "Ben puts them near the camps as markers. It also makes a home for *them*." He pointed down into the water.

David crouched down to look closer. A small, black blob darted around in the tiny pool of water. He looked up at Andy.

"Poison dart frog tadpole," said the guide. "The female brings them to the water in the bromeliads. They don't usually live here. Too wet."

"If this isn't where they live, why are they here now?" David asked.

"*Desconocido*. I don't know the word in English. Everything changes the further you go. It's dangerous to surround yourself with such magic."

48

Andy pushed past David and moved on, disappearing behind a large palm. Goosebumps rose along his skin when he brushed by him. Nelly passed next. She had been silent for the majority of the journey, pointing out the occasional wildlife sighting as they walked. David tried to ask her questions, but she refused to entertain him.

Dr. Morrow followed, stopping at the tree to reach down and touch the makeshift plastic bromeliad. She made eye contact with David, and sadness glossed over her eyes as she looked away and walked on. David's stomach knotted as he watched her. He knew she felt responsible for her former student but didn't know how to reassure her.

He flinched as fingers gripped his arm, and glanced up to see Marisol looking down at him. "Do you think you can take my tent for a little while? I feel like I'm moving at a snail's pace."

David's back already ached. He opened his mouth to protest, but quickly shut it when he looked at her. She looked exhausted. Her hair was in her face with pieces pulled out of place from being snagged on twigs. She rubbed at her neck, tilting her head from side to side, stretching the muscles. *I hope I don't look that tired.*

"Just give me your bag," he said, offering a small smile. His hand dropped as the weight hit his palm. He set it on the ground and removed his backpack. Using the bungee straps from his hiking bag, he secured Marisol's as best he could to his before replacing it on his shoulders. He tipped backward slightly, losing his balance before leaning forward to counter the weight. He looked around him, but Marisol had already started down the path behind the rest. *Thank God nobody saw that.*

They passed more water bottle pieces attached to the trees the longer they walked. David peered into them as he passed by, fascinated by the occasional tadpole swimming in the green water. The sun was starting to set, turning the already dim lighting of the rainforest to an all-encompassing dark shadow. Dr. Morrow and the guides had stopped fifty yards ahead. A large, nylon tent stood in a small clearing. Large, green patches of algae splattered the exterior. Fresh and bright green vines grew over and around it, making it look like the forest was reclaiming the space taken up from the unnatural furniture. Water pooled in small ruts dug out around the base of the tent, attracting swarms of mosquitoes which hovered nearby.

Dr. Morrow unzipped the front flap and peered inside. Stacked inside were three large, plastic bins. The outside of the bins were spotted with mildew, obscuring the contents. She stepped inside, collapsing a spider web that draped along the ceiling of the tent. Dr. Morrow unsnapped the lid of the first bin and reached inside. A stack of black three-ringed binders sat inside. She pulled out the first one, gently flipping it open. The binder was filled with page protectors, each one containing a plant pressing, ID tag, and field note card. She looked closer at the last page, reading the index card containing the relevant field notes.

October 13, 2019   #001025A

Site C - Possibly N-NW Sector   SSP???

Woody branches thin, 2mm.
Green, Laceolate leaves.
Small red seed-like buds. No flowers.
Igapó GPS not reading at Site C - no
coordinates-three specimens collected.

"October 13th...he would have been on his way back to the lodge," Dr. Morrow mumbled to herself. She put the notebook back, resealing the lid before opening the next one. She grabbed the next set of binders, flipping through, scanning for dates and locations.

The flap of the tent opened as Marisol peeked her head

inside. Dr. Morrow faced her, tears starting to flow down her cheeks. Marisol took the books from her hand and placed them on the nearest bin. She pulled Dr. Morrow in for a hug, letting the professor melt into her, sobbing.

"It's going to be okay," Marisol said as she ran a hand along her back. "Don't worry."

"He was my responsibility," she cried into Marisol's shoulder. "He was here. He must have turned around."

"If he did, I'm sure there was a good reason," she replied. "Maybe he lost track of time. You said he was fairly self-sufficient out here. I'm sure someone like that would know how to take care of themselves."

Dr. Morrow righted herself, blotting her eyes with the cuff of her sleeve. "I'm sorry I'm so emotional. It's not like me. If I had known earlier, we could have—"

"You can't think like that. What matters is that we're here looking for him now. Besides, we need you. I need you. You can't leave me out here to look after David. He'd never make it."

Dr. Morrow laughed as she brushed the tears away. "Thank you. It's been a long day. Let's get everyone settled in before it gets too dark."

Sounds of zippers and hammers on metal pins filled the clearing as the team assembled their tents. While made for one person, each tent still took up a decent footprint. To make room for five, they needed to spread out. Nelly and Andy worked on clearing ground space to accommodate everyone. Marisol and Dr. Morrow set up next to each other, helping one another stretch the aluminum poles through the frame of the tents.

Marisol jumped as she heard a loud growl from the other side of the camp, followed by the clashing of metal. She looked up to see David red-faced and glowering over the tent crumpled at his feet. He kicked the bundle of nylon before plodding away behind the nearby trees. Marisol and Dr. Morrow looked at each other and then to David's tent pieces.

"I'll go get him," said Marisol. She stepped around the poles and fabric and headed into the woods. She could see the back of David's head a few yards in. He was slumped over, sitting on a fallen log, his head in his hands. "Hey there," she said as she came up behind him.

David's back heaved as he let out an exasperated sigh. "Really?"

"I saw you storm off. I wanted to see if I could help."

"I don't want your help," he said stiffly. He lifted his head, turning toward her. "You know, I thought we were getting over this whole thing with you and me. I actually thought things were getting better…that this trip might not suck so damn much."

Marisol winced at his tone. She hadn't heard him angry before. "What are you talking about?"

"Oh, come on! 'You don't want to have to look after me…I'd never make it.' It's a freaking tent, Marisol, not a soundproof room."

"I…I didn't mean it like that. I was trying to lighten the mood. I'm sorry."

"I'm so *sick* of you saying you're sorry," he said, turning his back to her.

The air between them was palpable. Marisol stood frozen behind him. Her face burned, and her eyes welled up. She waited, trying to force herself to say something. She was embarrassed that he overheard her joke and ashamed that it had caused him to get so upset. She knew better. Humor was always her way of solving an uncomfortable situation, and she knew she sometimes did it at the expense of others. Now he sat there, silent, staring down at his feet. She wanted so badly to apologize but knew that would make it worse. Wiping at the tears forming at the corners of her eyes, she turned quietly and walked back to the campsite.

She stopped at David's area and looked at the mess of discarded tent pieces before picking up the scattered aluminum poles. Working silently, she grabbed the fabric and slid the poles through the corners, creating the frame. Emptying the remainder of the bag on the ground and grabbing a mallet, she pounded the stakes into the soft dirt, wedging them between roots to add some stability. She stood back, making sure the tent was complete. Leaving everything in place, she straightened her posture and wandered over to the research tent to join Dr. Morrow.

Dr. Morrow sat on the floor of the tent, binders spread around her on every side. She had a notebook in her lap and was scribbling furiously. "...lost GPS on day 2...increase in growth...SAT solar disabled...Site D?"

"Julia?" Marisol stepped into the large tent, carefully maneuvering around the scattered binders.

Dr. Morrow set her pencil down and looked up at Marisol with worried eyes. She offered her an index card, covered front to back with messy handwriting. Marisol held it up, trying to make sense of the small notations.

"What exactly am I looking at?"

"There are several of these that accompany the last couple weeks of Ben's field notes. I'm trying to make sense of them."

"I thought there were only three research camps. What is Site D?" Marisol asked.

"I guess he pushed on to another grid sector. We weren't projected to do that until after this next flood season. I'm trying to filter through some of the botanical notes and copy down some of the stranger observations."

"Stranger observations?" asked David quietly, sticking his head into the tent.

Marisol shuffled around the contents of the tent, making room for David while avoiding eye contact as much as possible. She handed him the notecard Dr. Morrow had given her. He pulled out a penlight from his pocket to get a better view.

"Rapid regrowth. Accelerated beyond normal parameters. Impenetrable. Extensive reach," David read aloud. "Everything is segmented, almost manic. The notations are written in the margins even. Why bring his notes all the way back here?"

"Normally, we bring all of our field binders back here first. We then go to the lodge and have some of the guides come out and help us bring all the essentials back. It doesn't make sense for him to bring so much back here and not have a check-in at the lodge."

"Do you think you have all of his notes here? We can go over them tonight. Maybe he left enough information to track where he is?" David offered.

Dr. Morrow shrugged and exhaled deeply. "They should all be dated. Why don't we go through them after dinner? There's a pond nearby. Nelly, Andy, and I were going to fish before it got too dark…hopefully give us a break from some of those dehydrated meals. You're more than welcome to come along."

"I think I may take some time to get off my feet for a bit," David replied.

"Same. I wouldn't mind trying to catch a cat-nap," added Marisol.

"No worries at all. I figured you both may be pretty tired." Dr. Morrow stood up, looking down at the cluttered floor. She rubbed her temples, taking in a big breath.

David placed a tentative hand on her shoulder. "We'll go through it all. We're here to help."

A soft laugh escaped her lips. "You're here to help me catalogue new species and solidify your own projects, not go on the hunt for a missing person."

"I'm sure we can manage both," said Marisol.

"Well, the least I can do is get you some good catfish for dinner," she said, giving them each a sad smile. "Go relax and take some time. We'll come back to this with fresh eyes."

David paced the area outside of Marisol's tent, walking up to the door before quickly retreating back several yards. After walking back and forth at least a dozen times, he approached the door one final time and took a deep breath, steadying himself.

"Hey Marisol?" he called out. "Can we talk?"

The zipper slid along the track and the door flap fell open. Forcing himself to move, David bent down and peered inside.

"Come on in," Marisol said quietly.

David slid off his shoes, leaving them outside of the tent before entering and plopping down next to her. He looked down at the floor, the door, and anything else that wasn't Marisol. After what felt like an eternity, he cleared his throat while trying to suppress the constant fiddling of his hands.

"Dr. Morrow said you put up my tent. Thank you."

"Yeah, no big deal."

David sat a while longer, the silence making him anxious. "Look…I'm sorry I snapped at you earlier. You didn't deserve that, and I shouldn't have yelled at you. I couldn't figure out the stupid tent. I was hot and tired and hungry. Apparently not a good combination for me. I-I just wanted to say that I'm sorry."

Marisol's face flushed a dark red, barely noticeable in the fading light. She swallowed hard and cleared her throat. "No, I'm sorry. I shouldn't have made you the butt of a joke. That wasn't right."

"You weren't wrong. We both know that I'm not the outdoorsy type. I don't even know why I'm out here. I would give anything to be sprawled out on my bed right now."

"Honestly…" Marisol hesitated. "You're handling this way better than I am."

"That can't possibly be an accurate statement."

"It is. I couldn't even carry my own bag that last bit." Marisol reached around David and pulled her picture frame close to her chest before holding it out and looking at her family photo. "And this is the longest I've gone without talking to my family. I used to call or text Matty every day. And I normally don't go more than a couple of days without talking to my dad." She ran her finger along the faces in the photo. "So, yeah, you're handling all of this better than me."

"That must be really hard."

"I didn't mean to say that you don't miss your parents. I guess it hit me harder than I was expecting."

David adjusted in the small tent, pulling his knees up to his chest. "You know, I can't even remember the last time I talked to my family. I sent them an email telling them about this trip a few months ago. I don't even think I got a response."

"Really? I can't imagine what that's like. I'm sorry."

"Oh, there's no reason to be sorry. It's just the way it is. So... who is who?" David nudged her picture frame and smiled, trying to divert the attention away from himself.

Marisol sat up straighter and held the photo between them. "This is my dad; he's the one that bought this really kitschy frame. And Ricardo, he's a few years older than me. Sebastian was after him...and then that's me and Matty, er, Mateo."

"Matty? That's a cute nickname."

Marisol sat up straighter, smiling at David. "It all started with *my* nickname, actually. My brothers call me Sunny. Ricardo came up with it when I was little. Marisol means the sea and sun, and that's what my dad always calls me: 'my sea and sun.'" She paused, smiling to herself. "Ricardo took that and made it Sunny. Me and Mateo always did everything together, so naturally, we matched nicknames. I'm Sunny, and he's Matty."

"Well, sunny definitely matches your personality," David said, bumping her with his shoulder.

"That better not be sarcasm," she laughed. She handed David the frame, pausing. "I think I hear everyone coming back." Marisol leaned out of the tent and saw Dr. Morrow and their guides walking through the trees with a handful of fish skewered on a thin branch. "Guess it's dinnertime," she said as she slipped on her shoes. She looked back to see David still looking at her family photo. "Hey...you coming?"

5

Dim light filled the research tent. A small solar-powered lantern hung from a hook attached to the poles on the inside. Dr. Morrow, Marisol, and David sat side by side in a semi-circle. In front of them lay over two dozen index cards, each with a varying amount of text scrawled across them. David reached out, moving them around, aligning dates and marking the listed locations in his notebook.

"We still have a gap between September 27th and October 3rd," he said. David touched each card, counting the dates in his head. "Are there any binders we haven't gone through yet?"

Dr. Morrow looked at a composition notebook by her feet, flipping back and forth between a few pages. "I have every week accounted for. I can go back through the bins again, but we've already done it twice."

"Alright," David said, a pencil between his teeth. He reached across Marisol and plucked the index card dated September 27th. He had looked at this card several times already, noting the increase in notations compared to the cards with earlier dates. The September 27th card was the first to mention Site D.

The scrawled handwriting spread over the margins and spilled onto the back of the page. Most of the notes were segmented, small glimpses into a train of thought. David scanned the card again, searching for a sign that may lead them toward wherever this new location could be.

New vine ssp? Abnormal growth pattern. Spreading throughout trees. Parasitic? Thick layering. No sun, dark—new ecosystem? Encompassed tent—lost part of camp. Dense vines, can't slice. Tried for new growth clipping.

David set the card on his notebook and picked up the index card dated October 3rd. Yawning, he flipped it over to see the back. He cut his yawn short with a frustrated huff. "And back at Site C." David groaned and pressed his fingers over his eyelids, rubbing hard. "There's just no information here. We have ten days of field notes after this and all it does is end on the 3rd without any direction. Everything goes back to normal with the sample pressings. The notes are still a little manic, but it's all in order. This 'Site D' is mentioned in passing, but nothing is as detailed after that day in September. I don't know what else to look at." David rested his head in his hands as another yawn escaped his mouth.

"Maybe there's nothing to find," Marisol said. "I feel like we've looked at this a dozen different ways. I don't know about you two, but I can barely keep my eyes open."

"No one writes little asides like this without a reason," David mumbled into his hand.

Dr. Morrow closed her notebook and stretched her arms up toward the top of the tent. "We may need to accept that there isn't a smoking gun in Ben's notes," she said. "We've transcribed all of them...more than once. Maybe there will be more information at the next camp."

Dr. Morrow reached down and started compiling the index cards, collecting them into a neatly stacked pile. David handed her the two he was looking at, lingering an extra few seconds with the September 27th card. There was something different about it...if only he could place it. He shook it off, thinking it was his brain working on overdrive from being so exhausted.

"What time are we up and at 'em again?" Marisol asked.

"Too early," replied Dr. Morrow. "We'll need to dip back

around to the pond to get water and boil it down to take with us."

"I can do that if you want," said David. "I wouldn't mind getting up before everyone and rinsing off anyway. I feel like I need a dozen showers after today."

"At least promise me you'll collect the water *before* you bathe in it?" said Marisol.

"I can send you with Andy in the morning. There's no way you can carry it all by yourself, and it's best not to wander off alone as it is." Dr. Morrow placed the notecards in the plastic bin before turning back to David. "We keep the buddy system."

David laid in his sleeping bag with his headlight shining from his forehead. He had made sure to purchase the nicest model he could find. It ran on solar with a battery back-up and had three light settings: bright, dim, and red. He kept the red light setting on in the tent, not wanting to attract bugs or keep the others awake. He held his notebook up, shining his light on the pages as he read his transcriptions of Ben's field notes.

> *He took clippings of five previously undescribed and unidentified flora. An epiphytic fern, an aroid — possibly a new species of philodendron, an Arecaceae (palm), a particularly prolific ficus/strangler fig, and an unclassified bush. Ben marked at least a dozen other plants but didn't give a classification nor make any remarkable notes about descriptions or location. The greatest number of clippings came from the bush, which didn't seem to fit into a classification. All of Ben's notes were neatly organized and concise. Most of the writing in the margins was of unimportance to the species classification and phenotype. The most hectic notes focused around the strangler fig and was the only specimen described from Site D. Crazy notes = excitement? = worry? = ???*

Bird calls rang through the trees as the songs from the evening's insects faded away. David opened his eyes, hearing a light rustling against the tent. Marisol's voice called softly through the vinyl door. "You awake?"

David managed a couple of half-words, half-grumbles in response. He lifted his head and immediately scrunched his eyebrows, feeling an unusual pressure against his forehead. The headlamp was still strapped to him while his notebook lay open on his chest.

"David? You said you'd be up early," Marisol called out a little louder.

"Yeah, yeah, give me like five minutes," he replied, peeling the headlamp off. He ran his hands through his hair, scratching his scalp before trying to smooth out his bedhead.

It was barely light outside, the sun not yet making its way above the trees. David unzipped his tent and was greeted by Marisol and Andy standing in the doorway.

"Jesus," said Marisol. "You look like crap. Did you even sleep?"

"Oh, thanks. Just what I want to hear before dawn."

David threw his bag over his shoulders as they headed into the jungle and toward the nearby pond. The trail was mostly clear. David was thankful that it was an easy walk and didn't require the same effort as the day before. The pond was of average size but had a small river from a distant water source branching off from the north. David and Marisol unpacked their bags and carried the water bladders to the pond's edge while Andy grabbed some supplies and headed back down the path. He set up their portable campfire off the trail, removing debris to make a small clearing. A fallen log sat between some trees, creating the perfect spot to sit and wait for the water to be purified.

Between the bacteria, parasites, and insects, drinking unfiltered water from the ponds and rivers posed a high risk. Dr.

Morrow packed several portable campfires to use for cooking and boiling fresh water. The metal containers were filled with recycled paper briquettes and wax and had a burn life of up to five hours. Making a regular campfire was not only too risky for the potential starting of a wildfire, but most of the kindling remained too wet to even catch a flame. The tins were small, about the size of a small pan, but did the trick for what they needed.

Andy lit the fire and propped a 2-gallon pot above it using a small, metal stand. David and Marisol refilled the bladders, carrying them back one-by-one to Andy. By the second trip, David's forehead was already dripping with sweat. Before bringing back the last of the bladders, he pulled a large water bottle out of his bag. He tugged at the lid, separating the bottle into two pieces. He took the outer shell of the bottle and dipped it into the pond.

"I hate to be the one to tell you this," Marisol said, watching him, "but the whole point of this is to boil the water so we can fill our bottles and *not* get giardia."

David stuck the other end of the bottle into the cup portion and pressed down hard, leaning his body weight against the top of it. "It's a self-filtering water bottle," he said, popping open the spout to take a sip. He handed it to Marisol while he picked up the remaining two water bladders.

Marisol rotated the bottle in her hands, the letters GRAYL were plastered on the side. She followed behind him as he headed back down the trail. She flipped the cap open and cautiously took a sip of water.

"This literally cleans your water for you?"

"Mhm," David grunted as he readjusted the heavy water bags.

"How?"

"Can it wait?" David reached the log where Andy sat tending to the fire. He dropped the remaining bags at Andy's feet and took the bottle from Marisol before downing half of the water inside. Wiping his mouth with the back of his hand, he said, "You fill the cup piece up with water. The other piece has a filter, so when you push down, it forces it through, cleaning it as you go."

"Oh, so rich people toys," Marisol said with a small shrug.

David rolled his eyes and tucked the bottle back in his bag. He threw one strap over his shoulder and started walking back toward the pond. "I'll be back in a bit!"

David stood waist-deep in the murky pond, slowly cupping the water in his hands and running it over his arms and chest. The morning air was chilly, bringing goosebumps to his skin as he bathed. He stayed a few yards offshore, too nervous to venture any deeper into the unknown waters. David closed his eyes, lowered himself down, and held his breath as he ducked his head underwater.

"Woo!" he shouted as he hopped back up to his feet, shaking the water from his hair and running his hands along his arms.

"That cold?"

David ducked back below the surface as he glanced up to see Marisol at the edge of the pond. She kicked off her shoes while setting her bag on the ground. She lifted her shirt off, revealing a black sports bra.

"What are you doing?" David asked, his head sticking up out of the water.

"You think you're the only one that's completely covered in sweat? I feel so gross." She slipped off her pants and placed them neatly on her bag, stopping to look at him. "Are you going to watch me or are you going to turn around?"

"Oh, obviously…sorry," he stammered as he faced away. He dipped his head back under as he heard her enter the water.

"You weren't kidding," Marisol said. She shivered as she crept deeper into the pond. "This is so cold."

David chuckled. "I'd like to think it would be really refreshing several hours from now when we're sweating again."

"How deep does it get? Or is it all pretty shallow?"

"I haven't the slightest. I'm honestly a bit terrified to go any further in. I'm not sure I feel like getting eaten by a caiman or chewed to death by piranha."

Marisol waded in the water behind him. "I think that may be a tad dramatic, don't you think?"

A loud scream came from the nearby trees, making David's hair stand on end. He jumped up and focused his eyes on the tree line. The call intensified as another round of screams joined in chorus. David scanned the trees, looking for the source of the calls. His heart dropped into his stomach as something cold brushed against his arm.

"What do you think it is?" Marisol whispered, now standing next to him.

"Jesus! Don't sneak up on me!" David hissed. He blinked, staring back at the shore, and pointed to the top of the nearby trees. "Ooh, look!"

The branches and leaves dipped and shook as the wings of a large bird stretched out into the skyline. The bird, gray with white splotches on its chest, wobbled up the thin branches and perched on the top of the tree, its size emphasized by the small leaves underneath it. It threw its head back, stretching its long neck, and let out a call. Its feathers ruffled as it adjusted its feet on the top of the tree. The bird shook its head before bending its neck backward and releasing another loud scream.

A shadow passed across the water in front of them. David lifted his head up to see another large, gray bird gliding above them. He followed it as it landed gracefully on an adjacent tree. The two birds took turns making screaming and whooping calls. David thought it was loud enough that Nelly and Dr. Morrow could probably hear it back at the camp.

"Well, Mr. I almost got a PhD in zoology?"

David looked down at her to give a snarky response, but quickly looked away. Her arms were crossed, covering her bare chest as they stood side-by-side. He shuffled his feet through the muddy sediment, trying to create a bit of distance. Her damp hair stuck to his upper arm as he pulled away slowly.

A smirk crossed Marisol's lips as she looked over to him shifting in the water. "Are you seriously slinking away from me right now?"

"No!" David froze in place. He searched for a spot on which to focus his attention but could feel her eyes boring into him. "Okay, fine, yeah…yes. I'm trying to be respectful. I mean, you're naked, so…yeah, I didn't want to come across—"

"You are *so* high-strung," she interrupted, trying to stop the verbal flood pouring from his mouth. "It's fine. I honestly don't care as long as you're not going to stare and gawk."

"I wouldn't do that," he said quickly. He focused his eyes on the birds still screaming over the trees. "Why don't you care, though? Am I that non-threatening?"

"You're totally not threatening." Marisol smiled. "But that's not it. The way I see it, is that no one goes anywhere alone, right? We're always in a buddy system. That said, I already assumed at some point we'd have to suck it up and be in this position together. I'm not saying it's comfortable for me—far from it—but I'm sure as hell not getting my limited supply of bras soaked because I'm too self-conscious. There is no way I'm hiking for almost twelve hours a day in a wet bra."

David lowered himself back down in the water. "I'd say I understand that, but I'm going to have to hike in drenched underwear after Paul's warning back at the lodge."

Marisol ducked down, crouching next to him. She studied him briefly, looking him over and wishing he didn't make things so awkward.

"Can't say I'd risk it if I was in your shoes either. Maybe try saving one pair for swamp baths?"

"Swamp baths? Way to make me feel even less clean." David laughed softly as he looked over at her and flashed a forced smile. "And I think they're horned screamers."

Marisol looked down at her chest and shrugged. "I guess I've heard worse nicknames for them."

"Oh my God," David snorted. "The birds. Horned screamers."

Marisol's lips curved upward in a satisfied smile. She was happy she was able to find a way to make him laugh, even if it meant making herself feel silly. She had hoped David would get more comfortable the longer they were together, but he was proving to be a challenge. He was a mystery wrapped in a nervous and constantly stressed body. She wanted to break through his shell without breaking him...and she was always up for a challenge.

They sat together in the water watching the birds until they flew off minutes later. The sun had risen over the tree line, and the temperature was already climbing. David turned away as Marisol got out of the pond and wrapped herself in a towel. He followed behind her, wishing he thought to bring his towel to the water bank.

"I didn't know you had a tattoo," he said as he slipped his pants on.

"And I thought you weren't going to stare," Marisol answered without looking up from drying her hair.

David's face turned beet red. He grabbed a clean shirt from his bag and pulled it over his head. As he tugged it on, he saw Marisol walking over to him.

"I wasn't staring, I promise. I barely glanced over."

"I'm just messing with you. Here." She lifted the side of her sports bra up to reveal an intricate tattoo painted on her ribcage.

"Wow. That's pretty cool. What is it of?"

"Mal de Ojo, the evil eye." She tugged her bra back down. "My family is pretty superstitious—my mom's side, especially."

"And you?"

"I'd like to say I'm not...but some things just stick with you. Mal de Ojo is definitely one of them. My abuela was the first on my mom's side to leave Puerto Rico. She helped raise me after my mom passed, so there were a lot of weird things she did to solve problems. She always made me put a glass of water behind my bedroom door to ward off any evil spirits." Marisol paused

65

as a thin smile crossed her face. "I may or may not still do that in my apartment."

"Why do you still do it if you don't believe in it?"

"Memories, I guess. She was the only grandparent I had." Marisol crossed her hand to her ribs and touched her tattoo. "That and I guess you never know. It's less not believing and more of knowing that we really don't know what's out there."

"Is that why you got so freaked out when Nelly mentioned that curse?"

"I wasn't freaked out." Marisol's mood shifted and her smiled dropped. She crossed over to her bag and threw a tank top on unceremoniously. Her drying hair formed loose ringlets that fell down past her shoulders. She combed her fingers through her hair, pushing through knots, before fashioning it into a ponytail. "Okay," she said, turning sharply to face David. "I was a little freaked out. In my family, you don't talk about curses. It's best not to mess with that kind of stuff. Hopefully it's only harmless, local folklore, and we won't have to find out."

By the time they arrived back at the research camp, both of their tents had been disassembled and packed neatly away. David and Marisol walked together at the back of the line while Nelly led the way to Site B.

The hours ticked by as the temperature and humidity rose. David's limbs were heavy. He knew his lack of sleep from the night before was catching up to him. He wiped the sweat off his forehead with his shirt to find it was already completely saturated.

I have never walked this much in my life, he thought. *Or sweat this much before…or been so tired.*

He looked up at Dr. Morrow who had fallen back to be the second to last in line. She had perfect posture. He didn't even know how that was possible with all of the supplies she carried. He was envious of how well she handled herself. He straightened his back, emulating her. He made it about twenty steps before slumping his shoulders back down and leaning into the balls of his feet, forcing himself forward.

They came upon a large, hollow palm trunk and decided to break for lunch while they had a place to sit. The tree offered enough room for three of them. David plopped onto the ground, not even noticing the moistness of the dirt seeping through the back of his pants. Marisol sat next to him on the log while Andy and Dr. Morrow set up one of the portable campfires. Nelly sat on the far end of the log and sharpened her machete with a large stone she pulled out from her bag.

Dr. Morrow opened several foil packages of dehydrated food and poured a ladle-full of boiling water into each of them. She handed the ready-to-eat food packs to Marisol and David before sitting on the fallen palm and digging in. Marisol talked excitedly to her about the birds they saw when they went to the pond while Dr. Morrow shared stories of the different wildlife she had encountered in her multiple trips. Marisol was halfway through her favorite story about how iguanas were taking over Miami when she paused, a weight suddenly present against her leg. She peered down to see David's head resting against her thigh. Dr. Morrow leaned forward and saw his eyes closed and his mouth half-open. His foil food container was nestled in his hands as they rested loosely in his lap. His chest moved softly up and down with long, deep breaths.

"He did say he didn't get much sleep last night," Marisol said. "He was up going over Ben's field notes."

"Huh, he didn't say anything to me. I guess he didn't find anything new or useful. We can give him a few minutes. But we still have a lot of ground to cover."

Dr. Morrow gathered the trash and sealed it tightly in a plastic bag. Marisol reached down, gently nudged David's head, and was met with a small groan in response. She gave a sympathetic smile as he raised his head up with tired eyes.

"Oh crap. I'm so sorry," he muttered, still half-asleep. "I didn't mean to fall asleep on you."

"Don't worry about it. We're getting ready to keep going, though. You good?"

"Stellar," he said, finding his feet. Normally, he couldn't fall asleep anywhere that wasn't a bed. He remembered how agitated he was when Marisol fell asleep almost instantly on the flight to Peru. He couldn't imagine how tired he must be to fall asleep sitting up in the middle of the rainforest.

David grabbed his machete and joined the guides, swinging away at a mess of thin vines that draped down from the branches overhead. The vines broke easily, leaving stringy, red tendrils by their feet. As they were cut away, more fell down from the trees, taking their place. They chopped relentlessly, slicing away vine after vine. Even taking turns, it felt like they had been hacking through layers for hours. David's eyebrows pinched together as he followed the source of the vines up the trees. They stopped at a large and thick trunk-like vine that blocked the pathway. Its hollow interior was filled with colorful bromeliads, mosses, and rotting leaves. Dr. Morrow and Marisol joined the guides, trying to cut through the latest obstacle.

There has to be an easier way around, David thought.

He spun in place, surveying the different paths. Behind him, Nelly was whispering harshly to Andy as they worked on pushing through the trail. David noticed Nelly had become increasingly agitated the farther along they traveled.

"Hey guys," David said with his back facing the group.

The sound of metal ricocheting off the impossibly solid vine echoed around them.

"Guys," David repeated, trying to talk over the noise.

Nelly took a final swing and threw her hands up in frustration. Her machete remained in place, wedged into a sliver of the wood. David heard her arguing with Andy as Dr. Morrow's voice raised between them.

"Surely we can climb over. It may be a pain, but it's doable," said Dr. Morrow.

"Not with our supplies. It's best to cut through," Nelly said.

"It's not working. We need another route."

"Guys!" David yelled with his back still turned.

Nelly turned toward David and fell silent. Marisol dropped her machete on the ground and quietly walked up to stand next to him.

"What the…" Marisol's mouth hung open.

"It's the forest. We are not meant to be here," Nelly whispered.

"Enough of this nonsense!" Dr. Morrow growled.

Marisol pointed a shaky finger ahead. "But how do you explain *that*?"

Hundreds of small vines filled the space behind them. The path they had cleared moments before was obscured by a wall of red, hanging shoots. The remnants of the sliced plants still laid on the ground in front of them. David cautiously stuck his arm out and pushed his machete into the vines. With a quick snap of his wrist, he sliced through them horizontally. The vine ends fell to the ground in a small heap. He glanced over his shoulder and saw the group staring at him. He crept forward, keeping his machete in front of him, slowly slicing away to make a path. Marisol's hand jutted into the vines to take a hold of David's backpack.

"Don't," she said, her voice wavering.

Nelly spoke angrily to Andy, the Spanish a blur to David. She lifted her machete from where it had stuck on the vine, pushing past David as he watched the vines fall away around her until she was out of view. A defeated look spread across Andy's face as he made eye contact with Dr. Morrow.

"Go," she said. "We're almost there. We'll be fine. You can't let her go back alone."

He took his backpack off and placed it on the ground next to her. "If you insist on staying, take the extra food." He reached out and shook her hand before turning and disappearing into the vines after Nelly.

Dr. Morrow shoved her and Andy's bag through the gaps in the large vine. "Let's go."

David and Marisol exchanged a nervous glance. Marisol's

eyes were wide and her feet were rooted to the ground. David rested a hand on her arm and gave it a light squeeze.

"It's either back or through," he said, releasing his grip.

She moved forward, removing her backpack, and pushed it through the mud behind Dr. Morrow's and Andy's. She watched as Dr. Morrow pulled herself up on top of the vine and then disappeared to the other side. She anxiously looked back to David, hoping for another option. The area that he had cut away moments before was regrown again, blocking the way back once more.

He met her eyes, seeing the panic forming there. "I know."

Marisol knew she had to keep moving forward, but the thought of venturing deeper into a supposedly cursed jungle had her frozen in place. Her stomach ached with dread.

David stepped toward her. "I can help you up."

Marisol nodded stiffly as she faced the vine. It stood slightly below her head; she guessed around five feet tall. It was the size of a tree trunk, but had large holes speckled throughout it. She had seen this type of vine before and had even studied a similar species as an undergrad. It was a strangler vine—a type of parasitic plant that fed on its host and grew around the trunks of trees, strangling the life out of them. Once the host tree died and disintegrated, the vine itself stayed in place, a ghostly shell of the life that was once there. She always felt admiration, thinking they were morbidly beautiful. Now all she felt was fear.

Her grandmother always spoke of signs and omens. She never put much stock into those beliefs, but she wasn't so sure she could dismiss those feelings now. She had a sinking feeling in her gut that this vine, this elaborate coffin, was just a warning of what was to come.

6

Dr. Morrow tucked her head against her chest as a constant flow of rain poured off her wide-brimmed hat. She watched as David chopped through branches and hanging roots to clear the way forward. The sound of raindrops slapping against the palm fronds and ficus leaves drowned out any chance at conversation.

She knew the kids were worried. She also knew that at their age, they weren't kids; they were adults who made a choice to come on this trip. Not only that, but they were adults who knew better than to believe in ghost stories.

She swore under her breath at the sheer frustration she felt with Nelly. She had worked with her for years. She was a great woman to have as a companion in a male-dominated field. She had never mentioned curses or lore or stupid superstitions before. Why now?

The rain began to fall harder, sending thick sheets of water down through the trees to pool at their feet and soak through their shoes. She saw David stop up ahead and hold his hand over his eyes to block the water. It was already dark, and it was only the late afternoon. It was going to be difficult for them to keep trekking along in this weather. Dr. Morrow joined David to monitor the trail conditions ahead.

In front of them lay a large section of ground, free from any obstruction. Tall trees with enormous buttressing roots encircled the clearing. Dr. Morrow pulled the compass from her pocket and waited for the needle to find its course.

"This can't be right," she muttered to herself, tapping the glass front of the compass.

David skirted the base of one of the trees to get some cover from the onslaught of rain as Dr. Morrow took over. His foot brushed against something hard, and he tripped forward, catching himself on the large trunk. Looking down, he saw something shiny sticking out of the muddy puddle at his feet. He stuck his hand in the water, getting on his knees to investigate further, and felt something smooth and about the size of a water bottle sunken below the surface. He wrapped his hand around it and pulled, dislodging it from the thick mud, before rinsing it off in the dirty water and rolling it back and forth in his hands.

"Dr. Morrow!" David yelled over the rain.

Dr. Morrow's hat fell to the ground as she hurried to meet David's calls. He handed the object to the professor, using the tree as leverage to pull himself out of the sticky substrate. As he stood, mud sloughed off in clumps from the legs of his pants, now blackened with dirt. Marisol appeared next to Dr. Morrow, her drenched hair plastered to her face.

"What is it?" she asked.

"It's one of our flashlights," said Dr. Morrow. Her eyes darted back around the clearing, searching. "I don't understand. This looks like our second camp, but it should still be a day or two away."

"Maybe we accidentally took a shortcut?" David asked warily.

"But if this is the second camp," Marisol said, "where is all of your stuff?"

"I don't know." Dr. Morrow clutched the flashlight to her chest and stepped out into the clearing.

A gust of wind shook the leaves, splashing more water down below. Marisol attempted to fix her hair, pulling her soaked curls into a new ponytail. As she raised her head, she saw David take off around the other side of the tree and into the thick brush. Spindly twigs scraped at her arms and face as she followed, trying to keep up with him.

"What on earth are you doing?" she asked. "You can't just run off like that!"

David's head arched back as he stared into the branches overhead. The right side of his face was streaked with blood. Several long scratches brandished his cheek and neck, where sharp twigs had snagged his skin.

"Do we tell her?" David asked quietly as Marisol came up beside him.

Suspended above them in a mass of winding vines and limbs were the tattered remains of a large vinyl tent. Thin roots dangled from the fabric like a beaded curtain, worming their way in and out of the torn material. The brown, plastic remnants of the tent were stained green from algae and moss.

"H-how did you know this was here?" asked Marisol.

Rainwater dripped off David's face. The blood from his cheek washed down his neck, staining the collar of his shirt.

"I didn't," he said with a shrug. "The rain sounded different. It sounded like it was hitting a tarp or something. I guess I was hoping it was something else…I don't know what."

"How did it get up there?"

"I don't know." He gingerly ran his fingers along his cheek and held his hand out in front of him. Droplets of diluted blood ran off his fingertips. Sensing Marisol watching him, he hastily wiped his hand on his pants before shoving it into his pocket. "We have to have her come look. Maybe it's not their tent. Maybe someone else came through here?"

"Oh yeah, I'm sure it's Joe Shmoe's tent," said Marisol. "Stay here. I'll go get her."

David removed his backpack and leaned it against the tree. He shook his head vigorously, flinging water droplets all around him. The rain was easing, and the light pitter-patter of occasional raindrops on leaves filled the space around him.

Securing his headlamp around his forehead, he looked up at the entangled tent. Green, leafy vines poked holes in the fabric and intertwined with each other before crawling back up into the bough of the tree. The leaves on the vine seemed familiar, eerily similar to several of the plant pressings they reviewed in Ben's notebooks.

He grabbed his machete and stood under the lowest hanging vine. It draped through the bottom of the tent and wrapped around the trunk a few feet above his head. David wielded the machete above him as he leapt upward. The blade skirted the arm of the vine as he landed. He fell backward, nearly colliding with a cluster of bamboo. The spines protruding from the stalks stabbed at him and tugged at his shirt as he pulled away.

"Are you okay?" Dr. Morrow asked as she pushed through the branches with Marisol at her heels. She reached toward the scrapes brandishing his face. "You have to be careful out here."

"I, um, I-I'm fine," said David. He brushed at his cheek, now flushed from where the professor nearly touched him. "It's just some scratches."

"Marisol said you found something?"

"We don't know how to ask this...but is that yours?" Marisol asked, nodding her head to the mangled tent.

Dr. Morrow's eyes narrowed as she looked up at the hanging remains. She paced around the trunk of the tree, studying the way the vines twisted in and throughout the fabric. Her shoulders dropped as she turned to Marisol. "Yes. That's the research tent. Have you found anything else that could indicate that Ben—"

"No," David interjected quickly. "It looks like it's been up there for a while, probably more than a couple of weeks. And we know he went back to the last camp, right? Surely that means whatever happened here happened after he left?"

"You're right. We don't have reason to assume anything worse than we...*I* already have. I would, however, like to try and get this down, see if anything was left inside."

"I was looking it over, and it seems like the trunk of the vine runs along the length of this tree trunk and then the arms branch out over the limbs, through the fabric, and then over to this neighboring tree. I was trying to snag a piece to compare it to the notes, but I can't reach it," David said.

Dr. Morrow unsheathed her machete and held it in the air, gauging the distance to the nearest connection. The tent itself appeared to be suspended by a singular rooted vine with the arms and tendrils poking through the fabric, holding it to the tree.

"David," she said, turning to him. "Do you think you could lift me? Only a couple of feet so I can reach the key points. Obviously, you're the tallest, but if you can't reach it, I don't know the odds of Marisol or me giving you a boost."

David's eyes flitted between Dr. Morrow and the tree. He shifted his weight back and forth on his feet as he contemplated how many ways that suggestion could go poorly for him. His eyes settled back on the professor. He bit down on his lower lip and nodded nervously several times. "Yeah, okay."

Dr. Morrow stood to the right of the tent, looking up to where the vine bridged to the next tree. David came up behind her, still shifting anxiously. Her head barely came up to the bottom of his chin. He could see the strawberry blonde streaks that ran through her hair. He crouched down, bringing his head flush against her hip, positioning her buttocks between his neck and shoulder. She rested her weight on him and kept her hand out toward the tree. David could feel the heat rising in his face. He hoped Marisol wouldn't look at him and point out how red he looked.

"Just be careful and don't cut me with that," David pleaded as he wrapped his arms around her hips. He tried his best to focus on anything except where his hands were placed. "You ready?"

Dr. Morrow held on to the tree trunk and steadied herself as David lifted her up on his shoulder. He lowered his head and straightened his knees, pushing her up toward the branches. With one hand pushed against the tree, she used the machete to cut away at the thickest part of the vine. She yanked at the rootlets, peeling the sticky tendrils off the tree. Once cleared, she reached up and began pulling the freed vine from the tent.

David dug the balls of his feet into the mud as Dr. Morrow reached higher, tugging at the tent. For every bit she loosened, she chopped away more of the vine. The thin green shoots fell and tickled David's face as more of the vine came free. She took one last swing with her machete and sliced through a thick portion of the vine, dropping the tent to the ground. Dr. Morrow leaned back to avoid the mess of leaves and tendrils coming down with the torn fabric and support poles.

David grabbed her legs and waist as he tilted along with the professor. He pulled her down from his shoulder, sliding her forward as he fell backward into the nearby bamboo clump. He yelped as the large, black spines pierced his shirt and stuck into his back between his shoulder blades. Marisol rushed over and grabbed his shoulder, helping him right himself.

"You okay?" she asked. Marisol spun him around so that his back was facing her. She began to slide the back of his shirt up to assess the damage.

"Hey! Stop!" he protested, yanking the shirt from her hands and spinning back to face her. "Barely grazed me."

"You should let me take a look," Dr. Morrow said, freeing her feet from the tangle of vines now clustered at the bottom of the tree. "Those spines can be really nasty."

"Guys...I'm fine." David adjusted his shirt, still sopping from the earlier rain. Small throbs emanated from his back where the needles had stuck him. He was thankful his shirt was both dark and wet because he had a sneaking suspicion that he was bleeding. The last thing he wanted was any more fuss over him after the past couple of days. "So, are we going to check this tent out or what?"

Dr. Morrow lifted the top of the tent while Marisol felt around the outside for the door. The fabric was heavily worn and ripped in several places. Algae on the outside left her hands covered in a thin slime. Marisol found the zipper and pulled it open to reveal the mildew-filled interior. Thin sheets of paper stuck to the moist fabric and covered the majority of the floor. Two small, wooden plant presses lay open, half-obscured by the loose blotting papers. Marisol climbed in, carefully sifting through the papers, looking for any kind of remnants left behind.

Seeing that the two women had the tent taken care of, David turned his attention to the discarded pile of plant matter. He pulled his bag over and removed a large Ziploc baggie before he sifted through the vines, flipping the leaves over to inspect the color and shape. He grabbed a section of the main trunk and counted three separate arms, each covered in dark green, diamond-shaped leaves. David opened the plastic baggie and carefully coiled the vine inside. As he tucked it back into his backpack, he heard a shrill scream behind him. He whipped around as Marisol tumbled backward out of the tent.

"What is it? What happened?" Dr. Morrow asked, dropping and collapsing the tent onto itself.

Marisol was brushing at her arms frantically and shaking out her hair. "There's a giant spider in there! I was feeling around for equipment or something and, ugh, I feel like I have spiders crawling all over me!"

"But, like, how big was the spider *really*?" David asked. "Or are you just scared of spiders?"

"I am *not* scared of spiders!" Marisol snapped back. "It was fucking huge." She stood up from the mud and shook her arms and legs, still jittery. "You're more than welcome to go look."

David rolled his eyes and let out an agitated breath. "Dr. Morrow, would you mind holding it back up?"

David slowly crawled into the tent on the lookout for a

spider big enough to warrant that kind of response. *Why are girls always so freaked out by bugs? I can't believe this is how I'm spending my time out here, as a bug catcher. There's nothing even in here. A billion pieces of paper...mold...pressing boxes...no 'giant' spider.* David collected the two wooden plant presses and secured them closed before backing out of the tent. "Maybe you're just paranoid," he said, turning to Marisol. "Only some supplies and a lot of wasted blotting sheets and...what?"

Marisol was staring at David, her eyes the size of saucers.

"What?" he asked again, his annoyance rising.

"Uh, David...don't move," said Dr. Morrow from behind him.

David turned his head to look at Dr. Morrow but froze in place as Marisol screeched, "She said don't move!"

"Would one of you please tell me what the problem is?" David asked.

David's shirt prickled against his upper arm. Tiny tugs at the fabric moved down the front of his shoulder and to his collarbone. He shifted his eyes to look down at his chest and sucked in a quick breath as he saw a large, hairy spider walking along the front of his shirt. It was about the size of his palm and covered in thick, black hair. The ends of its legs were light pink, a stark contrast to his dark shirt.

Marisol held her hands up, her voice barely above a whisper. "Don't. Move."

"It's okay," David said as he exhaled. His heart raced in his chest. "It's just a tarantula."

"*Just* a tarantula?" Marisol's eyes were glued to the massive spider. "I don't want you to get bit. It's huge," she added in a whisper.

"I just need to scoot him off...slowly. You don't have to whisper, but don't come near me. I'm going to hand you these boxes, okay?" David made eye contact with Marisol. He hoped that he didn't look as nervous as he felt. He extended his arms out slowly, trying to move as little as possible. His fingers trembled as Marisol lifted the plant presses out of his hands. He slowly breathed out, gathering himself. "Okay. Okay. Um, go in my bag. There's a folder in there."

Dr. Morrow crouched down and sifted through his backpack before pulling out a dark green folder with a sticker across the front labeled *DISSERTATION*. She came around in front of him with the folder in hand. David's eyes were closed, and he was mumbling to himself under his breath.

"South American tarantulas have urticating hairs. They flick them off for protection. If they don't sense danger, they won't get defensive. Just breathe. You can do this." David opened his eyes to see the two women staring at him. He caught Marisol's eyes and forced a small smile. "You were right. It's a big fucking spider."

"My guess is you want to get it on the folder, right? That's a smart plan." Dr. Morrow's voice carried an overly calm lilt as she spoke. A sympathetic smile crossed her face as she swallowed. "Would it help if I told you it was a pink-toed tarantula?" she added softly.

"Why-would-that-help-me?" he squeaked in a single word as he eyed the spider.

She shrugged. "You've been asking about each species we've seen. I thought it would help. But you know what? Don't worry about it. We've got this and it's going to be fine."

She inched up to David with the folder outstretched flat toward him. As she got closer, the tarantula began to move down his shirt toward his stomach. Each of its eight legs pulled gently at the fabric of his shirt as they lifted and stretched. David clenched his muscles and squished his eyes shut. Dr. Morrow pulled the folder away and stepped back. David's breathing quickened as he opened his eyes and looked down to see the spider resting right below his chest.

"What if we put the folder underneath it and then kind of just—I don't know—herd it down?" David hoped he had said the words out loud and that he wasn't completely frozen in fear. He pulled his vision away from the tarantula and focused on Dr.

Morrow. "You can use the stuff in the folder. Just go slow and…
please be careful."

Dr. Morrow opened the folder and pulled out a stack of
papers held together by a paperclip. She balanced the folder on
the palm of her hand, rested it directly under David's belt, and
held the bound papers up by his chest. She took the papers and
moved them down along his chest and toward his stomach. The
tarantula shifted again, slowly moving away and toward the flat
surface of the folder. Dr. Morrow nudged the back of the spider
with the stack of paper. With a soft plop, it landed on the folder.
Dr. Morrow spun away from David and toward the tent, flicking
the folder up and sending the tarantula into the tangle of vine
clippings.

David heaved a sigh of relief as he relaxed his muscles and
let his shoulders slouch. He looked up and saw Marisol still
staring at him, unblinking. "Told you it was okay," he said
jokingly as he waited for his pulse to return to normal. David
took his folder and papers and returned them to his backpack,
hoping neither of them would notice his still shaking hands.

"You handled that really well," Dr. Morrow said from behind
him. "We run into tarantulas all the time around here. Usually,
they're just hanging out on tree trunks and out of the way. I've
never had to get *that* close."

"You see them all the time?" Marisol asked, surprised. "I
mean, I'm not generally scared of spiders, but tarantulas are
different than the big Huntsman and wolf spiders we get in
Florida."

"The thing to be worried about is their hairs," David interjected from over his shoulder. "You *do not* want to get those in
your eyes…or anywhere else, really."

"You were talking about urticating hairs, right? Is that
anything like the urticating hairs on nettles?" Marisol asked.

"Exactly like that, actually," David said, facing them and
trying to ignore the wobbling in his legs. "They use their legs to
send their hairs flying into the air. It's like tiny pieces of fiberglass that lodge into your skin. I remember going over stinging

nettles in one of my classes, but it's the same physical reaction as brushing up against one—irritation, rash, all of that." David's hand subconsciously reached up and touched his shirt where the tarantula had been moments before.

"My thesis is actually on plant defenses. Trichomes, the 'tarantula hairs' of the plant, are one of my areas of focus. I'd love to pick your brain about the correlations between the two. I wonder if I can add something like that to my paper and—"

"I appreciate the excitement and passion," David interrupted, "but do you think we can dial it back a notch until we know what's going on?"

"Oh…yeah, of course, obviously. I know I can get a little carried away. Dr., er, Julia, where *do* we go from here? Do the tent and random supplies mean this used to be your second research site?"

Dr. Morrow looked at the two of them and let out a heavy sigh. "I really don't know. It seems like it, but it doesn't feel right. I don't know how our things would have ended up in a tree. We don't even get heavy winds or intense storms in this area."

"So, what do we do?" David asked.

"Well," Dr. Morrow said, "since we're all drenched and covered in mud, I say we set up our stuff back in the clearing and give ourselves a bit of a reset. I'd like to boot up the SAT phone and double-check our coordinates, compare it to the grid map. If we did somehow cut multiple days off our walk, then I guess we can't complain."

Marisol showed David how to set up his tent before working on her own. They each took a corner of the clearing with their tents set up against the large trees. Dr. Morrow erected her tent and unfolded a laminated aerial map of the region. The map itself was only the size of a sheet of legal paper but encompassed the entire Tamshiyacu-Tahuayo region. Marisol sat on the ground outside of Dr. Morrow's tent and leaned over, examining the map.

Gridlines were drawn in wax pencil over the mass of green trees. The research lodge was visible at the edge of the map, the only indication of human interference within the blur of fuzzy, green splotches. Three squares marked with large Xs dotted the first quarter of the map, extending out from the lodge. The first marked square, labeled X_a, was four grid boxes away from the lodge. The second square, labeled X_b, was six boxes away from the first. The final marked box, X_c, was another six grid boxes away from the second. Each square pushed further into the unknown wilderness.

Dr. Morrow removed the satellite phone from a case on her hip and pressed the power button. She set it next to the map and ran her finger over the grid, mimicking the path they had taken.

"It's hard to believe how large the jungle is," Marisol said. "There's so much out there and yet we're barely on the outskirts."

"This conservation region is over one million acres in size," said Dr. Morrow. "No one has explored as deeply as we have... and we haven't even scraped the surface."

"Why haven't more people been here?"

"The reserve itself is almost impenetrable. You see how long it's taken us to get the tiny distance we have so far. Not to mention the area is fiercely protected. We obtained special permissions through the government and the research lodge owners to conduct our studies. I've been hoping to wrangle Dr. Courtman from the biology department in to expand on the animal side of things. There's a greater diversity of plants and animals in this area than any comparable-sized place in the world. It's ripe for exploration."

"You sound so passionate." Marisol raised her head and made eye contact with Dr. Morrow. "I just want to let you know how much I look up to you. Your research out here, discovering new species, going into places no one has been to before. It's all so exciting...minus the tarantulas."

"You sound like Ben. He loved the idea of adventure and exploration. It's nice to see the same passion in so many of my students. Now, if we could only figure out where exactly we are, we'd be set." Dr. Morrow scooped up the SAT phone and punched a series of buttons. Her face scrunched up as she looked from the phone screen to the grid map. "Oh, weird…"

David took the plant presses and set them up outside his tent. He removed the plastic baggie from his bag and carefully extracted the vine. To his right, he had a small pencil case and a stack of fresh blotting papers. He stretched the vine out and laid it across the top of the wooden boxes, then slid his notebook out from his bag and flipped through the pages of dictations.

"Here it is," he whispered to himself.

VINE SPECIES INFO
Prolific vine species first noted by Ben at site C. Possibly new species of strangler fig – part of ficus family. New growth seen throughout branches surrounding both site C and D. Only sample mentioned was within the most recent camp. Wide- spread growth pattern – thick trunk, extensive arms, no notice- able fruiting. Long leaves, set of four to five dark green, diamond leaves, waxy.

David looked from the page to the specimen laying out in front of him. *Sounds the same,* he thought. David reached into his bag and pulled out a small but thick botanical encyclopedia. He flipped through the pages, settling on the section labeled *Ficus.*

David scanned the pages, eyeing the different species and descriptions, stopping at the section that described strangler vines. Small black and white photos were peppered between the dense lines of text. All the photos were similar, but each had a slightly different appearance…and yet none of them matched the sample he had in front of him.

He opened the pencil case to his side and extracted a small razor blade. David placed the blade to the trunk of the vine and sliced at a 45-degree angle, severing the excess plant material. He tossed the discarded vine pieces past the trees and into the brush. Holding the trimmed plant in one hand, he opened one of the plant presses and laid a layer of blotting paper inside. He carefully and delicately positioned the vine on top of the paper before adding another two sheets on top and closing the box. David used the two leather belt straps on the outside of the box to tighten the pressure. *Well, that's at least one more specimen for the count.*

David looked up to see Marisol and Dr. Morrow hovering over the tiny screen of the satellite phone. He retrieved a clean shirt and pants from his bag and ducked around the back of his tent to change. He winced as he peeled the wet shirt off over his head. The small punctures on his back from the bamboo spikes throbbed with his pulse. He bent his arm behind him, stretching to try and feel the wound, but was unable to reach. Frustrated, he yanked the dry shirt over his torso, hoping it would scab over by the morning.

Marisol glanced up to David and waved him over as he crossed the clearing toward them. He crouched down and looked at the aerial map and markings.

"The GPS says we're right on top of the second campsite," Marisol said. "But she was right about us being way ahead of schedule."

"When you were leading, you kept a straight northeastern route with the compass, correct?" Dr. Morrow asked him.

"Yes. I thought that's what you wanted me to do. Did I get us turned around somehow?"

"Not at all. Here, look." She angled the map to face him. She tapped her pointer finger on the square marked X_a. "This is where we started this morning." She slid her finger diagonally along the map, passing over the empty boxes of the grid and tapped her finger again over the box labeled X_b. "And this is where we are now."

"Okay? I guess I don't understand," David said.

"It's impossible to move in a straight line, like the route I just showed you. There are small rivers and lakes and dense foliage all throughout here. The reason it takes a day or two or *more* between locations is that we have to navigate off the direct path and course-correct along the way."

Marisol leaned over the map. "We calculated how long we've been walking, accounting for error and rerouting—which is inevitable, and we should be somewhere in one of these sections." Marisol tapped three empty grid squares on either side of the second campsite. "It's virtually *impossible* for us to have ended up here when we did."

David's brow furrowed as he scrutinized the map. "What's the distance between grid markers?"

"Almost five kilometers," Marisol said. "We already did the calculations twice…and don't even think of trying to mansplain the measurements to us."

David laughed and pushed the map back towards Marisol. "I wouldn't dream of it." He stood and looked around the clearing. "Would it be wrong to call this good fortune? We can spend the rest of the day relaxing some, maybe reserve some energy for tomorrow? I wouldn't mind taking the time to try and piece together Ben's notes with where we are."

"I think that may be the only choice we have." Dr. Morrow folded the laminated map back into a small square. "Better to stay settled here than end up trying to navigate our way forward in the dark."

The late afternoon sun glinted through the thick leaves of the towering trees. The dusky veil that encompassed them during the rain had lifted, giving way to brightly colored red and orange shoots that hung from the nearby branches. Leftover water droplets clung to the leaves of the ferns that covered most of the jungle floor. Dr. Morrow walked the perimeter of the foliage, occasionally staring up into the canopy of the trees. The sound of rustling leaves pulled her attention past the ferns and into the dense wood. Excess rainwater trickled off the leaves through the forest and carried throughout the camp. She listened closely and smiled, knowing the sound well. She turned as David ambled over from his tent and edged up to her.

"What do you think they'll be?" he asked, trying not to sound too excited.

"My guess would be squirrel monkeys...and a lot of them," she answered, flashing David a smile.

The rustling grew louder as the leaves on the trees in front of them shook, dropping water from the branches. David couldn't help but grin wildly as a troop of small, orange and white monkeys bounded overhead in the treetops. David counted at least fifteen of them as they gathered around the canopy. Every so often, one of them would grab a large leaf and pull it to its mouth to lap up the water. The squirrel monkeys jumped around the limbs along the perimeter of the camp, stopping to watch the humans below. A few stragglers lagged behind, keeping their distance.

David looked up as a branch snapped overhead. A large brown monkey leaped from one tree and into the middle of the troop of small monkeys. The squirrel monkeys didn't pay any mind and continued to forage through the leaves. Soon, the large monkey began picking at the leaves with them while hopping in and out of the different levels of the canopy.

"That's so interesting," Dr. Morrow whispered to David. "That's a brown capuchin. Monkey species don't usually mix. He must be adopted...found family if you will."

David reached into his back pocket and pulled out his small notebook and pencil and quickly scribbled down *brown capuchin.*

One of the monkeys made a shrill chirp, the call echoing throughout the trees. Every member of the troop chirped back before they disappeared up into the trees and away from the camp.

"Always coming and going," Dr. Morrow chuckled. "I think

the squirrel monkeys may be my favorite out here. They have such silly little personalities but are always on the go." She looked out past the trees, squinting into the mass of limbs and leaves. "What are your thoughts on taking another look around that tent? I feel like there's something we're missing."

"With two stipulations," David said, watching as she maneuvered her way into the thicket. "You're on tarantula duty...and you owe me some dry clothes." David hiked up his pants, pulling the cuffs up above his boots. "I also want to get a closer look at the vine we cut down. I'm almost certain it's the one from the research notebooks, but I need more than the small sample I scooped up earlier." David pushed the branches aside as he followed Dr. Morrow past the trees. He craned his head over his shoulder to look back at the camp. Marisol sat near his bag, holding his notebook filled with the transcripts of Ben's notes.

"Hurry up! It's going to be dark soon," Dr. Morrow yelled to David from several yards ahead.

He couldn't see her but followed her voice past the ferns and hanging shoots. He almost knocked into her as he pushed his way through some low-hanging branches. He began to apologize but froze before the words could escape his mouth. His gaze drifted above Dr. Morrow and to the high canopy of the tree.

Dangling, suspended by curling, green vines, hung the remains of the torn and dilapidated research tent.

7

"What do you mean it's back in the tree?" Marisol asked. "And can you stop? You're driving me crazy."

David paced tightly in front of her. "It's like we never cut it down. That's impossible, right?"

He had returned to the campsite with Dr. Morrow and immediately cornered Marisol, explaining their findings. Dr. Morrow had insisted on seeing the pressed specimen he had prepared earlier. She quickly retreated to her tent with the vine and his encyclopedia. David's stomach was in knots. All he could think about was turning around and heading home.

"Would you please just sit down?" she asked, setting aside David's notebook.

David stopped and looked down at Marisol, let out an agitated sigh, and plopped onto the ground, sitting cross-legged across from her. His knee bounced rapidly as he bit at the corners of his lips.

"Thank you...although you're still a bit neurotic," she said, eyeing him. "Look, I was reading over your summary of the field notes and saw you copied down that Ben wrote multiple times about accelerated growth in a new vine species. You said it looked similar to the one by the tent, yeah?"

David nodded. "But accelerated...what even is *accelerated*? Not, like, two hours and bam! Back to normal."

"Okay. I get it. I don't have the answers. Why don't we go take another look?"

"I don't want to go back there," he said quietly.

"It really freaked you out that much?"

"I don't know." He looked down at the ground and picked at his shoes, avoiding eye contact.

Marisol grabbed his notebook and stood up, brushing the soggy dirt off her pants. David lifted his eyes to watch her as she turned to leave.

"So, that's it?" he called after her.

"No," she said, spinning to face him. "I'm going to go check it out myself. What can I say? You've piqued my curiosity."

"You didn't have to come with me," Marisol said, ducking under a branch that David held up above her head.

"Buddy system, remember?"

The light under the canopy was diminishing quickly. Marisol swore under her breath as she repeatedly tripped on the bulging roots underfoot. They approached the hanging tent as the last vestiges of sun shone through the crowded leaves.

"You weren't kidding," she exhaled. She leaned into the trunk of the tree, studying the tent as it dangled a few feet above her head. "Fascinating."

Marisol stepped back, arching her neck as she studied the tendrils. She paused, feeling a light crunch as her foot pressed into the mud. David raised his eyebrows and tilted his head, silently questioning her.

"There's something here," she said, squatting down.

David joined her as they sifted through the wet dirt and old leaves. Marisol lifted her hand in a fist as she shook off the mud. She uncurled her fingers, revealing a small, black tube.

"What is that?" David asked, plucking it from her hand. He

rubbed it against his shirt, wiping away the mud. One end of the tube was rounded and closed, but the other was open with metal threading on the inside. "I think this is an antenna."

Marisol pushed her hands back into the mud. She was accumulating a small pile next to her of twigs, leaves, and hard clumps of dirt. She looked up at David and shook her head. "Nothing."

David stepped forward, extending a hand to her. Marisol reached up and clasped her hand in his. His foot sank into the ground and jammed up against a hard object buried in the mud. He quickly stepped back, releasing Marisol's hand and sending her toppling back into the dirt.

"Seriously? What the hell, David?" she growled as the mud splattered her pant legs.

David ignored her, and instead dropped to his knees and submerged his hand in the muck, reaching past the squishy dirt and deeper toward the firmer layers. As he raked through the mud, his hand brushed up against something hard. He wiggled his fingers, feeling around the object. It was smooth, different than the rough, uneven tree roots. The tip of David's tongue stuck out of his mouth, a look of concentration on his face as he dug deeper. The mud reached halfway up his forearm. The pressure of the wet dirt piled under his fingernails as he pinched the edges of the object. He pulled up, the mud suctioning around his hand, not wanting to let it go. With a loud pop, his hand came loose. David unclenched his jaw, his lip throbbing beneath his teeth. He ran his tongue along the small indent that formed on his bottom lip.

"Oh my God," Marisol whispered.

David looked down at his hand. He was holding a satellite phone, the same model they were all carrying. He brushed the dirt off the front and pushed the power button. Nothing. He pushed the button again, holding it down longer. The screen and buttons remained black.

"This has to be his," David said, making eye contact with Marisol.

"Maybe it needs the antenna?"

"That's not really how it works."

"Well, I *know* that. But can't you just try?"

David pulled the antenna out of his pocket and screwed it onto the open port at the top of the satellite phone. He waited several seconds for the phone to reset before pressing his finger against the power button.

"Nothing," he sighed. "We can try and charge it back at the tents, but honestly it's not going to tell us anything. It's not like you can get a history from these thin—"

David stared at the phone, his mouth parted from stopping mid-sentence.

"What?"

Marisol leaned down to catch his eye.

"David? What is it?"

He slowly lifted his head and gazed past her. Out of the corner of her eye, she could see his hand tightening around the phone.

"He said it stopped working," he mumbled. He looked back down to the phone and then up to the tent still hanging above them. "In his notes. He said the SAT phone stopped working."

Marisol followed David's eyes to the tent. "What does that mean, though? They're solar-powered. They don't just stop working. These things are like $600 a pop."

"I have no idea, but that's what it said. I literally reread it last night. If he thought it was broken, maybe he left it?"

"Wh-what if ours stop working?"

"That's what I'm worried about." David pocketed the phone. "We need to get back. It's already almost too dark to see, and I didn't bring a flashlight. Did you?"

"No," Marisol said, hesitating. "I really don't have a good feeling about this, David."

"There's not much we can do about that now. Best we can hope for is…" He shrugged and shook his head. "Well, I don't know what we can hope for. I guess for our phones to work long enough to get us back out of here."

David stood and held out his muddied hand to Marisol. She narrowed her eyes at him and scowled dramatically before getting up on her own.

"Really? I didn't mean to drop you before."

Marisol's eyebrow twitched as she waved her arm out in front of her. "After you."

Sighing, David wiped his hand on the back of his pants and patted the broken phone in his pocket. Grabbing his machete off the ground, he started to push his way back through the branches.

"I'm worried about—" Marisol let out a high-pitched shriek.

David jerked backwards as Marisol's hands gripped the back of his shirt. He spun around and dropped his machete, catching Marisol as she plummeted forward into him. She clawed at his arms, pulling herself up his body. Tears were streaming down her face as she continued to scream.

"Whoa, whoa, whoa!" David wrapped his arms around her, trying to get her on her feet. "Calm down! What is happening right now?"

Marisol kicked and shook her right leg while clinging to David's torso. She frantically pulled her leg up, jutting her forward as she fell into him. She wrapped her arms around his back and started sobbing into his chest.

David put a hand behind her head and held her against him until her breathing started to settle. She trembled against him as her hands gripped the back of his shirt in tight clumps.

"What the hell was *that*? Are you alright?"

Marisol slowly loosened her grip on him and lifted her head to meet his worried gaze. Her eyes were red, with tears still piled up in the corners. She sniffled and wiped her face with the back of her hand.

"S-s-something was wrapped around m-my ankle," she whimpered.

David peered down over her head. "I don't see anyth—"

"The vine was wrapped around my ankle, David!" Her voice was an octave higher than normal and shaking with each word.

"It-it was pulling me! I couldn't get it off. I—" Marisol leaned back into him, crying again.

"Okay…okay. Look, don't psych yourself out. I'm sure your foot got tangled up in all the shit we cut down earlier, that's all. There are piles of it under the tree."

"It wasn't tangled," Marisol murmured, her face still planted into his shirt.

"Do you want me to look?"

Marisol peeled herself off him and glanced behind her to the tree, the tent, and the pile of leafy debris underneath. "No. Let's just get out of here."

David crouched next to Dr. Morrow as she poured some rice into a metal pot above the campfire. He reached into his pocket and pulled out the dirty satellite phone.

"We found this when we went back to the tent."

Dr. Morrow took the phone from David's hands. She turned it around in her palm like a fragile heirloom, as though it would break if handled indelicately.

"It doesn't turn on. I thought we could charge it, but…" David could see that her mind was somewhere else. He began to stand when Dr. Morrow reached out and placed her hand on his knee.

"Can I show you something?" she asked.

Dr. Morrow led David into her tent. Next to her sleeping bag and personal backpack was the plant pressing box David used earlier. It was open, the leather straps trailing along the floor. He crouched alongside her as she crawled over to her sleeping bag and pulled the box toward them. Inside the box laid David's clipping. It was placed exactly the same as when he had trimmed and positioned it. David leaned in closer and whispered under his breath before turning to face Dr. Morrow.

"How is that possible?" he asked, reaching out and prodding the vine with his finger. At the base of the vine, where he had sliced the excess stalk away, was a protruding bright green stem.

"I was hoping you could help me figure that out," she replied. "We can grab Marisol and maybe do some brainstorming after dinner."

"I..." David's gaze drifted in the direction of Marisol's tent. "I told her I wouldn't say anything...but she's convinced that one of the vines from that tree, like, coiled around her ankle or something. I don't know. I'm not sure she'd be comfortable doing that tonight."

"The jungle *is* known for playing tricks on people," said Dr. Morrow half-heartedly.

"Like dragging you to your death?"

Dr. Morrow laughed. "More like mind games. Once you're deep enough in here, everything looks the same, and you start to let your mind play tricks on you. The sounds can be disorienting and frightening. It's not easy when people first come out here. You don't realize how small you are until you're just one more organism among thousands of others just trying to survive in the wilderness."

David's eyes lingered on the clipping before passing the box back to Dr. Morrow. "I don't even know where I'd start with this. You've seen way more than me and obviously have so much more experience."

"It's not about experience," Dr. Morrow said as she followed him out of the tent. "You were at the top of all of my classes. Do you remember the paper you did on air potatoes?"

"Of course. *You* remember the paper I did on air potatoes?" He was surprised she even remembered him taking one of her classes.

"I do," she chuckled. "You wrote about the voracity of the plant and its impact on native flora...and how without much effort, an entire ecosystem could be taken over by one singular creeper. It was very good."

"Do you think this vine is similar? I mean, I don't think this is at all invasive. How could it be? But growth wise..." David walked off past his tent and to the remnants of the vine he took the clipping from. He picked it up from the dirt, but stopped, feeling resistance.

Dr. Morrow squatted next to him and traced her hand along the root until it disappeared beneath the dirt.

"It re-rooted itself," David said, his eyes widening. "It's been maybe three hours, four at best. I've never heard of that happening before. I wouldn't even know how to quantify this kind of growth." David began to pace back and forth. His hands drummed against his thighs. "Air potatoes can grow up to eight inches in a day. Kudzu tops the charts at a foot. I don't even know how it propagates to be able to explain how it's rooted back into the ground."

Dr. Morrow carefully plucked the vine out of the dirt. "Only one way to find out, right?"

David watched as she brought the vine back to her tent. She disappeared behind the door flap and emerged with two small cardboard pots and a miniature spade.

Marisol stuck her head out of her tent and slowly walked over to David. He noticed her normally bubbly demeanor was dampened, subdued. "Hey. How you doing?" he asked.

"Fine. Jittery." She hesitated, brushing her foot along the ground. "I'm sorry for causing such a scene."

David looked down at her and smirked. "Don't be silly. I knew you had to be a *little* crazy."

Marisol met his smirk with her own. "What's she doing?" She nodded over to Dr. Morrow, who was filling up the pots with dirt and setting them on the ground against her tent.

"The vine I took a clipping of—the one from the tent— showed new growth where I dissected it."

"New growth, like, from inside the press?"

"Yeah. I know, it's weird, right? Even weirder is that the parts I discarded were rooted back in the ground. We thought we may be able to measure the growth rate to be able to compare it to other quick-growing species. She took a couple stalks and is transplanting them now."

"Does that mean we're staying put until we figure it out?"

"Honestly, I have a feeling she thinks Ben may be a lost cause. She barely even looked at the phone when I showed her. I wouldn't be surprised if we hang here for a couple of days and then head back to regroup," David said.

"I hope so."

Dr. Morrow brushed her hands on her pants as she walked toward them. "I guess we'll see what a little bit of measured control can do for us," she said to David before catching Marisol's eyes and offering a reassuring smile. "Oh shit!" Dr. Morrow's hand flew to her forehead as she dashed over to the pot of rice which was threatening to boil over. "Guess that's what I deserve for getting distracted." She pulled out the portable campfire and slid the lid over it to extinguish the flame. She glanced over to David and Marisol, a breathy laugh escaping her. "I hope some overcooked rice will work for dinner?"

David sat on top of his puffy sleeping bag, headlamp strapped to his head as he held a small mirror in his hand. Marisol and Dr. Morrow had retreated to their tents shortly after dinner. It was already pitch black by the time they had finished eating. David shuffled through his first-aid kit and cleaned up the scratches on his face and neck. The small amount of blood had already clotted and left dark red streaks across his pale skin. *Maybe I'll finally get a tan being outside every day*, he thought.

He winced, closing his eye as he dabbed the scratches on his cheek with an alcohol wipe. He turned his face in the mirror, waiting to see if they were going to begin bleeding again. The last thing he wanted was to make another wardrobe change. He was already feeling the effects of the rainforest's humidity on his clothes. Everything in his bag was damp, even his clean laundry. He slipped on a plain white t-shirt and some grey sweatpants after dinner, but he still felt slick with sweat. If he was home, he'd sleep in his underwear, but the idea of bugs and vines and swamps from the past few days left his uncovered skin itchy and uncomfortable.

He placed the mirror down and paused. Light scratches came from the thin, vinyl tent walls as a shadow moved on the other side of the door. He held his breath, his heart pounding a little heavier at the sudden presence of something outside of the tent.

"David?" a voice whispered.

David released his breath, leaned forward, and unzipped the tent, tilting his head up to see Marisol standing outside. She threw her hand in front of her face as the headlamp shone into her eyes.

"Sorry!" David whispered. He swiveled his head, looking around outside before glancing back up at Marisol. "What's up?"

Marisol bounced lightly on the balls of her bare feet. She was wearing short gym shorts and a thin, lavender tank top. Her knees bobbed up and down in front of David's face. He could see she still had muddy stains on her shins and ankles. She was nibbling at her bottom lip, picking the skin off with her teeth.

"Can I come sit with you for a bit? I mean, I saw the light...if you're going to bed, I can just—"

David nodded his head to the inside of the tent. "Come on in." He scooted to the back, clearing some room for her to enter as he picked up the scattered items from the first-aid kit.

Marisol ducked into the tent and crawled against the side. The inside of the tent had enough room for a sleeping bag and a couple of backpacks. Even sitting out of the way, her knees still knocked into his. A small smile broke across her lips as he juggled holding a couple rolls of bandages and a tube of Neosporin.

"Do you mind?" David asked, angling an elbow her way.

She followed his elbow to a red and white box labeled MEDIC KIT wedged behind her. Marisol slid it out and laid it open as he dropped the random supplies back inside and snapped the lid shut.

"So..." he said, not looking up.

Marisol adjusted her knees and sat up a little straighter. She started chewing at her bottom lip again.

"We don't have to talk," he added quickly. "I was about to read for a bit, actually. I have plenty of reading material if you want to make yourself comfortable."

Marisol nodded. "Sure."

David dragged his backpack over and pulled out a worn, maroon hardcover book. The spine was decorated in embossed gold font. The cover frayed at the corners, and the edges of the paper were colored a tea-stained brown. He slid his backpack over to Marisol as he laid back on the sleeping bag and rested his head on his bag of clothes. He adjusted his headlamp so it angled down toward the book.

"Take your pick," he said as he gently flipped the cover open. "I can't promise any of it is exciting. If you want something to make you sleepy, you're more than welcome to my dissertation." He shot her a grin and a wink.

Marisol quickly sifted through his backpack before setting it aside. She scooted over next to him.

"What's this book?" she asked, leaning in to see closer.

David flipped back a few pages. *"King Solomon's Mines."* He left it open to the bright red cover page. "By H. Rider Haggard. First edition."

"Never heard of it."

"It's old. 1885. It's my dad's. Well, mine, I guess. He gave it to me when I graduated high school. I really wanted his *Tarzan* collection or any of his stuff by Jules Vern. I used to spend hours reading all the books in his library. I think this is the one he was most willing to part with."

"Can't relate," Marisol said dryly. "You do realize you're talking about a library? In your house?"

David closed the book and laid it on his stomach. He could feel the familiar tightening in his chest, that feeling of his heart being squeezed. He closed his eyes and breathed in slowly through his nose before opening them again. He focused his eyes on his feet and let the tightness slowly subside. He took another breath.

"You know…" His voice came out louder than he intended. "I know I come from a rich family—and I know you like to give me shit about it—but I would trade all of that for what you have."

"Oh, come on, really?" Marisol sat up straighter, always poised for a debate. "You'd seriously trade all of your fancy stuff and your lifestyle for what? Student loans? Debt?"

"…friends, family," David said almost silently.

"Everyone has friends somewhere."

David lifted his arm and placed his hand behind his head. He turned to look at her. "I take the money because it's how my parents show that they care." David flexed his feet anxiously. He could feel his heart start to speed up again, the squeezing getting more intense. His face was burning. He stared up at the ceiling of the tent, his head cradled in the palm of his hand. "In 5th grade, I was invited to Tommy Bannor's birthday party. It was the first time anyone invited me to a party where it wasn't a general 'everyone in the class is invited' thing. I told my mom how much I wanted to go. He was going to have a Carvel cake and *two* Slip-and-Slides. You remember those? Anyway, my mom said I could go, and I was really excited because I thought, for the first time, other kids wanted to hang out with me. So, that Saturday comes and I throw on my bathing suit and pick out my clothes and go running downstairs. No one was home. I went to the kitchen, and on the table was a big, wrapped box with a note next to it. It was from my mom. It said that she had to make an emergency lunch date, and that she got me a little something to make up for it."

"What was it?"

David's face was on fire. "A Slip-and-Slide." He bit down on his lip. "She thought I wanted to go because there was going to be a Slip-and-Slide. I never even opened it." David cleared his throat, trying to shake away the lump growing there. "Anyway, yeah, can't say I was invited to anything after that. Always been the spoiled kid no one wants to hang out with. I guess that's carried on into adulthood, too."

Marisol scooched down until she was lying next to him. She laid her head in the crook of his neck and wrapped her arms around him as best she could.

"I'm sorry," she said quietly. "I didn't know that."

David blinked, a couple of tears running down his cheek. He tilted his head to the side, resting it in the curls of Marisol's hair as he brought his arm around to rest on her back. He closed his eyes and focused on pushing away all his bad memories. He glanced down as the heavy, leather-bound book shifted on his stomach. Marisol's fingers ran over the edges as she lifted it up. He held the other side with his free hand as Marisol steadied it and flipped the pages carefully to the first chapter. They read in silence as the sounds of the jungle drowned out the quiet turning of the pages.

Bright light flooded the tent as bird calls echoed throughout the trees, signaling a new day. David blinked his eyes open as he ran a hand over his face, wiping away the sleep from his eyes. He glanced down to see the top of Marisol's head still curled up on his chest. He inhaled, taking in the scent of her hair. She smelled like the jungle, dewy and earthy like a rainy day by a pond. He yawned and stretched his arm out, tucking it behind his head. Marisol shifted and groaned softly.

"Morning," David said.

Marisol tilted her head up and rubbed her eyes. "Morning." She rolled onto her back, nestling her head higher up on David's chest. "Sorry I fell asleep on you."

"I'm pretty sure I fell asleep first." A large smile spread across his face. He slept like a rock and finally felt well-rested for the first time since leaving California. His smile dropped when he saw her watching him. "Um, look..." He scrunched his eyebrows. "About last night...I, uh, I don't want you to think that I was, like, trying to, I don't know, make a move on you or anything." David licked his lips. His mouth was bone dry. "Not that you're not pretty or anything...you are. You're just not really my type."

"I'm not *your* type?" Marisol raised an eyebrow as she sat up to stare at him.

David sat up and stared back at her, weighing his next words. "I mean, if it was like a one-night thing and we never had to really see each other again..." He instantly regretted his choice. "It's that...I don't know, you're kind of mean and, like, super intense," he blurted out.

"*I'm mean*?" Marisol asked in feigned anger. She forced her lips into a straight line, attempting to stop the laughter threatening to spill out.

David's eyes darted down to the floor. "Sorry. I didn't mean it the way it came out." He saw something at the top of his peripheral vision and glanced up. It was Marisol's hand.

"Friends?" Her hand was extended out for a handshake.

David smiled, breathing out the tension. He clasped his hand in hers and shook. "Friends."

They pulled their hands apart, laughing at their awkward handshake. Marisol reached up and pulled the hair-tie out of her hair and began securing it back up into a fresh ponytail. David ran his hands through his hair in response, assessing his bedhead.

"Thanks," he said, catching her eye. "For not teasing me last night."

"I only tease in good fun," she said as she tightened her ponytail. "I could never make fun of something like that...I'm sorry if that's what you expected. And also, just for the record, you're not my type either. You're *also* super intense. Not bad. Just...a lot."

David laughed. "That's fair. I'm happy that's out of the way then. Now...do you maybe think you can head back to your tent so I can get changed?"

Marisol crawled over and crouched by the entrance. "Why? Back to being shy all of a sudden?"

"Friends don't watch friends get naked."

"How would you know? I thought you said you never had any friends before."

David slapped his hand across his heart as he pretended to be wounded by an imaginary bullet. "Ouch. Too soon!"

Marisol giggled as she unzipped the tent flap. David turned and fished out a set of fresh clothes from his bag.

"David?" Marisol asked, almost breathlessly.

"I'm just asking for five minutes of privacy," he called out, his back to her.

A harshness floated through her tone as she repeated his name. "David."

"What?" he said, rolling his eyes and turning toward her. He could see the bottom half of her legs on the other side of the door. He crawled over and stood up beside her, the humidity outside hitting him like a wave. "What the—"

His eyes widened, the air evaporating from his lungs. He spun slowly, catching Marisol's gaze.

The clearing was gone, their camp swallowed. Large trees extended around them on all sides. Branches arched overhead, creating an umbrella of leaves and fronds. Winding vines draped between the branches and crawled around the tree trunks. David stepped forward and looked down as his feet brushed up against loose, rubbery tendrils. He lifted his foot to see the green curlicues stop a few inches from the tent.

They were completely encompassed by the jungle. His tent and the two of them, were the only things in view. He glanced back at Marisol. He wasn't even sure he was breathing.

"Where's Dr. Morrow?"

8

D avid ripped through his backpack, digging out his SAT
phone from an inside pocket. He jammed his finger onto
the power button and stared, holding his breath while he waited
for the phone to boot up. Marisol knelt outside of the tent,
watching him through the door.

"Come on…come on," David grumbled under his breath. The
screen slowly brightened, the logo appearing briefly before tran-
sitioning to the main menu. "Yes!" David sat on his ankles and
scrolled through the contact list.

Berkley Office
ARC Lodge Paul
ARC Lodge Claudio
Marisol SAT
David SAT
Julia Home
Julia Cell
Julia SAT

"Thank God!" he said as he pushed enter under the last
contact name. The display turned white as black letters popped
up on the screen:

Julia SAT…dialing.

David spun on his knees and pushed past Marisol to the outside of the tent.

"What are you try—"

"Shhh!" David hissed, waving his hand at her. He held his breath, straining his ears. "There! Do you hear it?"

"You're a fucking genius, David!"

A sequence of three beeps on a loop, each a higher tone than the last echoed back from behind the trees. The ringing continued, repeating for several rounds. David sighed and pushed a red button on the phone. The faint chirping of Dr. Morrow's SAT phone faded and gave way to the sounds of the birds and breeze.

"She didn't pick up, though," David said, his shoulders dropping. "Here, take this." David shoved the phone at Marisol while he disappeared back into the tent.

He climbed back out moments later in a long-sleeved shirt and khaki pants. He pulled on his hiking boots and grabbed the machete from around the side of his tent.

"Dial it again," he said.

Marisol stepped in front of him. "You're not going out there on your own."

"*She's* out there on her own. I can move easier if I'm not worried about you getting lost behind me. And look at you, you're wearing practically nothing. You'll get torn to shreds pushing through there," he said, nodding his head toward the forest.

Marisol narrowed her eyes and stared him down as she clenched her jaw. "Fine."

"Just keep it ringing."

David jogged forward and disappeared behind the first set of trees, leaving Marisol alone with the tent. The distant pinging of Dr. Morrow's satellite phone competed with the heavy thuds of her heart. She closed her eyes and took a deep breath, recognizing the tension spreading throughout her muscles. Marisol dropped her shoulders and wiggled her jaw as she heard the ringing go quiet. Lifting the phone back up, she pushed on Dr.

Morrow's contact again, bringing back the beeping triplicate to ring throughout the trees.

Sinewy vines surrounded David as he swung his machete and sliced his way forward. There was no path, not even an old, overgrown one for him to follow. He had heard Dr. Morrow's ringtone stop and start twice already, and yet he didn't feel any closer than when he started.

Sweat poured from his forehead and down his neck, the collar of his shirt matting to his chest and back. He ran the bottom of his shirt over his face and tried to ignore the burning as the sweat rubbed into his eyes.

He stopped slicing through the foliage and stood still, listening. The ringing had disappeared, the only sounds the heavy breaths escaping his lungs. He strained his ears but was met with silence—not even the usual background noise of birds rustling the branches or wind brushing the leaves.

Come on, Marisol, he thought. *Keep it ringing.*

David's heart sank as his hand released the machete, sending it clattering to the ground. "Fuck," he swore under his breath. He spun around, his breath quickening and becoming ragged. His hands instinctively reached down to his pants, fingers probing his pockets. He crouched and lowered his head between his knees as he stared at the ferns below. He squeezed his eyes shut.

You gave your phone to Marisol. Screw finding Dr. Morrow, you don't even know how to find your way back. What kind of moron runs off into the fucking woods without anything on them? What are you doing? You're going to be stuck out here.

David opened his eyes, the dark green ferns in front of him turning to fuzzy splotches. He blinked, trying to get them to focus. His breaths were shallow and rapid in his lungs, like an invisible weight was bearing down onto his chest. He struggled to get enough air. Icy chills rolled in waves along his skin as sweat beaded along his brow. It had been years since his last panic attack.

He fell off his heels as he pushed himself against a tree, his back flush against the trunk. He brought his knees up to his chest and held them there as he tried to focus on steadying his breathing. David rested his head on the top of his knees and closed his eyes. His clammy hands trembled against each other as he intertwined his fingers behind his head and squeezed them tightly together.

Beep...beep...beep - beep...beep...beep

David's head jolted up from his knees as he stared out into the jungle. "Dr....Morrow's...phone," he panted. He tried to move his legs, but they were frozen in place. "You have...to get up," he said aloud, still trying to fill his lungs with air.

Beep...beep...beep

David shut his eyes and lowered his hands into the dirt, focusing on the sensations that crawled over his skin and around his body.

Cool dirt, rough roots...

His lungs accepted more air, filling more each time he named his surroundings.

Dripping sweat, sharp twigs, crunchy leaves, hot air...

David opened his eyes, his breathing slowly returning to normal.

Trees, ferns, leaves, green, brown, tan...

The weight continued to lift from his chest. He leaned his head back against the tree and inhaled deeply through his nostrils.

Beep...beep...beep

David pushed himself to his feet, ignoring the wobbling in his legs, and brushed his hands off on his khakis. He scrunched his hands into fists to try and push away the trembling that remained there. He focused on listening, trying to determine where Dr. Morrow's phone could be as he bent down and retrieved his machete. His jaw tensed while he took a deep breath and headed off to his right, slicing away at the thin branches and stepping deeper into the brush.

Marisol paced in front of the tent, David's phone in her hands. She could hear the ringing reverberating through the trees.

"Where are you? It's been almost 20 minutes," she grumbled to the bright screen.

She looked down at the words *Julia SAT…dialing*. David should have found the phone by now. And if he found the phone, he should have found Dr. Morrow. After all, yesterday the tents were only twenty or thirty feet away from each other.

He should have been back forever ago. She knew she should have never let him go out there on his own. She needed something other than her bare feet and pajamas.

She gritted her teeth, pushed the red button on the face of the phone and cancelled the call. The ringing vanished a second after, surrounding her in silence. She used the pad on the phone to scroll up until she saw *Marisol SAT*. She pushed the call button.

Marisol SAT…dialing.

Marisol knew they were supposed to keep the phones off unless they were being used, but they ran on solar power…why not leave it on all the time, if only for emergency's sake? She didn't plan on using it, but she was homesick. She thought maybe if she were desperate enough, she could call Matty late at night to hear his voice, a tiny piece of respite to keep her going.

Off to her left, the telltale beeps echoed out of the trees. Marisol glanced back to the tree line before turning on her bare heels and ducking through the thick palm fronds, away from David and toward the sound of her SAT phone.

Marisol carefully stepped through the dense foliage, trying her best not to accidentally brush up against any of the spiny trees and bamboo. The left strap of her lavender tank top slipped off her shoulder and tickled the top of her arm. Her feet were caked in dirt. She winced as she walked, every twig and leaf jabbing at the soles of her feet. The ringtone was getting louder and clearer.

A wall of bamboo stood before her, large, black spikes protruding out from the green stalks. Tall and skinny trees surrounded her. She had seen them throughout their walk as well as around the research lodge. Dr. Morrow had called them walking palms. The trees themselves stood up out of the ground on several long, thick roots, giving the appearance of legs. Dr. Morrow had told them the roots would shift toward healthier soil and sunlight, making the trees slowly walk throughout the forest. Marisol stared at them, wondering if they walked here, trapping them outside of David's tent.

That would be ridiculous. They're not sentient, they're just trees. Tall jungle tales.

Marisol got on her knees and sized up the spaces between the giant, exposed roots. She was petite, but she didn't know if she would be small enough to squeeze through the dozen or so roots. She peered through the legs of the palm and gasped when she saw the edge of her tent barely visible beyond the trees. She held the phone out in front of her and cancelled the call to her phone. She knew where she needed to go.

The contact menu popped back up on the screen. Marisol scrolled down and dialed Dr. Morrow's number again before slipping the phone into the pocket of her shorts.

Marisol was no stranger to squeezing into tight spaces. She and her brothers still played hide-and-seek when she would come home to visit—granted, nowadays they usually played after a few rounds of drinks. Because she was small enough to fit in places her brothers couldn't, she always found the best places to hide and claimed victory almost every game because of it. Short and skinny was the perfect combination for hide-and-seek, and hopefully the perfect combination for rescuing her supplies.

She sat on the ground and leaned forward on her right hip. Marisol lowered her shoulder and extended her arm between the closest set of roots. She laid down, almost flat on her side, pushing her head between the largest gap available. Once her head was through, she slid her other arm behind her, stretching in between her head and the tree. Roots and detritus dug into her exposed skin and pushed against her hip bone as she squeezed through the gap. Marisol's eyes darted between three sets of roots as she gauged which one to tackle next.

She tried the same maneuver, sticking her arm and shoulder out and through the gap, but grimaced and withdrew her hand when sharp stabs pierced the tips of her fingers. Blood began to seep out, pooling in small dots along her fingertips. They throbbed as Marisol stuck them in her mouth, the metallic after-taste lingering on her tongue. She laid down flatter and craned her neck to see through the palm legs. More rows of spiky bamboo were growing on the other side. Marisol twisted and bent her neck to get a better view, the muscles straining until she thought they might snap. Then she saw it: a clear path. She just needed to think skinny.

Marisol squeezed her head through the next set of roots, repeating the same tactic from the first. She pulled her arm up and over her head, rotating her torso to squeeze through the small opening. Her arm scraped along the tree's legs and she gasped. The space between the roots kept her arm pinned above her head, and she lay there, stuck in motion, half-contorted. Her breath quickened, panic setting in as she jerked her body, trying to push the last of her arm through. She knew if she could get her shoulder past the gap, then the rest of her body would fit enough to get to the other side.

Marisol gritted her teeth and pulled, her muscles burning from the strain. She propped her feet up against the roots and pushed, letting out a deep growl as the skin of her arm scraped along the rough bark of the root, leaving it ablaze from the friction. A loud pop in her shoulder caused Marisol to yelp as tears automatically welled in her eyes from the pain. Deep aches radiated down her neck and to her arm as it pushed past the root, allowing her body to slip through the palm legs and into a pile of soggy leaves. Marisol cradled her arm as she sat up.

She looked down at the outer side of her bicep. A large, red rash covered the skin like a bad rug burn. The longer she looked at it, the more she thought she could see the burning sensation as it moved along her skin in boiling waves. She reached up and gingerly touched her shoulder, letting out a soft sigh of relief upon finding it was still in place and not dislocated. Marisol stumbled to her feet and looked down to see one of the spaghetti straps had been torn off her tank top. She smiled at her disheveled clothes and mud streaked skin. Even though it hurt, she found solace in her ability to act under pressure. Pushing away the pain, she reached into her pocket and fished out the phone, redialing Dr. Morrow's number. *Hang in there David. I'm coming.*

Thick, green vines fell into a messy pile at David's feet. He wiped the sweat off his forehead with the back of his hand, his machete still clutched in his fist. It seemed like he had been searching for an eternity, following Dr. Morrow's ringtone deeper into the rainforest. David glanced down at his watch. He couldn't remember if he had looked at the time when he left the camp, but he knew it was the morning…and now it was mid-afternoon.

He was getting closer to narrowing down Dr. Morrow's phone, the sound ringing louder as the minutes ticked by. Nothing but the electronic beeping returned his calls as he shouted her name. It was eerily quiet. An occasional group of macaws would noisily pass by overhead, but outside of that… nothing. David raised his machete and chopped at the last curtain of vines which hung in his way.

"Oh my God," David gasped as the tendrils collapsed into a heap. Scattered across the dead leaves and mud were Dr. Morrow's ringing phone, one of the plant presses—strewn open—and one of her small backpacks. "Dr. Morrow!" David screamed, turning in a tight circle, scanning for any signs of movement or noise. "Dr. Morrow!"

David bent down and scooped up the phone. He pressed the green button and held it up to his ear. "Marisol?" Static and crackling echoed through the speaker and back into his ear. "Marisol?" David's heart thrummed faster with each second that passed. "Marisol? Can you hear me? Marisol?" David could feel the weight piling back onto his chest. He quickly hung up the phone and opened up the contact list, scrolling to *David SAT,* and pressed the call button.

A brief screeching noise screamed out from the speaker, followed by a series of monotone beeps. He hung up and tried again. Still busy. David exited to the main menu. He hadn't read the manual that came with the phone. He didn't think he'd need it. Dr. Morrow had said it was for emergencies only. What kind of emergency could they possibly get themselves into? She was experienced, had been out here well over a dozen times. Where was she?

He scrolled to the section labeled *GPS* and selected it. A small map appeared on the screen with longitudes and latitudes dotted across it. A little black dot appeared on the map, blinking slowly. David held the phone closer to his face to see the map details.

Great...all this shows is that I'm somewhere in the goddamned rainforest. Obviously. I wonder if I can hone in on the lodge...but I have no idea how to do that.

David jumped, almost dropping the phone as the ringtone blared from the speakers. He fumbled the phone in his shaking hands and pressed the answer button. "Marisol?"

Marisol's tinny voice crackled through the speaker. "David? Is that you?"

"Thank God! I found Dr. Morrow's phone and...well, some of her things." David hesitated, pausing before diving into any details. He didn't want her to worry her, and the last thing he wanted was to try and calm both his nerves *and* Marisol's. "I-I'm still looking for Dr. Morrow. She's got to be somewhere close."

"You should come back."

"I can't leave her out here, Marisol. She wouldn't have left her stuff."

"Trust me...you're going to want to come back. Scratch that. You *need* to come back."

He knew she wasn't telling him something. "Why? What's going on?"

"I'm sending you the GPS coordinates to the camp. I'll tell you more when you get here."

The line went quiet. David glanced from the phone to the bag lying on the ground. He grabbed Dr. Morrow's backpack and secured it around his shoulders. The plant press laid open a couple of feet away. David walked over and nudged it with his foot. He scrunched his eyebrows and leaned in, looking closer. The vine clipping had stayed in place, even with whatever had happened there. *What* did *happen here?* He blinked, quickly jumping back. He shook his head and squinted, his gaze affixed to the vine draped over the box.

Di-did that just move?

David took a step forward and squatted down. He nudged the box again and waited. He leaned in closer and prodded it yet again, waiting for the briefest movements from the plant matter. This time, he got on his knees and brought his face inches from the box.

Beep beep be-beep, beep beep be-beep

David jerked, dropping the phone into the dirt. "Jesus Christ!" he swore out loud as he brought his hand to his chest, his heart racing against his palm. David wiped the dirt off the phone and looked at the screen. A map appeared showing the same blinking, black dot...only this time, a small, dotted line crossed over the map leading to a blinking red dot. David gave a sideways glance back at the plant press before he stood, steadied himself, and followed the dotted line toward his way out.

9

Marisol waited in front of David's tent as he clumsily stumbled out of the trees and into the campsite. Small, dark leaves stuck out of his hair, the black and browns peppering his light-blond strands. His shirt was soaked through and his face was streaked with dirt and sweat.

"Oh, thank God!" Marisol shouted, running to meet him. She reached out to hug him but pulled back when she saw the state of his clothes. "Here, have some water."

David grabbed the water bottle out of Marisol's hands and upended it, nearly draining the entire thing. "Thanks," he said, lowering the bottle. He stared at her, looking her up and down before slowly turning his head to look at the rest of the campsite.

Marisol slowly raised her palms toward him, poised like she was about to calm a wild beast. "I can explain," she said, her tone careful and deliberate.

David brought his eyes back to her and glared, biting down on his bottom lip to keep himself in check. He knew he was two seconds away from blowing up at her. He had spent at least half of the day wandering the jungle, had his first panic attack in over two years, and managed his way back without anything but a machete, and here she was, in new, clean clothes, her tent set up next to his, and she had the nerve to stand there in front of him and pretend nothing was happening? His blood was boiling.

"David," she said with a soothing lilt. "I was worried about you, and you were gone a long time. I thought I could just get my stuff and—"

"And what?" David growled through his teeth. "You could have gotten yourself lost! Hurt! What the *fuck* was I supposed to do if I got back here and you were gone?" His hands shook at his sides as he tensed them into fists. He wasn't sure if it was anger or anxiety or a culmination of everything over the day, but he didn't care. He was mad, and she needed to know that. "The whole world doesn't revolve around you, Marisol!" he yelled. "I know you think you know *everything*, but you can't only think about yourself!"

Marisol lowered her eyes as he yelled at her. "I know." She swallowed hard before lifting her eyes back up to meet his. "But you were only thinking of *you* when you ran off."

"Are you serious?" He shook his head. "I was thinking of all three of us! You were safer here. It would have been too dangerous for you to go out there with me."

Marisol stood up straighter and raised her voice. "I'm not some girly girl who can't handle herself! I managed to find my tent and all my stuff. All on my own."

"And that was stupid. You don't think we would have done that next? You think I would have ignored the fact that all your stuff was out there? How conceited do you think I am? How does that even benefit me? I know you're capable, *clearly*, but do have any idea how reckless that was?"

David's eyes burned with tears forming at the corners as he stormed past her and to his tent. He didn't want to yell, or cry, or be angry. He wanted to go home. Once he got to his tent, he kicked off his shoes and sat down on the wet ground before peeling his wet shirt off over his head. Balling it up, he threw his saturated top to the side, reached into the tent to pull his bag over, and retrieved a clean shirt from inside. David laid it on the ground as he lifted his knees to his chest and folded his arms on top of them. With a breath, he lowered his head, resting it on his arms. The likelihood of another panic attack was high and giving in to the stress of dealing with Marisol on top of everything else would only make it worse. He let out several shaky breaths and focused on the dirt piled up on the edges of his shoes, noting the color changes as the mud dried. Crunching leaves filled the silence between breaths as Marisol crossed the camp to stand next to him.

"I don't know what I would have done if something had happened to you," he said into his lap as he lifted his head and looked up at her.

"Same," Marisol replied quietly, meeting his eyes. She lowered herself so that she was sitting beside him. She reached over and put her hand on his leg. "But we're both okay, right?"

"Yeah," David whispered, swallowing the lump in his throat. He leaned over, resting his head on Marisol's, needing the comfort of touch. "I'm glad you're alright."

"I'm glad *you're* alright," she said back, giving his leg a reassuring squeeze. "So…"

David lifted his head and looked over at her.

"There's more." Marisol grabbed the bag David brought back from the remnants of Dr. Morrow's supplies and brought it over to his tent. She scooted over so she was seated across from him. She pulled the satellite phone out of her pocket and laid it between them.

"Okay," she said, taking a large breath. "Before I sent you the coordinates to the camp, I called the lodge. I thought if I could get them to send out a search party, then all we would have to do is stick tight here, right?" Marisol picked at the inside of her cheek with her teeth.

"And? What did they say? Are they sending the guides back to get us?"

"Here's where it gets a little crazy." Marisol raised her eyes, looking directly into David's. "Claudio said when Andy and Nelly came back, he sent a couple of other guides back in to gather the research from the first camp. Normal recon, right? He said they came back within hours—said that they haven't been able to find it."

"Find what?"

"The first camp, David. They can't find it. Now, it's clearly mapped *and* marked, but Claudio said all of the trails are different. *Changed.*"

"You know that sounds like absolute horseshit right? They're probably just sitting on their asses laughing at us for being dramatic."

"I'm serious, David," Marisol snapped. "He wasn't joking around. If the same thing happened there…"

"Uh huh," he said narrowing his eyes at her. "You honestly think they can't do what they're trained to do and follow an already mapped trail? It doesn't just disappear."

"Why would he lie? He said that they followed the trails and that they looped back."

David arched an eyebrow. "Looped back?"

"Yeah. Looped back. As in it took them in circles. Look around us, David. Dr. Morrow is gone. We're surrounded by trees that weren't even here yesterday. How can you think it's just some prank?"

"So, you really think they can't come help us? And what exactly were we instructed to do then?"

"Stay hydrated. Be safe. Try to follow anything that looks like a trail or looks familiar. Claudio said he called for assistance, but since this is protected land, there's not much they can do except keep trying on their end."

"You're really serious, aren't you?"

Marisol nodded as she shifted on the ground. She reached into Dr. Morrow's backpack and pulled out the folded grid map. "We can use the GPS on the phones to track where we are on the map, make sure we're going in the right direction…or any direction, I guess."

"I'm not so sure we should leave where we are. Isn't the number one rule of getting lost in the woods to stay put? Especially when people know your last known location?"

"Maybe, but I don't think this is a normal situation. I mean, we literally got separated from each other by the rainforest itself."

"That's insane," David deadpanned. His mind wandered to the plant press he shoved with his foot. *There's no way I saw what I think I saw. This is just our minds playing tricks on us.* "I'm sure it's just your mind playing tricks on you. Dr. Morrow said it happens all the time out here. You get disoriented, everything looks the same…"

"Well, either way, I'm not staying here and waiting for the trees to come waltzing any closer."

"I mean this in the nicest way possible, Marisol," David said, "but you sound like a fucking lunatic."

"You don't think I know that? But can you explain how my tent ended up completely surrounded by those awful walking palms with no way in or out? And you. You were out there for a half a day…to what? Walk what should have been like 20 feet? Something happened here, David."

"I think we're tired, and I think there's no help in getting all worked up. There's always a reasonable explanation. We're scientists for Christ's sake."

"I wasn't raised as a scientist, though. I believe there are other things out there, things science can't explain. I've had a horrible feeling about this ever since those guides left. I'm not going to stick around here and wait for something to happen. I never wait for shit to hit the fan. I take action. And we're heading back whether you like it or not."

David sighed and folded up the map, sticking it back into the backpack. "Alright. Well, we're not going to make it far if we start now. It's three o'clock. We should wait until the morning." He tugged his clean shirt over his head and winced as the fabric brushed along the punctures between his shoulders.

"What's wrong?"

"Nothing," David lied. "Just sore."

Marisol eyed him, scanning him like a human lie detector. Resigning, she said, "You're probably right about not starting now. And we should eat first anyway. If we're spending the night here again, we need a plan."

"A plan?"

"Yes. A plan," Marisol said matter-of-factly. "We should tie our tents together, make sure they don't go anywhere. And we should split up our supplies—some in your tent and some in mine. We should stay in the same tent again, God forbid. And we need to measure out our water—"

"Jesus, Marisol." David stared at her, wondering if she had prepared this list in advance. "You'd think we're heading into war. It's literally a single night. You sound crazy."

"I'd rather sound crazy then end up like Dr. Morrow."

"For all we know, she's working her way back to the lodge. Or she's sitting out there testing us and determining if we're capable of hacking it. And by some miracle, I'm not the one being called crazy this time."

"This isn't funny, David."

David put his hands up in front of him in mock surrender. "Okay, okay. We'll batten down the hatches, Cap'n. Whatever you want, as long as there's a little less spooky campfire stories and more quiet."

David poured the last of the water from the near-empty plastic bladder into his water bottle, tucking it neatly into his backpack. Marisol insisted on having everything "ready to go" as a just-in-case.

"How much water do you have left?" she called from inside her tent.

"One bottle," he called back. "You?"

"I have a full water bladder, but I haven't filled my water bottle yet."

David paused, his stomach hardening in a tight knot. "Have you been drinking?" He waited. Left without an answer, he got up and peered into her tent. "Well?"

"I haven't *not* been drinking," Marisol said, looking up at him from the floor of her tent.

"You know how important it is to stay hydrated out here. With the humidity and everything…it's dangerous."

"I know, I know."

"Drink a bottle now." David crossed his arms. "And don't worry about rationing. It's more important for you to drink."

Marisol rolled her eyes and let out an annoyed sigh as she filled her water bottle. She waved it back and forth in her hand, raising it to David before taking a long swig. "Happy?"

"The whole thing."

"Fine!" she huffed as she chugged the rest of her water in long sips. Once empty, she turned the bottle upside down and held it outside of the tent in front of him. "One bottle of water, sir!" she said as she saluted him.

"Don't be an ass." David turned and headed back to his tent.

He packed the rest of his things in his backpack and turned on his small lantern. It was getting dark quickly, and he wasn't ready to admit that he was just as nervous, if not more so, than Marisol. During her initial run-through of prep work, she had brought her sleeping bag and laid it next to his. Peeking his head out of the tent, he saw Marisol's silhouette moving inside her tent as she continued to pack her things. Ducking back inside, he slipped into his sleeping bag and closed his eyes, trying not to let his mind wander off too far. David kept spinning the possibilities around in his head of where Dr. Morrow could be, the odds of them finding her, and if she was okay. He kept bringing his mind back to one thought: he couldn't afford to panic.

The tent door unzipped and Marisol carefully crawled inside. David squeezed his eyes shut tighter in the hopes she would leave him alone if he seemed fast asleep. He grunted as she pressed her knee into his leg while trying to maneuver around the tent.

"Sorry!" she whispered, as she crawled over him and into her sleeping bag.

David felt her adjusting every few minutes. She would occasionally kick her knee into his back or shove her arm against his. After what he had calculated to be approximately one hundred annoying instances, David rolled onto his back and opened his eyes.

"Are you awake?" he whispered. The sleeping bag rustled next to him as Marisol continued to shift.

"Yeah," she sighed, rolling onto her side.

David flipped over to face her, tucking his arm under his head. "Everything is going to be fine," he said, his face inches from hers.

"Maybe…" she said, her voice trailing off. "I just want it to be tomorrow. And I want to walk out of this tent and have everything look the way it did yesterday."

"I've been thinking." He adjusted in his sleeping bag. "What if we're just crazy dehydrated and going a little stir crazy…or whatever the opposite of stir crazy is. What if we're just psyching each other out?"

"What do you mean?"

"Well, like, what if this wasn't Dr. Morrow's second campsite? You both said we were still days away, right? What if Ben set up a peripheral site near the first one? We already know he broke ground on a new site. What if *this* is Site D?"

"Why would he do it within the same grid sector?"

"I don't know the guy, who knows? But wouldn't it make sense that *if* we've only been hiking a few days, but moving at double or triple the pace, that really the lodge was only a day's hike away to begin with? That maybe he's the one that got turned around and made a new camp just miles from the first one?"

"What about all the plant stuff? The trees and vines? You know damn well that they don't grow out of nowhere."

"I think that's where the mind games come in. It was raining pretty bad, right? Maybe we stumbled into a highly prolific area of the jungle? It's possible. Kudzu can grow a foot a day. Who knows what species are out here and what their untapped potential is?"

Marisol turned onto her back and stared up at the roof of the tent. "…maybe."

"What can I do to ease your mind a bit?" he asked, leaning up on his elbow.

She rotated her head and looked up at him. "Can we keep reading your book?"

David smiled. "Of course."

David lifted his arm gently, trying not to disturb Marisol. She had fallen asleep laying on his chest shortly after they began reading. He spent the rest of the night staring up at the ceiling, listening to the chorus of bugs singing their evening songs to one another and going over dozens of scenarios and possibilities to explain the last couple of days. He turned his wrist over to look at his watch. *4 am.* He was anxious to step outside, to watch— although he wasn't sure what he wanted to see or what he expected. *Maybe,* he thought, *the forest was moving, the trees creeping and stepping into new positions.* He told himself that this wasn't one of the books he used to read—that there were no such things as magic and curses, only science and tactile, physical facts.

David lowered his arm back down around Marisol and let out a deep sigh. Marisol squished up against him in response, nestling her head into his chest and tightening her grip around his waist. He smiled and closed his eyes. It had been a while since he had shared a bed with anyone and even longer since sharing a bed led to *actually* falling asleep with someone. Despite their differences, he was comfortable with her. He was happy she wanted to be friends and happy that the pressure of being anything else could go away. He only hoped she meant it…that they could be friends.

David let his thoughts drift back on the numerous times he tried to make friends throughout school. High school was a wash. He skirted by through college, but nothing ever stuck. He was always too focused on studying and trying to be the best in every class. That meant friendships and relationships took a backseat, which usually left him alone. He wondered about what would happen when they finally left here and traveled back home. Would Marisol still want to be friends, or would she be just as happy to leave him behind for her old ones?

Marisol shifted, pulling her leg up and over his, curling up against him tighter. He let his fingers run over her back in little circles. Marisol moaned into his chest as she lifted her tired eyes to his.

"Hey," he said, softly. "You can keep sleeping, but I'm going to go stretch my legs."

He slipped out from his sleeping bag and crawled over to the flap of the tent. He looked over his shoulder as Marisol rolled over, covering her head with the top of her sleeping bag. He waited a few moments until he heard her soft snores and saw her breathing deepen, then slid out of the tent and quietly zipped the door back up.

David squinted, waiting for his eyes to adjust to the shapes and shadows of the forest. Everything seemed to be the same as it was when they went to bed. The sky was a light purple—not quite sunrise, but not deep evening. The water he downed before settling in for the night was finally getting to him. David wandered a few feet away to a nearby tree to relieve his bladder. Dehydration had been one of his biggest worries. He had read countless articles about what to look for and how much to drink based on humidity, heat, and exertion. He knew not having to pee after drinking lots of water was a telltale sign. He had never been more thankful for a full bladder.

A swift breeze blew across his skin and stirred the leaves. The chirps and buzzes of the insects grew louder and then ceased completely as the wind whipped through the trees. David glanced up to watch the palm fronds sway in the wind, the leaves rustling loudly as they brushed together. The branches clacked against one another, filling the air with a flurry of sound. As soon as it had come, the breeze vanished, leaving David standing in an eerily still picture of trees and darkness. Unease crept over him, and his mind wandered to all of the grim possibilities hiding beyond the brush, but Dr. Morrow had mentioned the unpredictability of the weather here. At least it wasn't more rain.

David yawned, feeling even more exhausted than before. He made his way back to the tent and snuck inside as quietly as possible. Marisol was still turned away, sound asleep. David laid on top of his sleeping bag and curled up against her, draping his hand over her side and resting his head up against her frizzy hair.

"David! Wake up!" Marisol said, as she shoved his back, shaking him awake.

David groaned loudly and cracked his eyes open. He was curled up against Marisol's bunched up sleeping bag, his arms wrapped tight around the glossy fabric. He lazily rolled over to see her crouched over him. Her dark hair was down around her face and she was still wearing her clothes from last night.

"Get up," she commanded.

David rubbed his fingers over his eyes and stretched his arms up over his head, yawning. "What catastrophic event has happened now?" he mumbled through his yawn.

"There's a trail," she answered, straight-faced.

David laughed as he sat up. "What?"

"There's a fucking trail, David. Straight through. Clear as day."

"Just relax." He checked his watch. *6am.* "I was literally out there two hours ago to take a leak. It's probably what I cut down yesterday on my way back."

"Then look for yourself." Marisol swept her hand toward the door for him to follow.

David sighed and crawled out of the tent with Marisol sticking close behind. His hair was matted on one side, the other sticking up at awkward angles. He brushed both hands through his hair until it all fell together in a shaggy mess. David walked out toward the tree line and glanced back over his shoulder at her, raising his eyebrows in question. Marisol grabbed his shoulders and turned him around. She jutted her hand out and pointed past his tent.

"Did you come back from *that* side of the woods?" she asked, setting her hands on her hips.

"Huh," he said under his breath. "You sure this wasn't here yesterday?"

"Even if it were, that would be weird, too. It certainly wasn't there when we set up our tents, was it?"

David rubbed the back of his neck. "No…it wasn't. But how?"

He walked past his tent, still barefoot, and stood in front of a break in the trees. The palm fronds and branches were parted, giving way to a small, clear path leading straight into the jungle. The limbs of the trees arched above the trail, looking as if it were carved out by a knife. David turned back to Marisol, who waited several feet behind him.

"Well?" she prodded.

Well, I guess there goes my theory about this being all in our heads, he thought. *Either that, or we've both gone completely crazy.*

"Claudio did say to follow the paths," he said with a shrug. "Guess it's time to pack up."

10

They trudged through the rainforest, taking turns leading the way. Every couple of hours, the breeze would shift and rattle the leaves and branches like a ghostly whisper following them deeper into the wood. The path continued for longer than either of them had suspected. The occasional tree limb or thin curtain of vines would block their path, but nothing like what they had dealt with thus far. Marisol insisted that she saw the branches moving, making room for them as they passed. David ignored her superstitions for the most part but found himself doing doubletakes after seeing things shift out of the corner of his eye.

David continued to force Marisol to drink water as they moved, knowing she was probably already behind on what she should have been taking in. With each passing hour, he watched as her hair and face slowly became saturated with sweat. They stopped to rest by early afternoon. When Marisol ducked behind some trees to go to the bathroom, David transferred his remaining water to her drinking bottle. The last thing he wanted to deal with was her getting heat stroke or passing out on him. He was thankful that she didn't seem to notice that her bottle had refilled itself—either that, or she was too distracted to care.

"Do you think we made a mistake leaving Dr. Morrow?" David asked as they skirted around a deep puddle.

Marisol shrugged, balancing on a root to keep her shoes from sinking into the water. "Maybe. At the same time, staying put could have endangered us more. We could have disappeared just like her."

"Do you think she really disappeared, though? What if she tried to get back to us and got hurt? What if we're doing it all wrong?"

"I don't know, David." Marisol sighed and turned to face him. "I know that if anyone was going to be fine hoofing it in the rainforest, it would be her. I think the best thing we can do is take care of ourselves right now. Asking a million what-ifs isn't going to do anything other than add more stress."

"I just worry…"

"Me too. But we'll be okay. We just need to stick together."

By the time the early evening came around, they had slowed to a crawl. David thought he may as well have had lead weights tied to his shoes, each step taking more effort than the last. They decided to stop for the night and attempt to set up camp. David grimaced as he lowered his backpack. He could feel the wound on his back throbbing as soon as the weight of his pack had been lifted off. He reached his hand around but couldn't get far enough to reach where it hurt. He looked over at Marisol and debated having her take a look.

She'll just blow it out of proportion. Or call you a wuss or make some kind of smart aleck remark about sucking it up.

As David rested, Marisol took the time to clear a small section of ground as a campsite. Given the lack of space on the trail, they had opted to set up only a single tent. She used the extra anchors from her pack to secure the ends of the rope against the thick roots protruding out of the ground. While not necessary, she thought it may at least provide warning should the trees decide to move in the middle of the night.

Marisol wondered if Nelly's talk of this area being cursed was due to upset forest spirits, or if someone or some*thing* cursed the land. Her mind drifted to her ritual at home of putting a glass of water behind her door to ward off evil spirits. With a quick glance to David, she pulled the water bottle out of her bag and set it inside of the tent by the door before setting up the rest of their supplies.

On the other side of the trail, David fished his SAT phone out of one of the side pockets of his pack and turned it on. The home screen blinked on and flickered briefly before settling on the main menu. David scrolled through the menu to find and open the GPS to compare it to their map. As the loading screen started, the ringtone went off, startling them both. Marisol rushed over and leaned in to see the screen.

"It's the lodge!" she squealed. "Pick it up!"

"Hello?" David said as he answered the phone.

"Ye—Davi—wanted to—on—way," the voice crackled through the speaker.

"I didn't catch that…you're breaking up," David said, louder.

"What are they saying?" Marisol asked.

David waved a hand at her to be quiet while he pressed the phone tighter to his ear.

"Stay—on our—ay," said the voice. "St-y a—th—site."

Loud static and feedback blared through the speaker. David yanked the phone away from his ear. The bright home screen flickered for a few seconds before going completely dark. David hit the phone against his hand, trying to jiggle it back on.

"What did they say?"

"Something about the site? It kind of sounded like they said they were on their way? It was so garbled, I-I really don't know," he said, defeated. "Go get your phone."

Marisol grabbed her phone out of her bag and passed it to David. He pressed the power button, but the screen and keys remained dark. He rubbed one hand over his face in frustration, looking at the dead phone in the other.

"When did we charge these?" he asked.

"I plugged them in when we took a break. Maybe a few hours ago, tops?"

"And yours has been off this whole time? None of that bull-shit like before?"

"I swear. It hasn't been on since yesterday."

David paced as he gnawed on the corner of his mouth. His hands tapped at his sides as he ran through their options.

"Okay," he said, stopping and looking at Marisol. "Say they said to stay at the site, and that they're on their way. I don't know. I kind of think we should head back. It's cooler now, and I know we're tired, but if they're coming and we're *not* there when they get to it…"

"It's already almost too dark to see." Marisol turned, looking into the dense thicket. "We can leave first thing in the morning."

"You don't think first thing in the morning is too risky?"

"I thought you didn't believe in any of this stuff."

"I don't know what to think. But we have headlamps and flashlights. Even if we're slow, we'll make it there by morning."

Marisol let out a small groan as her shoulders sank. "I already set up the tent."

"So leave it. We're only using the one anyway. It'll help your back not having the extra weight."

They stood in silence. David's heartbeat thumped in his ears as he waited for her to give any kind of reasonable alternate suggestion. After a few minutes, Marisol sulked over to the tent, packed up her bag, and rejoined him. She strapped her head-lamp around her forehead and adjusted it over her hair. David did the same in response, shouldered his backpacks, and turned back down the way they came.

David led the way slowly but steadily with Marisol close behind. He had a harder time navigating the way back, tripping over roots and stumbling over his own feet as he tried to stay focused. His head ached the further they walked, small and persistent throbs pounding in his temples and behind his eyes. David repeatedly reached for the SAT phone to check the GPS, only to be met with a black and unresponsive screen. He swung his machete at a set of small, woody branches that had fallen across the pathway. As he swung down, the machete slipped off the branch and against his leg. He gasped as the machete grazed his pants, fraying the fabric and creating a small slit. He stopped in place, his hand shaking after almost slicing into his leg.

"Um, are you okay taking over for a bit?" he asked shakily, turning to Marisol.

Marisol nodded, eyeing David's torn pant leg as she stepped around him. "You should be more careful. That could have been really bad."

David let out an agitated breath. "That's why I asked you to take over."

"I'm just saying…"

David trudged behind her, his legs barely lifting off the ground as he marched forward. He stepped on Marisol's heels and apologized before realizing she had stopped walking. He looked past her to see the tent she had set up an hour prior.

David's eyes were heavy and his head pounded in beat with his pulse. "Did we turn around?"

"No. Well, I don't think so," Marisol said, looking down at the compass on her belt. "I've been following the same direction."

"Maybe we should wait until the morning."

"I thought you said that was a bad idea?" She turned, her eyes scanning him. "Are you feeling okay? You look awful."

David let out a tired sigh. "I'm fine, worn out. I just don't think I can walk another hour, especially if we're starting over."

"Okay." Marisol looked him over. "We don't have enough water to boil anything for dinner. I have our emergency fiber bars that we can break out."

"I think I may skip dinner and go lay down," David said, the words a slow drip off his lips. He dropped his backpack off his shoulders and rubbed his temples.

"You're really giving up that easily?"

David shrugged and shook his head. "I don't know what else

to do. I'm beat and really don't feel like pushing it. Let's aim for the morning. We can make quick time, and at least we won't be moving at a snail's pace."

"Okay." Marisol stared after him as he kicked off his shoes and disappeared into the tent. "Morning it is."

Marisol sat on the ground outside of the tent with the beam of her headlamp focused on the two satellite phones in front of her. She had almost disassembled the first one trying to troubleshoot it with the manual, and now she sat staring at the second. In a final attempt to get it working, she pressed the power button over and over without any response. She tossed it to the side, knowing there was no chance of sleeping soundly tonight.

Marisol had concocted several plans to try and debunk everything that had happened, but kept circling back to the phone call earlier. If help *was* coming, they needed to get back to where they were this morning...and soon. She pushed the SAT phones back into her bag and grabbed a flashlight out of David's pack. She was ready to test her first theory. She peered into the tent to see David curled up in his sleeping bag, his chest rising and falling softly as he slept.

"I'm going to figure this out. Don't worry," she whispered. Marisol stood outside of the tent and stared off into the trees. The knot building in her gut felt like an anchor tethering her to the ground. She let out a shaky breath and eyed the tent a final time. *He's going to kill you if he wakes up and you're gone again. But if this works, you'll be back, we'll get rescued, and it'll all be worth it. It's going to be worth the risk.* "I'm gonna figure it out, David. Just trust me." Marisol's words spilled out into the night, barely registering above the whirring insects. Tiptoeing away from the tent, she slipped her bag on, headed down the path and into the forest.

Marisol held the compass in front of her and followed due south. After going over the grid map, Site B should have been directly south of them, give or take some inevitable turns. She was revitalized after her brainstorming and determined to get them back to camp, but also wanted to prove herself. She was okay with David leading the charge, but she knew she was just as capable and rational...even if she still believed there was more at work out there aside from research papers and scientific discoveries.

Marisol trudged on in the dark for a half an hour before coming to a fork in the path. She didn't remember taking a fork before. She checked her compass. Due south. She turned back to the direction of their tent and checked again. Due south.

"Are you kidding me?" she said to the rainforest, exasperated. She looked around for any indication or sign of which way to go. Each path was the same, nothing but layers of dark trees and shadows. With a shrug, she veered off to her right and down the trail. As she pushed through clumps of ferns at the end of the path, she came upon a small pond, the surface slick and still. She shined her flashlight over the water and sucked in a quick breath as she saw several pairs of red eyes reflecting the light back at her.

"Oh shit," she whispered. "Caiman."

Marisol inched backward as the red eyes shifted, moving in silence across the tranquil water. She had more than enough experience with alligators back home to know not to mess with their South American cousins. Turning quickly, she made her way back to the fork, choosing to take the left path away from any more nighttime predators. Before she had time to compose herself, she found herself approaching her tent, complete with David's pack—exactly how she left it.

Marisol made her way back through the trail, rushing along the footpath despite her feet getting snagged on roots along the way. She stopped in her tracks as she found herself, yet again, at the same destination. *There is no way I'm taking the wrong direction. There has to be an explanation.*

She tried again, and then again two times more, even going so far as to skirt around the pond and its glowing, watchful eyes.

On her last round, she collapsed on the ground as she saw the tent come back into view. Marisol pulled her backpack and head-lamp off, chucking it into the leaf litter. She pushed the backlight on her watch to check the time. *12 am.* She had been walking non-stop for hours with nothing to show for it. Resigning, she kicked off her shoes, crawled into the tent—carefully climbing over David—before quickly succumbing to sleep.

Marisol's eyes fluttered open, the humidity of the day already seeping through her clothes and into her skin. She stared at the dew drops as they ran down the vinyl siding of the tent. It took several minutes for her to fully wake up. She figured the stress of yesterday and anxiety over today had to have been enough to knock her out last night. Soft moans from behind her brought her back to the present. She flipped over to see David laying on his back, covered in a thin sheen of sweat. He let out a quiet moan as his lips shivered and eyebrows pinched together. Marisol rubbed his shoulder to wake him.

"What? What's wrong?" he mumbled, his voice cracking from sleep. His eyelids drooped as he opened them.

Marisol stared down at him. "You sounded like you were having a bad dream."

David groaned and closed his eyes, running a hand across his forehead, wiping the sweat away. "I'm freezing. When did it get so cold?" He shivered as he pulled the sleeping bag higher to his face.

Marisol's stomach sank as she watched him bury himself in his sleeping bag. She reached over and placed the back of her hand on his forehead and ran it down to his neck.

"Stop," he whined. "What're you doing?"

"You're burning up." She reached over him and unzipped his backpack, pulling out the first aid kit. She unsnapped the container and rifled through the different supplies. She grabbed a small paper package labeled *ibuprofen* and ripped it open, shaking out two small, white tablets. "Take these. Where's your water?"

David sighed and looked up at her. "I don't have any," he said weakly.

Marisol snatched her water bottle from the front of the tent and unscrewed the lid. She shook the bottle and screwed the lid back on before pulling the top of his sleeping bag down. "Mine's empty, too. We need to cool you down."

"I'm fine," David said, sitting up. Each movement was at half-speed, pained and slow. His chin rested on his chest as his eyes closed. "We need to keep moving."

Marisol reached out and put a hand on his leg. "You're not going anywhere like this. And technically I don't know if either of us are going anywhere. I, um…I need to tell you something. I tried to go back last night."

David's head shot up. "You what?" he said angrily.

"Not, like, to *leave you*. I wanted to test something and…I don't think we can go back."

David pushed the heels of his hands against his eyes as he rested his head in his palms. Marisol waited for him to argue, but he sat quiet and still. She would have preferred the yelling.

When he didn't jump in, she continued, "Don't be mad. I was safe. I went back down the trail, right? There's a fork. One side kept circling me back to the tent and the other led to this lake or pond or something, but there were a ton of caiman out. Luckily, they just stayed in the water."

David lifted his head again. His jaw tensed and one of his eyes twitched at the sudden movement. "Wait…you found a pond?"

"Yeah, but here's the thing," she said, talking quickly. "Claudio said the guides kept ending up back at the lodge when they tried to get to the first camp…that the trails looked all different. It's like the same thing is happening here. I don't know why, but clearly we can't go back to—"

"But there's water," David said, looking at her.

"Caiman-infested water."

"Caiman are more active at night. Paul said that. I say we go refill our water and then work through whatever it is you were talking about." He forced each word out with more effort than the last.

"I can do it. You should stay here." Marisol moved to the door of the tent.

"I don't think so," he said, holding her by the arm. "It's a lot to carry, and we shouldn't split up anymore. I'm fine...really." He smiled weakly as he tossed the pills into his mouth and swallowed them dry.

David followed Marisol down the forked path to the small pond. Marisol slowed as they approached, watching the water. The surface of the pond was covered in thick, green algae and small water plants. David plodded to the edge of the water and sat down on the bank. He fumbled with his water bottle, trying to take it apart. She came up behind him and reached down, taking it from his hands before unscrewing the body of the bottle into two pieces. She dipped the cup into the water and pressed the top filter down, securing the pieces back together, and handed it back to him. David tilted the water bottle up and drank the contents in two long gulps. He leaned back on his elbows and stared out over the quiet water. Marisol lowered herself and sat next to him as a group of macaws cawed and passed by overhead.

"It's really beautiful," he said, not breaking his gaze.

Marisol glanced over at him. His breathing was different, more labored. He leaned forward to sit back up, pulling his legs up to his chest. She watched as he closed his eyes and struggled to open them again.

"We should probably rinse off while we're here. The water would help cool you down," Marisol offered.

David grunted and nodded his head, shifting to kick his

shoes off. He stopped to take several breaths before moving to stand.

"Let me help you," Marisol said, standing and grabbing his arm.

"I'm not dead, Marisol. I'm achy. I'll be alright."

David slipped off his pants and lifted his shirt over his head before wading into the shallow edge of the pond.

"David! What did you do?"

Her hands groped along his back between his shoulder blades before he even had time to turn around. He winced as her fingers brushed the spot where the bamboo had stabbed him.

"When did this happen?" she asked, pulling her hand away.

David turned to face her, but kept his vision focused on his feet. "A couple of days ago," he said quietly. He slowly raised his eyes to meet hers.

"And when were you going to say something?"

"It's not a big deal. I fell into some of the bamboo back at that camp. It's nothing. It stings, probably from the sweat, but it's not that bad."

"Not that bad? David, it's swollen and oozy."

"Oozy?" David said, scrunching his face. "Gross."

"More than gross. Infected. It needs to be cleaned up." Marisol stormed off to get the first aid kit and came running back with alcohol wipes and gauze. "Sit," she ordered.

David grumbled and sat on the ground, his feet resting in the cool water. Marisol sat behind him and ripped open the alcohol wipe packet. Keeping it flat, she moved it down David's back and over the wound.

David gasped and jerked away, pinching his shoulders back to stop her.

"Oh my God, I'm so sorry!" Marisol said, reaching towards him and putting her hand on his shoulder.

"Just don't touch me! That hurt *so* bad!" he growled, balling his hands into fists and pounding them into the dirt.

"You can't leave it like that."

"Yes, I can. Keep that shit away from me." David pushed up onto his feet and strode into the water.

He lowered himself to sit in the thick sediment of the pond, cupping the stagnant water over his face. The sun beamed down onto the water, heating the surface. David laid back, dipping his back and head into the water. His muscles and joints ached, but the water seemed to help. He let his eyes close as he took slow breaths.

Marisol waded through the water toward him and crouched next to him, her head peeking out above the smooth surface. David opened one eye to look at her. He pushed his hands into the silt and sat up, facing her. She eyed him with her nose crinkled and eyebrows arched with concern. David let his shoulders fall with a sigh.

"I'm fine. I don't want to have to keep saying it."

Marisol returned his sigh with an exaggerated one of her own before rolling her eyes and ducking further into the water. David moved to his stomach, laying horizontally in the shallow bed. Despite the sun pounding down on his back, the deep cold persisted. He couldn't shake the clammy feeling under his arms and down his back. He ran his hands over his body, trying to wipe away the grime. Hearing Marisol leaving the water, he flipped over to his back, closing his eyes as the warm water lapped at his skin. David took a breath and ducked his head under the water one last time before walking back to his clothes.

They moved past the tent from the night prior, choosing to leave it behind. Marisol insisted on carrying the heavier bag despite David's repetitious claims of being fine. She had been around her brothers and father long enough to know that men didn't so easily admit that they weren't fine. At least they had water, having boiled it down from the pond to refill their supplies. Unfortunately, that added several pounds onto each pack. Marisol led the way, following the path that was laid out for them. She had tried the phones again but decided that it was useless to keep attempting to turn them on.

She spent the walk letting her mind wander, thinking of what meaning these occurrences could have. She imagined her older brother, Ricardo, would have said it was a dark entity bent on drawing them in to never escape...but he was always a fan of the macabre. Sebastian would never have believed her. Matty, on the other hand, would find the good in it all, probably spinning it into some communion with nature and the wild. She didn't know what she believed, if she believed anything at all.

Dr. Morrow would have come up with some amazing scientific explanation with whimsy and wonder...and then would most likely turn it into a class that Marisol would have to sit on a waiting list to attend. Her dormmate, Tif, would suggest getting high and listening to the spirits of the forest. Marisol giggled to herself as she pictured that conversation. Tif would be sitting on their couch, bong in hand, spouting off some crazy philosophical nonsense about space and time and Mother Earth.

Her giggle gave way to a small frown as she thought about getting back to her life. Her family. Marisol slowed, looking down at her feet as they kicked up the leaves. It was quieter than when they started, less crunching and shuffling. She stopped, realizing the footfalls ended with her. She turned around to see David stopped several yards back. As she moved toward him, she saw him lean over the edge of the trail and vomit into the ferns. She ran to his side, but he held out a hand to stop her.

"Just give me a minute," he mumbled, spitting saliva and bile onto the ground.

He was sweating; small rivers pooled down the side of his head and onto the ground. Her stomach twisted in worry as she studied him closer. His face was almost pure white, but his cheeks were flushed a hot pink. He breathed heavily as he wavered on his feet.

"We should stop for the day," she said, reaching out to touch his arm.

"No," he croaked. "If I stop now, I won't have the energy to get back up. We need to get to the next research camp...like an actual campsite."

"We don't even know if that's the direction we're heading. How about food? We should eat. It's been at least six hours of walking."

"You can eat. I'm not hungry."

"Then we keep walking. If you won't eat, neither will I." She turned on her heels and continued down the path.

David wiped his mouth with his hand and trudged down the trail, calling after her. "You know that's stupid!"

They made their way deeper into the jungle, stopping twice for David to get sick. Marisol watched with worry as he struggled more the longer they walked. She wanted to force him to take a break, to drink, to eat...anything but walk. He continuously refused.

The plant life changed as they moved further inland. Large palms gave way to tall flowering trees and colorful crotons. As the sun set, light broke through the canopy, highlighting the oranges, purples, and pinks of the flowers and air plants which draped off the trees. The ferns they had pushed through during most of their time in the jungle turned to sharp, brightly colored bromeliads. The pointy and needle-ridden palm trees still dotted the landscape, but the atmosphere felt less formidable than it once had.

David called Marisol's attention to a nearby tree. It had large, pink flowers cascading from the branches and reached far into the canopy overhead. David staggered over to one of the lower branches and pointed.

"What are those?" he asked.

Marisol joined him and looked into the limbs of the tree. What looked like a wind chime, made from blackened bamboo pieces, hung from the branch by a piece of vinyl twine. "I have absolutely no idea. It's definitely man-made."

"Maybe we're close to the next camp."

"Or maybe people *do* live out here and Dr. Morrow had bad intel," Marisol suggested, glancing over to him.

They moved on past the tree and further down the cleared trail. More of the bamboo chimes hung from various branches, each suspended by a string of red twine. Soon, the trail widened into a small field of colorful ferns, flowers, and orchids.

"Wow," Marisol said, spinning in a circle. "It's so beautiful. What do you think? This is the perfect place to stop and set up camp."

David grunted in response as he unshouldered his backpack and plodded over to the edge of the clearing. A large, fallen trunk squashed the ferns and penetrated the serene field. He knew he'd have to give in and stop soon, though he wasn't sure if Marisol's nagging or his body would make him bend first. With an exhausted breath, David sat on the log and observed Marisol taking in the scenery. *It is quite beautiful*, he thought, despite the circumstances. He ran his hands along his arms, trying to chase away the shivers he had yet to shake. His arms were weak, and he let them collapse onto his legs. Bits of sunlight twinkled through the trees and covered the ground in glittering flashes. It was almost mesmerizing. David tore his eyes away from the glimmers of sun and watched as Marisol pitched the tent and set up their supplies. She had become adept at building up the small campsite, even now, while checking on him every few minutes to see if he needed anything.

Marisol walked over in front of him, holding up two sealed foil packets of dehydrated food. David took a slow breath in, readying himself for her next barrage of questions. As she approached, he could see her mouth moving, but her voice sounded like she was underwater. He squinted, thinking maybe he could hear her better if he focused.

"David? You need to eat. Just pick one," Marisol said, getting impatient.

David leaned in, staring at her mouth move. Even her movements were slowed.

"Are you alright?" she asked, "David?"

Black clouds crept in from his peripheral vision, closing in and around his line of sight. He squinted harder as she became smaller and further away, like he was looking at her from down a long tunnel. The blackness closed in around his vision as his eyes rolled back in his head. He was falling down a black hole, his head spinning and his body in free-fall. He felt it all at once, his body going numb as it hit the ground below.

11

A soft groan escaped David's lips. His pulse radiated in his temples as he lay on his back. He tried to lift his head but couldn't get his body to listen and respond. His tongue dragged across the dry roof of his mouth and to his lips, the chapped skin flaking away. He tried to open his eyes, whimpering at the amount of effort it took to move a single lid.

"Hey," Marisol's gentle voice called out, floating in the air around him. "There he is."

David opened his mouth to speak, but it was as dry as a desert, his words like cactus spines against his throat. He kept his eyes closed, still unable to find the strength to open them.

"Can you get him some water?" Marisol asked.

David swallowed hard, trying to moisten his throat enough to talk. The mouth of a water bottle pressed up against his lips. He leaned forward as the bottle lifted up, warm water pooling in his mouth and down his throat. David felt the water drip down his chin and onto his bare chest. His hand reached up weakly and touched the droplets of water that were now dripping down his side.

"Where's my shirt?" he asked, his voice hoarse.

"That's what you say?" Marisol laughed. "How are you feeling?"

He felt a soft hand rest on his shoulder and give a light squeeze. David peeled his eyes open. Marisol was leaning over him, her big, brown eyes and curly hair a comforting sight. He shifted his weight, feeling rough planks against his spine. David turned his head and winced at the tight muscles in his neck. He was under a canopy and propped up a few feet off the ground. A basket made of woven palm fronds sat on the ground next to him filled with pink-stained gauze. Marisol's hand cupped his face to turn his head toward her.

"How are you feeling?" she repeated.

"My head hurts," he groaned. "Where are we?"

"…the jungle?" she answered hesitantly.

A small smile crossed David's face as he let out a half-hearted laugh. "I know that…but where?"

Marisol reached out and helped him slowly sit up. Small cracks popped in his back as he leaned forward. He looked around to see a couple of tents set up a few yards away from the canopy and a fire pit roaring with a large pot hanging above it. He glanced at Marisol, awaiting an answer.

"Well, you're not going to believe me," she said, raising her eyebrows.

"What isn't he going to believe?" a deep voice said from David's other side.

David turned his head and glanced up at the tall, muscular man walking toward them. His near-black hair fell around his face in messy waves. David's eyes moved to the intricate black lines of flowery tattoos that sprawled across his toned chest and wrapped around his shoulder and upper arm. He found his gaze drifting down to a six-pack as he followed the deep v-shaped grooves on either side as they disappeared below the waistband of a pair of dirty cut-off shorts.

"David? You still with us?" Marisol waved her hand in front of David's face.

David blinked and shook his head gently. "What?" he asked, continuing to stare.

"David…this is Ben. He saved you."

David blinked again, this time directing his eyes up to Ben's face. "*Ben* Ben?"

"Nice to meet you. Officially, that is," Ben said, cracking a soft smile. "How are you feeling?"

"Thirsty," David answered.

Ben let out a light laugh as his wavy hair fell around his eyes. "You're probably pretty dehydrated after being out for a few days. Let me grab you some more water." Ben reached over David and grabbed the water bottle from Marisol before turning to cross the clearing.

David watched him walk away before looking over at Marisol. "I have so many questions."

A smile spread across her face. "I had a feeling you would. Long and short of it? You've been in and out of consciousness for a few days. Four to be exact. As far as Ben...well, it turns out his camp was right along where we stopped for the night. I guess there's lots of nice little clearings here. He heard me yelling at you to wake up after you fainted, and he came running. He was expecting Dr. Morrow...so that was hard to explain."

"He's, uh...he's not exactly what I was picturing."

"Oh, you mean drop dead gorgeous?" Marisol laughed as her gaze shifted in Ben's direction.

David raised his eyebrows at her. "Are you two already a thing then? I pass out and you're ready to leave me in the jungle for a hot guy?"

"He swings for the other team," Marisol said with a disappointed sigh. "I don't have a chance. Such a waste."

"What's a waste?" Ben asked as he ducked under the canopy to hand David a refilled water bottle.

"That as the only girl stranded in the rainforest, neither of you are a possibility," she answered nonchalantly.

Ben's eyes darted over to David and lingered before turning back to Marisol. "Sorry about that," he said, still smiling. He turned his attention to David. "If you're okay with it, I'd like to check you out."

"What?" David asked, looking up at him.

"Nothing major. I want to do a little bit of a check-up—temperature, rebandage your back, heart rate. The usual, now that you're awake."

"I'll leave him in your very capable hands then," Marisol said. She patted the back of Ben's shoulder, ducked out of the canopy, and strolled back across the camp.

"Can you scoot to one side?" Ben asked, straddling the thin boards of the cot. David shifted back a couple of feet, allowing him room. "It's easier for me to do when I don't have to be crouching over you." Ben reached out and cupped his hand on either side of David's neck, feeling down the side and around his throat. "Any pain?"

David shook his head as he withdrew his hands. Ben reached to the ground and rose with a notebook in his hand. He slid a pencil out from behind his ear and scribbled on the paper.

"Wrist."

David extended out his hand as Ben placed two fingers along the inside of his wrist and eyed his watch. After a minute, Ben released David's wrist and made another marking on the paper.

"What was wrong with me?" David asked as he watched Ben marking notes on the notepad.

Ben looked up, making eye contact with him. His eyes were a deep blue, like gazing into the ocean. David stared into them, forgetting whether he had already asked any one of the hundreds of questions that he had floating in his head.

"You had a really nasty infection with a dangerously high fever."

"Infection?" David asked, arching an eyebrow.

"Yeah, that crazy wound on your back? It had formed into a pretty decent abscess. No surprise, really. I pulled out a couple of pieces that worked their way in there fairly well."

"Worked their way in there?"

"Mhm." Ben nodded. "You had two little spines in your back. Marisol said they were from the bamboo, but I haven't seen anything like those before. Are you sure that's what happened?"

"I mean, I think so. Fairly positive. How could you not have seen them before? Those bamboo clumps are everywhere."

"Well, yeah, but these spines were barbed. My guess is that as you left them, they slowly worked their way deeper into your skin. I had to really dig to get one of them fully out. But don't worry," Ben added with a smile, "you're all patched up."

"I don't want to come off as ungrateful...but are you *qualified* for that? You were in Dr. Morrow's classes. She doesn't exactly run a medical program."

Ben laughed and put his notebook down between them. "My specialty is in botanical pharmacology. I was pre-med for a bit, but I wanted to study how we use certain plants for medicine. The people of the Amazon have been using natural, native cures for everything from malaria to cancer for generations. That's why I'm out here."

"That's cool." David glanced down at Ben's notepad between them. "Wait," he said as his head shot up. "The spines were *barbed*?"

"Weird, right? I've never seen a spine or thorn like that before...that's why I wanted to ask if it was maybe something else. Not that I didn't believe Marisol, or you, but you never know." Ben tapped the end of his pencil against the notepad as he looked David up and down. "So, please don't think I'm weird or anything, but I did save them if you want to see."

"You did? Of course I do...as long as you don't think *I'm* weird for wanting to look at them."

"Hardly! Here, come with me!" Ben said as he swung his leg over the cot and strode out of the canopy.

David studied him for a second before straining to stand up. His legs were weak under him as he leaned his hands against the cot, looking down at his bare feet pressing into the dirt. He heard footsteps rushing through the leaves as Ben came jogging back and pushed his shoulder under David's arm to support him.

"I'm *so* sorry. I totally forgot you haven't stood up in a few days. That was stupid. Let me help you."

"No, I-I'm okay," David stammered, pulling away as he

stood up straighter. "I probably just need a minute to walk around, make my legs stop wobbling."

Ben shrugged, taking a few steps back. "Okay." He lingered, waiting to see David take a few steps. "I'll be over in the research tent—that big one over there—when you're ready. But if you need help, just shout, okay? Don't want you falling and hurting yourself more."

David nodded and flashed Ben a quick smile. As he left the canopy, David lifted his head to see large flowering trees woven overhead. Various colored orchids clung to the branches and trunks, dotting the bright green trees with splashes of pink and white. Dangling from the trees were dozens of bamboo chimes hanging at various lengths. The bamboo stalks ranged from bright green to black and were all suspended by the same vinyl twine they had seen earlier.

David turned, noticing a large tent, open and filled with binders and plastic bins as well as two personal tents on either side of the campsite. David thought it looked like a scene from an elaborate painting. He didn't understand how something so beautiful could exist after spending the last week trudging through dark, damp forest.

"It's pretty amazing, isn't it?" Marisol said, walking up to him and leaning her head against his arm.

"Very. Ben's...*interesting*."

"Interesting?"

David toed the ground, brushing up against the leaves and dirt. "I don't know. Never mind."

"You're just jealous because he's all hunky. But don't worry, I'll still hang out with you even though there's someone more 'interesting' now."

"You're so generous," David laughed. "He said he was going to show me the bamboo spines that he pulled out of my back." He shivered as he thought of something digging into his skin for days without him knowing.

Marisol straightened and swiveled to face him. "Did he tell you about them?" she asked, her face serious.

"I mean, a little, just that they were—"

"Barbed! I know! All I could think about was you going on and on about that porcupine and fishhooks and…" Marisol squirmed. "It was *not* pleasant."

"I can't imagine it was. And it *would* be the same principle, I guess."

"I'm still mad at you for not telling me." Marisol pursed her lips and glared up at him. "You could have killed yourself."

"I know, and I'm sorry. I didn't want you to worry about me."

She threw her hands on her hips. "So you make me worry *extra*?"

"I promise if anything happens again, I'll tell you. No matter how small. I have a feeling you're not going to let me forget this one."

"Not in a million years." She reached an arm around him and pulled him in for a hug.

"Hey, you coming?" Ben called out from the large tent.

Marisol removed her arm from his waist and feigned gagging. "I was there when he pulled them out." She gestured to the tent. "It's all you."

Inside the tent, Ben hunched over a small plastic petri dish. He held a large magnifying glass in his hand as he waved David inside. He placed the magnifying glass next to the petri dish and picked up a small jar, unscrewing the lid.

"I got a little too eager about these that I forgot to check your back. Turn around." Ben reached out for David's shoulders and spun him around.

David's skin pulled taught between his shoulder blades as Ben peeled something away from his skin. He winced as Ben poked around the inflamed area.

"It looks so much better," Ben said.

David could hear the smile in Ben's voice. Normally, he

would be pulling away and trying to avoid anyone being in his personal space, but Ben made him feel almost at ease. David scrunched up his face as he felt a sticky substance spread along his back. He flinched, jerking his body away as Ben pushed his finger hard against the healing wound.

"Shit, sorry," Ben said, through gritted teeth. "Forgot you've been out cold when I've been doing this. You alright?"

David nodded sharply, his back still facing Ben. "Just stings a bit. What are you putting on it?"

"A paste made from the bark of a tawari tree and the lapacho plant. Both have properties that fight infection and help with pain and inflammation. It's worked wonders. Your abscess is almost healed after only a few days. Interesting that it stings, though…" He turned away to jot something down on a piece of paper.

David turned to face him. Ben was bent over a stack of plastic bins, scribbling quickly with his pencil. David looked to his side to see the petri dish, grabbed the magnifying glass, and looked closer at the specimens. The two spines, blackened with old blood, were about a half an inch long and barely the width of a thin blade of grass. Looking at them in the dish, he was surprised he didn't feel them at the time. He moved the magnifying glass toward the end of the spine, watching as it came to a crooked, hooked tip. David's eyes darted up as Ben leaned his head in next to his.

"It's different, right?" Ben asked, touching the spines with his fingertip.

David straightened and leaned away, handing him the petri dish and catching a flash of his blue eyes. "Definitely different…"

That night, the three of them gathered around the campfire, taking turns spooning rice out of the boiling pot and into the crude bowls Ben had handed out earlier. Marisol bragged to

David about how Ben had carved them out of tree bark. She wasted no time in catching him up on everything he had missed.

The air was thick with humidity, but no longer held the same oppressive heat as it had during the day. The chirps and whirrs of hundreds of different insects filled the empty spaces around them. David had changed into a pair of sweatpants and a t-shirt, happy to be out of the shorts he had unknowingly been in for days. Marisol's hair whipped loose around her shoulders as she ate and shared stories of the last few days. Ben sat across from them, cross-legged on the ground in the same pair of shorts but was now wearing a black tank top. The front of the neckline was cut into a deep v-shape, giving way to the ink that decorated his skin.

"Marisol, I'm sure you'll be thrilled to be able to sleep in a tent again," Ben said through a mouthful of rice.

"What do you mean?" David asked, looking at Marisol.

"Well, she's spent all day and night over with you while you were out. I could barely get her to leave your side."

Marisol moved her head away from him, her eyes focused on her lap as her fingers played with the dead leaves littering the ground.

"You did?" David asked, keeping his eyes trained on her.

She looked up and stared at him. David swallowed as he saw the glossiness forming around her eyes. He knew that feeling all too well.

"I'm just glad you're okay," she said as a small smile crept over her lips. She leaned in and wrapped her arms around him, giving him a tight hug.

"You two are cute," Ben said, smiling at them.

David and Marisol pulled apart, chuckling as they went back to picking at the food in their bowls. Marisol wiped her eye, stopping a tear from dropping down her face.

"We're just friends." David smiled at her. "Trust me, she would just as easily kill me or leave me out here to starve."

"Well, now I want to know more," Ben said, leaning in.

"Oh, there's nothing to know," Marisol said, shaking her

head. "He's being dramatic. I mean, he's cute and all but super neurotic and shy and awkward and nerdy—"

"I think he gets the idea," David said, cutting her off.

"I had a few more, but you'll figure him out soon enough." Marisol stood up, leaning both hands on David's shoulders. "I can't wait to sleep without having to worry all night. I'm turning in." She pushed off of him and sauntered into their tent.

David stared at the last few grains of rice in his bowl. The fire crackling in front of him left the exposed skin on his arms tingling from the heat. "Sorry about that," he said, looking up at Ben. "She's a little much sometimes. I'm not *that* neurotic."

"Don't worry about it." Ben stood up, reached down, and took David's empty bowl from his hand. "I think it's cute."

David glanced up as Ben gave him a wink, the side of his mouth curving up in a small grin. David watched as he walked to the large tent and emptied out the bowls, pouring water over them to give them a quick rinse. He set them upside down on the plastic bins and sealed the flap of the tent.

"I'm going to turn in, too," Ben said, coming back from the tent. "Try not to stay up too late, and make sure the fire is out before you go to bed. And if you need anything, I'll be here. Sleep well." Ben crossed the camp and ducked into his tent, zipping the door shut behind him.

David sat in front of the fire, staring at the shadows dancing across the ground. He scooped up some dirt and threw it onto the fire, slowly smothering the flames. As the fire died, he looked back across the way to see Ben's tent lit up with a dim light.

What did you just get yourself into? He took a deep breath and closed his eyes. *Please, please, please don't make this more awkward than it needs to be.* Checking that the fire was out, he pushed himself up and headed over to join Marisol in their tent.

12

David crawled out of the tent and into the soggy morning air. He hadn't slept well, tossing and turning as he thought about how he had missed the last four days of his life. Marisol was deep asleep next to him as he watched the hours tick by. He was worried he might wake her but was desperate to stretch his legs. As he stood outside of the tent, he cracked his neck and raised both arms up, interlocking his hands in a stretch.

"Morning!" Ben called from the middle of the camp, waving.

David adjusted his shirt, pulling it back down from where it had lifted from his stomach. He walked over to Ben, who had resumed sharpening the machete in his lap with a smooth stone, and glanced down to the campfire, noticing he already had a small fire burning. Ben set the machete aside as David sat down across from him in the dirt, pulling at his pant legs to get comfortable.

"Coffee?" Ben offered.

David's eyes lit up. "You have coffee?"

"Yep! Here, I just poured this one. I'll grab another." Ben grinned as he thrust a metal thermos into David's hands. He twisted himself up on his knees and headed toward the research tent.

David watched as he trotted off. He was wearing sweatpants

and another tight tank top. With so much skin exposed, David wondered how he avoided being constantly covered in mosquito bites. He cupped the thermos in both hands and bent over, inhaling the bitter aroma as the steam tickled his nostrils. He looked up from his cup as Ben plopped down next to him, and grabbed the metal pot hanging over the flame to pour the hot brown liquid into a stainless steel cup.

"Sorry, I can only offer it black," Ben said, blowing at the steam billowing out of his cup before taking a sip.

"It's how I normally drink it, actually. I don't like it all sugary." David held the thermos up, still relishing in the comforting smell of freshly brewed coffee.

"Me too!" Ben said, perking up. "I have a killer sweet tooth... just not with my coffee." He flashed David a toothy smile before lifting the cup to his lips. "So, I know we didn't get a chance to really get to know each other yesterday afternoon," Ben continued, putting his coffee down, "but Marisol talked a lot about you while you were out."

"Oh? I wouldn't believe everything she says."

"She said you're a bit of a bookworm," Ben said, uncrossing his legs.

David let out a small laugh. "To say the least." He took a sip of his coffee. "Okay...maybe she's a *little* bit believable."

"I'll settle for a little believable. And don't worry, she didn't say anything *too* salacious. I'm glad that's true, though. It's nice to run into fellow bibliophile."

"People say that, but they rarely mean it—*bibliophile*. They read three or four books a year and think they're blowing through the library. Me? I feel like my entire life has been nothing but devouring books."

"I get that. I tend to go through three or four a month. What really interested me, though, was that Marisol said you carry a really old book around with you. She couldn't remember the name of it...said she didn't feel comfortable going through your stuff to find out, but I've been kind of dying to know."

David grinned. "Yeah, I do actually. It's a first edition of *King*

Solomon's Mines. I know it's stupid and impractical, but I bring it with me everywhere I go."

"Wow, first edition? Seriously?" Ben asked, leaning back with surprise. "I read that one back in high school. Very old school. My oldest sister got me really into adventure books as a kid. I mainly read that or sci-fi...or high fantasy. And between you and me, I may dabble in romance novels as a guilty pleasure. But anyway..." Ben laughed, a slight blush building on his cheeks. "Is that one your favorite? Is that why you carry it around?"

"Nah, not really. It was one of several my dad had. My favorite was always *Tarzan*. You know, the series. Not many people know them. They're a little campy, but I always loved those little books."

Ben smiled, his eyes twinkling in the morning light. "No way. Hold that thought." He jumped up in one quick motion and dashed over to his tent, disappearing inside. He came jogging back not a minute later with his arm tucked behind his back as he plopped back down across from David. He pulled his hand from around his back and held a thin book out in front of him.

"You're shitting me," David said, his mouth stuck in a wide grin. "Are you serious right now?" He reached out and took the book, running his hand along the familiar cover. The edges were worn and the gold letters spelling *Tarzan of the Apes* were faded into the burgundy background.

"It's no first edition, but it's something." Ben beamed.

David looked up at him, awestruck. "I haven't seen this book in *years*. I-I can't...I mean, what are the odds?"

"I know, right? Kinda serendipitous. About had a heart attack when you mentioned it just now. Most people make fun of me for toting around the same book over and over again. Kinda why I had to ask. It'd be nice not to be the only weirdo out here. No one ever knows it when I mention it. They always think Disney or Brendan Fraser...never the book series."

"This book made me want to explore the jungle. Be Tarzan," David said as he smiled to himself.

"Really? See, I always wanted to be Jane and get rescued by Tarzan." Ben shrugged, laughing.

"By looking at you, I'm pretty sure you're Tarzan."

"Maybe on the outside. But inside, I'll always be damsel in distress, Jane Porter, just waiting to be rescued by the ape man," Ben said wistfully, staring into the flowers draping the canopy above them.

David's stomach fluttered as he watched him. It was rare for him to let his guard down around a complete stranger, especially a complete stranger found in the middle of the jungle. Not only that, but he hadn't met anyone even remotely as interested in books as he was, let alone his favorite book. If anything, that topic was often used against him, a mechanism for teasing and poking fun.

Ben lowered his head, redirecting his gaze from the trees overhead. He smiled at David, catching him staring at him.

David returned the smile, digging the side of his foot into the dirt. "I, um—"

"Morning boys!" Marisol shouted as she came up behind David and gripped her hands around his shoulders.

"Morning," Ben said, tearing his eyes away from David.

"And what are you two up talking about this—oh!" Marisol reached down and scooped the thermos off the ground in front of David. "Coffee!" Marisol dropped onto the ground between them and took a slow sip from David's cup.

David and Ben locked eyes over the thermos as Marisol downed several more sips, oblivious to her interruption. Her curly hair was frizzy and secured in a low and loose ponytail, the bottom of which was plastered with static cling to a blue oversized t-shirt.

"Mmm, exactly what I needed this morning. I see you've started a two-man book club," Marisol said, nodding her head toward the book in David's lap.

"A book club which is run solely on coffee," David replied, snatching his thermos out of Marisol's hands.

Marisol pouted her lips and gave David her best puppy-dog

eyes. "But you've been basically asleep for almost a week. You're plenty rested and energized. Besides, don't you get off on old books anyway? Who needs coffee when you have…*Tarzan of the Apes*?" She made a face as she leaned over to read the book cover.

He rolled his eyes and shoved the thermos back into her hands. "Ugh, fine."

"Thanks! I'm going to take this back to the tent and get dressed," she said as she hopped off back to their tent.

"You're welcome!" David called after her, as he heard the tent flap unzip.

"You two are like an old married couple," Ben said with a cheeky smile.

David shook his head and breathed out a light chuckle, offering a slight smile to Ben from the corner of his mouth. "So, what's the deal with all of these wind chimes anyway?" David looked up, pointing to the hanging bamboo stems overhead.

"For when the jungle moves," Ben answered without looking up from the cup pressed against his lips.

David's heart dropped into his stomach. "What did you just say?"

Ben looked up, perplexed, as he lowered his coffee. "I thought you and Marisol knew about it. I assumed that that's how you ended up in here. They let you in."

"*Who* let us in?" The air was draining out of David's lungs as the question passed over his lips.

"The trees."

"For the hundredth time, no," Ben said, watching David walk in circles around the middle of the campsite. "I don't have any idea how or why. If I did, I'd tell you!"

"I don't understand why you wouldn't say anything," Marisol said to Ben. David had pulled her out of the tent midway through getting dressed to hear about 'Ben's trees.'

"And David, for fuck's sake, just sit down. You know I hate when you get like this."

David stopped in his tracks and glared at her. "So, you're going to get on *my* case when we're trapped in the goddamned rainforest by what? Killer trees?"

"Look, both of you just calm down," Ben said, holding a palm up towards each of them. "I'm sorry. I figured you knew. That's on me."

"So you were never really missing then?" David asked, bringing his eyes to Ben. "We're out here for nothing?"

"Not nothing. And it's more complicated than that." Ben's shoulders dropped as he let out a heavy breath. "Before I was due back at the lodge, I started noticing weird things with this vine I was tracking. I thought maybe I came across a novel species and I could do more research on it. But I don't know. I got stuck, I guess."

"Stuck. Great," David huffed, taking a reluctant seat on the ground. "Well...what do we do now?"

"That's what I've been trying to figure out," Ben said, joining him. "Once I realized what was going on, I couldn't get up and leave. I had to know why it was happening, you know? This is new territory, completely unexplained. And then you showed up and introduced these new bamboo spines, and somehow you were able to make it this far in. I haven't been able to get further than a few miles outside of this camp. The jungle won't let me."

"I can't. This is crazy," Marisol said, throwing her arms up and turning on her heels, stomping back to the tent.

"Marisol, wait!" David called after her. He got up to follow her but stopped when Ben's hand held tight at his arm.

"You get it, though, right?" Ben asked, staring up at him. His blue eyes reflected the bits of sun that broke through the leaves.

David hesitated. "I-I don't know what to think right now." A sadness crossed Ben's face as the words left his mouth. The hand on his arm dropped away, giving him permission to move again. "I have to go check on her...but it's not like we're going anywhere." David reached the front of the tent before he turned and jogged back toward Ben. "Hey…if you're anything like your field notes, and you probably are, I assume you've already done a lot of research to test and prove your theories about..." He waved his hand to the canopy.

Ben nodded. "I have."

"Then let me take care of Marisol for a minute. When I come back, why don't you show me what you have so far. Maybe I can help." David's lips lifted into a slight smile before he spun around and retreated toward the tent.

David ducked as Marisol whipped her sleeping bag toward his head as she straightened it out and began rolling it up.

"What are you doing?" David slid around her and onto the floor of the tent, trying to avoid another near miss.

"What am *I* doing? *We're* getting the hell out of here," Marisol said without stopping. She grabbed a small pile of her clothes and shoved them into her backpack, pounding them to the bottom with her fist.

"Slow down. I…I think we should hear him out."

Marisol let go of her bag, dropped onto the floor, and looked at David with her mouth open. "*You* want to hear him out? *You*?"

"Well, you don't have to say it like that," David said, shrinking back.

"You don't even want to be out here!"

"It's not about that. You have to admit, it's…*interesting*. Scary, yeah, but interesting." David licked his lips and stared at the ground between them. "It's just that…I've been reading all of Ben's notes since we got out here. He's smart. And capable. He's clearly okay out here and has a grasp on this place. We don't. Do you really want to go wandering around on our own again? You want to avoid anything else happening, right? I think he's our best bet."

"I can't believe you," she spat, turning and throwing more

miscellaneous things into her backpack. "And what's changed? Why now? What happened to our minds playing tricks on us?"

"Marisol..."

"Well?" She stopped, narrowing her eyes onto him.

David averted his eyes and half shrugged. "The way he said it."

"Okay?"

"I don't know." He let his hands fall to his sides. "If anything, isn't it just confirmation? That *obviously* something is happening out here?"

"Maybe. But you don't mess with things like this, David. Nothing good comes of it, and I refuse to have us find out the hard way."

"At least hear him out." David stared as she pushed the last of her belongings into her bag and zipped it shut. "He saved my life, Marisol. And made sure you were okay. Don't we owe him a day to explain?"

"One day," she said, holding up her pointer finger. "Then I'm out."

David and Ben stood in the research tent, hunched over a handful of open plastic bins. Ben laid out several binders containing pressed plants, note cards, and journal entries. David tried to catch all the information as he listened. Ben flipped the binder pages, almost ripping them off the rings as he listed off every detail he had noted since venturing deeper into the reserve.

"...and then by the third day, I knew it wasn't just me seeing things. Like here..." Ben flipped the page to show a pressed vine positioned neatly on a piece of paper. "I *finally* got a usable clipping. But when I woke up the next morning, the entire camp was covered in these things...and I mean *covered*. I cut them all back and went to go check for a pond or lake or something in the area, and when I got back—boom!" Ben flipped to the next page to show a series of Polaroid photos lined up in a sheet protector.

"You documented it? Like in photos?" David asked, turning his head over his shoulder. "Marisol, come over here! You should see this!"

David leaned in closer, looking at the photos. The first Polaroid was dark and blurred, but he could make out a large shape suspended from gnarled and branching vines. Specks of light and dust obscured parts of the photo, reminding him of the types of things shown in ghost hunting television shows— ghostly orbs and longing spirits plaguing innocent homeowners via shoddy film exposure. The second and third photos were clearer. Bright light illuminated the twisting vines. He assumed Ben had shone a flashlight on the subject after seeing how the first photo turned out.

The remaining two photos focused on a tent—the same tent they had visited only days prior, except that it looked brand new, no mold or mildew staining the surface. Though unscathed by algae, the fabric was torn and pierced by vines. The tendrils wormed through the fabric and around the trees, suspending the tent several feet off the ground. David tore his eyes away from the pictures and faced Ben.

"We saw this," he said. "Right before we got separated from Dr. Morrow."

Ben pinched his eyebrows in concern. "You guys tried to break through the vines, didn't you?"

"Oh my God," Marisol breathed, leaning around David. "Is that *the* tent?"

David ignored her and nodded to Ben. "We needed to know if there was any sign of you there, any clue to point us in a direction, and I had been reading your notes and the vine sounded similar to what you had noted. So, I took a clipping and then it began propagating. Dr. Morrow transplanted some of them into the compostable pots and—"

"You transplanted them?" Ben interrupted.

"Yeah?" David said, almost in question. "But then the next morning—"

"Damn!" Ben cursed under his breath and slammed his fist down onto the notebook, making both David and Marisol jump.

"I mean, we didn't have the chance to follow through or get any additional information. Once Dr. Morrow disappeared that morning, I honestly kind of forgot about it," David continued.

"That makes sense," Ben said, only half-listening as he bent down and lifted another plastic bin and pried the lid off. Inside lay stacks of cardboard planters. "I never thought of transplanting them."

"You're not thinking of doing that are you? After what happened?" Marisol asked from the other side of David.

"We don't have to do it anywhere near camp. I have chimes set up all over this section of the grid. We can take a clipping, transplant it, and then watch it around the clock. It's the perfect way to see how this all operates on the simplest level."

"And *why* do we need to know how this operates? The guides at the research lodge said this place was tierra maldita, cursed earth. Clearly, they were right," Marisol said, her anger rising. "Dr. Morrow is *gone* because we didn't listen to them. We barely made it this far, and now you're telling us we're trapped. Dr. Morrow could be out there trying to find her way through, and you want to research it? I know about tall tales, and I know about superstitions. There is something else at work here and none of it makes sense. We're just three people with limited supplies. We can't explain any of the things going on here."

Ben replaced the lid on the container and turned to face her. "Every superstition is steeped in a scientific truth. Superstitions are what people create to explain what they don't understand. People use God and Jesus to explain miracles. Natives throughout North America use spirits to explain the wonders and awe of nature. The Greeks used the gods of the Pantheon to explain human behavior. The Egyptians worshipped gods to bring them fertile land and life after death...it's all just stuff to explain the unexplainable. There is always an answer. You just have to be smart enough to look for it."

Marisol crossed in front of David, biting down on her lower lip as she stared up at Ben. Her head came up to the top of his shoulder, but she had never let her small stature make her a weak adversary. She knew what he was saying made sense, but the voice of her grandmother still stuck in the back of her head. The thought of the jungle swallowing them up made her queasy, but she wasn't about to walk straight into a trap, especially if she didn't know what the trap was or who was setting it. She knew better than to be the bait.

"Look," Ben said. "I'm not trying to argue. And you're right. Julia is out there, but if we can figure out why all of this is happening, then we might have a chance to make a break for it... and maybe help her in the process. I've been out here for a long time, and I haven't made any progress. This is the best, maybe the *only* chance we have to help all of us. We don't have to do it if it makes you uncomfortable, but we have to do something. I've run out of things to try. Like I said, I've only made it a few miles forward and back. You both are more than welcome to take some of my supplies and try to hike back out of the reserve. There's no reason for me to stop you."

Marisol ground her molars together, disappearing inside of her head. She thought of her family and of David. It could have been her that was hurt; it could have been both of them dead among the leaves if Ben hadn't been there, and this may be their only chance of getting home in one piece.

"Fine," Marisol said, giving a curt nod. "But we do it somewhere as far away from here as we can. And I don't want anything to do with it."

Ben looked from Marisol to David. "And you?"

David inhaled and held his breath. His heart quickened at the thought of ending up injured again. He glanced to Marisol, her eyes trained on him. "Let's go for it," he breathed. "Where do we start?"

13

Marisol puttered around the camp as she watched the numbers on her watch change with each passing minute. David and Ben left earlier in the morning to scout out areas for Ben's half-cocked experiment. She refused to go with them. While she didn't want to be left alone, she also didn't mind the break to be by herself for a while.

Marisol had pulled the makeshift cot Ben had made to take care of David out into the middle of the camp and reclined on top, gazing at the flowers and leaves shimmering in the light breeze above her. She closed her eyes and let several relaxing breaths flow in and out as she focused on the air filling and then emptying her lungs. She'd yet to take advantage of the scenery and was determined to do so before the other two came back.

The whining caw of a hawk soaring above the canopy brought a smile to her lips. She glanced up, hoping to catch the beautiful, rust-colored bird overhead. They had seen the species throughout most of the journey, always crying as they flew from branch to branch. Andy had said the local nickname for them was, Mama Vieja, "old mother", due to their nagging squawks while in flight. But the birds looked anything but old and whiny, the black-collared hawks were stunning with their mottled copper and black feathers, and nothing but grace when perched in the treetops. Marisol closed her eyes as the calls faded into the far reaches of the jungle.

The squawks weren't the only fading noise. As Marisol reclined, she noticed even the peeps of the colorful songbirds had disappeared. Within moments, silence filled the clearing. The sudden absence of noise sent a cold flush over her body. She held her breath, about to get up, when the knocking and tinkling of hollow wood filled the camp. Marisol's eyes shot open as she sat up and twisted her head, trying to find the source of the sound. Above her, Ben's windchimes clacked, though the breeze had long since died down. The leaves were unmoving, yet the bamboo chimes continued to stir, leaving a dull clinking haunting the clearing. She jumped off the cot and spun when a soft thud sounded from her left. Marisol exhaled and shook her head, chuckling at her jumpiness. A small heap of black fur lay on the ground several feet away. She craned her neck, seeing a long tail curled up against its body.

"Just a tiny monkey," she whispered, approaching the hairy creature huddled on the ground. Marisol inched closer and cooed to it in a sing-song tone. The animal, hunched over and bent at the waist, let out a small chirp in response. She reached forward, hand outstretched, and gently touched its back. At her touch, it whipped its head up, revealing a white, furry face. Marisol gasped as it looked up at her. Its eyes were swollen shut. The hairless skin circling the eyelids were red and puffy, making it look like blood was pooling around the sockets. The animal opened its mouth, emitting a loud, shrill shriek.

Marisol yanked her hand away and stumbled backward, falling onto the ground. A chorus of loud trills and screams erupted from the branches above her. Wet leaves stuck to her knees and legs as she pushed herself to her feet and backed away from the monkey. She stared in horror as it pulled itself toward her, using its arms to drag itself along the ground, its tail and legs leaving an indent in the leaves and dirt as they trailed behind. Marisol threw her hands up to her ears, trying to block out the deafening screams. She squeezed her eyes shut and shuffled backward, tripping over the cot, and falling back into the dirt.

As she hit the ground, the shrieks disappeared, leaving the canopy and campsite in complete and utter silence. She cowered, holding her arms against her head, tears silently falling down her face. Raising her head and opening her eyes, Marisol blinked away the blurriness from the tears to see the animal laying a couple feet away from her, prone and unmoving. She crawled on all fours toward the heap of fur, her hands shaking as her palms pressed into the moist, dead leaves covering the ground. She reached her hand out and pressed against the mound of black fur, flipping it over. The animal's face was motionless, contorted in frozen pain. Its mouth was drooped open, and a small stream of foam oozed out from the corner.

Marisol pushed herself back off her knees and onto her butt, holding her hands over her mouth. She tilted her head up as the branches rustled overhead. Dozens of black and white faces stared down at her from the treetops. Big, black eyes followed her as she forced herself to move. Marisol shifted, scooting herself along the ground an inch at a time. The eyes followed her, the animals' heads rocking back and forth, assessing her movements in quiet curiosity. She slid her hand along the ground until her fingers hit the metal pot next to the campfire. She lifted it and banged it against the rocks surrounding the kindling as she let out a loud scream. High-pitched chirps rang out as the branches bent and swayed, the faces disappearing behind the leaves and out of sight. Once the calls faded into the distance, Marisol brought her knees up to her chest and hugged her body tight as her chest heaved with silent sobs.

Ben lifted his foot up on a nearby tree trunk and adjusted his shoelaces. He and David had been walking for nearly an hour, taking note of the plant life and their proximity to the camp. David was surprised at how clear the paths were through the jungle. Ben explained that he made frequent rounds, making sure everything remained easy to travel through and that his bamboo chimes stayed in place. He pointed some out that needed continuous replacements due to troops of monkeys shaking them off the branches as they foraged.

They were headed to a small opening in the woods, a spot Ben marked for the next possible research site. "Without my GPS or compass, it's been near impossible to know when I'm at a grid point to know if I should move all of the equipment," he said as they continued to walk.

"You pack all of that up and transport it from place to place each time you move?" David asked.

"So far. I was hoping Julia would be bringing an extra camp-site's worth of stuff so I could leave this one intact. I'd be lying, though, if I said I wasn't getting comfortable there."

"Don't you miss being back home?"

"This is home enough for me. I miss my family, sure, but there's something about being out here. I belong out in the wilderness…challenging myself, you know?"

David walked in silence behind him, letting his machete brush against the ferns on either side of the trail. The sound of their footsteps allowed him to drift off into his thoughts.

"I take it that's a 'no,' then?" Ben said, craning his neck over his shoulder.

"What?" David drew his attention back to him.

"Liking being out here, having a challenge…"

"Oh," David said, contemplating his next words. "I'm not really the outdoorsy type. This is obviously a challenge, but probably not for the same reasons as you. Being out here kind of scares me. I don't know what I'm doing…" David trailed off. He stared down at the leaves crunching beneath his feet.

Ben stopped and turned to him, smiling. "I don't know. You seem like a natural fit."

"I almost killed myself my second day out here," he replied flatly, raising his eyebrows.

Ben's smile widened as he laughed, his wavy locks falling into his face. "But you didn't. Isn't that half the fun?"

"...not particularly?"

"Oh, come on," he said, playfully pushing David's right shoulder. "Let me show you something." Ben slipped off his backpack and stuck his machete in the ground, blade first. He turned his back to David and lifted up his shirt with one hand while pushing down on the waistband of his shorts with another. A long scar ran across his lower back next to his tailbone and down to the top of his right buttock. "Fell out of a tree on my first week out here alone. Landed right on a sharp branch. Took *weeks* to heal. And this one..." He turned back to David and pulled down the collar of his tank top to show his left pec. A series of thin, white scars blemished his tanned skin. "When I first tried hiking back to the lodge, I attempted cutting through some palms—you know the ones with the giant thorns? Squeezed through and scraped myself all up. Oh! And this one!" Ben held out his hand and tilted his palm up, highlighting a deep scar in the fleshy part at the base of his thumb. "Accidentally dropped a piranha off the hook and picked it up without thinking." He laughed to himself as he refitted his backpack around his shoulders. "There's a lot that can happen," he continued, "but sometimes you just have to try something that's a little scary."

"Guess I can check that box off then."

"Trust me," Ben said with a wink. "Nothing you can't handle." He turned around and continued down the trail.

David watched Ben navigate his way through the twisting paths. He was in awe of how easily Ben maneuvered through the roots protruding out of the ground every couple of feet; he figured he had managed to trip on every single one he came across. Soon they came up to a narrow trail. Skinny trees covered in woody thorns lined either side. Ben removed his backpack and turned sideways, holding it outstretched to his side. David stood at the entrance and watched him shimmy through.

"It's not as bad as it looks," Ben said, turning his head to see

David. "Follow me and shuffle sideways. Oh, and watch where you step."

"Is there not another way around?"

"Trust me, this is the easiest way."

David stayed unmoving, shifting the weight on his feet as he made a mental pros and cons list. Ben looked back and reversed, scuffling sideways and back toward David. He straightened as he came back out into the open next to him.

"Here, I can take your backpack. I promise it's not as scary as it seems."

"I'm not entirely sure I'll fit," David said, craning his neck around him to look down the path. "Next to you and Marisol, I feel like a whale."

Ben laughed softly. "That's ridiculous. Come on, we'll go through it together." He grabbed David's hand and pulled him forward as he headed back between the thorny trees.

David followed him, sucking in his stomach and standing as straight as he could to avoid leaning into the sharp spikes. He slid his feet over the leaves covering the ground as he watched the thorns cross inches away from his face. The path opened up into a bright clearing, and they found themselves in a field of ferns and flowering bushes. A small pond butted up against a break in the foliage. The still surface was covered in bright green algae and giant water lilies. Small birds darted in and out of the shrubs, their bright colors the only contrast against the mass of green leaves and white flowers.

"It's gorgeous," David breathed.

"Isn't it?" Ben said, facing him. "I sometimes come out here to read or watch the birds. It's pretty perfect."

David saw Ben watching him and averted his eyes, choosing a damp leaf at his feet to focus on. "And you're willing to use your perfect place for this? Won't it potentially be ruined?" He raised his eyes to see him still staring at him.

"Maybe. Only one way to find out."

David stiffened as a faint scream echoed through the trees. He looked past Ben and into the woods, back the way they had come. Ben tilted his head at the dim knocking of his bamboo chimes clanking in the distance. His muscles tensed when another scream made its way over the canopy.

"Marisol," David said in a near-whisper, feeling his stomach somersault. He swung the backpack off his shoulder and dove toward the narrow pathway into the thorns.

David and Ben sprinted through the pathways toward the scream. Branches scraped and pulled at their skin and clothes as they wove between branches. Ben pushed forward with David at his heels. David was barely breathing. His heart constricted with worry as he pictured a million possibilities as to why Marisol would be screaming so fiercely.

They burst through the brush and into the campsite to see Marisol curled up in the fetal position on the ground next to the research tent. David rushed to her side and placed a hand on her shoulder. She screamed in agony as his hand touched her skin. He jumped, pulling his hand away when Marisol curled tighter into a ball.

"Marisol, it's me. Talk to me. What's going on?" David pleaded over her whimpers and screams.

Marisol sobbed deeply. Her skin was red and inflamed with raised, white blisters broken out across the surface. She looked up at David with swollen eyes.

"Jesus," Ben gasped from behind David. "What happened?"

"The...ferns," Marisol cried, pointing past the trees on the other side of the camp. "It hurts so bad!" Marisol buried her face into the ground and continued to cry.

"Marisol, listen to me. You need to tell me more. What happened? We can't help you unless we know what's going on."

"I-I-I went into the f-ferns. A dead mo-mo-monkey got dragged away b-by a vine," she sobbed. "It-it was like a-a cloud of nee-nee-needles." She cried into her arm as she writhed on the ground.

David brushed his hand against her blistered skin, and she screamed out again. He grimaced and turned to Ben. "This might be a long shot, but this looks like a contact rash. A *bad* contact rash. You see it with plants like stinging nettle."

Ben's forehead scrunched as he shook his head. "We don't have those here."

"Well, it's something like it then, possibly worse by the looks of it. She said it was the ferns. If it's plant fibers, like a nettle, we need to get them out. Do you have any tape?"

"No...no, I don't have anything like that. Only adhesive bandages."

David's brain raced as he flipped through his mental rolodex. "What about wax? Something really sticky that can pull them out of her skin."

Ben closed his eyes and muttered a list of supplies. "I have some jars of sap from some rubber trees? It may be the best I have."

"Okay. Get it. And I need water." David pulled off his shirt and grabbed the water bottle from his backpack. "Marisol, I'm going to need to rinse and dry your skin, okay? I need to get a better look."

Marisol nodded and David pulled her gently into a seated position. She flinched under his touch, grimacing as his fingers grazed her skin. He sucked in a sharp breath as he looked at her fully. She wore a thin tank top and shorts, and every inch of visible skin was covered in large, white welts. David took a deep breath and opened the spout to his water bottle.

"I need to rinse out your eyes first," he said, gently. He lifted Marisol's chin and pried one eye open at a time, pouring a stream of water over each of her eyeballs.

Marisol bit down on her lip, her teeth piercing through the flesh as she held still. "It burns," she cried.

David released her head and watched as she fought back tears. "I'm so sorry." He dabbed the edge of his shirt against her lip, soaking up the blood dripping from where she bit down.

Ben appeared from the other side of camp with two large

containers of water and four mason jars filled with a white, viscous liquid. "Water is all sterilized," he said, leaving them next to David. He placed his hand on David's shoulder and crouched, leaning in closer to his face. "You're clearly thinking something. What is it?"

David shifted, facing away from Marisol, and spoke in a hushed tone. "It has to be some type of nettle. I don't know what else it could be, but the symptoms are the same. I've never seen a reaction this bad...not even when we were studying them."

"What do you need?"

"If we were back home..." David shook his head in question as he thought. "I guess other than tape, we'd need aloe or some kind of anti-inflammatory cream or baking soda mix—like an astringent, maybe. I don't know. Something to take the swelling away."

"I have a bunch of plants that can do that. Do you want a paste or just something topical?"

"Honestly? Anything you can manage. And as much of it as you can make."

Ben squeezed David's shoulder and moved around Marisol and into the research tent. David looked back to her. Marisol's eyes were less puffy, but still swollen. He offered her a small, reassuring smile.

"Okay," he said with a sigh. "This next part is going to hurt." David refilled his water bottle and began pouring it over Marisol's skin, starting from her face and moving down her arms and chest.

Marisol clenched her teeth together and balled her hands into fists as the water poured over her. David took his discarded shirt and soaked up the excess water.

"It's like sandpaper," she groaned through her teeth. She squeezed her eyes shut. "Or like a thousand tiny needles stabbing me all at once."

"I'm going to make it better, I promise." David stopped after her arms and stared at her. "I, um, I'm going to have to do under your clothes, too," he said, nervously. "Is that okay?"

Marisol nodded stiffly as she let David remove her tank top. She winced as she pushed up on her hands to allow him to remove her shorts. She sat, hunched in front of him, wearing a black sports bra and panties. David took a deep breath as he filled the bottle again and repeated the same procedure, rinsing her skin with water and drying it with his shirt. He moved from her chest and stomach down to her legs and feet. His heart hurt as he looked at her; the pain on her face made him feel like whispering a hundred apologies while knowing that it still wouldn't be enough to make it better. Ben edged out from the research tent and around Marisol, holding out two palm boots filled with a grayish paste.

"Can you put them in our tent?" David asked, glancing up at him.

Ben nodded, hurried over to their tent, and placed the palm pieces inside. He crossed back to David and stood over him. "What else?"

"The rubber tree sap, too," he said, tilting his head to the jars next to him. His attention moved to Marisol. "Do you think you can walk to the tent?"

Marisol shook her head, and he could see the fear in her eyes as they met his. David stood up and bent down, hooking her right arm around his shoulder. She dug her nails into him, muffling a scream into the crook of his neck. He pushed from his knees, lifted her off the ground, and carried her into the tent before placing her on their sleeping bags.

David saw her staring at him as he unscrewed the lids on the jars of sap. He held the jar up. "I'm hoping this will pull the plant fibers out." He glanced away and took another breath before facing her again. "You don't have to, but it would be easier without your, uh...well, without your bra."

A faint attempt at a smile spread along her face. "You remember the rules, right? Just don't stare." Marisol crossed her arms and pulled the bra over her head, grimacing as it brushed across her skin.

David dipped his fingers into the jar of sap and lifted them out, testing it, although he wasn't sure what exactly he was supposed to test. His eyes raised to meet Marisol's. "Here goes nothing." He reached over and spread the white sap along her arm. "I don't know how long this takes to cure, but hopefully not too long. In the meantime, tell me more about your thesis. You wanted to talk about it, right? Seems like ages ago now." He scooped another handful of sap and covered the reddened skin on her shoulders and collarbone. David smiled at her as he tried to ignore her flinching under his hands. "What better time to discuss it than now?"

"Is it feeling any better?" David asked, as he smoothed the plant paste across Marisol's ribcage.

"It stings a little less."

David peeled the drying rubber tree sap away while they talked and had applied Ben's plant mixture in its place. He reluctantly watched as Marisol tried to apply it herself, the pain in her hands preventing her from getting further than her palms and wrists.

David hesitated when he got to her breasts, but the white blisters spotted her skin even there. He was careful not to linger too long or make it seem like he was anything less than professional. Relief washed over him when she started teasing him about it, knowing it was a sign she was at least in less pain than before.

"Finished," David said as he ended at her feet, wiping his hands off with a towel. He twisted and cracked his back, stretching after being hunched over for so long. Marisol shifted out of the corner of his eye, angling herself away from him. He directed his vision away from her nakedness and slid her backpack over. "Want me to get you a shirt or something?"

"And get my clothes all covered in this crap? I think it's too little too late now anyway, don't you think?" Marisol smiled at him, though he saw her lifting her arms to cover herself.

David appreciated her effort to break the tension, so he forced himself to return the smile and held her gaze. "So," he said, raising an eyebrow, "you still haven't told me what happened. Not really."

"I feel stupid," Marisol said under her breath.

"Why?"

"Because I'm smarter than this." Marisol's eyes broke from David's. "And I'm so embarrassed."

"You don't have anything to be embarrassed about. You're such a badass."

Marisol chuckled as she looked back up to David. "Maybe next to you."

"Next to me you're a freaking superhero," he laughed. "So don't be embarrassed."

"If I tell you what I saw and what I think, you're going to think I'm crazy."

"I think after everything we've been through, crazy is a relative term."

"Okay," she said, taking a breath. Marisol explained her run in with the animals in the trees. "I freaked, which is stupid, but I did. But then after a while, I saw those vines from before. They were creeping along the ground, fast...you know, for plants. But before I could even process it, they were wrapped around the monkey and pulling it into the ferns."

"Like...you actually saw them moving?"

Marisol nodded slowly. "And I know I know better," she continued, "but I followed it. Once I got maybe twenty feet in, I started to feel itchy. I looked down, and all of the ferns were releasing these little hair-like spores. The more I moved, the more I kicked up. I couldn't see and it just burned so bad. It was like fiberglass. I ran and then I couldn't see and—" Tears started to flow again down her cheeks.

"Hey, don't cry," David said, wiping the tears from her face. "You're going to mess up my handiwork."

Marisol burst into laughter with David following suit. "Do you believe me?"

"Of course I believe you."

"Some ferns have trichomes to stop insects from preying on them. I did an entire section on it in my thesis."

"The tarantula hairs, right?" David welcomed the academic shift in conversation, always more comfortable than in those based on emotion.

"Exactly. But that many...I don't know. Enough to take down a monkey, clearly."

"So we stay away from ferns. The vine, though, is what concerns me. Carnivorous maybe? I'm not well versed in that."

"Carnivorous plants are touch-sensitive; they need a bug or lizard or something to land on them, so they know when to strike. They don't 'seek out' prey. But I've never seen anything like this."

"I guess we have more to figure out than we thought. I'm going to catch Ben up, if that's okay. Can I get you anything at all?"

Marisol shook her head. "I'm going to just sit here and pretend I'm in a spa having a mud mask treatment."

"Now that's the badass I was talking about," he said, winking at her before ducking out of the tent.

"Outside of being shaken up, how's she doing?" Ben asked. He and David huddled in the research tent, flipping through notes and encyclopedias to find anything on fern trichomes.

"Hard to tell. She's tough as nails, but those blisters were no joke. I can tell it hurts even though there's no way she'll admit to it."

"I'm glad you were there. I don't think I would have been able to come up with what you did. That was really impressive," Ben said, glancing up to David.

"Mostly just panic," David replied with a smile.

"You two must be really close. How long have you been friends?"

174

David laughed as he grabbed another reference book. "About two weeks—technically less if you count my time being unconscious."

"Really? That's surprising. It seems like you worry about her a lot for only two weeks."

"I feel like that's a pretty solidified piece of my personality: perpetual worrying."

"I like that. It's endearing."

David looked over to Ben and caught his eye, his stomach fluttering again. "Most people hate it. I've always been told to be tougher and more resilient," he said with a shrug. "She's definitely brought out the opposite in me, *and* she constantly teases me for it. Makes me feel like I have to buck up and take the lead…be more rough and tumble."

Ben reached out and placed his hand on David's, locking eyes. "Don't let anyone else's expectations of you mold the way you view yourself. You should be who you want to be, not what others expect or want. Besides, I think you're nice the way you are."

David slid his hand away as he looked into Ben's deep blue eyes. "Thanks…but you don't even know me."

"I'm really good at reading people. You're a good one. I can tell," he said with a reassuring grin. His eyes lingered on David's. "Anyone ever tell you that you have nice eyes?"

"…they're brown," David said, arching an eyebrow.

"Brown can't be nice?"

"Nobody thinks brown eyes are nice."

"Guess I'll have to respectfully disagree." Ben's eyebrow twitched, his grin growing.

David cleared his throat. "So, um, anyway…do you have supplies to make more of that mix for Marisol?"

Ben let out an inaudible breath and leaned back. "I think maybe enough for half of what I made earlier. Why? Do you think she'll need more?"

"I'd rather be safe than sorry."

"Well, I can always go get more. Probably not until tomorrow though since it's getting late. Most of those trees and bushes are scattered in different sectors."

"And we should all go together. If something happened to you while you were out there…"

"Do you think she can do that?"

"I guess we'll see tomorrow. Is that pond from earlier the nearest water source? I don't want to use all of our water on rinsing off that stuff."

"No, there's a closer one. I took her when you were still out, so she knows where it is. Up to her if she wants to make the trek. Are you wanting to go tonight?"

"Maybe tomorrow morning if she's willing to sleep in all that gunk overnight. Speaking of, I should probably get back to her. Mind if I take this book?" he asked, holding up an encyclopedia on ferns and epiphytes.

"Sure." Ben smiled as he watched David turn and walk away. "I'll be here if you need anything!" he called after him, raising his hand in a wave.

Ben sighed and ran his hands over his face before grabbing one of the open books and going back to flipping through the pages. He turned and looked at David's tent, seeing the open flap with two silhouettes against the lantern light. Without looking, he closed the book in front of him, zippered everything up, and made his way across the camp to his tent. Inside, he plopped down on his sleeping bag and pulled out David's copy of *King Solomon's Mines* from under his pillow. Thankful for the borrowed reading material, he ran his hand along the cover and flipped it open to a bookmarked page. With one more glance out of his tent, he began reading well into the night until the lanterns dimmed and his eyes forced themselves closed.

14

The cool water soaked into Marisol's hair as she submerged her head under the murky water. She had woken up to the dried plant mix flaking off in thin, papery sheets. Her body was sore, but she was relieved to see that the welts and swelling were no longer blemishing her skin. Red splotches on her arms, shoulders, and legs remained as she rinsed off the dried paste and watched it float away on the water's surface. The trip to the pond was a welcome excuse to get away from the dense jungle surrounding the camp. She swam out toward the middle, enjoying the calming sound of the birds in the nearby trees.

David and Ben sat on the shoreline as they watched a myriad of colorful butterflies land on the ground, feeding on the salts leached into the soil. David wiggled his feet through the silt at the edge of the pond, enjoying the cold water lapping up and over his ankles. A mint-green butterfly fluttered around his head as he leaned back on his elbows.

"I could see why you'd want to stay out here," he said, glancing over to Ben.

Ben smiled and laid next to David, bumping against his elbows as he leaned back. "It *is* magical." He turned his head toward David as he chewed on the inside of his bottom lip. "I'm sorry if I come off overly passionate sometimes." Ben adjusted his elbows and looked out over the water. "I know it bugs a lot of people, and I know there's strange and unexplainable things out here…but I'm not scared of any of it. It makes me want to know more—rush in headfirst. Maybe that's bad."

David turned to his side, leaning up on one elbow to face Ben. "I don't think it's bad. I'm jealous. I wish I could dive into something without worrying about every outcome first."

"But where's the fun in knowing how everything is going to turn out?" Ben asked, mirroring David's position so that they faced one another.

"Maybe that's why I don't tend to have a lot of fun," David said, cracking a smile.

"Well, you're right in the middle of it now. What better time to start?" Ben pushed himself back up to a seated position. "Why don't we start by teaching you how to fish? We're going to need lunch and dinner, after all." Ben stood up, looked down at David, and reached into his shorts pocket, pulling out a plastic baggie filled with fishing line and a hard-plastic case of fish-hooks. "Well, come on." He nudged David's side with his foot, nodding his head further down the shore.

David followed, using his machete to cut two small twigs off a nearby tree. Ben made a small notch in each and wrapped the line around it, attaching a hook to the loose end and knotting the other end to the stick.

"Voila! Fishing poles. Do you still have the palm nuts from the walk over?"

David nodded, grabbed a handful from his pocket, and handed them to Ben. Ben cracked open each nut and removed a white grub. He pierced one, sliding it onto the fishhook, and handed the pole to David. He repeated this for his own and pocketed the remaining grubs.

"Okay, I'm going to take a wild guess and say you've never fished before?"

"That obvious?"

"Do what I do, and you'll be good. Just watch, you'll end up some angler prodigy and show me up."

A smirk played across David's lips. "What? Don't like a little competition?"

"There he is," Ben laughed. "First one to catch enough for dinner gets to go swimming. Loser has to descale all the fish first."

"Okay," David smiled. "Deal."

Marisol kicked her feet, treading water as Ben swam over to her.

"David too chicken to swim past the shore?" Marisol asked between breaths.

"He's on fish duty," Ben said, grinning.

Marisol laughed. "Oh, he must be thrilled."

"Hey, he made a bet. I'm just a better fisherman."

"Has he even gone fishing before?"

"Well, no," Ben chuckled. "But it's good for him. Break him out of that cocoon a bit."

"Good luck. That cocoon is made of Teflon."

Ben laughed as he treaded water next to her. He glanced back to the shore to see David hunched over the pile of fish they caught. "If it helps, I already did over half of them when showing him how to do it."

"I'm amazed he agreed to it. I'd think he's way too fragile for that."

"Oh, come on...I wouldn't say that. He majorly stepped up yesterday when you needed it. You should have seen how fast he took off through the jungle when he heard you yell. He's tough."

Marisol raised an eyebrow at him. "I don't think 'tough' is ever a word I'd use for him. I'm not entirely convinced."

"You don't have to take my word for it," Ben said, half-shrugging while trying to stay afloat. "I think he's a lot stronger than you give him credit for."

"And you know that from only a few days?" Marisol asked, dryly.

"Know what?" David's voice rang out from behind them.

"You actually swam into the deep end?" Marisol asked. "Maybe Ben's right after all."

David looked over to Ben in question. "Stumble into some gossip then?"

"Not in a bad way," Ben answered before Marisol could offer a retort.

"Ben was saying how you were a knight in shining armor yesterday," said Marisol.

"Oh?" David tried to suppress the smile spreading across his face.

"I mean, kinda." Ben blushed.

"You two should get a room," Marisol teased. "And make me a reservation while you're at it. Meanwhile, I'm going to head back because I can barely kick anymore." She ducked underwater and swam toward the bank, splashing both of them in the process.

David ran his fingers over his eyes, clearing them of the pond water. He paused, seeing Ben looking over at him with a grin.

"What?" David asked, breathing heavily as his legs paddled beneath him, keeping him afloat.

"I just can't get a read on you."

"I promise I'm not that complicated." David panted, struggling to breathe. "And clearly not that fit. I'm going to head back, too. Luckily, I think we can skip the supply run. Marisol seems a lot better."

"Yeah, she does." Ben eyed David as a playful smirk crossed his face. "Wanna race?"

Marisol threw her head back and laughed, clinging to the towel wrapped around her. "You," she said, looking to David. "You thought you could beat *him*? First you lose in fishing, of all things, and then you try to out-swim him?" Marisol wiped a tear from her eye as she cackled.

"Hey now," Ben said, stepping over with a towel wrapped around his waist. "It was close!"

"You were already up here getting a towel by the time he even hit the dirt," Marisol said, catching her breath.

David was sitting next to Marisol, drying his hair off with his towel. He kept his head down, focusing on the flecks in the mud around his feet. Out of the corner of his eye, he saw Ben sit down next to him and watched as his hand came to rest on his knee.

"You're not an official judge, anyway. He could have had me," Ben said. He gave David's knee a small squeeze before taking his hand away.

David looked up to Ben and gave a small smile. "You don't have to be nice. Sports have never really been my strong suit."

"You say that like it's a bad thing. I mean, I never played sports growing up."

"I call bullshit," Marisol quipped.

"I'm serious! High school football, basketball, any of that stuff? Never been my thing. And yeah, I may work out, but I'm not a sports nut. Besides, no jock is going to want to talk about classic literature and prose. Call me a sucker for intellectual conversation."

"I had to be stuck out here with two nerds," Marisol joked.

"Don't pretend you're not one of us," David said, turning to face her.

"Yeah, yeah, yeah," she said, shoving his shoulder. "So then, fellow nerds, what's the plan? I know David wants to see this through, and as much as I don't want to stay, I'm not trying to go back alone." Marisol pulled her clothes on under her towel and gathered her things.

Ben slipped his shorts on and began sliding the fish, one by one, onto one of the fishing poles. He pushed the end of the stick through the gills and out through the mouth, stacking them like a totem pole. David grabbed the water containers they'd refilled earlier and brought them to the trailhead.

"I think we need to try and catch it in action," Ben said, threading the fish onto the stick. "I still like the idea of transplanting some of the vines, but it's not guaranteed, and I don't want to do anything dangerous." He glanced up to Marisol, giving a half-smile in apology for the day prior.

"If we do the transplant method, we're going to need to stay together. That means staying outside overnight—no cover and no camp," David said.

"And that's definitely dangerous," Marisol added.

"Your notes said that you saw most of the activity when you were first blazing trails, right?" David asked. "What if we veer off the path? Cut some new ways back to camp and see what happens?"

"That's actually a really good idea," Ben said as he attached the pole to his backpack, throwing it over his shoulder. "Certainly couldn't hurt."

"I volunteer for being in the middle," Marisol said, eyeing both David and Ben. "Safest spot."

"Whatever you want," David said, shaking his head with a smile.

Ben pressed ahead of them and down the path back to camp. He took out his machete and sliced through the palm fronds to forge a new trail. They steadily inched forward, cutting through the foliage, climbing around roots and large branches.

"No way!" Ben said, as he chipped away pieces of a woody bush. He ducked through a patch of bright green leaves and disappeared from view.

Marisol looked back to David and shrugged. "I'm not following him in there."

David side-stepped Marisol and climbed through the bush. Ben stood a few feet ahead, running his hand along a large, wooden vine. The trunk of the vine looped and folded around itself as if it were braided; multiple wooden spirals twisted around each other and up a giant tree trunk. The winding vine was as thick as a small tree, with the newer growth sprouting dark green leaves.

"It's an ayahuasca vine," Ben said, turning to face David, a smile wide across his face. "They're hard to find in this area."

"And that means what?" David asked.

"Depends on what you're into," Ben laughed. "It's used to make a psychotropic tea, mainly by shamans. It takes one other plant to make, but those are all over the place by the camp."

"And you learned this how?"

"I stayed with an indigenous tribe when I first stayed down here. I wanted to learn everything about the local plants, remedies, treatments, whatever. Well, they liked me, and I earned my keep. Next thing you know, I'm training with their shaman. I learned *so* much."

"Like how to get high on tree bark?"

"It's more complicated than that," Ben said, his smile fading. "It's a spiritual experience. Transcendent. Opens your mind… brings clarity and direction. It's a whole thing. Also, from a pharmaceutical standpoint, it helps with anxiety and depression, which is one of the main reasons it interests me."

David gave a light chuckle. "Sign me up then."

"I can always make a batch." Ben hacked his machete into the smallest section of vine. "I can't do any of the spiritual stuff— that's reserved for the shamans. But I can definitely make some." He continued to hack at the vine until several small chunks of wood lay at his feet. He gathered them up and shoved them in his backpack. "Shall we?"

"That's it? All that fuss for a handful of bark?"

"Well, there's only three of us," Ben shrugged. "Call it a little side project to learn more about how it works."

David raised an eyebrow at Ben.

"I'm not trying to roofie you or anything if that's what you think. I have other plants that can do that without this much work," Ben said with a cheeky smile. "Come on. Let's not leave Marisol waiting too long."

Ben climbed through the bush with David close behind.

Marisol was sitting on the ground and picking at the leaf litter on the small, newly cleared trail. She looked up at them as they stumbled back through the leaves and into the path.

"It's about time," she said, taking David's hand as he pulled her to her feet.

"Sorry about that," Ben said, smiling. "Rare find."

"Apparently, he's collecting supplies for some kind of psychedelic drink."

"Psycho*tropic*," Ben corrected.

"Nice," Marisol said, nodding to Ben.

"Glad we're all on board then," David said, shaking his head. "Doesn't seem like the safest—"

The dirt beneath their feet vibrated as a heavy crash thudded behind them. David spun, looking toward the area he and Ben left moments before. The leaves swayed as a gust of wind blew through the treetops.

"Look out!" Ben yelled as a loud crack sounded overhead.

Ben shoved David, his open palms slamming against his chest, as a large branch came crashing down between them. David tumbled backward through the bushes and onto his back. Marisol screamed as another branch snapped and collapsed between her and Ben, the thick leaves sending her tumbling to the ground.

"David! Ben!" Marisol called out, spinning around. "Are you guys okay?"

She was pressed in on all sides by the jungle, leaves and draping vines in every direction. Marisol reached her hands forward and pried at the branches. The sharp twigs scraped at her already irritated skin. She gritted her teeth through the pain and snapped off the small pieces she could get her hands around, pushing against the branches by her head as she held the leaves back. She leaned forward and peered through the gaps. More leaves. Attempts to swing her machete in front of her failed, unable to gain enough momentum to cut through the woody branches. Instead of clearing a way through, little pieces of wood chipped off in small pieces, flaking off and landing on the ground around her feet.

"This isn't doing *anything*." Marisol dropped the machete and cupped her hands around her mouth. "David! Can you hear me? Ben!"

She strained, listening for their voices. Her stomach knotted as she focused on her surroundings. She didn't hear anything. No voices. No birds. No insects. Dead silence.

"Marisol!" David yelled from the ground. "Ben!"

He scrambled to his feet and glanced behind him to see the small trail and braided vine he and Ben had left minutes prior. David faced the bush leading back to the trail and moved toward it, but his foot gave way underneath him as he stepped forward. Looking down, he found his left foot entangled in a web of thick, green vines.

David yanked his foot forward and shook, pulling and twisting his ankle, trying to loosen the plants. Despite his efforts, the vines tangled tighter against him, anchoring him to the jungle floor. Swearing under his breath, he lowered himself to the ground and unwound the tendrils one by one from around his ankle and shoe. For every piece he removed, there seemed to be five more in its place.

"Come on," David grumbled, unable to tear off the vine. He reached for his machete and slipped the blade between his foot and the vine, slicing up to sever the green shoots. They fell away easily and laid at his feet as he pushed himself up and headed toward the bush before him.

A light rustling erupted from behind the leaves as he approached. David paused. He took a step back, the rustling growing louder with each shuffle of his feet. The leaves fluttered on the twigs as a soft breeze blew through the wooded alcove.

Cautious, he held his breath and watched the foliage. Within seconds, the leaves fell still. The rustling disappeared. Creeping forward, David reached out and stuck the tip of the machete past the leaves and into the bush.

Ben reached a hand behind him and gingerly ran his fingers along the back of his neck. The branch had barely missed him, nicking him on the back of his head and sending him straight to the ground. His face was covered in mud and dead leaves; his head ached as he lay face down on the trail. He groaned and rolled to his side, staring at the leaves on the fallen branch before him. Bringing both hands up to his face, Ben smeared the mud away from his eyes and picked at the wet leaves still stuck to his forehead and cheeks.

"Okay," he said to himself, squeezing his eyes shut. White sparks flew across the inside of his closed eyelids, and his stomach turned. Ben opened his eyes and pushed himself up, wincing at the pain radiating from the back of his head. Despite the dizziness, he hunched forward, leaning his head between his legs and took several deep breaths.

Without raising his head, Ben shrugged the backpack off his shoulders and brought it in front of him. He reached inside and retrieved his water bottle, raised his head, and took a small sip. His eyes darted to the surrounding trees. The trail was gone. Fallen branches and thick, sweeping vines covered every available space. He took a deep breath before standing up and finding his feet. Closing his eyes, Ben tried to hone in on where the others were, but the only sound was the blood thumping in his ears.

"Fuck," Ben swore over a heavy sigh. He swung his backpack back onto his shoulders and unsheathed his machete before swinging it forward and into the dense jungle.

Marisol's arms burned as she hung by a large tree branch. After failing to cut through the branches around her, she'd shimmied up the trunk and was barely able to reach the branch. She used the blade of her machete to dig a couple of small toeholds to help. Marisol figured if she found the two guys, she would leave out how many attempts it took her to figure that bit out.

She clenched her muscles and pulled herself up, using her feet to steady herself against the trunk. Marisol walked her feet up along the trunk until she could wrap them around the branch with enough purchase. With a final heave, she swung herself around and rested her stomach on the scratchy bark.

"Now what?" she asked between heavy breaths.

Gripping onto the branch with both hands, Marisol pushed herself up until she was seated, straddling it between her legs. She gasped as her eyes scanned the ground. Small green and red vines twisted and weaved between the branches below, forming a large web that stretched the expanse of the area before her. She squinted, trying to see through, looking for any sign of movement...or any indication of what to do or where to go next.

Just breathe.

David stood in front of the bush, his machete at the ready. His heart pounded in his chest. He ran through his options: he could climb back through the bush and face whatever was behind it, or he could head backward and try to find another route through. This time, listing out possibilities didn't calm him. Instead of feeling in control, David felt the panic seeping in. He stared at his hand, watching the machete tremble in his palm.

"This is stupid," he said aloud. "Just go through. They're right there."

David stepped forward, sliced away the branches to the bush, and stepped through. The sharp edges from the cut twigs scraped at his face and ripped at his sleeves. His foot caught on the shrub, sending him tripping to the other side. He landed on his knees and toppled into the trail, rolling into the thick branch which had fallen between them. David narrowed his eyes as he looked through the leaves. Small, red vines encircled the bark of the branches and stretched up and into the canopy. David's eyes followed the vines until his head tilted back, staring up toward the sky.

"Holy shit," he whispered under his breath.

The canopy was no longer a lush greenery of arching trees and towering palms. The vines intertwined above him and spanned as far as he could see. Some of them hung down in thin sheets, reaching toward the earth. Spindly roots erupted from the tips like veins, attempting to connect back to the soil. David glanced back to the bush he had fallen through. Red vines encompassed the opening, slowly stitching it back together. David froze as he watched his way out slowly disappear.

"David!" Ben called out, cutting a trail to his left. "Marisol!" He paused, waiting to hear a response. To hear anything.

No matter how loudly he yelled, his voice was muffled, absorbed into the jungle. Ben knew it wasn't right. He had tracked monkey calls from miles away. He knew how sound carried and how important it *was* for sound to carry out here. Territories needed to be claimed each day, animals needed to find each other, warnings needed to be heard. His voice should be carrying more than enough to alert anyone or anything around him. Unless they weren't around him.

"Dammit!" he screamed, throwing his machete to the ground. He squatted and ran his hands along his neck as he breathed in deeply. "You've got this. Don't panic."

Ben sat down in the wet leaves and pulled a crudely drawn map out of his backpack. He scanned the page, looking at the markings scribbled in his handwriting.

Camp
Pretty pond
Deep pond (closest)
Plantains here

He ran his finger along the line that connected *Camp* to *Deep pond (closest)*.

"You can't be too far off from your path. We've been hiking maybe twenty minutes. Add ten for getting in this mess. But where the hell am I?"

A faint sound echoed from the distance. Ben dropped his map onto the ground and jumped to his feet. A light voice floated above the trees from the east. Ben grabbed his map from the leaf litter and shoved it in his pocket. Bending down, he ripped his machete from the ground and made his way forward, following the faint echo deeper into the jungle.

Marisol sat in the tree and continued to call out every few minutes. Despite ignoring David's warnings the last time they were lost, she knew the first rule of getting lost in the woods was to stay where you were. Don't wander. Don't get overconfident. She figured climbing a tree and yelling for help fell slightly under the realm of overconfidence. Get in a tree? Yes. Get help? That was to be determined.

Marisol cupped her hands around her mouth and yelled out again. "David! Ben!"

She slumped her shoulders and leaned her back against the trunk. It felt like hours had passed even though she knew it was probably no more than a half an hour, maybe twenty minutes at best. She tipped her water bottle up to her mouth and took a sip.

"Hello?" a deep voice called out from beneath the web of vines.

Marisol shot up, leaning forward and almost toppling out of the tree. "Ben?"

"Marisol?"

Ben's voice drifted up into the canopy, music to her ears. She cupped her hands over her mouth again. "I can't see you! I'm up in a tree!"

"Hang tight!" he yelled back. "Just keep talking to me!"

Marisol continued to shout down from the branch. Each time Ben responded, he sounded as far away as the last time. She wondered what was going on down there and if he would know how to follow her voice. He sounded distant, but she knew he couldn't be that far away if he could talk to her. She pictured him fighting his way through mats of vines and leaves and who knows what else down on the ground.

"Hey up there!" Ben's voice rang out.

Marisol jumped at his sudden presence. She peered down around the branch to see him staring up at her from the base of the tree.

"Thank God," she sighed. She leaned over, looking around him. "Where's David?"

"I was hoping he was with you." He spun, surveying the jungle before turning back to Marisol. "Can you get down?"

"Of course I can get down," Marisol said dramatically. She threw her backpack to the ground, laid on her stomach, and prepared to climb down. Her arms shook as she lowered herself. She never thought about how she was going to get down. Glancing down to Ben, she clenched her muscles, gripping the branch tighter.

"You sure?" Ben asked.

"Just give me a minute!" Marisol snapped. Closing her eyes, she counted to three before dropping her legs off the branch to hang by her hands. She inhaled sharply and let go, landing on her feet and quickly falling to her knees. She gasped as sharp pains shot through her kneecaps and up to her hips. "I'm fine!" she added, holding a hand up. "I'm good."

Ben extended a hand, helping Marisol to her feet. "That was impressive, going up a tree."

"I'm an impressive person." Marisol smiled as she brushed

the dirt off herself. "So..." she said, catching his eyes, "what *happened?*"

Ben glanced at the surrounding plants. "I wish I knew. But I have a feeling we got what we were hoping for...tenfold."

"From up there," Marisol nodded to the tree, "it looked like the vines were growing straight across the trail. I know I wasn't that high up, but I couldn't see *anything.*"

"It sounds a little crazy, but I think it's dampening the sound, too...if that's even possible. I was screaming my head off for you guys, and there wasn't so much as an echo. This is way more than anything I've documented. I don't even know where to—"

"Shhh," Marisol whispered, holding up a finger to Ben.

A soft hum filled the air. Ben and Marisol looked at each other in quiet acknowledgement. Ben tilted his head, listening.

"What is it?" Marisol whispered.

"I can't tell," he said, looking back to her as he walked up to the wall of leaves and broken branches, leaning his ear against it. He turned to face her. "What's your take?"

Marisol's eyes moved from Ben, to the tree, and to the path he carved through to get to her. She grabbed her backpack from the ground and brushed off the wet leaves and muck.

"I think we only have one choice," she said, steeling herself and nodding toward the sound. "It's the only way we haven't been."

"Agreed," Ben said, stepping back and reaching for his machete. "Now let's go find David."

15

David's heart thrummed in his chest as he slowly spun, finding himself enclosed on all sides by red, draping vines. He had watched as they slowly descended, reaching toward the ground and the fallen tree branches around him. He gripped the base of his machete with both hands, steadying himself as the blade quivered before him.

You have to do something, he thought. *You can't just stand here.*

David's eyes darted back and forth, watching the vines slowly creep in around him. His gaze settled to the vines on his right.

I can make a run for it.

David raised his machete, aiming for the red shoots. Taking a quick breath, he stepped forward and swung the blade. The section of shoots dropped away, cut clean from the sharpened edge. He lunged forward, ducking through the gap. As he pushed through the opening, there was a light tugging at his shoulders. David pulled forward, yanking against the resistance. He glanced over his shoulder to see his backpack entangled in thin, red rootlets. The vines climbed around his backpack, twisting around the straps, and clung to the fabric of his shirt. David leaned forward, pulling harder, the sticky rootlets stretching but holding strong. He gritted his teeth, leaned his weight onto the balls of his feet and threw his chest forward. A soft pop sounded behind him as he fell, the straps around his backpack snapping loose. David threw his hands in front of him and braced himself before hitting the ground.

Bright flashes exploded behind David's eyelids as his head slammed into a large tree root. He winced and rolled onto his back, the stabbing throbs in his head like an ice pick jabbing against his skull. Between the blinking stars and blurred vision, he could barely make out the red vines slowly descending around him. His eyes fluttered shut as his vision faded. Though he couldn't see, he could feel the cool tickling of the plants brush up against his skin and tug at his clothes.

"Careful!" Marisol yelled, ducking as splintered pieces of wood flew by her head.

"Sorry," Ben said, ripping his machete out from a thick branch. "I don't know if I can get through this one. We may have to climb over."

They had been following the humming noise and clearing the path as much as they could along the way. Marisol called out every few minutes for David, but was met only with the eerie hum and the hacking of Ben's machete. They had narrowed the noise down to the other side of a row of bushes and stout palm trees. It had grown to a steady buzz, getting louder as they chipped away at the shrubbery.

Ben handed Marisol his machete. "Let me see if I can get over." He placed his foot into a knot of branches, propelling himself up as he grasped at the leaves for balance. The buzzing grew louder as Ben pawed at the twigs, bending them back to gain a better vantage point. He turned his head against his shoulder and called back to Marisol, "I don't see anything."

"I do," Marisol said, looking up into the limbs above them.

Ben turned and followed Marisol's gaze above his head. Hanging off the branch was a large, white, cylindrical hive. Black and yellow insects moved along the surface, spotting the flaky shell with dark specs. Ben's heart sank in his chest.

"Paper wasps," he muttered, his eyes moving back to Marisol. "Don't. Touch. Anything."

Ben shifted on his toes, feeling underneath him for a foothold. The buzzing grew louder as he watched a handful of wasps fly above his head, diving downward from their nest and toward his face. He raised his hands, swatting them away, and quickly lost his balance, falling backward. Marisol's arms hooked around him as he tipped back, catching him before he hit the ground. More wasps emerged from the hive, the steady hum growing even louder. Marisol looked up as the swarm of wasps formed a noisy, thick cloud above their heads.

"We need to get out of here," Ben said, turning to Marisol. "Now."

Marisol turned and ran with Ben on her heels. She held up her arms, shielding her face from the twigs that reached out like spiny fingers into the trail. The wasps followed, occasionally diving into their path as they wove their way back through the trail. The toe of Marisol's shoe caught under a root, sending her careening to the ground. Without missing a step, Ben pulled her up by her backpack and shoved her into the ferns off to the side. He stepped around her, took the machete from her hands, and hacked into the jungle. He could hear the wasps behind them closing in.

"Go ahead. We need to get out of their line of sight."

Marisol froze, looking at the ferns surrounding her. Her hands shook at her sides. "We shouldn't move. The ferns the last time…"

His gaze focused behind and above her. "We don't have time to see if it's the same. It's either this way or get stung by a thousand wasps. I'm going with the harmless plants."

"Fine." Marisol whined softly as she side-stepped Ben and headed into the dense wood.

Ben bent and grabbed the branches he cut away, squeezed in front of Marisol, and held them up to cover the opening. He sucked in a quick breath as he listened to the swarm get closer. Marisol clung to the back of his shirt, her body pinned between him and the rainforest behind her. The buzzing passed in front of them and within a few minutes slowly faded into the distance.

Ben dropped the branches to the ground, letting out a heavy breath. "I hate those things, but I think they're gone."

"Ben…" Marisol said, tugging on his shirt.

She slowly twisted and pointed to the depths of the jungle behind her. Ben leaned in, his body tensing alongside her. The crunching of snapping twigs and breaking branches sounded beyond the trees and grew in intensity. Whatever it was, it was headed toward them, and quickly. Ben reached out to Marisol's shoulder and pulled her behind him. He backed up a couple of feet and raised his machete in the air, ready to strike. The rustling of leaves grew closer, and Ben could see a large shape making its way straight toward them. He swung his machete down, cutting through the ferns as the sound closed in from the other side. He raised the blade up again, poised to bring it down on whatever was coming at them.

"Whoa! Hold up! Hold up!" a voice stammered from behind the foliage.

"*David*?" Ben asked, lowering his machete to his side, and squinting past the leaves.

Two pale hands, raised in the air and speckled with mud, stuck out through the palms. David's voice squeaked from behind the foliage, "Please don't hit me with a machete." He slowly pushed himself through the fronds and into the small clearing. His blond hair was obscured with thick clumps of mud, and his clothes were tattered; small rips and holes spotted the fabric of his shirt and pants.

"What happened to *you*?" Marisol asked, peering around Ben's back.

"Long story." David eyed the machete in Ben's hand before looking up to them. "Bad news, though; I lost my bag. Good news…I found this along the way." David turned and reached behind the palms. He pulled up a stick covered in skewered fish.

"At least we won't starve?" He raised an eyebrow to Ben as he handed him the fish.

"My hero." Ben cracked a smile as he took the stick. His smile quickly faded as he cocked his head. "Is that blood?" He reached out to brush David's hair away from his temple.

The right side of David's hair was matted with dark, dried blood. Another dried trail ran down the side of his face and curled down around his chin.

"Here. Sit," Ben said, pushing down on David's shoulders.

"I'm *fine*," David said, folding under the pressure of Ben's hands.

Ben tipped his water bottle over the side of David's head, soaking his hair.

David shut his eyes as the water ran down his face. "Is this really necessary?"

"What happened?" Ben asked, pulling David's hair away from his forehead and temple. "You've got a decent gash here."

David hesitated, staring at Ben's shoes. "I fell."

"You...fell?"

"Yes, I fell," David said, glancing up. "I said it's a long story."

"Well, you better spill, because a hit like that to your temple is not something to blow off. And don't say you're fine 'cause it might not be. Now talk."

David's eyes drifted to Marisol. "I don't want to freak anyone out."

She shook her head. "If you've seen half the shit we've seen today..."

Ben brushed his fingers along David's hairline. "You're not going to freak us out. Promise."

"Okay, okay. Have you seen those reddish vines? Like the ones that hang down from the trees? They're kind of everywhere?"

Ben and Marisol nodded.

"Well..." David took a breath, watching them stare intently at him. "I saw them literally *moving* and closing off pathways. Like not normal growth rate kind of moving…like when you watch plant growth in fast-forward and you see it all squished together in real time? I tried to make a run for it, but they had wrapped around my bag. The whole thing was tangled up in them. Anyway, the straps broke, and that's when I fell," David said, almost in one breath. "I landed on a root—you know the ones that stick up out of the ground like pegs? Completely smashed my head into it and blacked out. When I woke up, I was covered in them…like *completely*. The roots were wrapped around my arms and legs and parts of my face." David stopped, his heart racing against his chest.

"Then what?" Marisol asked, sitting on the ground next to him. She placed a hand on his leg and looked into his eyes.

"I fought my way out. I didn't have my machete. I think it got dragged away, too…or I was stupid and dropped it somewhere. I just ripped at it until I could get free. I think it was mainly adrenaline."

"Wait. You hiked all the way through here without your machete?" Ben asked, his eyes glued to David.

"Uh, yeah," David said, lifting his arms to show the holes in his shirt. "Hence this mess."

"But you're okay?" asked Marisol.

"Shaken up and massively confused and terrified and exhausted, but yeah, I think I'm okay. You guys?"

Ben and Marisol nodded in response, still taking in David's disheveled appearance. Ben helped David to his feet, and they retreated back onto the trail.

"Since you blacked out, I say we play it safe and assume it could be more serious than just a cut on your head. You're going to have to be honest and tell us if you're feeling dizzy or anything. And make sure you're drinking." Ben handed David his water bottle.

Marisol nudged David's side and handed him her machete, offering him a weak smile.

"You sure you're okay?" David asked quietly, looking down at her.

"One hundred percent. A little sore, but we didn't get killed by wasps."

"Wasps?" David asked, eyes wide.

"Don't worry yourself about it," Ben interrupted. "Now all we need is to find our way out of here."

"I think I can get us back," said David. "I found our fish a little ways back through there." David pointed back behind the palms. "If that's where we all got separated, wouldn't that lead us back in the right direction? Or *a* direction at least?"

Ben's eyes shifted between them before turning back to the area where David had emerged. "It's the only plan we've got," he shrugged. "Let's go for it. But let's also take it slow. Nice and easy."

David raised his wrist to check the time, only to see the face of his watch cracked and frozen in place. They had been working their way in one direction for what felt like hours. The path cleared up after a while and merged into a trail with Ben's bamboo chimes lining the branches above. The overwhelming sound of birds and bugs was a relief to all of them. They hadn't realized quite how profound the silence was until they broke out into the open air with the cacophony of nature once again surrounding them.

"Thank God," Ben breathed, throwing his head back as they approached the edge of their camp. "I can't believe it."

They dropped their bags by the research tent and collapsed in a heap on the ground around the firepit. Ben glanced at his watch while kicking his shoes off and reclining back on his elbows. "It's getting late," he said, looking over to the other two. "I know today has been…a lot, but we should eat something."

"I don't think I have the energy," Marisol said, resting her face in her hands.

"I need to at least change," David added, looking down at his shirt. "And I'm using some of our water to clean up. There's no way I'm tracking all of this into our tent."

"Either way, we're eating. It's important. I can do all of the cooking, and you two can rest up."

"You need to rest, too," David said.

"Plenty of time for that later. If I take a break now, there's no way I'm getting back up to do anything. You both go clean up, I've got this."

David flinched as Marisol ran the edge of a wet towel along the large cut on his right temple. The swelling had gone down, leaving a jagged slice along the skin.

"You look better," David said, his eyes running along her exposed skin.

"I feel better." She gave him a small smile. "Feels like a bad sunburn now. Nothing I can't handle."

"That's good…" David said, trailing off.

"What is it?" she asked, dipping her head down to catch his eyes.

"I don't know. I just don't understand it, I guess."

"Well, with hive-like rashes, the skin stays irritated for—"

"Not you…the plants. How was it happening? It's almost like the jungle was *alive*."

Marisol studied him, her brows pinched together. "That's not for us to figure out right now. Let's just recoup, make sure you're okay."

"…what do you think it is?"

"I have no idea," she said, leaning back. "I've never heard of anything like it. Never seen anything like it. Your guess is as good as mine."

David stared forward, his vision passing through Marisol and past the fabric of the tent. He retreated into his head, flipping through the files in his memory, trying to piece the elements together.

"David?" Marisol said. "You still with me?"

David blinked, focusing back on Marisol. "What?"

"Maybe you *do* have a head injury. I was saying that Ben finished dinner. Food is ready."

"I don't have a head injury," he said, rolling his eyes. "I was just thinking."

"You know you're going to end up hurting yourself if you keep doing that. Come on."

The three sat in a semi-circle around the fire. Ben cooked half of the fish he and David caught earlier and laid it out in a small bowl of rehydrated rice. Ben had spent most of the meal postulating different theories about what had happened. Marisol refuted each point while providing references.

"But there's no pattern," David chimed in on the third round of debate. "It's not species-based, and there's no common denominator, at least that we know."

"...that we know," Ben repeated, waving a fork in David's direction.

"Right," David said, shaking his head. "You can't assume that you're going to break down a series of supposedly non-related events without first getting to what they have in common. Even if you went by phylogeny, none of the affected species are even slightly similar."

"Well, they're a *little* similar," said Ben.

"Okay, even if they're a little similar, there's nothing specific about them that indicates receptors or growth patterns or anything that can be attributed to what we just experienced," David argued.

"Maybe it's a rogue gene," Ben retorted.

"And you think we're going to be able to study a rogue gene without any equipment or expertise out here in the goddamn rainforest?"

"It could be environmental," Marisol interrupted. "Something about the climate and location that's different than other regions?"

"But is there even any difference in these climates to that of the rest of the rainforest here? I mean, it spans through several different countries," David said.

"We don't even know how many ecosystems there are out here to begin to know if that's a factor to consider," Ben jumped in. "Randall Myster, who wrote about the Igapó umbrella alone, said that there could be over 40 different ecosystems under that delineation. That's not even counting terra firma, aguajal, or restinga ecosystems. How on earth would we even begin to narrow that d—"

Ben stopped, turning to David as his bowl and fork clashed to the ground. He watched as David's eyes squeezed shut, his hand reaching up to clutch at his chest.

David's heart raced as he struggled to take a breath. He could hear Marisol and Ben talking, but their voices were muffled and distant. His chest rose and fell rapidly, his lungs gasping for air. He opened his eyes, seeing Ben and Marisol staring back at him, their eyes wide and worried.

David pressed his hand tighter against his chest, hoping it would slow his heart down. His other hand shook as it clawed at the dirt next to him. He tried to speak, but his jaw muscles refused to unclench. All he could do was gasp and choke on his own breath.

"David," said Marisol. "David, you're scaring me." She reached her hand out to touch his shoulder.

David flinched away from her, his shoulder yanking away from her hand like an opposing magnetic field.

"Don't...t-touch...me," he huffed between quick breaths.

Marisol reached out again, her voice saturated with a thick, calming tone. "It's okay. I'm just trying to help."

"I s-said don't f-fucking touch me!" David growled,

hunching over into a ball. He shut his eyes and tried to breathe, managing only quick, shallow breaths.

Marisol tucked her hand to her side and looked to Ben. "What's wrong with him?"

"Just leave him alone for now, okay?" Ben answered, watching as David straightened and struggled for air.

"I-I'm hav-having a p-p-panic attack," David said, forcing his words out between breaths. "I just…" David clutched his chest with both hands, pushing them hard against his ribcage. "I-I feel like I'm hav-having a h-heart attack." Tears rolled down his face as he tried to force a breath. His body shook, the tremors wracking his body. He tried to concentrate on the things around him, to focus his mind, but all he could feel was all-encompassing dread.

"Okay," Ben said, positioning himself in front of David. "Just look at me, okay? Breathe with me. Deep in through your nose…"

David sucked in five short breaths.

"And out through your mouth. Nice and slow, okay?"

David released his breath, but immediately breathed in, trying to get more air. "I-I just ne-need one br-breath. P-please. I ca-can't move."

"It's going to be alright. Try again. Watch me and do it with me." Ben breathed in and out again, and then several times more.

With each set of breaths, David was able to slow his breathing and fill his lungs. After several minutes and on a last exhale, his muscles relaxed, allowing his shoulders to sag and the tension in his legs to loosen. He hastily wiped at his still-flowing tears as he stared at the dirt and leaves on the ground before him. His heart still raced but was no longer pounding out of his chest. David raised the fingers of one hand to his head, feeling them trembling against his scalp as he tried to focus on his senses.

"Hey," Ben's voice drifted into his ears. "It's okay."

David raised his eyes to meet Ben's. He focused on the deep blue, on the comfort he found there.

"You alright?" Ben asked. He knitted his brows, his eyes filled with worry.

David nodded weakly as he chewed on his bottom lip. He couldn't stop the tears from flowing down his face. He wiped at them with the back of his hand, like a child.

"I-I'm sorry," David said. His voice was feeble and strained.

"No. You have no reason to be sorry," said Ben.

David shifted his focus to Marisol, moving only his eyes to look at her. She was curled up with her knees against her chest, her eyes red and puffy. A tear trickled down her right cheek.

"I didn't mean to yell at you," he sniffled, wiping at his nose.

"It's okay. Like Ben said, don't be sorry. I'm worried about you is all."

David lowered his eyes and went back to focusing on the ground before closing them and taking several deep breaths. Once his heart settled and the tremors died down, he sat up straighter and cleared his throat.

"What can we do?" Marisol asked, scooting closer to him.

"Nothing," David said, his voice hollow. "I just want to go to bed and disappear."

"I don't know about the disappearing, but we can definitely turn in for the night." Marisol glanced to Ben, who was already gathering up their dishes.

"I've got it," he said, scooping David's spilled food back into his bowl. "You guys go ahead."

David watched Marisol as she drifted off to sleep. Once he was certain she wouldn't wake up, he ducked out of the tent and into the night air. The sound of crickets and cicadas flooded his senses. He looked into the shadows of the trees and thought about how the busy noise of the rainforest distracted him from his thoughts more than his quiet apartment back home. He always had trouble settling his mind after an episode.

He wandered over to the research tent and turned on one of the lanterns overhead. He leaned both arms on top of the stack of bins and stared at the notebooks through the plastic casing.

"Can't sleep?" Ben said, coming up behind him.

David turned to see Ben, his hair scraggly and clothes disheveled. "No. You either?"

Ben shook his head with a small smile. "Are you okay?"

"Yeah, I'll be fine. Mostly embarrassed."

"Don't be. One of my old roommates back in sophomore year used to get panic attacks. His doctors put him on a few different SSRIs, but I don't think they really helped him. He got a medical marijuana card before it was legal to just go to a dispensary, and it helped him so much more than the pills. It's actually one of the few reasons I got interested in pharmacology and ditched pre-med. Wanted to try to figure out better ways to cope with different disorders without all the nasty side effects, you know?"

"Yeah, I know how that goes. I, uh, I was diagnosed with panic disorder when I was sixteen." David crossed his arms along his chest. "I've spent most of my life on some kind of drug or another. Zoloft, Prozac, Valium, Ativan, you name it. Though I don't know if they really helped at all."

"What makes you say that?"

"I always felt a bit numb on them, like I wasn't really *here*, you know? They did lessen the frequency, though. Less anxious, less attacks…was more just *existing* than anything else, really."

"Do you get them often? The attacks?"

David let out a small laugh. "Ironically, not so much anymore. I actually stopped taking my meds a couple years ago. I still get the occasional one or two every now and again, but I haven't really had any regular episodes. Plenty of anxiety through that time, don't get me wrong, but nothing like what happened earlier. I had one after Dr. Morrow went missing. I was hoping it was a one-off. Guess not."

"I'm sorry. It must be scary."

"It is," David said, uncrossing his arms. "Each time feels like the first time. No matter how many times it happens, and no matter how much I tell myself it's going to pass, it's always just as scary. Long term, it's only my pride that's wounded, especially if it happens in front of people. The whole, 'Oh my God, I'm dying,' thing only lasts a little while." David smiled sadly. He chewed the inside of his bottom lip before staring up at Ben's eyes. "Thank you, by the way. For helping me."

"Don't mention it," Ben said with a wave of his hand. "I used to help my roommate with his. It's about the only thing he said worked to slow it down. All about the calm breaths."

"It definitely helps." David toed the ground with his feet. "Hey, um, it may be a weird question, you know, with everything that happened earlier…but do you still have that stuff you said you could make into a tea. For anxiety? It's just…I start to hyper-focus on if I'm going to have another one, and then when, and then I end up shutting dow—"

Ben touched David's arm, stopping him. He tilted his head to the side as a smile spread across his lips. "I do. And I can, but it takes a few hours to make. Granted, it's more helpful in the long run and in small doses for things like anxiety. That said, I've never been against having a little fun, too."

David raised a questioning eyebrow. "Am I going to regret asking? I feel like we can't sit back and ignore what happened today either."

"I mean, I don't think we're in any immediate danger. I've never had any issues here at this camp." Ben grinned and gripped David's arm, giving it a reassuring squeeze. "And after all of this, I think we could all use a day to zone out. No problem solving, no experiments, and no research. So, go get some sleep because tomorrow morning, we'll have a chill, no danger, no craziness kind of day. You're in good hands."

16

David opened his eyes and stared at the top of the tent. He felt like he had been hit by a truck; his head ached, his muscles were sore, and all he wanted to do was hide under a pile of blankets in his own bed. With a groan, he turned his head to the side. Marisol sat with her back to him, rummaging through her bag. He sleepily pushed himself up and pulled the top of the sleeping bag down to his feet.

"Morning sleepyhead," Marisol said, turning to face him. "How are you feeling?"

"Okay enough." David hesitated. "About yesterday…"

"Don't," she said, holding up a hand. "There's nothing to say." Marisol wrapped her arms around her waist. "I've never actually seen anyone have a panic attack before. I'm sorry that happened…and that I didn't know what to do." She paused. A worried frown spread across her face. "Ben said you had another one out here. When?"

"He did, did he?" David let out a sigh and ran his hand over his face, wincing as his fingers brushed the now bruised cut on his temple. "It was when we split up and I went after Dr. Morrow."

"Why didn't you tell me?"

"Why would I have told you?"

"I don't know. I could have been there for you."

"I've handled them on my own forever. Despite what you think, I'm actually a very capable person."

"I didn't mean it like that."

David gave her a small smile and shifted, pulling the sleeping bag up into his lap. "I know. And I really am okay. They just come and go sometimes. I'm only sorry it had to happen in front of you guys."

"I'm glad it did. I can't imagine going through that alone."

"It's easier alone, at least for me. I even switched to online classes for the second half of freshmen year and all of sophomore year because I was too worried I was going to have them in the middle of a lecture hall. I've had more than enough people look at me like I'm crazy."

"I'm sorry," she said, fidgeting with her hands. "I want you to know that I've got your back…if you want it."

"I appreciate that."

"All of that aside, I heard Ben has a treat for us this morning at your request. So, why don't we put all of this away and forget our worries for a bit? We can all look crazy together."

David sat on the ground across from Ben and Marisol in the middle of camp. He watched through glassy eyes as the two engaged in deep conversation. He looked down at his cup. The tea inside swirled as glints of sunlight reflected off the brown liquid. The leaves and flowers above him danced in the breeze, the colors blending together into an intricate tapestry. He closed his eyes as the world moved around him. He could feel the wind dancing on his skin and the damp leaves nestled around his feet.

"You seem more relaxed."

Ben's voice flooded into David's ears, loud and deep compared to the all-encompassing sounds of nature. His eyes opened; the lids heavy as he let the brightness of the day back in. David smiled at the familiar eyes shining back at him. He could see the waves of the ocean within the deep blue, the sun reflecting off the surface. His gaze moved down to Ben's bare chest, following the tattoos across his pec and up his shoulder. The flowers drawn along his skin shimmered and blossomed, expanding out and along Ben's body. David watched in wonder as the ink rippled, forming new buds and leaves as the tattoos moved onto the unmarked skin, covering his whole body in blooming plant life.

"They're beautiful," David said, his voice flowing out of him like molasses. He brought his hand up to Ben's chest and brushed his fingers along the lines, tracing each flower with his fingertips.

"Thank you?" Ben smiled as David's hand ran along his collarbone.

"He is so far gone," Marisol said from over Ben's shoulder. "How much did you give him?"

Ben laughed, looking at David's cup on the ground between them. "Same as you. But he certainly didn't take his time drinking it like I told him to."

David continued to let his fingers run across the outline of Ben's tattoos. Every time his finger brushed a flower, the ink would explode in a rainbow of colors across Ben's skin. The flowers followed David's touch, spreading the ink like water-color paint down his chest and to his stomach.

"Okay then," Ben chuckled. "Getting a little handsy there." Ben gently grabbed David's hand and pulled it away.

"They're beautiful," David said again, blinking up at Ben.

"I seem to recall hearing that," Ben said, biting back his laughter. "Why don't I get you some water or something...and maybe take this cup away. Marisol, keep an eye on him, will you?"

Marisol laughed as Ben got up and crossed the camp. David's eyes slowly moved from Ben and settled onto her.

"Hey there," she said with a smile.

"Your hair is like fire," he said, his eyelids drooping.

"Is it?"

"It matches your personality," he said, the words barely audible. He stared into her eyes and smiled. "I'm tired."

"Okay." Marisol nodded slowly while she bit her lip, a small snicker escaping. "Let me clear off your spot in the tent. Don't move." Marisol walked over and ducked into their tent, moving David's clothes and books off his sleeping bag.

"You guys good in there?" Ben called from the other side of the tent flap.

Marisol stuck her head out of the tent, looking past Ben and to the campfire. "Shit," she cursed under her breath. She pushed past him and jogged to the center of camp. "David?"

"He's not in there with you? I told you to watch him," Ben said, his voice urgent. "He could have wandered off anywhere like that."

"I know! I'm sorry. He said he was tired. I was just trying to make a spot for him."

"David!" Ben yelled, jogging the perimeter of the campsite.

Marisol searched the inside of the research tent and behind the bins of notebooks and supplies. "David! Please answer us!" She pictured him wandering into the jungle and strung up by vines. And it would be all her fault. Her feet kicked up the wet leaves as she called his name into the trees behind the tent. Marisol jumped as a hand wrapped around her shoulder.

"I found him," Ben said, breathless. "He's fast asleep in my tent. It's okay. He's fine."

"Thank God. That was so stupid of me."

"No, it wasn't. You were trying to help. But he's sleeping and clearly *out* out. And you and I have the whole day ahead of us. Let's take a breather and let him sleep it off. He probably needs it after yesterday."

"Should we wake him?" Ben asked, looking over to his tent as he sipped hot coffee from his cup.

"Should we? It's almost five. How much longer could he possibly sleep?" Marisol asked.

"We can always place a pool and see who wins," he offered with a grin.

Marisol laughed as she cracked her neck and stood up. "I'll go check on him, I guess."

"Tell him I want my tent back!"

Marisol crossed the camp and peeked into Ben's tent. David lay on his stomach, his head at her feet. She crouched down, smiling as she looked at the small puddle of saliva pooling on the sleeping bag under his chin. She crept around him and sat, facing him, watching his back rise and fall with his slow breaths. She extended her hand and rubbed his back, nudging him awake.

David groaned, burying his face into his arm. "What?"

"You have to get up. You've been sleeping all day," Marisol said, her voice soft.

"Why? Can't I have ten more minutes?" David mumbled into his arm.

"Ben said he wants his tent back."

David lifted a hand to his face and rubbed his eyes, prying them open. He stared at Marisol for a minute before directing his vision at his surroundings. "This isn't our tent."

Marisol laughed. "I know."

David sat up. He yawned and stretched his arms across his chest. His muscles were weak, like he had taken a long nap and awoken too soon.

"How're you feeling?"

"Feels like I could sleep for a million years, but still somehow I feel totally rested."

"I think Ben is getting ready to cook up the rest of the fish for dinner, if you're interested in getting up."

"Dinner?" David asked as another yawn escaped his mouth.

"Yep. It's past five already. Like I said, you've slept all day."

"I'll have to have Ben bottle that stuff for later. I don't think I've ever slept that hard."

"I have a feeling you've never tripped that hard either."

"What do you mean?"

"You were high as a kite," Marisol laughed. "I didn't realize you were so into tattoos."

David arched an eyebrow and shook his head in question.

"You couldn't keep your hands off Ben's tats. I don't know what you were seeing, but it had to have been pretty spectacular."

"Great," he groaned, burying his head in his hands.

"It's not a big deal. Just fun to watch."

"I'm sure it was." David lifted his head. "Guess I'll go back to sleeping like crap."

"Either that, or I'll just lock you in the tent," Marisol joked as she slid past him and outside.

"Probably a good idea anyway," he muttered to himself, following her out into the humid early-evening air.

"Good morning," Ben said, smiling. He leaned over the campfire, rotating the rest of the fish over the flame.

"Sorry about crashing in your tent," David said. "And apparently also for accosting you."

Ben broke out into a fit of laughter. He pushed the loose hairs in his face back behind his ears. "You didn't *accost* me."

"Either way," David shrugged, "sorry."

"You apologize too much," Ben replied, pulling the fish off the fire and into a palm-woven basket. He stopped and pointed a finger at David, the fish steaming next to him. "Don't! I can see you about to say sorry for that."

"Fine." David let out a soft laugh and sat on the ground by the fire.

"Do you at least feel a little better, more relaxed?" Ben asked, grabbing a seat next to him. He handed him a makeshift plate with a small, scorched catfish on it.

"I do, actually. Sleep definitely helps. I don't tend to sleep much, especially since being out here."

"I gathered by our repeat late-night run-ins," Ben said. "I'm the same. Always thinking. Can't ever fall asleep."

"Exactly."

Marisol wandered over and sat on the other side of David. Ben reached in front of him, handing her a plate.

"Meanwhile," David said, "you have Marisol over here who can fall asleep at the drop of a hat."

"What can I say? It's a gift." Marisol said, picking the meat off the cooked fish.

"So, I know we said a day of no worrying or anything..." David started.

"Here we go," Marisol said, chewing.

"But what about tomorrow? And the day after? We can't stay here without anything forever. There has to be something we're missing."

"The whole point of today was to ease some stress. We can deal with it tomorrow," Ben said. "It's not good for us all to be this worked up. We won't think clearly."

David sighed. "There just has to be something."

"And I'm sure there is," Marisol said, eyeing him. "We don't need to rush it, though. We've all had close calls out here. We need to be more careful."

"Agreed," said Ben. "David?"

"Fine. Agreed."

The sound of turning pages filled the inside of the research tent. David leaned over a set of notebooks, the lantern light illuminating the handwritten observations jotted on the damp paper. The light was balanced on the empty space left on the top of the bins, the bright LED casting long shadows along the vinyl siding.

"I thought we agreed to wait," Ben said, yawning as he walked up next to David. "Marisol asleep?"

"Fast asleep. And I can't wait." David chuckled, shaking his head and looking up at Ben. "Curiosity."

"Seems about right. Anything I can help with?"

"Sure. You can point out the smoking gun in your notes and we can call it a day."

"That's the piece I was missing!" Ben flashed David a bright smile. "You should have asked for that days ago."

David laughed, hanging his head. "You know," he said, staring at the pages, "I think I finally get what you were saying yesterday...at the pond."

"And what's that?"

"That interest, you know? I think after today, I'm a lot less scared and a lot more intrigued. Like, it *is* scary, yeah, but it's also fascinating." David turned toward Ben, leaning his back against the plastic bins. "Before we left Iquitos, Dr. Morrow told me that it's good to try things that scare us and make us uncomfortable." David locked eyes with Ben and smiled to himself, feeling the relief and comfort in his company. "Turns out she was right."

Ben met David's eyes and the corner of his mouth upturned in a small smirk. "Had a little epiphany on the ayahuasca? Told you it was spiritual."

"Was a little eye opening," David admitted, keeping his eyes on Ben as he straightened, taking a step toward him.

Ben's eyebrows twitched as he inched closer. "Only about the adventure?"

"And a couple of other things..."

Ben bit down on his lower lip and closed the gap between them. With a breath, he leaned down, pressing his lips against David's. His hands gently moved forward and gripped David's waist as he tugged him closer. David breathed him in, returning the kiss and parting his lips to let his tongue probe against Ben's.

As if in a trance, his hands lifted to Ben's chest, his fingers tracing the outlines of his muscles before finding their way around to the back of Ben's head, pulling him in deeper. David kissed him harder, his hands sliding down his back and stopping at his waist as he pulled Ben against him, feeling him hard against his hip. He pushed into him, breaking away from his lips long enough to take in the sensation of his touch before leaning in for more.

David gasped as Ben's lips moved down, kissing along his neck as his fingers played along his waistband. Ben paused and brought his eyes back to David's, waiting. David nodded, allowing Ben to slide his pants to the ground as he leaned in for another kiss. Ben slowly kneeled, kissing along David's hip before taking him into his mouth. David moaned as he leaned his head back and ran his hand over Ben's head. He looked down, the waves of Ben's dark hair drifting through his fingers. Electricity sparked through his veins and goosebumps prickled along his skin as Ben's hands wrapped around him. He brought his hands down to Ben's shoulders and leaned him back, before pulling him back up to his feet and kissing him deeply.

"You want me to stop?" Ben asked, his mouth moving against David's lips.

"No." David smiled, Ben's breath hot against his face. "I'm just not ready for it to end yet."

Ben leaned in and nibbled on David's ear lobe. "Good," he whispered as he took David's hand and led him back to his tent.

David nuzzled his head into Ben's shoulder, catching his breath. "I've wanted to do that since I first saw you."

Ben tucked his hand behind his head as David adjusted onto his back, resting his head on Ben's chest. Strands of Ben's hair stuck to his forehead, both of them covered in a thin sheen of sweat.

"Really? I was beginning to think my radar was way off," Ben chuckled, leaning his head against David's. "You were sending some really mixed signals."

David cleared his throat as he stared at the top of the tent. "Sorry. I didn't mean to. Guess I was kind of scared."

"Scared? Why?"

"Seriously? Look at you. You're like a model or...I don't know, some Instagram fantasy guy. You've got this, like, perfect body, and you're outgoing and adventurous. Then I'm over here, just nervous, and awkward and...*average*. You take all of that and then picture being stuck out here with you and the possibility of being completely turned down. No one wants to be turned down when they're the only option."

"Wow," Ben said, blinking. "Um, I don't know what to say to that. That's a *lot*." He turned over and propped himself up on his elbow to face David. "For starters, I so don't look like a model. And I don't go out of my way to look like this...I'm also more than just my exterior. Sure, I work out a lot and am pretty physical, but I do it because it clears my head. I can push all that stress away for a bit when all I have to focus on is counting reps. I'm sure you get that. And secondly, I definitely don't think you're average."

"You'd be the first," David said, directing his eyes away from Ben.

"I guarantee I'm not. Even so, I think you're hot...not to mention crazy smart, which makes you *more* attractive. And I like that you're a bit shy. It's really cute. I also thought I was pretty obvious about being into you, but I'm sorry you thought I'd turn you down. I was honestly beginning to think I was reading you all wrong and that maybe you and Marisol—"

"No," David interrupted. "Definitely just friends."

Ben smiled and let out a breathy chuckle. "Good. Because I was super doubting myself earlier today. Marisol and I were sharing stories, and she was telling me about how you guys spent some time in the city. She said that you got crazy wasted and she had to drag you away mid-making out with some girl at a club. The entire time, I kept thinking I was so stupid for trying to flirt with you if you were straight. But at least I know now." Ben brought his hand to rest on David's side.

David's stomach squirmed as he bit down on the inside of his bottom lip. "Um..." He swallowed hard. "I'm, uh...I'm bi actually."

"Oh," Ben said, taking his hand from David and sitting up.

"*Oh* oh?" David sat up across from him, holding his arms across his stomach. "Is that okay?"

"Yeah, of course," Ben said, readjusting on the sleeping bag. "I've, um...I've just never been with somebody that's bi before."

"It's not any different."

"Right. Obviously. I guess I didn't expect that one," Ben blurted. "So, I mean, you *say* you and Marisol are just friends, but that could change, right? Like, it's not off the table?"

David's heart panged, his chest tightening. His nails picked along his arm, leaving small red specks along the skin. He swallowed, trying to ignore the lump forming in his throat. "You know, this was a bad idea," he said, shaking his head. "I'm just gonna get dressed." David grabbed his scattered clothes from around the tent, bundling them up against him as he turned away from Ben.

Ben leaned over to touch David's arm. "Whoa, David, wait. What happened? What did I say?"

"Nothing," David muttered, reaching for the tent zipper. "It's fine."

"It's not fine. I clearly said something. Talk to me."

"You didn't say anything wrong." David turned around, holding the pile of clothes tucked over his lap. "People always get weird when they find out. They always look at me different, like you are right now. And now we're stuck out here together. I shouldn't have kissed you back."

"But I really like you," Ben said, scooting closer to him. "I didn't mean to do anything like that. I don't care who you're attracted to."

"But you will," David said, his voice catching. "People I've been with assume I want something else. Something *more*. They think I want threesomes, or that I'm attracted to everyone I see, or that I'm indecisive and more likely to cheat on them, or that I just plain want to fuck everyone I meet." David's cheeks burned, and he could feel the tears threatening to burst out of him. He squeezed his eyes shut trying to stop them but failed. "I don't want any of those things."

He hated that he was so emotional, that he couldn't will the tears away. David cringed, hearing every teardrop falling and splashing onto the sleeping bag underneath them. He knew how this conversation went. He'd had it many times before and each time resulted in him going home alone.

This time, there was no going home. No sitting with a book and a pint of ice cream, no meaningless sex from an app, and no privacy to hide away from the world.

"Well, what *do* you want?" Ben asked, reaching forward and squeezing David's hands.

"I don't know," he whispered. "I want to be with someone who wants to be with me, *for me*, and I'm tired of trying so hard. I'm tired of being alone."

Ben raised his hand to David's face, lifting his chin to look into his eyes. "I can do that. You don't have to be alone," he said, his own eyes welling up. "I'm here." He delicately brushed David's cheek with his finger, wiping away his tears.

David closed his eyes as his shoulders shook. He could feel Ben's hand move to his arm and squeeze, holding it there. David blinked away the tears to see Ben's eyes staring back at him.

"I really do like you," Ben said. "I know it's weird circumstances out here, but I feel like we mesh. It feels like I've known you a long time even though we've basically just met—and *yes* I know that sounds really cliché." Ben looked down between them and wet his lips before raising his head to face David. "And… and I'm *really* sorry that I made you feel that way just now. It was shitty of me, and I shouldn't have jumped to any conclusions. I would be upset if someone did that to me. I did mean it when I said I liked you…and I also understand if I blew it. But," he hesitated, "if I *didn't*, I'd like another chance to show you that it doesn't matter to me…and won't. Honest."

David watched him for a moment. The thudding of his heart

beating in his ears slowed, Ben's eyes quelling his racing thoughts. He looked down as Ben took his hands and held them tight. David glanced up.

"Well?" Ben asked, raising his eyebrows in question. "What do you say? Stay for a bit?"

David stared at him and slid his hands away, placing them on either side of Ben. He pushed himself forward on his knees and pressed his lips against Ben's, squeezing his eyes shut. Ben's hands slid up David's torso, moving up his chest, and around to grope at his back. Goosebumps blossomed across David's skin as Ben's fingers squeezed at his hips, their lips still interlocked. David's body relaxed at his touch, the lingering feeling of past memories fading away like snow melting under the heat of the sun. He smiled against Ben's lips, his tears still staining his cheeks.

When he opened his eyes, Ben's were already gazing back into his. David melted in his arms, relishing in the touch of his body against Ben's. David leaned forward again, kissing him deeply as he pushed Ben onto his back and straddled him on the sleeping bag.

17

S un filtered through the fabric of the tent, bathing Marisol in a warm, comfortable light. She stretched her legs, her toes pushing up against the seam of the sleeping bag. She rolled over and opened her eyes, allowing her vision to adjust to the bright daylight. Her gaze drifted down to David's sleeping bag next to her, zipped closed and unmoved from last night. Marisol's heart sank as she pushed herself upright and laid her hand on his sleeping bag, the polyester cool against her palm.

Marisol ducked out of the tent and scanned the camp, her eyes taking quick inventory of every stick, leaf, and rock. Normally, David and Ben were up before her, but there was no sign of anyone. Moving to the campfire, she touched the damp logs and found they were still cool from overnight. Marisol tried to remember David coming back into the tent after ducking out last night. She knew he often snuck out when he couldn't sleep, though she always pretended to be asleep herself as he slinked off, flashlight in hand.

Marisol rubbed her jaw, realizing she had been clenching her muscles since she left the tent. Rolling her shoulders and taking a breath, she let her eyes wander over the trees, investigating them for rogue vines or strange movement. As her eyes settled on Ben's tent, she tiptoed over and listened for him.

"Ben?" Marisol called out, her voice meek. Her heart quickened as her thoughts flashed back to waking up to Dr. Morrow missing from camp. "Ben? Are you still sleeping?" Marisol inched closer and pressed her head against the fabric of the door. She heard a faint snoring from the other side. "Ben?" she called out again, getting agitated. She bounced on the balls of her feet before grabbing the zipper and pulling the tent flap open. "Ben, I can't find Davi—"

Marisol stopped in place as the door dropped open, her eyes widening. Ben and David were asleep—together—both naked, with their legs intertwined. Ben was on his back with David draped on top of him, each curled up in the other's arms. David lifted his head, half-asleep, and nestled tighter into the crook of Ben's neck. Marisol quick-stepped backward, knocking into the tent pole holding up the small weather guard outside of the door, pulling the fabric and shaking the tent.

"Shit," Marisol whispered, trying to back out of the small, canopied entrance.

Ben raised his head, blinking a few times, before his eyes settled on Marisol. "Hey," he said, his voice dry from sleep. "What's wrong? What happened? Is everything okay?"

"I'm sorry. Yes. Yeah. Sorry." Marisol scrunched her face in embarrassment as the words sped out of her mouth. She directed her eyes to the top of the tent, cringing at her intrusion. "I just…I woke up and David wasn't there, and I couldn't find him, and I panicked, and—"

"Are you talking to me?" David mumbled into Ben's chest. He tilted his head up and made eye contact with her. Both of them paused, staring at the other, painfully stretching the moment out.

"I'm-going-to-go," Marisol said all in one word, fumbling her way out of the tent.

David groaned, burying his head into Ben's chest. "Ugh, just fantastic."

"It's fine," Ben said, rubbing David's back. "It's not like it should be a big surprise to her."

"She doesn't know about me either," David grumbled. He pushed himself off of Ben and rummaged around the tent for his pants. "I have to go talk to her."

"Do you want me to come with you?"

"That sounds absolutely awful," David said, slipping his pants on. "No offense. But I should explain it on my own. It's awkward enough."

"Okay. I'll be here." Ben brushed his fingers against David's back as he ducked out of the tent.

David walked toward Marisol as she leaned up against one of the poles of the research tent. Her arms were crossed at her waist and her hair loose around her shoulders. David looked down at his bare chest and immediately regretted not taking the time to find his shirt. Marisol glanced up as he approached.

"Hey," she said, tightening her arms around her waist.

"Look, I can explain…"

"Nothing to explain," Marisol said. "Explains why you said I wasn't your type. I knew I wasn't *that* mean. So…you're gay then?"

David focused on his bare feet, his eyes tracing the outlines of the leaves underfoot. He hated this part, no matter how many times he had to say it. "Bi," he said, his voice eking out from his lips.

She put her hands on her hips and tapped her foot next to his. "Okay."

"Please don't be mad at me," David said, raising his eyes to look at her. "I'm sorry if you thought I was leading you on at all or lying. I thought we were on the same page. I'm sorry I didn't tell you. I-I don't want to lose you as a friend."

"You think I'm mad because you didn't tell me you were bi?"

"Wait…" David's eyebrows furrowed. "But you *are* mad. I mean, you *seem* mad. But that's not why you're mad? Then why?"

"David," Marisol said, grabbing his hand, "I don't care if you're bi, gay, straight, or whatever. I wish you trusted me enough to tell me. I'm *mad* that you didn't tell me you liked him."

"What?" David said, confused.

"I wouldn't have poked fun at you in front of him. I would have been a good wingman. Why wouldn't you tell me? I thought we were friends."

"We are," David implored. "I don't know how to do that. I... I've never had anyone to talk to about stuff like that."

"Well, now you do," Marisol stated with a curt nod. She squeezed his hand in hers. Before biting down on her lip, contemplating. "You guys could be cute together. Despite being a total hunk, he's about as dorky as you are."

"Thanks...I think? I don't really know what happens now, though. It's kind of like forced confinement in a way, like we *have* to be in each other's space, so I don't know...but, honestly, I'm kind of relieved it happened and that he felt the same way. Then again, it could all end in a total dumpster fire, so who knows."

Marisol laughed. "That was a lot at once. Your brain really is constantly running, isn't it? I'm sure it'll all be fine. And I'm glad he felt the same way, too. You deserve that." She let go of his hand before taking a step back and placing her hands back on her hips. "So, since we're now opening up and talking about all of these things...how was it? Is he just as impressive under the hood?"

"Oh my God, we are *not* talking about that," David said as his face turned bright red. "I take it all back. You can be mad at me."

Marisol laughed harder. "Not even a yes or no?"

"No!" David said, starting to smile. "You know I'm no different than before, right? It's not like I'm going to turn into some chatty gossip-type person. I'm still me."

"I know," Marisol groaned. "A girl can hope, though, right?"

David shook his head and stole a glance back at Ben's tent.

Marisol followed his gaze. "Go ahead and go back to him, lover boy."

"We're okay?" David asked, turning back to her.

"Right as rain...albeit a little jealous if we're being honest. I do have one more question, though."

"Oh, great."

"Does this mean I get my own tent again?"

The quiet smoldering of the firepit crackled over the occasional sipping of coffee as they sat around the fire, picking at bits of plantains for breakfast.

"Can I break this awkward silence yet?" Ben asked, putting his cup on the ground.

David closed his eyes. He could sense the tension moving throughout his muscles as his teeth ground together.

"We're all adults here," Ben continued.

"I already told David I don't care," Marisol said, popping a piece of the fruit into her mouth.

"So...everyone is good, then? David?"

"Mmmhmm," David hummed, nodding.

"There's nothing to be embarrassed about," Marisol said to David. "If y'all want space to work through it, that's fine."

David's eyebrows knitted together as he turned to her. "Work through it?"

"Well, I only mean if this is all new to you, that—"

David laughed and hung his head. "Marisol, I'm 27. I think I know what I'm into. This is definitely not something new, and *not* something I need to work through."

"Sorry, it's just you always seem...I don't know, kind of prudish."

"*Prudish*? Look, I may be shy and awkward, but I'm far from prudish."

She raised an eyebrow at him, sitting back. "I have a really hard time believing that."

"Why? We've been out here for, what, a couple of weeks? You barely know me. I mean, not that that's your fault. But do you even know how many classes we've had together? The times I've seen your profile pop up on Tinder or Hinge? I've been basically invisible to you for the last two years."

"I—"

"It's okay," David continued. "No hard feelings, but I'm not as innocent as you think. I tend to keep it to myself is all."

"Well, I'm sorry for breaking that awkward silence with *that*," Ben chuckled.

"I'm sorry I didn't notice you and get to know that guy," Marisol said, looking to David.

David shrugged. "I'm not. Our circles never crossed until now, anyway. But we make good friends and that's good enough for me. I think it's pretty clear we're not destined to know each other deeper than that."

"Destined, huh? So you believe in destiny?" Ben asked, clearing his throat and steering the conversation in a different direction.

"I do on some level," Marisol chimed in, taking the bait. "Maybe not love at first sight, but more like right place, right time."

"I don't." David gave another shrug. "I believe in science too much. Fate is just a series of choices and coincidences."

"That's so romantic," Ben joked. "I'm sure your past boyfriends loved to hear that on a first date."

"I don't have any past boyfriends, actually," David said, shifting his weight. "Girlfriends either really, before Marisol goes on another tangent about my lack of experience."

"Really? Not even one?" Ben asked.

"Do we really have to get into this?" David ran his hands along his face. "My longest relationship was only like two months."

"That's it? What happened?" Marisol asked.

"Oh, we're diving into this? Okay." David sat back and took a breath. "For that one, she said I was too focused on school. Said I cared too much about getting straight A's rather than taking her on the dates she wanted to go on. It was for the best anyway; she only wanted me to buy her things."

"One of those," Marisol nodded knowingly. She turned to Ben and nudged her head in David's direction, rubbing her thumb and pointer finger together. "He's loaded."

"Oh," Ben said. "Who knew?"

"I'm not loaded," David contested. "My parents are. I just don't turn it down."

"So that's at least one girlfriend. Why no boyfriends?" Marisol pressed.

"I don't know. Guess I've never met anyone that I clicked with or anyone that wanted more than a hookup. You know guys," David said, looking to Ben.

"And what about the other heartbreaks you've left in your wake?" Ben pried with a smile.

"Hardly heartbreaks," David said, rolling his eyes. "No one has ever stayed longer than a couple of weeks, except maybe one or two. I've heard a litany of complaints about myself, though. I read too many books; they want money or gifts or fancy dinners; I'm annoying because my thesis is too cerebral…"

"Wait," Marisol said, holding up her hand. "Someone dumped you because your thesis was too cerebral?"

"I know! In her defense, she was an art major. She was hot and a little crazy, but she wasn't the most complicated person on the planet."

"Harsh," Marisol said, taken aback.

"*She* dumped *me*! And she was definitely a nutcase," David laughed. "Anyway, there've been plenty of reasons to leave me and not many in my favor to make them stay. I haven't figured out if it's worth it to have someone if my entire being is just too much or too little."

"That makes me sad," Ben said.

"Why?" asked David.

"Because you haven't met someone who sees how special you are. They're missing out."

"And that's how you do it," Marisol grinned, pointing a finger at Ben. She nudged David with her elbow. "I like him. He's good for you. I approve."

David's cheeks flushed as he tried to suppress his smile. "I'll make sure to keep my thesis tucked away then. Just in case."

"So, I have an idea," Ben said, gathering the plantain peels and used coffee grounds from their breakfast. "What would you guys think if I went out and tried to go back to the pond?"

"Is that a serious question?" asked David.

"Hear me out. I'm talking only me. A quick trip. There and back." Ben gestured around the campsite. "Truth is, we're getting short on food. I wasn't exactly prepared to feed more people and not for this long. On top of that, we lost two of our water containers the other day."

"So, why can't we go together?" David asked.

"Because I know my way around." Ben's fingers picked at the pocket of his shorts. "And honestly, I haven't had any issues when I've been out alone. If something starts to go wrong, I'll come right back."

"It still seems dangerous," Marisol added.

"It probably is," Ben said. "But those plantains just now? Those were the last ones. We have almost no rice left, no dehydrated meal packets, and now we're short on water. That's definitely more dangerous than me trying to replenish what I can."

"How long?" David asked. "How long do you think it'll take you?"

Ben shrugged. "I don't know. Maybe a couple of hours max."

"Okay," David said with a stiff nod.

"Okay?" Marisol asked, surprised.

"Yeah. Okay," David repeated. "He's right. You know he's right. We can't stay put and expect food and water to fall into our laps. No food is serious, dehydration even more so. I lost my water bottle in my bag, otherwise I'd say we could collect the rainwater and use that. I don't think we have another choice."

Marisol's shoulders slumped as she hung her head, shaking it in disbelief. "Okay." She let out a heavy sigh. "Is there anything we can do here in the meantime to help?"

"Brainstorm?" Ben suggested. "Like David said, we have to be missing something. Let's find out what it is."

18

Marisol sat cross-legged on the floor of her tent, head leaning on the palm of her hand, and a collection of three books spread out around her. She scanned the pages, reading the paragraph headers as she went. Her eyes drifted up as David poked his head inside.

"Anything?" he asked, surveying the books on the ground.

"Nope," she sighed, sitting up straighter. "You can mark off *Neotropical Plant Families*, *Seeds of Amazonian Plants*, and..." She looked down and flipped the cover closed on the book to her right. "*A Field Guide to the Families and Genera of Woody Plants of Northwest South America*." She raised her eyes back to David, shaking her head in frustration as she shoved the book to the side. "Anything on your end?"

"Maybe?" David posed, side-stepping the books and sitting down across from her. "I did come across a book tucked into the bottom of the pile. *Amazonian Ethnobotanical Dictionary*. I'm only a little bit in, but it's by James Alan Duke from the USDA and Rodolfo Martinez, a former assistant curator of the Missouri Botanical Gardens."

"No way! I actually used Dr. Duke's *Phytochemicals Database* in my thesis. He's amazing. He's written so many incredible resources. I gifted my dad his book on the medicinal plants of the Bible. Don't know how well that went over, though."

"The only thing I've read from him is *The Green Pharmacy*. Went on an herbal remedy kick for a while, so I spent forever reading up on natural cures for everything. Thought I was well versed, but then Ben comes along..."

"Right? He's like a walking encyclopedia."

"Speaking of, he didn't exactly mention the downsides to our little drinking experience yesterday. This book opens with an explanation of the ayahuasca ceremony, and all I can say is that I'm happy I didn't end up with a bad reaction after that."

Marisol gasped, her eyes getting wide. "Oh my God. What did it say?"

"Let's just say it ended with warning about a 'mental one-way trip' and to 'beware.' Not exactly a caveat he touched upon."

"That's a little intense."

"I thought so," David laughed. "But you can read it if you want. I'm having a hard time focusing. I keep watching the clock. Ben's been gone a little over three hours."

"It's been that long?"

"And counting."

"I'm sure he's fine."

"I don't know," David said. "Doesn't feel right."

"How so?"

"He said a couple of hours tops. There's no doubt he knows his way around. If anything, he'd make better time than what he estimated."

"What do you want to do?"

David closed his eyes and let out a heavy sigh, pressing the heel of his hand against his forehead. As he breathed back in, he opened his eyes and looked at Marisol. "I think I need to go after him."

"You mean *we* have to go after him," Marisol corrected.

"You're okay with it?"

"I trust you. And he would do the same for us."

"Let's hope we're only being paranoid and that he's on his way back now. Maybe we'll meet him halfway."

"I'll grab some of his first aid stuff. We can't afford to lose him. Apparently, he's the only one that knows how to fish."

Mosquitos swarmed Marisol and David, lending a light and constant buzzing to the bird songs raining down from the branches above. They were able to follow Ben's trail without much effort and without having to cut back any overgrowth. David hoped the ease of the walk meant that they were heading in the right direction. He wasn't sure about any of the trails anymore, not after experiencing what they did the other day.

His mind drifted to the book he was reading before they left camp. It listed out the cultural uses of various local plant life. He named back the sections he had read in his head. *Timber uses in rural housing, the ayahuasca ceremony, how to make a blow gun out of a specialized tree in the nutmeg family, and the use of poison darts…*

"Poison darts," David mumbled aloud.

"What?" Marisol asked, stopping and turning around to face him.

David slowed to a stop and looked down at her, his face scrunched up in confusion.When she continued to stare at him, he raised his shoulders in question.

"You said something?" Marisol pressed. "What is it?"

"Oh." David shook his head in embarrassment. "I must have been thinking out loud. You can ignore me."

Marisol shrugged and went back to forging ahead. After a few minutes of silence, she slowed down, letting David walk next to her as they took their time stepping over tree roots while avoiding touching any of the peripheral vines.

"So, what were you thinking about?" she asked, continuing to walk. She kept her head down, focusing on her steps.

He walked in quiet contemplation for several seconds before answering her. "Duke's book."

"What about it?"

"You're going to think I'm weird."

"I think that ship has sailed," Marisol snorted.

He was only half with her, though he knew the small retreats into his own head were becoming more noticeable the longer they spent together—an unfortunate downside to having to be around people for increased periods of time.

Breaking out of his own thoughts, he said, "There was a chapter I was reading on poison darts. Like for blow guns by the indigenous people here. There are a lot of trees around here that have some pretty hefty toxins."

"And you're wanting to make poison darts?"

"No. I was wondering if somehow we came in contact with a poison like that. Maybe one that makes you hallucinate or something? What if the other day was an adverse reaction to something we all touched?"

"The classic 'the whole thing was a dream' plot-line. I mean, it's creative."

"I told you you'd think I was weird."

"Hey," she said, stopping and grabbing his arm. "I don't think you're weird. It's a good theory."

"Now you're just trying to spare my feelings."

"I am not! It's something we haven't thought of yet. It's not something we can test, though…not really." Marisol glanced up at him. "Doesn't mean it's a bad idea."

"I feel like I'm grasping at straws."

"You're not alone. None of us know how to broach this. We have to do what we do best: come up with a hypothesis, test it, and interpret the results. That's all we can do."

"I know I keep saying it, but I feel like there has to be something right in front of us, you know? Something we're obviously missing."

"Can I tell you a quick story?" asked Marisol as she continued down the trail.

"Sure?"

"So," Marisol started, "last year I was in a lab rotation, and we were focusing on plant-microbe reactions in certain crops in relation to environmental stressors—mainly drought. The secondary part of that research was looking at plant growth promoting microbes, PGPMs, and how to improve the abiotic stress response. The goal was to find a way to genetically manipulate the microbes to give advantage against specific stressors. Anyway, we're looking at different ways the host machinery can be manipulated by those PGPMs. We wanted to protect against drought, so we were looking at which combination would release the right hormones to increase nutrient uptake from the soil. I had to have spent hours upon hours stuck on the hormone outputs."

"And I thought I was done with classes."

"*Anyway*, I spent so many sleepless nights running data, doing calculations, re-evaluating the way I was looking at the genetics—you get the idea. Turns out, I was missing a major detail. I was running everything purely against the salinity of the soil and not accounting for the drought condition itself, which was the whole freaking point. I was so focused on all of the small pieces we were putting together that I missed a glaring mistake that took way too many days to discover."

"Your lab partners must have hated you."

"Not once I fixed it," Marisol shot back. She stopped walking and looked up at him. "I guess what I'm saying is, don't hyperfocus so much on what you think you're missing, looking at every detail and wondering how it all fits in. It makes you blind to the bigger picture. We're going to figure it out or at least get in the right direction. We just need to take a step back."

"That was a really long story to basically tell me to stop overthinking," David said, slipping around her to continue walking.

"Would you have listened to me if I told you to stop overthinking?"

David shrugged, his back to her. "Probably not."

"Exactly," Marisol said with a firm nod, following after him.

"I can't believe I'm biting at this…" David grumbled, shaking his head. "What did you find? With the microbes and drought?"

"Bite away! I could talk all day about it!" Marisol sped forward to catch up with him. "We were able to promote growth in the plant by manipulating the microbes to improve the nutrient exchanges and kickstart the production of phytohormones. There are still a lot of things that need to be studied on how the PGPMs can benefit the host plant, and I know the research project is still ongoing, but it was neat to see how those little genetic changes can impact an environmental response. When I left the rotation, we were able to effectively reduce the abiotic stress response and essentially make the plants drought resistant. It was really cool."

"So, the plant was able to sustain itself within the original environmental factors? Genetically altered, though, of course."

"Precisely," Marisol said. She sighed as David went silent. "You're overthinking again."

"I am not," David snipped. "Just regular thinking."

"Care to share?"

"I guess I'm wondering if that can be applied to other plants, but in reverse."

"You mean, like, to activate intolerance to an environment?"

"Exactly like that," David said, more to the air in front of him than to Marisol. "So, I'm studying invasive species, right? Hostile species. Parasitical. Domineering. What if there was a way to alter the genetics to make those species averse to their environment?"

"I wouldn't know. Definitely outside my scope, but it sounds neat. Maybe a post-doc research project?"

David continued forward in silence. Marisol trudged behind him as he side-stepped roots and sliced his machete haphazardly through the occasional dangling vine.

"What about other factors?" David asked, breaking the silence as he continued to walk. "Like non-environmental ones."

"What do you mean?"

"Well, your research is all about stress responses, right? Like, obviously there's a reaction to environmental stress—we see that in floodplains, after hurricanes, in snow...but is there anything else?"

"Seriously?" Marisol deadpanned, "I've told you about my thesis a million times."

"Humor me."

"Fine." She sighed dramatically, dropping her shoulders in emphasis. "There are a *bunch* of different stressors and responses associated with them. Stress can be abiotic, you know, with environmental factors like drought, or it can be biotic. Biotic stressors include herbivores, pathogens, things happening to the plant via living organisms."

Marisol waited for David to acknowledge her before she continued.

"That said, my thesis is on defense mechanisms mainly initiated by biotic stressors. The first ones I cover are trichomes, like what I think those ferns released near the camp. Trichomes are essentially little hollow hairs. You know a little about them at least, because of your whole 'I think tarantulas are cool' thing. They can range from things like irritating hairs in a stinging nettle or sundew, or sensory hairs in carnivorous plants like the Venus flytrap. The Venus flytrap has trichomes that alert the plant when touched. The plant then closes on the prey, lured in by nectar. Following?"

"Yes, I'm following," David muttered. "I've been in school longer than you have. I can follow a basic lecture."

"You never know," Marisol said, adjusting the backpack on her shoulders. "The second part is idioblasts. Idioblasts are mainly found in plants that need to protect themselves against grazers, things that eat them. The idioblasts are specialized cells. They can be used as storage cells, manufacturing cells, or as weaponized cells. I focus on the latter. The plants that use defensive idioblasts are filled with biforine cells. Those cells contain calcium oxalate crystals, a horrible irritant or poison depending on what the grazer is and what plant they're eating. What's cool is that those crystals have many forms. They can be needle-like or like a grain of sand. Either way, they're badass."

"It's neat to see you so passionate. I knew about some of—"

"I'm not done," Marisol interrupted and continued to speak over him. "The third, *and yes*, the last one I cover, is chemical signaling. So, get this...plants can communicate with one another. There've been studies where electrodes have been placed on leaves and scientists have been able to measure electrical signals traveling to other parts of the plant and even nearby plants like a nervous system. The plant cells actually pass charged ions between themselves to alert of certain dangers— say one leaf is getting eaten by a caterpillar and it wants to warn the rest of the plant to take action. Those other leaves will then start making compounds to make them undesirable for eating... could be poison, could just be a bad taste, but they communicate! It's fascinating. Plants have so much more going on than people give them credit for. Do you know how many people are accidentally poisoned or get severe reactions from their household or garden plants every year? People have no idea these living things can actually defend themselves and can do so violently and in coordinated attacks."

"Is it an attack if it's defensive?"

"Think of it like a provoked attack. If someone came up to you and shoved you, you'd shove them back."

David laughed. "Have you met me?"

"Well, maybe you're a bad example, but those are only stress *responses*. That's not even including external defenses, like thorns and spines. Plants are tough. They're constantly evolving, making cellular moves to ensure survival, creating and manipulating compounds to keep themselves alive even if it means a detriment to the plant itself until it can recover safely."

"I can see why you would want to write a thesis on it. It's really cool."

"It is, isn't it? No one ever wants to hear about it, but how could you not think it's interesting? People go to a hardware store and pick up some succulent off the discount shelf and bring it home or into their office. They have no idea what's going on in there. It's actively changing to suit its new environment;

it's probably rearranging cellular storage units to account for the fact that its new owner just drowned it near to death. All of these little micromovements and communications, all happening in some $5 plastic cup on some receptionist's desk." Marisol stopped walking and looked up at David. "I lost you again, didn't I?"

"No, I'm listening," David said, distracted. "Do you hear that?"

"...no?" Marisol answered, stepping up next to him. "I hear birds."

"It's not birds," David said, his head tilting to the side.

A light clinking of dry wood filled the air. The sound began to drift toward them from several yards down the trail. Marisol's hand shot out and grabbed David's arm, her nails digging into his skin. David held his breath as he arched his head back and looked above them. He trained his eyes on the bamboo chimes in the limbs above as they slowly knocked together, creating a rhythmic drumming against the normal clamor of the rainforest.

"We need to move. Go!"

Marisol jutted forward as David pushed against her back. She didn't look forward or back but kept her head tucked down, weaving and skipping over the exposed roots. The chimes clanked together above them every few yards as they ran. David lagged not far behind, his feet kicking up mud and leaves as he maneuvered the natural trip hazards of the forest floor. Marisol came to a screeching halt, the toes of her shoes buried in the mud. A string of curses echoed over her shoulder as David tried to avoid running into her.

"What are you doing?" he panted, breathless.

"Listen. What is that?" She held up her hand and pointed a finger down the trail before them.

A soft grunting echoed from behind the next set of trees. The bamboo chimes knocked together on the trail ahead, louder than the others thus far. David pushed past Marisol, holding a hand out for her to stay where she was. He moved forward, cringing every time he lifted his foot out of the mud; the squishing suction from his shoes pulling away from the mud sounded like cymbals crashing in his ears.

Barely breathing, David snuck down the trail and around the trees. The grunting increased in intensity the closer he inched to the bend in the path. His heart dropped to his stomach as he heard a familiar, but muffled voice from around the corner.

"Ben?" David called out, nervous. His heart beat heavily against his ribcage.

"David?" Ben's breathless and strained voice called out. "Oh, thank God."

19

Ben sat hunched on the jungle floor, the wet leaves seeping through the seat of his pants. He ground his teeth together as he rotated a switchblade in his hands. His wrists were bound with thick, green vines, which traveled up his arms and were encroaching on his neck. Grasping the handle of the blade in his palm, he slid it against the vines binding his wrist. The sharp blade sliced through the plant without resistance, cutting it away and into a pile of discarded tendrils. Ben had done this several times already. Each time, a new layer of vines took the severed one's place. He pulled his legs, the resistance from the vines looping and twisting around his ankles, anchoring him to the ground. The tendrils crept their way up his legs and around his calves, pressing against his muscles. He growled through his teeth as he yanked his limbs, trying to tear away the plants as they swallowed him up.

"Oh my God!" Marisol screeched as she and David rounded the trail.

David dashed to Ben, dropping to his knees next to him. He began detangling the vines, pulling and stretching them back over Ben's hand. As he tried to lift them away, dark red lines crisscrossed Ben's skin where the vines held onto his flesh.

"Man, am I happy to see you," Ben said, sucking in a quick

breath, the vines cinching tighter around his skin as he tried to wiggle free. "Ow!" He flinched and bared his teeth as David pulled tighter on the vines.

"Sorry." David moved his hands away. "They're not budging; it's too tangled."

"My other hand." Ben directed his head opposite David. "I have a knife. I think I've cut a little away."

David scooted on his knees to Ben's other side, taking the knife from his hands. "Marisol," David said, snapping her out of her shock. "Use your machete for the ones by his feet."

Marisol gave a quick nod and knelt on the ground at Ben's feet. She lined the machete up with the vine on his right foot, positioning it to cut where it emerged from the ground. With a careful swing, the vines cut away.

Marisol breathed a sigh of relief, looking between Ben and David. "I think this'll work!"

"Good." David met Ben's eyes. "Where's your machete?"

"I don't know." Ben winced at the pressure on his wrists. "I put it down on the trail before...this."

David positioned the knife back in Ben's hands, setting the blade against the tendrils around his wrist. "Keep cutting." He hopped to his feet, moved back to the trail, and scanned the ground.

Marisol continued to cut away at the vines by his feet. As she freed Ben's left foot, she turned to see his right tangled again. She gasped as she watched the vines squeeze around Ben's ankle, the skin above it turning a pale white. Ben moaned as they tightened their grip. Marisol watched as more thick vines emerged from the soil and began to wrap around his left foot, creeping around his shoes and ensnaring his calf. He frantically cut away at the vines by his hand, rotating his wrist, cutting away one tendril at a time.

"I don't...know what...to do," Ben panted between held breaths. He leaned his head back and squeezed his eyes shut in pain, sending a small trickle of tears running down his cheek.

"We've got you. Hang in there," Marisol said, determined.

She raised her machete and swung down, slicing through the vines at his feet before they had a chance to grow back.

Ben screamed out and the blade dropped from his hand. His arms yanked toward the ground, the vines around his wrists pulling him taut against the dirt. Small streams of blood seeped out where they sliced into his skin. Ben's muscles ached as they continued to squeeze around his arms, drawing blood and cutting off circulation. He looked down through watery eyes and saw the tips of the plant making its way up to his neck.

"Guys!" Ben cried as the vine tickled against his ear.

Marisol moved to Ben's hands and sliced the machete through the new growth coming from the ground. The tendrils on Ben's left hand fell away. As he lifted it and shook the vines free, a sharp pain shot through his legs. Hunching forward at the waist, he moaned as the vines encircling his ankles and calves tore into his skin.

"Jesus Christ," David gasped, as he rushed back to Ben's side, machete in hand.

"It hurts so bad," Ben whimpered. Small streams of blood poured from each of his limbs, the vines digging deeper and deeper into his skin.

"It's going to be okay," David reassured him. "Marisol, you get his feet, and I'll get the hands."

Marisol readied her machete and looked up at David. The blade shook in her hand as Ben winced and groaned in front of her. David met her eyes and gave her a firm nod. They brought their machetes down and cut away at the roots reaching up out of the dirt.

Ben writhed in pain as the vines curled up around his neck, wrapping tightly around his throat. He kicked out his free leg, trying to push himself away as he struggled to loosen his still bound hand. The more he struggled, the tighter the tendrils dug into his neck. He clawed at the vine around his throat with his free hand, trying to pry it away.

"You have to sit still," Marisol insisted, holding down his

foot. Marisol moved to Ben's other side and raised her machete and swung down again.

Ben let out a sharp yelp as Marisol sliced through the vine at his foot. He pulled his hand back from his neck, to see it wet and red with fresh blood. Ben reached out and tore at David's shirt, moving his hand back to his neck as his airway began to close. Raspy breaths escaped his lips as he fought to breathe between the panic and pain.

Marisol rushed to Ben's vine covered wrist and brought the blade to the roots.

"Wait!" David yelled, diving over Ben to grab Marisol's arm. "Don't." He held her hand steady, the blade frozen in the air.

"Let go!" she yelled. "It's killing him!" Marisol pulled against David's hand, ripping her machete away.

"Please," David said, his voice steady. He held up a hand, motioning for her to stop. "We're making it worse."

David brought his hand to Ben's throat, running his fingers along the vine cutting into his skin and crushing his windpipe. He looked down at the discarded plants that were already giving way to new growth. His gaze returned to Ben. The peaceful ocean in his eyes that was normally there was now a squall with violent tidal waves of fear crashing onto the surface.

"I've got you," David whispered. "Try not to fight it."

"David, no. He has to fight. What are—"

David held his hand up to Marisol again, cutting her off. "Listen to me," he said to Ben, not breaking eye contact. "Don't fight." He reached down and squeezed his hand. "You have to trust me."

Ben focused on David's eyes as he tried to slow down his thoughts and release the tension in his muscles. Shallow breaths filled and emptied his lungs as the pressure continued to bear down on his throat.

"Marisol," David said, his voice calm. "Go back to the trail."

"But I—"

"Do it," David commanded.

Marisol reluctantly stood from her knees and backed away

toward the trail. She clutched the handle of her machete, keeping her eyes trained on David and Ben. Her heart pounded in her chest, her pulse rapid and thumping in her temples.

David sat on the ground and held Ben's hand, squeezing it tightly as his eyes scanned the vines still clinging and wrapping around Ben's body. The pressure against his hand changed, followed by a loud gasping of air coming from Ben's lips. David sat up on his knees and leaned over Ben, who was now coughing and sputtering while trying to take in the extra air now flooding his lungs.

Streaks of blood dripped down his neck as the vines loosened their grip. David's hand shot out and grabbed at Ben, who was reaching up to pull the vines away.

"Don't," David said, shaking his head. "Not yet."

The two remained still and motionless. David continued to keep his hand in Ben's, his thumb rubbing a small pattern against the back of his hand as they sat in silence. After a few minutes, the remaining tendrils uncurled and fell away, becoming nothing but loose ringlets around Ben's legs, arms, and neck. David released his grip on Ben's hand and met his eyes once more.

"Here goes nothing."

David plucked at each vine, his fingers barely putting pressure on the shoots. He methodically lifted and slid each individual tendril off until Ben laid there, with only the red marks and smears of blood as evidence of the struggle. David stood, watching where he stepped, and offered a hand to Ben. When he pulled him to his feet, Ben immediately collapsed into David's arms as quiet tears fell down his face. He buried his head into the crook of David's neck and wrapped his arms around him as tight as he could.

"Are you okay?" Marisol asked, tiptoeing back toward them.

Ben lifted his head from David and let his arms fall back to his sides. His neck and arms were stained with ribbons of red and now drying blood. He looked from David to Marisol, and then to the ground, seeing the desiccated plants.

"Let's get the fuck out of here," Ben said, sticking his hand into David's and heading back to the trail.

They continued in silence, Ben insisting on heading away from camp and toward the pond to retrieve their water. David followed closely behind, with Marisol bringing up the rear. They soon came upon a fork in the trail; a snapped tree branch laid across it. Without hesitation, Ben stepped over and through it. As David began to climb up and over, Ben reappeared with a large water bladder in his hands.

"Found 'em," he said, handing one over to David. "Right where we left them." He hoisted the second over his shoulder and pushed past them to head back toward camp.

David furrowed his brow in concern as he watched him carry on. The usual joy in his voice and demeanor were overshadowed by a dull and sullen cloud. David worried for him. He wanted nothing more than to reach out, hold Ben tight against his chest, and tell him that everything was going to be okay. But he didn't know that. He didn't know if they'd ever be okay again.

They walked on, making their way back to the campsite. Once there, Ben emptied his backpack by the campfire. He dropped several bunches of plantains onto the ground followed by a dead pheasant-like bird. Marisol gasped as the bird thumped into the dirt.

"We need to eat more than fruit. They're easy to hunt." He shrugged.

David came up next to him and took the backpack from his hands. "I can handle it all. Why don't we clean you up and everything first?"

Ben's tired eyes bore into David's as tears built up in the corners. He gave a small and silent nod before sitting down on the ground at David's feet. Ben's gaze drifted down his arms, looking at the crisscrossed patterns still left from the vines. The hair on his legs was caked with dirt and blood; he couldn't even tell where he was bleeding from.

Marisol stepped in and took the bunches of plantains, arranging them in the palm basket on the other side of the campfire. Once finished, she cradled the dead bird in her arms and laid it on the ground by the steel cooking pot. "I hadn't thought about not knowing how to hunt. If we hadn't run into you…" Marisol looked back, but both men were focused elsewhere. She turned to the bird, nibbled on her lip, and mumbled, "We probably would have starved."

David gathered his first aid kit from his bag and sat next to Ben. He reached over and ran his hand along Ben's back, his fingers brushing over the fabric of his shirt. "You okay?" David asked, failing to hide the concern in his voice.

"How did you know how to do that?" Ben asked, his voice timid.

"I, uh…I guessed."

"You *guessed*?" Marisol asked, coming to join them.

"Like you said," he turned to look at Marisol, "come up with a hypothesis, test it, and analyze the results."

"You seemed like you knew exactly what to do," Ben said in barely more than a whisper.

"I didn't." David fidgeted with the snaps on the first aid kit. "But I had to do something. It was hurting you."

"What was the hypothesis?" Marisol asked.

"When we were talking earlier, you said plants can communicate, right? And they have provoked attacks?" David sat back and let out a frustrated breath. "I don't know, it seemed like every time we cut more away, it got worse. I thought maybe if there wasn't anything happening to it, and if everyone just let go, maybe it would stop." He looked to Ben, his worried eyes moving over the streaks of blood along his limbs. "I had to try. I promise it wasn't, like, an experiment or anything. I didn't know what else to do."

"I wasn't thinking that," said Ben. "I'm really lucky that you were there."

"But we made it so much worse before it got better."

"But it got better," Ben said, giving David a weak smile. "I-I wish I had listened to you and not gone alone."

"What happened?" Marisol asked. "How did you even get all tangled up like that?"

"I wish I knew. I don't understand it. I stopped to tie my shoes and get some water." Ben shook his head in disbelief. "I cleared out a spot off to the side of the trail so I could have more space. I don't even know what happened, really. I was sitting, taking a breather. I may have dozed off, I don't know. I didn't even feel it. I went to get up, and they were all wrapped around one of my hands and both of my ankles. I tried to rip them off, but..."

"That made it worse," Marisol finished for him.

Ben nodded. "I don't know what I would have done if you guys didn't come get me."

"Don't think about that," David said, reassuring him. "Let me clean you up and maybe you can talk to Marisol about whatever she needs to do for us to eat that pigeon thing." David motioned his head toward the campfire.

"Me?" Marisol gulped.

"Yes you. I had to descale all those fish the other day, and Ben gets the night off. It's your turn."

"You're lucky I'm a team player."

"Glad nothing changed while I was gone." Ben laughed, wiping the corner of his eye. "And thanks," he said, catching David's gaze. "I really am glad you were there."

"Me too."

"I guess this means a few more scars to add to the collection?" David asked, looking at Ben in the lantern light as he got undressed and ready for bed.

"I'm sure I'll be completely covered by the time we're out of here," Ben said, collapsing onto his sleeping bag next to him.

"You really think we're going to make it out of here?"

"I do," Ben said, looking over at him. "I don't know how yet, but between the three of us..." Ben shrugged his shoulders and exhaled. "We have to."

"Are you okay?"

"You know that has to be the hundredth time you've asked me that tonight."

"Sorry." David adjusted on his back. "I just know I can't stop thinking about it, so I figured—"

"I can't either," Ben interrupted. He rolled onto his side to face David. "I can usually handle anything. I don't think I've ever been so scared."

"Do you want to talk about it?"

Ben shook his head and raised his eyes to meet David's. "Can I just snuggle up to you instead?"

David smiled and scooted closer to Ben, lifting his arm and placing it behind his head. Ben leaned in, rested his head against David's chest, and curled his leg on top of him. He closed his eyes and took a deep breath. The steady beat of David's heart drummed steadily against his ear. He wrapped his arm around David's torso and held him, pressing against his bare skin until they could no longer take the heat coming off them in the oppressive humidity.

David smiled down at Ben as he tilted his head up from his chest to meet David's eyes. Leaning down, he kissed Ben's forehead before taking his hand and brushing the loose strands out of Ben's face.

"I'm happy I ended up out here with you," Ben said, leaning his head into David's hand. "It may not be the best of circumstances, but I'm glad we met."

"I am too."

David reached over him and flipped the switch on the lantern, entrenching them in darkness. David pulled Ben tighter against him as the sounds of singing insects filled the air and lulled them to sleep.

20

A light froth foamed over the edge of the stainless steel pot as it hung over the dimly lit fire. David dipped a spoon in, breaking up the foam and mixing it back into the pot. Steam billowed from the spoon as David held it in front of him. He blew on it, watching the steam dissipate before sticking it into his mouth.

"I don't think you're supposed to use the same spoon you cook with to taste the food," Marisol said as she came out of her tent and walked up behind him. She leaned down on his shoulders and peered into the pot. "What *is* that?"

"I was kind of hoping like a porridge?"

"That doesn't make me nervous at all." Marisol came around to sit next to him. "What does 'like a porridge' mean?"

"It's mashed up rice and cooked plantains." David ran his hand through his hair and chuckled. "I wanted to make a decent breakfast, but it turns out that it's another thing that's *not* my strong suit out here."

"I'm sure it'll be...edible," Marisol said, scrunching her face at the pot as it began to froth again. "Where's Ben?"

"Still sleeping. I figured he could use it."

"It's nice of you to make him breakfast."

"You know it's for you, too."

"I know, but the thought was for him. And that's nice. I think you two are good together." She paused, watching as he tended to the boiling pot. "I was impressed by how you handled that yesterday. I probably would have gotten us all killed."

"Not killed," David said without looking up. "Maimed maybe."

"Hey!" Marisol shoved him. "But I'm serious. I'm happy for you."

"Thanks. We'll see."

"What's that supposed to mean? You want to break up already?"

"It's been a couple of days, Marisol. I don't even know what it is. I don't even think there's anything *to* break up."

"So you *do* want to break up?"

David sighed into his hands. "Oh my God. It's not even dating yet." David lifted his head and looked at her. "I haven't really felt this way about anyone before. He's kind of perfect... like, too good to be true, you know? And we're trapped out here in the middle of nowhere. I guess I'm second guessing myself. Someone like him wouldn't even have noticed me back home."

"You don't know that," Marisol said, becoming serious. "And who cares? You're not back home. I may poke fun at you, but you don't give yourself enough credit. He's lucky to have you."

David shrugged his shoulders in resignation. He grabbed the bowls and filled them up with the rice and plantain mixture from the pot, handing one to Marisol and placing the other two at his side.

"I do mean that," Marisol continued. "Why don't you serve him some breakfast in bed? That's romantic."

"I'm not trying to be romantic," David grumbled. "I'm trying to get through one day at a time."

"Maybe you should *try* being romantic." Marisol lifted the bowl to her mouth and took a sip, resisting making a face as the rice hit her tongue. She took the bowl and placed it on the ground. "He likes you. Go make him forget about yesterday for a while."

David glanced over to her. "You just don't want to hang out with me."

"True. I also don't want you to watch me dump all of this out." She knocked the bowl with her foot. "Because it's a crime against both rice and fruit."

Ben rubbed his fingers against his closed eyes, brushing away the sleep as he rolled over onto his side. A smile broke across his face as his eyes focused on David. He was sitting on the other side of the tent, notebook in hand, scribbling away. A yawn escaped Ben's mouth as he stretched his arms and legs under the cover of the sleeping bag.

David smiled, looking over at him. "Hey."

"How long have you been up? What time is it?"

"A while now...and around ten-ish."

Ben's voice crackled from sleep. "Why didn't you wake me?"

"You deserved some extra sleep. Here, saved this for you." David grabbed a plantain and handed it to Ben. "So...I wasn't going to admit it, but I tried to make breakfast, and it ended up a total disaster. I was really hoping not to have to give you a single plantain."

"You tried to make me breakfast?" Ben grinned. "That's so sweet."

"As long as you know it's the thought that counts. My execution could use some work."

Ben laughed and sat up, peeling the plantain. "Of course it's the thought that counts." Ben bit off a piece of the fruit. "How'd you mess up breakfast?" he asked, his mouth half-full.

"Don't ask," David laughed. "I promise I'm way better in an actual kitchen."

"Are you one of those guys whose mom taught them how to cook when they were little?"

"No..." David trailed off, going quiet. "Taught myself."

Ben grimaced. "Did I hit a nerve? I didn't mean to. I was assuming—"

"You didn't. It's okay. My parents weren't around a whole lot. Just don't really have stories to share."

"Well, I'm sorry either way," Ben crawled over and sat next to David, letting his knee rest against his. "Mine have always been over-involved. There never seems to be a happy medium, does there?"

"Over-involved?"

Ben laughed. "Oh yeah. Always interested in everything I'm doing. Coming to every event, no matter how small. They showed up and waited in the parking lot the day I had to defend my dissertation." Ben's smile faded, and he began to pick at his fingernails. "They're planning on coming down here to stay for a week on the off-season. Want me to be their guide and show them around."

David rested his hand on Ben's knee. "We're going to get back there. You can still do that."

"I know they worry. All I can think about is them getting a phone call that I'm 'missing.' They'd be down here on the next red-eye. They already worry enough about me living down here. I don't need them to know about all of this."

"We'll get back to civilization, or at least the lodge, long before any of that. Then they can just worry about you being out here under normal circumstances."

"Knowing my mom, she'd change her tune and be fine with me being out here once I tell her about you."

"Me?"

"She'd probably go on about how I met this dreamy guy in the middle of the rainforest, tell all of her friends, plan a wedding..." Ben glanced up, smiling at David's panicked eyes. "She's really anxious for me to settle down. But don't worry, I'm not crazy like that. I heard how that came out." Ben swallowed hard as he watched David. "Can I start over?"

David let out a nervous laugh. "Not exactly what I expected to hear, but it's all good."

"Guess I'm lucky that they're so supportive. I wish they'd ease off some and stop freaking my boyfriends out, but it's kind of sweet in a lack-of-boundaries kind of way. What about yours?"

"What about mine?"

"Do they pressure you to get married or are they accepting of you being a bachelor out on the town?"

"I've never actually talked about it with them."

"Well, I know it'll be one of the first things my mom asks. I can finally tell her I met a cute boy in the jungle, and you're proof that I'm not delirious from malaria." He studied David as he talked. His eyebrows bunched together as David chewed the inside of his cheek. "I'm sorry if I'm making you uncomfortable. I can talk a lot."

"You're not," David mumbled. "I'm having a hard time picturing a mom like that. Honestly, my parents would probably cut me off forever if they knew I was seeing a guy let alone some guy who lives in the rainforest."

"They don't know? About all of that?"

"We don't really talk. When we do, it's about school or what I'm going to do once I get my PhD, whether I'm going to be successful or start a business. They don't ask, and I don't share."

"I'm sorry I brought it up." Ben scooted over so that he was sitting behind David, his legs draped on either side of him. He wrapped his arms around his chest, hugging him from behind.

"Don't be." David reached up to grab Ben's arms as they held him. "I'm liking learning about you."

"Speaking of learning, what are you writing in there?" Ben leaned his chin on David's shoulder, looking down into his lap. "Diary? Manifesto?"

"Oh, definitely a manifesto." David laughed as he placed a hand on the notebook. "Trying to connect dots. Come up with a theory. You know, light reading."

"Whatcha got?"

"Not much." David pushed the notebook off his lap and leaned his head back against Ben's shoulder. "I'm not even sure what I'm looking for. I have a million little notes, but they're all so disconnected."

"You know it's not on you to figure it out alone, right? Here, let me see." Ben reached around David and picked up the notebook. He held it out in David's lap as he flipped the pages, reading over his shoulder.

David's stomach fluttered as Ben leaned against him. His dark waves tickled his face as they brushed along his cheek. He closed his eyes, hoping to slow his heartbeat, worried that Ben would be able to feel it beating through his back and against his chest.

"You're missing a big piece," Ben said, pointing his finger at a bulleted list on the page.

"What? Where? What do you mean?" David stammered, snapping back to the present.

Ben backed up from David and slipped out of the tent. "Don't move."

A minute later, Ben reappeared and plopped down in front of him. He carried a stack of notebooks in his hands. He set the stack down next to them and grabbed the first one, flipping it open.

"You wrote down the details from my notes that I dropped at the first site, yeah? Well, you only have the one in here from the end of September."

"That's all there was…"

"I wrote *a lot* more." Ben flipped to the middle of his notebook and splayed it open. "I wasn't planning on heading back to the lodge, at least not right away. After seeing everything out here, I had to know what it was. I knew Julia was coming with new people, so I left the one for this new site to let her know I progressed to the next grid. I didn't exactly expect to be stuck out here so long. I was hopeful I'd meet everyone back halfway by the time she came around. Turns out, the jungle had other plans."

"Why didn't you tell me before?"

"Because it wasn't relevant. I never narrowed it down and

eventually I stopped taking samples and stopped recording down the species. I figured if I was going to get anywhere, I had to be *in* it, not just observing it. But," he said, pointing back over to David's notebook, "your theories in there…they're definitely missing my notes."

David's hand blurred across the page in front of him. Messy scribbles decorated the paper, bullet points connected with lines and arrows and tiny notes in the margins crossed over the hurried handwriting. The pencil in David's hand came to a halt as Ben jabbed a finger down at one of the bullet points.

"Add one here about the spines from the bamboo. The ones you fell into."

"You think it's related? It doesn't fit."

"I know it doesn't fit. They're different, though. I think we should account for anything outside of the norm."

"But how are you judging the norm? The whole point of having a research team out here is to help catalogue new species. How can we tell what's a new species and what's a variant? We're working with a barely known baseline."

"Then put it down with an asterisk," Ben sighed, waving it off with his hand. "I think we need to put everything on the table and then walk it back from there."

"Alright." David rolled his eyes, giving in. "Bamboo spines are on the list."

David glanced up as he heard Marisol call out from the outside of the tent. He watched the zipper glide on the track around the door as Marisol's head appeared, peeking into the tent.

"I thought I'd be walking in on something completely different," she joked, surveying the two of them with notebooks strewn around them.

"David's trying to hash out a solid theory," Ben said, tilting his head back to look at Marisol.

"And Ben's adding more complicating factors into it by the minute," David added.

"And I wasn't invited?"

"It just kind of happened," Ben said. "We can make room. Grab a notebook." Ben stacked the scattered notebooks into a pile and pushed the sleeping bags into a mound at the corner of the tent.

"What exactly is the process here?" Marisol asked, peering over at the chaotic writing on the page in David's notebook. "*Is* there a process?"

"There *was* a process," David said, raising his eyebrows at Ben.

"Lover's quarrel already?" Marisol smirked.

"Different academic approaches," Ben answered. "Hardly a quarrel."

"Right. So, I wanted to list out all the things we've come across that we could consider 'active' and narrow down individual instances and species and what we know about them," explained David.

Marisol nodded. "Okay. I'm with you."

"*I* think we should have everything on the table *first*, and then backtrack from there, eliminating plants and instances that don't fit or have no correlation to what we're looking at," added Ben.

"And what *are* we trying to look at?" asked Marisol, looking to David.

"Ideally? Things that are clearly hostile. Plants like the vines that got a hold of Ben, for instance. And Ben wants to add the bamboo spines that messed me up—I don't think it's relevant, but we added them anyway. I haven't figured out if the fern incident was just a normal species of fern that has trichomes or if it's something purposeful."

"Well, it's all purposeful," Marisol said matter-of-factly.

David let out a heavy sigh and put his pencil down on the page. He ran his hands over his face and up through his hair to rest on the back of his neck.

"I think you broke him," Ben said, looking at Marisol.

Marisol reached over and took the notebook from David's lap. Her eyes scanned the page as she read the bullet points and timelines between the rest of the markings.

"Well?" asked David, raising his head and letting his hands drop into his lap.

"Well..." Marisol said, drawing out the word. "I think it's a good start. I also think that you're missing a good chunk of the point."

Ben's eyes darted over to David as Marisol finished her sentence. "Before we throw it all out, why don't—"

"Oh, nothing needs to be thrown out. It's good work, it really is. It's that you guys didn't take into consideration the factors behind the incidents or any data to help support your end theory —assuming the end theory is that the plants are, in your words, 'hostile.'"

"And what data is that?" David said, frustrated. "We don't have any data!"

"Sure we do. Like here." She pointed to the bullet point marked *Ben-Vines*. "You have the incident listed, right? But you don't have the why's and how's."

"Were you not there? We don't know any of that," David argued.

"I beg to differ," Marisol retorted. "We know that they were most likely chemically signaling to one another. It was coordinated in some fashion. We know that damage to the plant caused an adverse reaction, i.e. they increased restriction and force. While we don't know *what* provoked it, we do know what affected it *once* provoked. Then again, I could argue the entire theory of plants being 'hostile' in general, but I'm not going to argue semantics."

"So, if we go back through and try to narrow down the why or the how, we'd be able to see a pattern?" Ben asked.

"In theory. I honestly don't know. The least you can do is make sure you have all the data and information for everything listed here."

"We've been at this for at least a couple of hours," David groaned, leaning his head back into his hands.

"Take a break, then. Go stretch your legs. It's not like we're on a deadline. I'm happy to take over for a bit," Marisol offered.

"The last thing I want to do is go walk outside. Especially with everything going on."

"To be fair, we could always use one more really detailed incident and data point to add to the chart," Marisol half-spoke, half-sang to him with a cheeky smile.

Ben's cheeks flushed a hot pink as he tamped down his smile. Marisol's joke created a harsh silence between them, everyone waiting to see the other's response. Marisol's smile grew, her eyes twinkling with her well-aimed hit. Ben bit down on his bottom lip and stifled a laugh as David's eyes narrowed onto her.

Ben cleared his throat and forced a straight face. "You could always take a nap or something."

"Yeah," Marisol joined in. "You were up early slaving over breakfast anyway." She caught his eye and winked.

"So glad you two are teaming up now," David said. He leaned his neck to the side, stretching out the tight muscles.

"Really though, take a break. You know staring at the same thing for hours doesn't do anyone any good," Ben said.

"Are *you* taking a break?" asked David.

"I will in a bit," Ben answered. "Promise."

"Alright, fine," David caved. "I'm going to go read up on your why's and how's. Consider it a working break. Shout if either of you have an epiphany."

"We'll be fine!" Marisol insisted. "Go refresh. Ben and I will crack the books and spend some nice, quality time together."

"That's what I'm worried about," he said, arching an eyebrow toward Marisol before ducking out of the tent.

"You're saying your first experience with weird things going on was only a couple of days in?" Ben asked, puzzled.

Marisol sat across from him, David's notebook in hand. The space between them was covered with splayed notebooks, loose pages, and binders filled with plant pressings. Marisol adjusted her legs, trying to maneuver within the cramped space. She flipped the pages in David's notebook, going back to the beginning. Her eyes moved over David's notes, detailing their travels so far.

"Right before we got to the second campsite, with the tent in the tree, we got boxed in by those red shoots...the ones that drape down from the trees."

"I didn't notice anything strange until I was out this far," Ben muttered, jotting down notes.

"When I spoke to Claudio, after Dr. Morrow but before the phones died, he said his guides couldn't even get to the first site."

"I remember you saying that when we first met. So, whatever is affecting the jungle is moving and getting more widespread?"

"You're assuming it's something affecting the jungle?"

"Wouldn't it be?"

"Not necessarily. I mean, it *could* be. Could be something like a parasite, an organism that affects the host and triggers these reactionary mechanisms. It could also be something as simple as variants in the species and how they grow. Either way, we need to look at it from an unbiased lens."

"No, I know," Ben agreed. "It's frustrating, though. I feel responsible, especially for you both. You wouldn't be in this if it weren't for me. I should be able to figure it out."

"That's silly." Marisol reached out to rest a hand on his leg, hesitating as she saw the bruising and scrapes from the vines etched across his skin. "You're not responsible, and this isn't on you, just like I know you probably said it wasn't on David, just like it's not on me. There's only so much you can do as one person."

"I could have followed the protocol and gone back to the lodge."

"You could have, but I'm pretty sure there are no actual protocols. You did your job, and you followed your gut to understand something you discovered. Any of us would have done it."

"Not so sure David would have."

"That's true," Marisol laughed. "But if it were up to him, he'd probably still be back home in Cali."

Ben stared down at his notebook in contemplation. The sudden silence made his skin crawl. "I'm sorry if I made things weird," he said, the words falling out all at once. "You know, with David."

"You didn't. Can't say it didn't surprise me, but it seems like a nice change for him."

"How's that?" Ben asked, meeting her eyes.

"As you've clearly seen, we're relatively new friends. Not only that, but the time we've spent together has forced us to get close, fast. He always came off a little sad. Since running into you, though, he's been brighter."

"Really?" Ben asked with a smile. "He's different. Honest… and sweet. It's refreshing. Being around him makes me nervous."

"Nervous?"

"In a good way," Ben added quickly. "Butterflies kind of nervous, you know? A good nervous, where I want to say the right thing or make him smile…I don't know."

A wide smile spread across her face as he spoke. "That's really sweet. You're both really genuine. Good hearts. That's hard to come by."

"Thanks," Ben smiled. "I don't know why I'm telling you all of this."

"I'd like to think it's because you and I are friends," Marisol chuckled. "But I also know I'm the only other person out here to talk to. That's not lost on me. Talk away."

"We're definitely friends. And thank you...again. So," he paused, "you think he feels the same?"

"It's not really my place." Marisol picked at her lip with her teeth. "But let's just say I don't think you have to worry about it."

Ben breathed a sigh of relief. "Good." He picked up the pencil from the spine of his notebook and set the tip to the page. "Alright, enough of this sappy talk. Read me off the next incident."

Marisol brushed her finger along the page with a swoosh. "Sappy talk checked off the list. Next." She looked down and scanned her page. "Speak of the devil." She glanced up with a grin. "David and the bamboo."

21

D avid stared at the shadows dancing along the ground. The sunlight shined through the canopy above, casting a kaleidoscopic pattern over the dead, fallen leaves and soggy earth. He listened to Marisol and Ben talking a few feet ahead of him as they made their way out of camp and back into the trails.

After a night of combing through notes and interpreting data, they started their morning already on edge. By the time they called it a night, David had written five pages of separate incidents, ranging from Marisol's second-hand information from her call to the lodge to their last 72 hours. Each incident appeared unrelated, and they ended the night more frustrated than they started.

They decided as a group that they would spend the day visiting the pond Ben and David had traveled to the day of Marisol's run-in with the ferns. It seemed like weeks ago since they had last traveled there, but Ben was steadfast in his opinion to steer clear of the normal pond and his favorite fishing spot. David and Marisol were quick to agree, knowing the risks from his last trip.

"You joining us for fishing this time, Marisol?" Ben asked, leading the way.

"I'm sure I can catch more than David," she said, raising her voice loud enough for David to hear as he trailed behind them. She twisted her head to take a glimpse behind her, sighing as she saw him several feet behind, trudging his way slowly after them. Marisol turned to Ben and muttered, "Deep in thought again."

Ben slowed and let her pass as he waited for David. "Hey there," he said, catching his attention as he approached.

"Hey?" David said, confused, redirecting his attention from the ground to Ben.

"You alright?"

"Yeah, why? *You* alright?"

"You were lagging behind and kind of zoned out. Wanted to make sure." Ben gave David's arm a quick squeeze.

David flashed him a small smile. "Just thinking."

"Want to walk together and you can talk to me about it?"

"Sure." David continued down the trail. He glanced up, seeing Marisol several feet ahead of them. "I have an idea, but you may think it's stupid," he said under his breath.

"I'm sure it's not stupid."

David stuck his hands in his pockets and fiddled with the hemming. "I want to try and prove some of the things we recorded yesterday. An experiment."

"...okay."

"I brought some petri dishes with me. I want to take random samples of the different flora—some we know have led to direct interactions recorded in the data and others we've never mentioned."

"And what are you trying to prove...or disprove?" Ben asked, wary.

"One of the hypotheses we discussed was a parasite or bacterium, something that's affecting the plants and is spreading throughout the forest."

"Right, but we don't have the equipment to look at things like bacteria. I don't know how yo—"

"I won't need to. I was reading one of the books about plant diseases. Most of it's fungal, and honestly not particularly helpful for much else. It said, though, you'd notice discoloration on the leaves or failure in the roots and stems. Some have flowers that grow malformed because of a parasitic fungus. We have photos and descriptions of most of these plants. If I take samples from several species—leaves, roots, stems, whatever, then I can see if any of them exhibit similar physical affects." David picked at his pockets as he waited for Ben to respond. "You think it's stupid."

"No, I don't. I-I just don't know how it helps."

David shrugged his shoulders. "One more thing to cross off the list."

"Say you do it and it is something like that. It's not like we can treat it."

"I know. That's what I've been trying to sort out in my head. If it's proven, what are the repercussions? What is the action plan? What does it mean for us and how does it work as a widespread thing? Is it a detriment to the plants? To the things that eat the plants? Does it change the ecosystem? Does it go out even past this reserve and across borders and—"

"Whoa there, killer," Ben said with a laugh. "Your brain really doesn't stop, does it?"

"Always on the lookout for an off-switch."

"Look, you can't be worrying about all of those things all of the time. It's bad for you, okay? And I'm going to be completely honest with you here. I don't know if it's worth pursuing. For one, it's risky. We don't know what sets this off, and I don't think I can do that again...I'm still kind of shaken up. Second, we need to come at this together. I don't want you taking unnecessary risks, and I know Marisol doesn't want that either."

"Alright," David conceded.

"Alright? Just like that?"

"Just like that." He turned, walking to catch up to Marisol.

Ben grabbed David's arm and pulled him to a stop. "Are we okay?"

David turned, looking Ben in the eyes. "Yeah, we're great." The corner of David's mouth turned up into a small smile. "I appreciate that you guys care. And you're right. It should be a group decision. I'm not used to that. I also know it's easy for me to get lost up here," he said, tapping his head. "I'm trying to work on that. I'm glad you can call me out on it."

"It wasn't a bad idea."

David's smile grew a little wider. "I know. I never said it was. I said *you* might think it's stupid." He leaned in and pecked Ben on the cheek. "I don't sit and think for hours to come up with bad ideas."

Ben let out a sharp laugh and shook his head as a large smirk crossed his face.

"What?" asked David, cocking his head.

"That was hot," Ben said through his smile. "That confidence is sexy."

"I wasn't trying to—"

"Shhh…" Ben held a finger up to his mouth. "Just let me have it."

David's cheeks flushed as he turned around and faced Marisol, now staring at them from down the trail. He took a deep breath and bit down hard on his bottom lip. He counted each step as he headed toward her, his cheeks burning as he tried to suppress the smile forcing itself across his face.

"You're getting scruffy," Marisol said, running her hand along David's face.

"I know. I hate it." David scratched at his face where Marisol had touched him. "My razor was in my bag that's now lost out here somewhere."

He looked out at the pond sprawled in front of them. It was every bit as beautiful as the first time he saw it. It was a true oasis. David took a few steps into the pond, letting his legs adjust to the cool water.

Marisol droned on next to him, studying his shaggy cheeks and chin. "Normally, I'm all for a little scruff, but I think you're meant to have a clean face."

"I wholeheartedly agree," David replied, half-listening. He couldn't tear his eyes away from the landscape, taking in the giant expanse of brackish water, the smooth surface nearly smothered by flowering water lilies and reeds.

"Hard to believe this all exists sometimes." Ben's deep voice chimed in from his other side. "I've swum pretty far out. There's a small tributary on the other side that empties into here. Harder to fish, but it makes the water perfect."

"It's amazing."

"It almost makes you forget all the craziness, doesn't it?"

"Almost." David frowned as his eyes moved over Ben's body. Dark purple bruises lined his arms and neck. He knew without having to look that they extended down and around his legs as well.

"It looks worse than it is." He brought his hand to David's face and lifted it to meet his eyes. "Stop worrying for a little bit."

"I don't know what to do if I'm not worrying."

"Well, let's change that," Ben said with a grin. "Let's go swim and shake off all of the grime and stress. Let's just *be* for a little bit."

Marisol swung her feet over the side of a fallen log as she perched a few feet above the pond. Water droplets dripped from her toes, causing ripples to expand outward on the smooth surface below. A light breeze blew over the water, bringing goosebumps across her skin. She ran her hands over her arms, rubbing the chill away.

Marisol let her vision drift to David and Ben swimming off in the distance. She reached behind her and fished a notepad and pencil out of her backpack. Flipping to a blank page, she set the pencil to paper and began writing. She spoke the words aloud as she wrote, measured and slow.

"Environmental factors: strange defensive-like reactions shown in primary forest, little to no human interference over time, tropical climate, soil compounds and alkalinity unknown." Marisol brought the end of the pencil to her lips and nibbled on the eraser. "How can I narrow you down?"

Hearing her name being called across the water, she glanced up, still chewing on the pencil. She saw the guys waving their arms, trying to get her attention. She raised her hand in the air and waved back, lifting her shoulders and shaking her head, questioning them. Ben lifted his arm high in the air and pointed behind them, to the middle of the pond. She followed his direction and brought her hand up to her mouth, suppressing a squeal. David waved his hand, calling her down and to the water.

Marisol scrambled off the log and down to the water's edge, kicking off her shorts and tank top. She slipped into the water and swam toward them, making sure to not make any splashes or loud noises. As she approached, David held a finger up to his mouth, gesturing for her to be quiet.

Marisol spun around as a spray of water erupted behind her. Her mouth dropped as a large, grey-ish pink mass popped up out of the water. Its small eye met hers before it disappeared again below the surface. She gasped as something slick and rubbery brushed up against her feet.

"This is wild," she whispered, her eyes the size of saucers. "Are they dangerous?"

"You ask that *after* you get in the water?" David whispered back. "And I hope not. It's been circling us for a few and nothing has happened so far."

"We're actually swimming with dolphins!" Marisol screeched, trying to keep her voice down.

Ben flinched as another spray of water splattered his back. He turned and stuck his hand out toward the dolphin only a few feet away from him.

"Be careful," Marisol hissed, as Ben's hand brushed against the dolphin's head.

The dolphin descended again, knocking into their legs as it dove beneath them. Water erupted several feet away as the dolphin jumped out of the water before disappearing beneath the surface. Several minutes passed as they waited, watching the water for movement, yet the pond remained still, save for the small ripples shimmering around their torsos.

"That was...I don't think I have words," David said, breathless. He sat on the shore, his feet digging into the warm mud.

"I'm happy to call it an afternoon after that," Ben said, a giant smile plastered on his face.

"Maybe it wanted the fish we caught," Marisol added, staring out at the still water.

"Or it saw you sitting all alone," Ben said, arching an eyebrow her direction.

"What do you mean?"

"The legends of the river dolphin." Ben turned away from the water to face her. "You said you know all about superstitions, right? Well, the Amazon is rife with cautionary tales and creation stories. The river dolphin appears in a ton of different oral histories. Here, for example, indigenous peoples throughout the Amazon believe the river dolphin has the ability to change into a very handsome man. He comes out of the river at night and preys on young women. He impregnates them and then returns to the river by morning, becoming a dolphin once more."

"Uh huh," Marisol said, raising an eyebrow. "And what exactly is the purpose of that one? All tales and legends have a purpose."

"Missed opportunity," David chided. "Should have said porpoise, not purpose."

Ben and Marisol stared at him, each shaking their head in feigned disappointment.

David held up his hands, containing a giggle. "Sorry. Go ahead, then."

"Horrible pun aside," Ben continued, turning back to Marisol, "it was mainly used as a way to explain unexplained pregnancies. It's different per region. In Brazil, they refer to a fatherless child as the son of a *boto...boto* being dolphin. On the flip-side, some think that the spirit of the river dolphin protects young boys while they're out fishing."

"So, we shouldn't leave Marisol alone, then? At least near a river?" David joked.

"Definitely not," Ben said, shaking his head dramatically. "It's also said river dolphins abduct lone swimmers and whisk them away to Encante, the underwater city. That said, you're also not supposed to look them in the eyes, or you'll have horrid nightmares for the rest of your life."

"Didn't you look it in the eyes when you touched it?" Marisol asked.

"Oh, please," David interjected.

"I didn't actually," Ben said, becoming serious. "I've spent enough time with the people here that I wouldn't risk it."

"You're kidding me," David scoffed.

"I know, but hear me out," Ben said, straightening and preparing for debate. "I spent months training with a shaman and learning the culture and the stories and the medicine. I experienced things I couldn't medically explain. It doesn't mean I'm not with you. I believe in science...*obviously*. It's just—"

"Why test it?" Marisol jumped in.

"Yeah," Ben nodded. "We know that the story was born out of a need to explain women getting knocked up. There are stories like that all over the world to cover up most of the unsavory things about humankind. I still stand by my thinking that there is always an explanation for superstition, but sometimes it's better to play it safe. I mean, I wouldn't be going and breaking a mirror on purpose just to test it."

"I'm not going to argue you," said David. "Just because I don't see things that way, doesn't mean you can't."

"Okay, but hold up a sec. Those cautions don't transfer over to locals calling this area cursed earth?" Marisol rebuffed.

"I'm not saying *not* to be cautious," Ben said. "We did go out of our way to come this way today. We don't know the why yet.

We don't know *why* they gave it that name or what it even explicitly refers to."

"I think it pretty explicitly refers to the fact that the plants out here have a mind of their own," David said.

Marisol released a heavy sigh as her eyes narrowed and bore into David's.

David leaned his head back, sighing. "What'd I say now?"

"I think I've been pretty clear about plants having a mind of their own. That's the whole point of what I've been saying this whole time."

"I didn't mean it like that. Obviously they do. I'm saying that to them, they didn't have the pleasure of listening to your thesis over and over again. Therefore, cursed earth refers to the fact that they can't explain why the plants here are like this."

"You didn't *have* to listen to my thesis 'over and over' again," Marisol said, rolling her eyes.

David's shoulders slumped. "Can we please not argue? We got to swim with a wild dolphin, we're in this beautiful little alcove in the rainforest, and no one has almost died today. Can we not appreciate that for a just a moment?"

Marisol side-eyed David as she went back to facing the water. "That doesn't sound like you."

"I'm trying to work on worrying less." He glanced over at Ben, who was already smiling at him. "Besides, this is the perfect place to sit back and brainstorm."

"I'll take notes!" Marisol beamed as she snatched her notebook and flipped it open.

"Do you two ever take a break?" Ben asked, laughing.

"I already gave in yesterday with taking a break and all it did was have us up late," said David. "You don't get anywhere if you're not working hard enough. Breakthroughs don't come from breaks. That's what my dad always told me when I was a kid."

"He said that to you as a *kid?*" Ben asked, his eyes wide.

David shrugged his shoulders in response.

"Breaks help keep the mind sharp," Ben continued. "That's a shitty thing to instill on your kid, that you can't take breaks."

"It got me this far," David said with another shrug.

"This far? You're up all hours of the night 'brainstorming.'" Ben threw his hands up in frustration. "You get panic attacks and crazy anxiety over not being able to solve problems and forcing yourself to work, I—"

Marisol grabbed at Ben's arm, cutting him off.

"I-I'm sorry," he stammered. "I didn't mean—"

"You're not wrong," David said. "It's okay."

"It's not okay. I shouldn't have said that." Ben's eyes welled up and he moved his mouth, as though he wanted to speak but couldn't find the words. He took a breath as he reached out and grasped David's hands in his. "It's just that I hate the idea of putting that kind of pressure on someone—especially a kid. You're smart, but you're also so much more than that. You don't need to push yourself that hard."

"It's all I know." David's eyes lifted to Ben's face. "I don't need you to worry about me."

"I want to worry about you," Ben said, holding onto David's hands even tighter.

Marisol leaned in and clasped her hands on top of both of theirs. "Friends worry about each other. I know you two are more than that, but at the base, it's friendship. David, you don't have to be what your dad or anyone else wants you to be, at least not while you're out here with us. If you want to lay back and get a tan and forget everything for a day, we can do that. If you want to brainstorm more ideas, that's fine too. But we're certainly not expecting you to work your ass off for us. We're in it just as much as you are."

David's eyes glanced from Ben to Marisol, both still holding his hands in his lap. He ground his teeth together, the muscles on his cheeks flexing as he clenched his jaw.

"I appreciate that," he said, letting each word drip off of his tongue, "but I don't need to be coddled." David pulled his hands out from under them and pushed up to his feet. He forced his shoulders down from his ears and looked down at the two of them. "I know you both think I'm fragile and maybe I'm a tad over-sensitive, but I don't need the two of you babying me."

"I wasn't trying to," Ben said, looking up at him from the ground.

"I know," David said, staring down into his eyes. "I'm gonna go for a walk. Clear my head."

"It's not safe," urged Marisol.

"I'll be fine. I'm not going anywhere."

Ben and Marisol exchanged a look as David walked off, heading for the edge of the tree line. Ben dropped his head into his hands as David's silhouette blended and disappeared into the tall palm trees ahead.

"I can't believe I said all that," he moaned into his palms.

"It's okay. He's not going to stay mad. He knows you care and that it comes from a good place."

"Does he?" Ben sighed, exasperated. He moved his hands up and through his hair, pushing the waves behind his ears.

"If he doesn't, he will. We've been cooped up together for a while now. Maybe he needs a little space."

Ben, stared out at the trees, trying to track David's path. "Should I go after him?"

Marisol shook her head and ran her hand across his thigh. "Give him a little time. He'll be okay."

22

D avid rolled a dark red seedpod in the palm of his hand. The outer shell was rough and lined with thick and black prickly hairs. He cracked it open between his fingers, the thin shell splintering to reveal dozens of hard red seeds. They tumbled out of the pod as he watched them land on the ground by his feet.

You shouldn't have walked off, he thought, digging the toe of his shoe into the wet dirt and burying the seeds. *They're going to think you're throwing a fit...a temper tantrum.*

David ran his hand along the shrub in front of him, his fingers brushing against more dangling seed pods. He crouched down and followed the stems down toward the ground.

"No mold," he muttered to himself. "No discoloration. Perfectly healthy."

He looked out behind the shrubs and into the dense jungle before him. His eyes followed stubby, green stems covered in bulbous red flowers to thin, orange vines draping down from the tree limbs. Small ferns at his feet obscured most of the ground ahead, and colorful bromeliads clung to the trunks of the distant trees, adding splashes of whites and purples in the dim light. David took a quick glance behind him before stepping over the ferns and into the thicket. He parted the vines as he stepped through, letting his fingers run down the rubbery shoots as they brushed along his face and shoulders. David squeezed past the crowded trees and crept further into the jungle.

He yanked on the vines, snapping them from the tree. David held them up to the small amount of light glittering through the canopy and inspected them. Using his nail, he peeled away the bright orange exterior to reveal the innards of the vine. He yanked more down from the tree and compared them. David wasn't sure what he was looking for, but he knew the vines were at least on the "known" list in his notes. The only notable difference he could decipher was the color variation. He reached into his pocket and pulled out his small notepad. His fingers flipped through the pages and stopped on a blank page. David fished a small pencil out of the same pocket and began writing.

Similar vine species – maybe the same. Color variant. Orange morphology in lieu of red. Could be due to exposure to sun. Nothing remarkable about location, condition, or description.

David snapped the notepad shut and returned it and the pencil to his pocket. He jumped up and pulled one more handful down, snapping them from the limbs above.

"I'll just save you for a sample later," he said, sticking one of them into his pocket and tossing the rest to the ground.

David eyed a flowering bush beyond the next set of shrubs. Little white flowers littered the ground and stood out amongst the myriad of brown and black leaves coating the jungle floor. Leaning his hand against a tree trunk for balance, he stepped over a pile of fallen and decaying branches, keeping his eyes on the ground. David gasped as his hand pushed, no, *sunk,* into the bark of the trunk, stopping him and sending his feet crunching into the branches underfoot. He lurched forward as the surface collapsed against the pressure and engulfed his hand.

A sudden warmth spread across David's skin and he yanked his hand away, losing his balance and falling through the branches. The wet and fragile wood snapped under his weight, sending him crashing to the ground. He glanced up at the tree to see a large hole in what he thought was part of the tree trunk.

David squinted his eyes, looking closer; his heart sank at the realization. It wasn't the tree trunk he fell through. It wasn't even part of the tree at all. Rough, brown, and bulbous, it surrounded the trunk, though now most of it had been disintegrated by his hand, leaving a gaping hole. The inside of the collapsed nest oscillated, the walls moving and wavering as he stared, his pupils dilating as they homed in on the source of the movement.

David's stomach flipped over on itself as his skin began to prickle and crawl. His eyes darted to his hand. Thousands of small, black termites covered his pale skin and skittered along his shirt sleeve, burrowing under the fabric and crawling along his arm. David shouted and flailed his arms, attempting to shake the termites off. He tore at his shirt, pulling it off and whipping it against himself, flinging the insects away.

"Fuck!" David yelled as the termites flew around his head, swarming the area around him. "Fuck, fuck, fuck!"

He dropped his shirt and swatted at his face and hair as termites bounced off his skin and landed around his eyes and mouth. The broken branches scratched at him as he pushed himself to his feet and dove through the trees and ferns. He backed out of the thick forest and into the open air, clawing at his neck and chest, the feeling of bugs tickling his skin still lingering. Goosebumps exploded along his skin as a cool sensation ran along his back and up to his shoulder. David yelped, whipping around.

"Whoa, it's just us!" Ben shouted, ducking as David turned, swinging an arm toward his head.

David stared wild-eyed at Ben and Marisol. He ruffled his hair with his hands and swatted at his arms. His heart pounded so quickly, he could hear it in his ears and feel it throbbing in his temples.

"You okay?" Ben asked, a look of concern spreading across his face. "We heard you yelling."

"Where's your shirt?" Marisol asked. "What the hell happened?"

"Nothing," David said, pushing past them and near-jogging

toward the water. As he got to the bank of the pond, he ripped off his pants and underwear and strode into the water without hesitation.

Ben and Marisol watched as David dunked his head under the surface.

"What was *that*?" Marisol asked.

"I have no—"

They both flinched as David's head reemerged and a loud, frustrated growl escaped his chest. Marisol looked sideways at Ben, who was still staring at David with a deep concern.

"Should I still be giving him space?" Ben asked, not breaking his gaze.

"I'd maybe go check on him." Marisol turned back to see David scratching at his neck and arms. "Let me know if I need to come in, too!" she yelled after Ben as he pulled off his shirt and headed into the water toward David.

"Please tell me there aren't a million bugs all over me right now?" David asked, squirming in the shallow bank.

"I don't see anything," Ben said, his tone cool and collected. "You want to tell me what's going on?"

"Termites," David shivered, closing his eyes. "Fucking *thousands* of termites." He brushed his hands down his arms and along the back of his neck.

"But you're okay?"

"Yeah, I'm fine." David rolled his shoulders and shook his head violently. "Still feels like they're all over me."

"Want me to check more thoroughly?" Ben parted David's hair while leaning on him, forcing David to lower himself into the water. "I still don't see anything." He ran his hands along David's shoulders as if to smooth out the goosebumps that still lingered on his skin.

David twisted around to face him. "Thanks."

"About before, what I said..."

"Don't," David spoke over him. "I know all of those things are true, but it's also who I am. And I wasn't mad. I'm not mad. I-I need…"

"Needed some space?"

David nodded. He stood up and leaned into Ben, embracing him. The cold wetness of Ben's body quashed the crawling sensation still vibrating along his skin.

"I'm working on it," David said into Ben's shoulder. "I don't want you to think I was upset with you."

Ben squeezed him back and then pulled away, resting his hands around David's waist. "It's a hard topic for me." Ben's eyes fixed on the water lapping at their legs. He hesitated, clearing his throat. "My high school boyfriend—we were still closeted at the time…he was never good enough for his parents. It was one of the reasons why he couldn't come out. He needed straight A's and to be the top of all his extracurriculars. 'Ivy league or else' type of mentality, you know? It was either perfection or getting shamed into feeling like he was stupid and worthless. It really messed him up."

"That sounds awful, but…it wasn't like that for me." David lifted his hands to Ben's arms. "My mom honestly didn't care what I did, but my dad always lectured me about working as hard as you can and that real success takes doing things for yourself. It made me feel shitty at the time, but it's made me get to where I am, and I'm okay with that."

"I'm glad…even though you shouldn't have had to put up with that. No one should. Ever since…well, ever since that time, I swore I'd never be hard on anyone like that. My parents were always encouraging and forgiving. But his…they never let up. He was sarcastic and so funny and kind. And they took that all away because they wanted him to be perfect. Their version of perfect, at least."

"I didn't know all of that. I'm sorry."

"It's okay. He crosses my mind every now and again. He, um…he killed himself senior year." Ben looked up at David with watery eyes. "He got two rejections from Princeton and Yale—

his mom and dad's schools. I'd never seen him so upset. Not only was he worried they'd hate him for being gay but then there was the fear of being a disappointment to them. I always hoped his parents never stopped hurting for making him feel like that. All for what, you know? Their idea of success that they forced on him?"

"I'm so sorry," David whispered, pulling Ben in and hugging him tight.

Ben leaned in tighter, talking into the nape of David's neck. "No one should have to feel that kind of pressure to be perfect. But I shouldn't have said those things to you."

"Well, I'm not going anywhere. I can't control when I get things like panic attacks, and I know that I should be less anxious...like a *lot* less anxious. But like I told you before, I've dealt with this stuff since I was a teenager, and who knows where it came from. Maybe my parents, maybe genetics, maybe it's because I didn't know how to be who I am...but it's never stopped me. It may feel like the end of the world sometimes, but there's plenty of good, too."

Ben lifted his head from David and wiped at his eyes with the corner of his hand. "Promise me you're going to take it a little easier on yourself?"

"Okay." David forced a small smile. "I promise."

"I can't believe I told you that. I don't think I've ever talked about him with anybody."

"I'm glad you did." David looked back toward the tree line and saw Marisol sitting on the ground with her notebook in hand. "I'm happy I met you guys."

"Same. Now that I've made this more awkward than it needed to be, what do you say we head back to camp and call it a day? I think it's safe to say we've had enough stress for one afternoon." Ben grabbed David's hand and intertwined his fingers with his. "Times like these, I really miss being able to go have a stiff drink."

A light drizzle of rain started as they made their way back to camp. By the time they made it back to their tents, it had become a full downpour. David peeled off his pants and left them hanging from the weather guard leading into the tent. Ben sprawled out on his sleeping bag in his briefs, a book in hand. The slapping of the rain against the tent drowned out the noise from the jungle, leaving him and David encompassed in a constant din of water ricocheting off the vinyl fabric.

"I can't believe I'm down another shirt. I think I'm officially running out of clothes," David groaned as he dug through his backpack. "Between losing my bag with my extras and now today…"

"Well, you won't find me complaining," Ben smirked. "But you know you can always wear any of my things."

David laughed, looking over his shoulder. "Oh, like your tight-ass tank tops? No thanks. Maybe if you want them permanently stretched out. I couldn't pull those off if I tried."

Ben stretched his leg out and pushed at David's back with his foot. "I wouldn't mind seeing you in a tight shirt."

"Yeah, then Marisol wouldn't let me hear the end of it. She'd somehow magically have a goddamn camera and post it everywhere."

Ben nudged David harder with his toes. "I'd just buy the rights to them then. Problem solved."

David shook his head while continuing to laugh, happy that Ben wasn't dwelling on their conversation from earlier. "Do you ever stop flirting?"

"Depends. Has it stopped working?"

"…not yet."

"Then no. My goal is to see how red you get."

"That wouldn't take much," David said more to himself than to Ben.

Ben crawled over to David and pulled him backwards and

onto the sleeping bag with him. He tugged at his rain-soaked underwear while kissing along the back of his neck.

"Why are you even still wearing these?" Ben asked, grinning.

David pushed his back into Ben and turned his head to kiss him. "Because I'm trying to see how many I have left so I can plan accordingly. I like to be prepared," he said, pulling his lips away.

"Can't that wait until morning?" Ben leaned in for another kiss. "Besides, I'm not letting you curl up with me in those. You're cold and wet." Ben moved his lips to David's collarbone. "So? Can you please take these off and worry about that tomorrow?"

David sighed, letting Ben slide his briefs off. "Fine." He yanked the sleeping bag out from under them to cover himself. "You're impossible to say no to."

Marisol sat in her tent with her sleeping bag wrapped over and around her head, forming a tight ball of nylon around her. Small stacks of books surrounded her, illuminated by the LED lantern at her side. Long shadows stretched and danced along the inside of the tent as the rain continued to fall in heavy sheets outside.

She watched the shadows waver as the vinyl siding of the tent vibrated from the unrelenting raindrops. Her eyes moved to the space next to her, now filled with a pile of clothes and assorted textbooks. She missed David's company, even his complaining and moping. A night like this, with the rain and the wind, she pictured them tucked into their sleeping bags reading the next chapter of *King Solomon's Mines* as David pointed out which sections were based on actual expeditions and which were fiction. She found her gaze drifting to the other tent, beyond her own and across the clearing.

Marisol let out a soft sigh before redirecting her attention to the book in front of her, flipping it closed and stacking it on top of the others next to her. She laid down, pulling the cocoon of her sleeping bag tighter against her body before flipping the knob on her lantern, plunging the tent into darkness. Closing her eyes, her mind drifted to Dr. Morrow as she wondered if she was still out there somewhere. Images of the professor wandering the trails and being snatched up by the surrounding plants sent a shiver down her spine. After all of their struggles, they still weren't any closer to figuring out where she went and if she was okay...or if they'd ever find her. She felt guilty for finding moments of enjoyment, for laughing and having fun between the feelings of fear and worry. Those feelings were enough to haunt her thoughts most nights, but Marisol knew Dr. Morrow's best chance was if they could get out and find help. With a sigh, she tried to clear her head, shifting her focus from all the what-ifs and onto the loud thudding of the rain.

"That was...amazing," David said, breathless.

"Yeah it was," Ben said, his lips curling into a satisfied smile. His eyes bore into David's as he propped himself up on his elbow and hovered over him. "I could lay here and look at you forever."

David felt the air leave his lungs as the words left Ben's mouth. "I...uh," he fumbled, his face flushing. He wasn't even certain his heart was still beating. "I—"

"Should I not have said that?" Ben asked, biting his bottom lip, the look in his eyes changing from desire to concern.

"No, I..." David stammered. His stomach fluttered so intensely that he wondered if there was a name for it. He knew butterflies didn't swarm. Maybe, instead of butterflies, it was bees or locusts or bats. Definitely not simple butterflies. "I, uh...I don't really know what to say to that."

"You don't have to say anything." Ben blinked, hesitating. "But you can kiss me."

David stared up at him, expecting a cheeky grin or a subtle wink, but all he saw was Ben looking down at him, truly *at* him.

The sound of the rain faded into the distance. All David could hear was the thumping of his heart against his chest.

"That I can do." He pushed himself up on his elbows and pressed his lips against Ben's. He smiled against his lips as Ben's hair fell over him and tickled his face. He kissed his way down along his neck and to his shoulders, taking a minute to press his hand against Ben's chest to feel his heart beating alongside his. He held it there, lingering, feeling their rhythms create a chorus together—a steady thrumming that mixed with the rain and filled his entire body up until they were synchronized and singing together. He lifted his head to catch Ben's eyes, still staring down at him. He smiled.

Ben matched the smile with his own. "You okay?"

"Never been better."

23

"Stop," David whined, adjusting in his sleep, and tucking his right foot back under the sleeping bag draped over him.

Ben cuddled closer against David under their makeshift blanket. His leg draped over David's as he held him close along his waist, nuzzling his head into his chest. David's arm rested along his back, keeping him pulled tight against him.

A light tickling brushed against David's ankle as his foot shifted out from the sleeping bag. He moaned as he pulled his foot back, tucking it again under cover.

"I said stop," David grumbled, his eyes still shut. He lifted his arm off Ben and shifted, rolling over to his side.

"Stop what?" Ben groaned into David's back, turning to spoon him. He pressed up against his back and threw an arm back around his waist.

"Nothing. Go back to sleep."

David's breathing slowed as he felt Ben's heart beating steadily against his back. He let his body relax again to try and fall back asleep as Ben's soft breathing filled his ears. David huffed a frustrated sigh, feeling a small pull against his calf. Annoyed, he tugged his leg up and away from Ben.

"Dude," David whined against the sleeping bag, adjusting again. "Stop touching me."

Ben let out a small groan, rolling away from him and onto his back. "Sorry," he muttered, still half-asleep.

David flipped onto his back in response. He rubbed his eyes and opened them, looking up at the top of the tent. He tilted his head as he yawned, seeing Ben beside him, mouth hanging open and his chest rising and falling in a quiet rhythm. Despite his frustration, he smiled as he watched Ben sleep, and the agitation of being woken up melted away.

David's smile morphed into a frown, feeling the same pressure against his leg again. His eyes moved down Ben's body under the sleeping bag and to his legs. He laid sleeping, perfectly still. David's heartbeat hammered in his chest as he stared at Ben, the pressure returning, now a creeping sensation, moving up his leg and along his skin. He ripped the sleeping bag off and looked down.

"Oh shit!"

Marisol shot up from her sleeping bag, jarred awake by David yelling out from across the camp. She fumbled at the zipper to her tent and tripped out into the damp morning air. Her bare feet slid against the wet leaves, kicking her feet up from underneath her and sending her careening into the wet mud. Marisol yelped, a sharp pain radiating up her arm as she hit the ground. Her head whipped forward, hearing David and Ben's voices shouting over each other from the tent. Cradling her arm, she pushed herself to her feet and ran toward them.

Slick, rubbery plant matter squished under her feet as Marisol approached the tent. Gasping, she skid to a stop and looked down, lifting her foot to see a trail of vines twisting their way past the zipper and into the door flap. She yanked the zipper open and ducked her head inside.

"Oh my God!" she yelled, covering her mouth.

David had pushed himself up against the back of the tent. The vines snaked along the floor and up and around David's right leg. The green tendrils spiraled around his foot and up past his knee. Marisol's eyes darted to Ben, who had his hands, along with David's, wrapped around David's leg, trying to stop the vines from moving any further up his body.

"What do I do?" Marisol asked, trying to stay calm.

"Did you see where it's coming from?" David asked, grimacing. "If there's one, maybe we can uproot it."

Marisol rushed out of the tent, nearly ripping the weather guard from the poles, and followed the vines, tracking them as they lead under David's still-soaked pants from the day prior. Rushing, she snatched at the khakis, pausing as they caught in her hand when she lifted them, somehow tethered to the ground by the unrelenting plants. She dropped to her knees, ran her hand along the roots and traced them as they stretched from the ground and through the fabric of the pants. Marisol's face scrunched in confusion as the rubbery shoots wove through the fabric of the khakis and into one of the pockets. She attempted to rip the pants away from the vine, but the tendrils held it secured to the ground. Helpless, she resigned with a hefty sigh and crawled back into the opening of the tent, only to see the vines continuing to creep up and along David's legs, overtaking their hands.

"They're coming from right outside. I couldn't see where it started, but they're woven all in the pants you left drying from yesterday. Do you want me to try and uproot it?"

"There's no time. We need to get him out of this, fast," Ben said, pushing down against the encroaching vines. "These are really tight."

"I keep telling you to move your hands!" David snapped.

"No! They're just going to keep going, and you don't want them any higher."

"It'll be fine. You have to trust me." David looked up at Marisol, wincing as the vines tightened around his leg. "Please."

Marisol's eyes were wide as they moved over David. "I...I think we should listen to him."

"Are you crazy?" Ben pushed harder against the vines, eliciting a small yelp from David.

Marisol's eyes flickered to David's. His chest heaved quickly with shallow breaths as he met her eyes, pleading with his own. With a steadying breath, she clambered over and grabbed onto Ben's arm, trying to move him off David's leg. "You're making it worse," she cautioned.

Ben shook her off and continued to push down on the vines. "I can't just sit here and watch him get hurt."

"He did it for you," she said, her voice stern and steady.

David moved his hand to Ben's and squeezed. "It'll be okay. Please trust me."

Ben looked from David to Marisol and back to the vines gripping at David's flesh. He released his grip on David's leg and sat back, pulling his knees up to his chest and wrapping his arms around his legs.

"Okay," David breathed. "We're going to wait."

Marisol sat next to Ben. He leaned into her while they watched the vines dig tighter against David's skin. She held her arm, rubbing her sore elbow as she nibbled her bottom lip.

David glanced over to her. "What's wrong? Did you hurt yourself?"

Marisol forced a smile. "Don't worry about me."

A choking laugh slipped from his lips. He flinched, and Marisol saw his hands contract into fists alongside him. "Well, I have to worry about someone other than me. I need the distraction."

"Then you'll have to find something else. It's nothing more than a bruise. I swear."

"I hate this," Ben quipped. "How can you two pretend everything is okay right now?"

David stared at Ben, holding his gaze. "What else am I going to do? There's no use fighting it. We know that."

"How do we know it's the same? That's a wild assumption."

David looked down at his leg. The vines had made their way to his mid-thigh. "It has to be. I think it stopped climbing. I mean, it still hurts, and I can't really feel my foot or the bottom half of my leg, but I don't think it's progressing anymore."

"Really?" Marisol asked, leaning up on her knees and looking over David. "Fascinating."

David glanced over to Ben, hearing him let out an angry huff in response. He directed his eyes to Marisol and raised his eyebrows. Marisol pushed herself back beside Ben and rubbed her hand between his shoulder blades.

"Why don't we go make David a hot cup of coffee?" she asked, leaning her shoulder into Ben. "We should have enough for a few more cups, don't you think?" She raised her eyes to meet David's.

"I would love that actually," David added. "If you don't mind."

Ben narrowed his eyes, glaring between Marisol and David. "I know what you're doing."

"So, that's a 'no' on the coffee then?" asked David.

"Fine," Ben sighed, unwrapping his hands from his legs. "Let's go figure out why it takes two people to make a cup of coffee that he's clearly not even going to drink."

"You said it was nothing more than a bruise," Ben said, as he applied gentle pressure up and down Marisol's arm.

Marisol winced as Ben prodded around her elbow. "I don't need him worrying about me."

"You can move it, but that doesn't mean it's not a fracture. I can make you a sling if you want it. That's about all I can do."

"No, I'll be fine. It hurts like a bitch, but it's nothing I can't handle."

"David did say you were tough as nails."

"He did?"

"Yep. Although I'd say the same thing about him. I know how much pain I was in the other day, and he's not even showing it."

"You really care about him."

Ben nodded. "I keep having to tell myself that we basically just met. He has me kind of hooked."

"I think that's nice." Marisol folded her legs and tossed her hair over her shoulder. "I hate to admit it because of my oh-so-cool reputation and all that, but he's grown on me, too. I was thinking last night about how much I missed having him around in the evenings. It's stupid, but being out here together, we were more or less forced to become fast friends."

"Sorry if I got in the middle of that."

"He needs someone like you. Someone to loosen him up some. I tried, but..." Marisol shrugged. "So, don't go thinking you got in the middle of anything. It's nice to see him smiling."

Ben blushed as he looked back toward the tent. "Do you think we waited long enough? Can we go check on him?"

"Sure." Marisol laughed, pointing to the thermos by Ben's feet. "Don't forget the coffee."

Ben grabbed the pot from over the fire and poured the coffee into the thermos, raising it up to Marisol. "Fingers crossed?"

David looked up as they ducked into the tent, a loose vine dangling in his hand. He sat cross-legged against the back of the tent, the rest of the vines around his legs in small heaps. Aside from the red impressions still lingering on his skin, he was no worse for wear.

"What...I..." Ben started, his jaw dropping.

David smiled out of the corner of his mouth. "I told you to trust me."

Marisol rushed forward and into David's arms, giving him a hug and ignoring the sharp pain in her arm. "I am so glad you're okay."

"I think I figured it out," he whispered into her ear as a grin stretched across his face.

She pushed herself away from him, practically sitting in his lap as his hands rested against her lower back. "Figured what out?"

David smiled wider as his eyes moved between her and Ben in the small tent. "The whole thing."

Ben and Marisol collected the detached vines from the tent. They carried them a few yards into the jungle and left them, not waiting to see what would happen if they lingered too long. They found David pacing in a circle around the campfire when they returned, the thermos of coffee still clutched tight in his hands.

"Well?" David asked, stopping and watching as they approached from the surrounding trees.

"We didn't hang around to see if anything happened," Marisol said, walking up to him and holding out her hand as David passed the thermos to her.

"I wanted to," Ben added. "But after everything, it seemed way too risky."

"I agree," David said. "I'm glad you're both safe."

"Yeah, yeah, safe is great and all, but you can't drop a bombshell like knowing what the hell is happening and expect us to sit back and pretend this is going to be a normal conversation," Marisol pressed.

"Just promise me you'll have an open mind," David said, sitting down on the ground and motioning for them to join.

"I think it would be impossible not to," said Ben, plopping down across from him.

"So," Marisol said as she sat next to Ben and took a sip of coffee from the thermos. "Lay it on us."

"Okay. Hear me out." David took a deep breath. "To distract myself from what was going on, I started thinking back to the other day when you were talking about the why's and how's of each incident we have recorded. I realized that we came up with the how's, right? Like, the vines on Ben loosened when we didn't mess with them. The how was the vines falling off and we *thought* the why was that they were being injured or felt threatened."

"But that was the direct correlation. That's a why," Marisol said. "The vines reacted that way because of the physical stimulus."

"Maybe at *that* stage of things," David continued. "But the real why is unknown. The question isn't why did they fall off of him, the question is why did it happen in the first place? Why have any of them happened?"

"But none of our incidents were linked that way," Ben said. "You said yourself that they weren't related."

"I was wrong." David grinned. "They were. Marisol, if you hadn't explained your thesis to me a dozen times over, I would still be lost."

"I think we're *all* lost right now," Marisol said dryly.

"You basically read me your thesis verbatim, laying out the processes of what goes on in the plants and when they use their defenses. If I understood correctly, and I think I did, it explains almost everything. Some plants change their composition to deal with the environmental changes they're facing, and some deal with direct threats, right?"

"Right?" Marisol echoed back, confused.

"You said people don't even know what's in their own gardens, that plants are constantly evolving and changing to their surroundings, protecting themselves."

"But how is that relevant? We're not in a botanical garden or studying some retiree's window box," Ben interjected.

"No," David said, looking at Ben, "we're in something way bigger. But say we were looking at a smaller scale ecosystem, a home garden—let's look at foxglove, for instance. To protect against natural predators, like deer, it creates volatile chemicals to discourage consumption. Marisol, you told me about trichomes and how they basically are meant to impale insects that are trying to eat the leaves of the plant or like Venus flytraps which move when the trichomes are touched by prey. And then chem—"

"Are you just going to cite my entire project back to me?" Marisol asked, impatient.

"Chemical signaling," David pressed on, raising his voice and talking over her. "Plants warning each other of an impending attack from things like caterpillars or browsers. All of these different methods of protecting themselves from predators and potential danger are inherent."

"What are you getting at, David?" Marisol sighed, crossing her arms. "None of this is new information."

"You're right. It's not. These are all normal things in the majority of plant life anywhere in the world."

"I'm not getting it," Ben said, shaking his head.

David looked back and forth between them, taking another deep breath. "*We're* the why."

"What?" Ben and Marisol said in unison.

"It's us. We're the common denominator. We're the threat here. Not herbivores. Not insects. Us."

Ben and Marisol glanced at each other out of the corner of their eyes before turning their attention back to David.

"Think about it," he said. "The plants are using their normal defenses, just at a larger scale. What they use on bugs and monkeys, they're using on us but magnified. We're at the cusp of a million acres of rainforest previously untouched by mankind. Never explored. Never studied. We're the biggest threat to this ecosystem right now. Ben didn't run into trouble until he pushed further in. He traveled deeper into the gridline and into territories people have never seen. We come in with our machetes and clear paths and make camps. Hell, our tent over there is complete with binders filled to the brim with samples we've cut from different species. We've hacked these plants into pieces to study them. We're here with the intention of learning about them, but all we're doing is endangering them." David ran a hand along the back of his neck. "I'm not crazy."

"I don't think you're crazy," Ben said, slowly. "It's that, well..." He trailed off, looking to Marisol to jump in.

"It...it kind of makes sense?" Marisol turned from Ben to

David. "I mean, most of what's happened has come after we've blazed trails, uprooted different plants, or taken samples, right?"

"It has to make sense," David jumped back in. "And I'm the prime example. Those vines came from the pieces I took yesterday. They had to. With everything that happened yesterday, I forgot I put them in my pocket. And then after the rain, I stripped down and left them outside the tent. But this is where it hit me...my feet were right next to Ben's. He was actually closer to the door than I was, but they wrapped around *my* leg. It targeted *me* as the danger." He turned to Ben. "You cut an alcove off the trail to take a break before they got to you. And you," he said, looking over at Marisol. "You said those ferns didn't start releasing fibers until you were several feet in. If they released trichomes on touch alone, you would have activated their release on your first step into them. It all fits." David tapped at his legs, picking at the khaki fabric. "This whole section of the jungle, shit, maybe even the whole reserve, is defending itself. Only instead of defending itself from normal, everyday things it encounters, it's protecting itself from *us*. Maybe that's why it's been unexplored for so long."

"Or if it has been explored, no one has been able to make their way back out," Marisol added. "Nelly did say, before she left, that this place wasn't meant for us. Maybe that's why they think it's cursed. It repels any advances, like one giant organism communicating within itself to stop the threat."

"I don't know, guys," Ben said, shifting in place.

"I know it sounds crazy..." said David.

"...but it actually does make sense," Marisol finished for him. "When we all got separated, it was after we cut down a ton of stuff, like we were slicing and dicing our way through the woods. Ben, you said that the most activity you recorded was after you made a new trail. And Dr. Morrow..." Marisol lowered her eyes, letting the thought go. "Look, as someone who lives and breathes this area of study, I have to say, what David says tracks."

"I trust you, I do. It's just a lot to consider." Ben rested his head in his hands as he took a deep breath. "I guess it's no stranger than stories I've heard from the indigenous tribes. Like I said before, superstition is steeped in truth, no matter how bizarre those truths may be. A cursed jungle could easily be the excuse for an inhospitable environment or hostile landscape. For all we know, there were telltale signs the local guides knew that we overlooked—things that have been passed down, things we would easily ignore if we didn't know the local lore." Ben combed his fingers through his hair, tucking it behind his ears. "If I had only waited…"

"Would you have listened to them?" Marisol asked.

"Honestly? Probably not. But, tell me this…if we're such a negative impact on the ecosystem here, why wouldn't the jungle let us leave? Why not push us back out?"

"Maybe it's like a pitcher plant. Keeping us in until we eventually succumb," said Marisol.

"What it comes down to," David interjected, "is if it *is* keeping us here, what do we do? Fight our way out? Give up? Do we try and prove it?"

"Proving it sounds dangerous," said Ben.

David pushed himself up to his feet and paced back and forth in front of them. "I have an idea. It's potentially dangerous but could kill two birds with one stone."

"Probably not the best turn of phrase to use there," Marisol chimed.

"If it works, we could prove it *and* get ourselves out of here."

Ben sat up straighter and nervously bit at his lip. "What is it?"

David rubbed his temples and closed his eyes. He opened them to see Ben and Marisol staring back at him. A heavy sigh escaped his lungs as he crossed his arms in front of his chest. "I say we try to hike our way out."

24

D avid crossed the camp, taking soft and careful steps across the slippery leaves. A constant, light rain caused a misty haze to hang over the camp, as though it were trapped in a dense cloud. The crickets and cicadas were deafening in the night air, their chirps flooding the foliage encircling the camp. He glanced up into the limbs above, squinting against the gentle raindrops, taking in the handful of stars peeking through the small gaps in the canopy.

He approached Marisol's tent. A faint glow illuminated the fabric and projected her silhouette against the vinyl siding. "Marisol?" David called out, his voice low and hushed. "You still up?"

"Um...light's on, isn't it?" Marisol replied back flatly.

David unzipped the door and crouched down, sticking his head inside. "Well, I know that. I didn't know if you had fallen asleep or not. Can I come in?"

Marisol scooted over, making room, and David crawled into the tent and sat across from her.

"Can't sleep?" she asked.

David shook his head. "Too anxious. Do you think we're doing the right thing? What if my plan gets us worse off than we are now?"

"Are you second guessing yourself?"

"No...yes...no...I don't know. I'm not second guessing myself per se, more like dwelling on everything that can happen or go wrong. When I came up with this plan a week ago, I was sure it was the right thing. We've spent this whole time whittling down our supplies, batch-cooking those grubs as trail mix—which don't even get me started on—condensing what we need to take with us, trying to troubleshoot potential problems. What if by doing all of that, it was a week wasted? What if this all ends in a complete disaster?"

"You know you can't control the outcome no matter what we choose to do, right? It's a solid plan, and yes, there are things that can go wrong in any scenario, but you can't worry about that."

"I know."

"Do you? Because you haven't been up wandering around at night in almost two weeks." Marisol narrowed her eyes at David, raising her eyebrows in question. She softened at the look of perplexity taking over his face. "I know you used to get up and go slink around the camp in the middle of the night. You don't have to pretend."

"I always assumed you were sleeping," David said, lowering his eyes. "And I wasn't *slinking*. I don't sleep well, especially not out here."

"You seem to have been sleeping fine lately."

He looked back up to her. "Haven't been in my head as much, I guess."

"And you're back to overthinking because of us trying to leave in the morning? We have it all planned out. Like you said, we've been planning this whole week, and it's going to be fine. It's worth the shot."

"I don't know what I'm doing, though. I'm trying to grapple with things that I don't understand and that I'm not comfortable with."

"What do you mean?"

"Marisol, I'm not Ben...or you. I've been floundering here

since we got off the plane. I'd feel better if this were a plan from either of you, not me."

"I am actually going to stop and disagree with you there," Marisol said, straightening her posture. "I think you've really come into your own since being out here."

David arched an eyebrow. "Seriously?"

"This week, I have seen you more sure of yourself and you have shown more confidence than I ever thought you could." Marisol rested a hand on David's knee. "Me and Ben? We believe in you. You jumped in and took care of me when I was hurt. You saved Ben, all on your own. You put the pieces together when we couldn't. I don't think you realize how much of us getting through this has been on you."

David's eyes focused on Marisol's hand resting on his knee. His thoughts raced as he tried to find the words to express his worry and hesitation.

"Hey," Marisol said, bending forward to catch his eye. "I mean it. And I'm sorry if this makes you uncomfortable, but ever since getting together with Ben, you've become more...*you*."

"Maybe," David shrugged. "You didn't even know me before."

"I knew you when you bitched the entire layover at the airport, or when you wouldn't look me in the eye until we were almost tearing each other's throats out. I may not have known you back home, but I've spent enough time with you out here. And trust me, you're different when you're with him. You're brave. You're adventurous. You seem happy." Marisol's eyes bore into him.

David looked up to meet her eyes. "I am happy. I'm just...I'm scared."

"Of what?"

He hesitated, licking his lips before picking at the small flakes of peeling skin with his teeth. "I'm worried I'm going to lose this feeling, that I'm being stupid because everything here is so overwhelming, scared because we're constantly facing some kind of danger. What if I only feel this way because of all that? And what if I ruin it? What happens if this all works and everything changes?"

"Not that this comes as a surprise, but I don't think I'm following you. What feeling? Being scared?"

David shook his head and stared at the cover of the sleeping bag tucked underneath them. "With Ben." His fingers picked at the skin of his arms as he raised his eyes to Marisol. "You know that feeling you get when you're on a roller coaster? Like when you're going down a big drop and your stomach kind of floats for a second in mid-air? It feels like that."

Marisol took in a breath as a smile spread across her face. She squeezed her hand where it still rested against David's knee. "It sounds like love."

"It's not love," David scoffed.

"And why not?"

"Because I've only known him, like, a little over two weeks. You can't be in love with someone after two weeks."

"Sure you can. There's no rulebook for falling for someone. And face it, you two are perfect for each other. Yeah, it's a little much to be around twenty-four hours a day when I can't exactly escape it, but you're a perfect match. He brings you out of your shell, and you let him be all gooey and mushy. You guys fit."

David's eyes shifted as he stared back down between them. "But what if he doesn't feel the same way?" He half-whispered the words, barely saying them aloud. "That's what scares me. What if I only feel like this because of the situation we're in? What if *he* only feels the way he does because I'm the one person out here to settle with?"

"First of all," Marisol said, reaching up and grabbing his upper arm to catch his attention, "he could never be settling with you, okay?" She waited for David to acknowledge her. "Second, I think that's something you're going to have to risk. To me, it doesn't matter if you met him on campus or an app or in the middle of the jungle. That doesn't change anything about you except that maybe you're a little more daring because you have to be. I can't tell you what to do.

You're going to have to trust your gut. If your gut says you're in love with him, then you're in love with him. And it's okay to feel that way. There's no *right* way to feel, you know?"

"But...I've...I've never said it to anyone. I don't even know if that's what it is. And that's not even trying to figure out how any of this would work."

"Not everything is planned out in a list, David. And I don't care what you say, but you two have this insane, albeit sometimes sickeningly annoying chemistry. You really do. You have to stop living your life being scared of trying things, of experiencing things. He brings that out in you. You should hold onto it. Jump off a cliff every now and again."

David's eyes welled up. He closed them and swallowed, his throat tightening in response as he tried to stop the flow of tears he knew were inevitable.

"I don't know how to do this, though. I don't..." David stopped, the warm trickle escaping down his cheek. He brushed it away, getting angry. "I'm sorry for constantly being so goddamn emotional. It's so annoying. It's just...this is all so overwhelming."

"So, don't worry about it right now. I know it may not help, but I know he likes you. Like, he like-likes you. And I truly don't think you have to worry about his feelings toward you. He likes you for who you are, even all of this," she said, waving her hand up and down in front of him.

David laughed through his tears and wiped at his face with the side of his hand.

"Even if he didn't tell me, *which he did*, I see the way he looks at you. You've got nothing to worry about."

"Thanks." He looked at Marisol through his teary eyes. "I miss this, you know. Hanging out together one-on-one."

"Yeah," she smiled, "I've missed this too."

"I know I basically made a fool out of myself right now, but can I stay in here tonight, for old time's sake? The thought of shrinking down to one tent after tonight makes me claustrophobic, and I don't want to pass up on a little extra time together. May be our last chance."

"I would love that. And it *is* going to be our last chance because your plan is going to work. Next thing you know, we'll be at the lodge, in real beds." Marisol turned, looking around her. "I do only have the one sleeping bag, though."

"That's okay," David said, running the palms of his hands over his face, wiping away the wetness. "Ben literally takes both of ours by the middle of the night. I'm used to it."

"And that's what you want to stick with? A blanket thief?"

David laughed as he shimmied down on the floor mat and laid next to Marisol. "Eh…the other perks make up for it."

He reached over and turned the lantern off, the LED light leaving small flashes in his vision as his eyes adjusted to the pitch black. David lifted his arm as Marisol sidled up to him and rested her head on his shoulder. David could still feel the tightness in his chest as he thought about embarking tomorrow, his plan a week in the making. He hoped he wouldn't let them all down—or worse, get anyone hurt.

"So," Marisol said into the dark, interrupting his spinning thoughts. "Talk to me about these other perks."

"No!" David laughed, feeling Marisol doing the same against him. "Go to sleep."

David was awake and pacing around the middle of the camp before the sun came up. He watched the canopy lighten, shifting from light orange-pink to baby blue as the sun burnt away the sunrise. His stomach had been in knots all morning. He couldn't tell whether he wanted to vomit from the nerves or curl up in the corner of the tent and fall asleep forever. David watched Marisol sleep for a bit but couldn't get comfortable. He tried deep breathing, but that made him more anxious. After what felt like laying and staring at the roof of the tent for hours, he got up and went outside, and had been pacing ever since.

His stomach lurched as he heard a zipper pull off to his right. He spun on the balls of his feet and saw Ben stepping out of the tent, his arms stretched above him mid-yawn.

"It's about time." David marched over and pushed past him into the tent.

Ben tilted his head in confusion and turned, following David back into the tent. He watched in silence as David began rolling up the sleeping bags.

"Did you even sleep?" Ben asked, trying to break David out of his frenzy of activity.

"Not really." He sat back on his heels and looked up toward Ben. "How are you so calm?"

"Because everything ahead of us is out of our hands. May as well get some sleep and take our time heading out."

"We should be starting as early as possible. Hell, we should have already been on our way."

Ben sat down next to David and put his hand on his shoulder. "Relax. It's not a race. We'll know within an hour if this has the potential to work, right? We talked it all out."

"And if it does work, those lost hours are going to mean a whole lot more."

"David, look at me." Ben spun David to face him. "You can't get this worked up. You just can't. It's not good for you, and to be honest, it's not good for me or Marisol either. We need you at your sharpest, not most anxious."

"You think I want to feel like this?"

Ben sighed, taking him in. "Of course not. It's that…I guess I want you to realize that you're feeling this way and that we're here to help you reel it back."

David locked eyes with Ben as he released another breath. He started to pick at his bottom lip, the skin now red and chapped.

"I may seem calm," Ben sat back, adjusting. "But I'm so scared."

"You are?"

"Yes! How could we not all be scared? We're about to go trekking deep into the jungle, and we're doing it without using machetes or anything else. That alone is terrifying. Tack on the fact that I still get flashbacks to those vines wrapped around me. It's not easy."

"I didn't know you felt like that."

"You think you're the only one that deals with anxiety? Yeah, yours may be worse, but we'd be crazy not to feel that way right now. We're attempting to travel back with limited supplies, we're all going to be sharing a tent, and we have no idea what we're about to run into. It's fucking scary. But..." Ben smiled. "We're in it together. If I had to be out here with anyone, I would choose the both of you. I know we can do it."

"Will you still let me obsessively pack our stuff?"

"I wouldn't even think of trying to stop you," Ben chuckled. "You'll get it done in half the time it would take me anyway." He leaned in and pecked David on the forehead before heading back out into the humid morning air.

"You two are already packed and ready to go?" Marisol gasped as she stepped out of her tent. "I didn't realize I was so behind."

"You're not," Ben said, handing her a plantain. "David did it all in like ten minutes."

"Oh. Yeah, that sounds about right. Where is he anyway?" She turned, taking in the camp.

"Bathroom break." Ben looked to either side of him before leaning in toward Marisol. "Are you as nervous as I am?"

"Mmmhmm," Marisol nodded, her mouth full of food. "But I have faith. This is going to work. I can feel it."

The corner of his mouth turned up in a small smile. "I don't know if that makes me more or less comfortable."

"Me either," Marisol laughed.

"Oh good, you're up," David called out, emerging from the woods. "Your stuff packed?"

Marisol looked to Ben before glancing back to David. "Would you leave me behind if I said I hadn't started?"

"Do you want me to do it?"

"It's up to you, but you don't have to. I don't want to put more work on your shoulders."

"It's fine. It'll be easier for me anyway."

David trudged over to the tent and crawled inside. Marisol looked back to Ben as she took another bite of her plantain.

"What?" she shrugged with exaggerated innocence.

"Subtle," Ben smirked. "Making my boyfriend do all the work so you can sit back and eat breakfast."

Marisol wiggled her eyebrows. "Oh, we're official now?"

"Shut up." Ben blushed as he suppressed his smile. "We haven't really talked about it."

"Well, I'm using it," she said, sticking out her chin. "And yes, your *boooyfriend* is definitely going to speed things up. I'm terrible at packing. I will say, though, I think it's going to be nice carrying substantially less than we did on the way here."

"I hate leaving all of this behind. It's so much work, just gone." Ben looked over to the research tent and back to Marisol. "I know it would be impossible to pack all of this up with what we're doing, but I hate leaving stuff out here. It's like the ultimate form of littering."

"We're sealing it all up and doing our best to preserve it. We'll make sure it's extra secure, so nothing gets tangled up in it." Marisol spun around as David ducked out of the tent and jogged over to them.

"If you want to do a quick look around your tent to see if there's anything I missed that you want to bring, now's the chance. Everything else we can box and stick with the rest of the stuff in there." David pointed to the research tent. He bounced nervously on the balls of his feet, waiting for a response.

Marisol looked him up and down. "You haven't stopped all morning, have you?"

"Don't start with me," David said, his voice flat.

"I'm not!" Marisol held her hands up in surrender. "I don't want you wearing yourself out by the time we actually have to start hiking."

"I won't. It's better for me to stay busy, anyway. I say we get going with wrapping this all up and plan to head out in twenty. I have the checklist, so we can go through that as soon as we're finished."

"Sir yes sir!" Marisol yelled, standing up straight and raising her hand in a salute.

Ben held his hand up, covering his laugh as Marisol marched off toward her tent. "You good? You know she's only teasing." He reached an arm around David's waist and pulled him in.

"I'll be fine once we get going. It's the waiting that gets me."

"I know." Ben leaned over and rested his head on David's shoulder. "Soon enough."

25

D avid tapped the tip of a pencil against the open page of his notepad, reading the list over and over in his head. Three backpacks, equipped with the rolled sleeping bags and mats, lay at his feet. He looked up from the notepad to see Ben shoving the collapsed tent into the vinyl carrying case as Marisol shouted directions to him. They had broken down the other tent and stashed it inside of the research tent, zippered it up, and then secured it by adding extra ties on the stakes for additional protection from the elements. The tent and the fire pit were the only things remaining to indicate their presence.

"Alright," Ben said, dropping the bagged tent into the pile of backpacks. "Last piece."

"I think we should rotate who carries the tent," Marisol said. "I don't think it's fair for one person to have extra weight when we can split it."

"Ben and I can rotate then," said David. "I don't want you hurting your arm any more. It's almost better and there's no need to risk it."

"Carrying the tent on my back isn't going to affect my arm."

"Why don't we wait and see how it goes?" Ben said, stepping in. "So, Mr. Checklist, let's run it down."

"Okay," David breathed. He placed the tip of his pencil to the first checkbox and read off the list. "One: inventory supplies. Three jars of cooked palm grubs," David squirmed as he read it aloud, "two bunches of plantains, and three full water bags."

"Check!" Marisol called out.

"Two: pack bags. Minimal clothes, first aid kits—including some of Ben's concoctions, necessary personal items, sleeping bags, and mats."

"All packed and ready to go," Ben chimed.

"Three: disassemble tents. Carry one, pack the other and place in sealed research tent. And four: store the machetes on our bags so we don't accidentally use them."

"Done and done," Marisol said, the air becoming thick with apprehension.

"So...are we really ready to do this?" David asked. "We head back toward the lodge. No clearing our way through. We take our time, and we do it carefully."

"I think we're ready," Ben said with a curt nod. "What's the worst that can happen from trying?"

"You should know not to ever say anything like that." Marisol slapped his arm with the back of her hand. "Despite that *horrible* omen, it's now or never."

Ben held out his hands for balance as he walked across a fallen log. The frequent rain had flooded much of the forest floor, leaving only the occasional fallen tree and stump to walk upon. Raindrops trickled down through the canopy, creating ripples along the flooded ground.

"You should see it during the wet season!" Ben shouted behind him. "Watch your step and take your time."

David wiped at his face, shaking off the water dripping from his hair and into his eyes as he followed a few feet behind Ben. Keeping his eyes on his feet, he moved one foot in front of the other, his legs trembling with each step. He gasped, leaning hard to his left as his right foot slipped on the wet bark. David's legs wobbled like gelatin, and he squeezed his eyes shut as he balanced in place.

"You okay back there?" Ben called over his shoulder.

"Yep. Good," David said, taking a breath before moving forward. "Marisol?"

"I'll be good as long as you keep moving," she pressed from behind.

Ben jumped down onto the ground, his feet splashing in a shallow puddle. He reached his hand up to grasp David's, helping him down. Ben walked forward, eyeing the way ahead.

"This area seems a bit drier, although the further we hike into Igapó territory, the wetter it's going to get," said Ben.

"Based on your outings," Marisol said, coming up next to him, "have we made it further than your previous attempts?"

"It's hard to tell. We've been at this for a couple hours, maybe a bit more. The rain slowed us down some, not to mention having to climb over and through every obstacle, but I'm hopeful."

"Then let's keep going," David said. "The further we can get, the better. It's what? Almost a week out to the lodge?"

"Assuming we don't get turned around or slowed down too much," Ben retorted. "But you're right. We need to keep moving."

Ben stood with his hands on his hips as he investigated the potential paths forward. Large ficus trees interspersed with spiny bamboo clumps boxed them in. The sound of raindrops hitting the leaves and small puddles filled the air. Ben shook his head as he mentally tallied all the possibilities.

"I honestly don't know how to get through this without cutting some of it down." He turned to face the other two. "Look at what happened to David with those spines before. We can't afford to take that kind of risk."

"Could we go back around?" Marisol asked. "I know it's a pain, but maybe there's a better way?"

"I doubt it. This was my worry. It's about as close to impossible as you can get to travel through the rainforest without clearing your way through."

David nodded. "Contingency plan. Minimal damage, minimal impact. We do *just* enough to get by. At least, if you think it's truly necessary."

"I think it may be," Ben shrugged. "I'd be lying if I said it didn't make me really nervous."

"What will we need to get rid of?" asked David.

"With our fully-loaded bags in tow? Maybe three stalks of bamboo? But that's getting us only to the next section."

"Do we have a choice?" Marisol asked, eyeing Ben.

Ben shook his head in defeat.

"Only one way to find out," David said, taking a deep breath. "Everyone, cross your fingers."

Marisol stood with her arms folded across her chest as she watched David and Ben assemble the tent. Their clothes were matted to their bodies, and their pants and sleeves were caked in mud. It had rained on and off over the several hours they had hiked. After the last bout of rain, they decided to stop at the next suitable spot and make camp. A crack of lightning flashed through the leaves above.

"Again?" Marisol whined, looking up to the dimming sky. She hugged her arms tighter around herself as the rumbling echo of thunder rolled over them. "Can we get this up before it starts again?"

"Just about done," said Ben, hammering the last stake into the wet earth.

The forest lit up again, a huge clash of thunder shaking the ground beneath their feet as the sky opened up once more.

"Everyone in!" Ben called over the pelting rain. He waved Marisol forward, holding the door flap open for her.

She ducked under the small weather guard in front of the door and kicked off her shoes, scooping them up as she entered the tent. David followed suit, toeing off his shoes before peeling his muddy pants and shirt off. He tucked his clothes into the frame of the weather guard, the mud immediately sloughing off and onto the ground. Ben did the same, hanging his clothes opposite David's as he grabbed his muddied shoes and slipped into the tent.

"Well, this is going to be very cozy," Ben said, scooting back into a corner. His knees knocked into David's as he tried to create as much space as possible.

"Cozy is such a nice way of saying everyone is going to be touching everyone else constantly," Marisol said with a laugh. "This is going to suck."

"While I don't disagree," David said, "it's still a lot safer than being apart. And we only have to carry the one tent."

"It definitely sounded great on paper," Ben said, pulling his knees up to his chest. "I have no idea how we're going to sleep."

"On top of each other," Marisol joked.

"No kidding," Ben said. "Marisol, you're closest to the bags. Mind getting me and David some clothes from ours?"

"You mean you're not staying in sopping wet under—"

Marisol let out a scream as a sudden flash illuminated the tent. She jumped as a deafening bang of thunder shook the ground and rattled their bones. David threw his hands up over his head, ducking down. A loud snap sounded off to their right, and the side of the tent caved in. An impression of a leaf-covered branch pressed up against the vinyl, missing Marisol's head by inches.

Ben dove toward her and pushed against the limb, trying to shove it off the tent. Marisol turned and pushed with him, but the branch wouldn't budge.

"I'll pull on it from outside!" David yelled over the rain hammering against the tent. He moved to the front and began to unzip the door.

"David, no, it's too dangerous!" Ben yelled back. "That was too close!"

He reached his hand out to grab David's arm, but he had already unzipped the door and dived out into the rain.

"Shit," Ben hissed, turning and pushing his weight against the branch.

David held his hand over his eyes, trying to look through the downpour. The sky flashed a bright white as another round of thunder crackled nearby. He moved around the side of the tent, cursing as he assessed the situation. With a turn, he darted back to the door and popped his head inside.

"I don't know if we can move it," he said, voice raised and shaking the water out of his face.

"What if I come lift it with you? Like if we can shove it off to the side?" asked Ben.

"Worth a shot." He looked behind Ben to Marisol. "Marisol, go to the opposite side of the tent and stay out of the way so you don't get hurt."

Ben followed David outside and around to the fallen limb. "Holy shit!" Ben shouted over the rain.

"Told you!"

The top of a branch leaned onto the tent, the leaves and twigs pressing against the side. The main trunk of the branch was almost a foot wide and longer than the two of them combined.

"Let me get under it, and I'll lift up! You come behind me and push! We'll see if we can inch it off!"

Ben dropped to his knees and crawled under the leaves. His drenched hair clung to his face, obscuring his vision. Sharp twigs scraped along his back, stinging his skin as he clawed his way further under the branch. Peering over his shoulder, he saw nothing but dark and dripping leaves. David had simply disappeared behind the foliage. He looked up at the main trunk and positioned it above his shoulder, gripping it with both hands. His jaw clenched as he pushed up from his legs, pressing his body weight against the branch.

The bark dug into his skin as he pushed up, his feet sinking and slipping in the mud underfoot. Air flooded out of Ben's lungs as he felt the weight shifting. He pushed harder, his knees burning under the strain. Rain slammed against his back as the tree slid away from him. Shoving against the branch, the leaves slowly dragged over and away from him, scratchy against his skin. Ben collapsed onto his knees as the limb crashed into the mud beside him.

David knelt down in the mud next to him and spun him around. The rain streamed down his face as he looked Ben over, his eyes searching every inch of him. The jungle was cloaked in a dark shadow, the last of the sun blotted out by storm clouds and rain. Pulses of sheet lightning over the canopy lit up the rainforest in ghostly waves.

"You okay?" David shouted, the rain and his own pulse overtaking his hearing.

"Good teamwork!" Ben yelled back.

Even through the dark, David could see the smile playing across Ben's face. Before he could ask why, Ben leaned forward and kissed him, the rain pouring in rivers down their faces.

"Always wanted to kiss someone in the rain!" Ben leaned back, resting his hands on David's muddied thighs. "Didn't feel as romantic as the movies!"

"Because normally they're not about to get hit by lightning!"

Ben smiled and pushed himself to his feet, extending his hand to David to help him up. David rubbed at his legs, flinging the mud off along with the rainwater. He looked up as he felt Ben pluck a couple of leaves out of his hair. Ben looked about as disheveled as David felt, and he wondered if he looked the same or worse. After a quick glance to the persistent lightning, they crawled back into the tent, leaving a trail of muddy water behind them.

"You guys okay?" Marisol asked over her shoulder. She knelt in a small puddle, a piece of bandage tape in her hand. The fabric of the tent in front of her had several pieces of tape already stuck to it.

"Oh no, no, no," David said, crawling over to her.

"It's not that bad," she said. "I think it snagged a few times. The rips aren't that big."

"Big enough to get water in here."

Marisol shrugged. "At least we won't be squished to death."

"David, here," Ben said, throwing a towel to him. "She's got it. Get dry and throw some clothes on. Don't want to end up sick because we stayed soaked."

"I *do* have it," Marisol said, looking over to him. "Go on."

"You say 'go on,' like we're not going to be two feet away from each other," David huffed as he crawled closer to Ben. He ran the towel through his hair, patted himself dry, and let out a sigh of relief as he tossed on a pair of sweatpants.

Ben grabbed the towel from David and dried off before slipping on a dry pair of briefs. "I can set up the sleeping bags and everything if you want to help Marisol."

"I don't need any help," Marisol said, sticking her chin out. "But you can clean up this water while I get changed. You're not the only two that are drenched."

David stared into the dark, sandwiched between Ben and Marisol, listening to the rain and wind as the thunderstorm raged on overnight. Ben's back pressed up against the wall of the tent, his arm and leg draped over David's right side. Marisol laid to his left, with her head nestled into his shoulder and her arm tucked up against his chest. They decided that lining up next to each other was more advantageous than trying to sleep with their packs between them. David figured it was the lesser of two evils, though he didn't quite anticipate being touched from every which way throughout the entire evening.

By the time morning came, David was fast asleep, curled up against Marisol. He groaned as the sunlight filled the tent. He turned onto his back, feeling Ben wiggling behind him.

"Morning," Ben whispered. "I think I'm officially stuck over here."

"I can move," David grumbled, curling his legs up toward his chest.

"Thanks."

David pulled the sleeping bag up to his neck and closed his eyes before sighing and shoving it back down, curiosity getting the better of him. Still groggy, he slipped past Marisol and followed Ben outside. He shuffled around the side of the tent to see Ben surveying the damage from overnight.

"Oh my God. Your shoulder," David gasped, closing the gap between them. He reached out and brushed his hand along the area between Ben's neck and shoulder. The skin was black and blue with deep red blotches spotted throughout. "Is that from last night?"

"Yeah." Ben ran his fingers along the skin. "But look what we moved. This thing is massive."

"You can't carry your bag like this," David said, ignoring Ben's topic change.

"I'll be fine. It's tender, but not too bad."

"It looks awful. There's no way you're not hurting. Let me take your stuff today."

Ben reached up and cupped David's face. "I love that you're trying to be a gentleman, but I've got it."

"You're being stubborn."

"I am. You're no less stubborn. You'd do the exact same."

David shook his head and sighed in resignation. "Alright. If you decide you don't want to be stubborn anymore, you know you can ask me to help."

"I know," Ben said, giving David a smile.

He looked past Ben and to the tree branch. "We totally did that."

Ben let out a barking laugh. "We totally did." Ben shifted the weight on his feet. "Do you think it had anything to do with all of this?"

"It was a lightning bolt. I think that's a little beyond the scope of reason."

"Is it? I have to wonder."

"Well, we can wonder while we get far away from here. I'll

go wake Marisol, and we can get started. Hopefully we can skip the rain today."

"Hopefully." Ben waited until David walked away before approaching the branch. He moved to the end and crouched down, leaning in to investigate the base of the limb. The bark was splintered away in jagged spikes. He muttered under his breath, "Except lightning usually leaves burn marks."

26

David and Marisol watched from the tree line as Ben walked around the familiar clearing. Rows of walking palms lined the outskirts of the old campsite. David gripped the straps of his backpack, the tension in his muscles traveling from his neck and down to his legs. He scanned the clearing, remembering the fear that ran through his body the last time they passed through this section of the grid. Part of him had hoped they would stumble upon Dr. Morrow and her tent, unscathed and waiting to take them back to the lodge. Instead, they were met with a dense and overgrown camp that once was.

"I was really hoping she'd be here," Marisol said, looking up at David.

"I don't know what I expected," he replied, his eyes trained on the trees. "I'm not exactly relieved to be back here." The muscle in his cheek clenched with the tension in his jaw as he went quiet.

Marisol gently touched his arm. "We don't have to spend the night here."

David glanced down at her as his tongue wetted his chapped lips. "I don't think we have a choice. It's going to be dark soon, and this is better than anything we'd find."

"You guys have a preference on where you want to set up the tent?" Ben called to them from across the way.

"Just say the word and we can keep going," Marisol whispered to David. He hesitated before shaking his head and letting out a small sigh. "Wherever you want!" she called back to Ben, then turned to David and whispered, "Doesn't mean you can't change your mind." She lifted her hand from David's arm and walked over to help Ben with the tent.

David closed his eyes, trying to block out the worry. He was met with images of himself crouched down in the jungle, his heart beating against his ribcage and his hands shaking. He could still hear Dr. Morrow's satellite phone ringing throughout the trees. He squeezed his eyes shut tighter, seeing Marisol wide-eyed and scared as he emerged from the trees with nothing to show for his efforts but an extra, useless phone.

"Everything okay?" Ben's voice rang out, snapping David out of his thoughts.

David's eyes sprang open to see Ben standing in front of him. He gave a quick nod as he swallowed, his heart pumping in his chest. He released his grip on the straps of his backpack, wiggling his fingers to relieve his joints, sore from clenching the fabric. Ben's hand clasped around his shoulder, massaging the muscle.

"If staying here again is too much…" Ben started, but trailed off, his eyebrows pinching together in concern.

"It's not," said David. "I'm just a little on edge."

"Understandable. You guys weren't kidding when you said this placed swallowed you up. I know it's been a while, but our second site was definitely a *lot* bigger than this."

"We woke up completely surrounded." David's voice was soft, distant.

"At least we know better this time." Ben removed his hand from David's shoulder. "It's been a couple of days now, and nothing. Just a couple more, and we'll be out of here. We're just here for the night."

Marisol stared into the darkness of the tent. She waited for her eyes to adjust, the seams of the fabric slowly taking shape around her while the sounds of the rainforest filled her ears. The mix of insects became a sort of white noise in the evenings, something to drown out the thoughts and concerns of the day.

She shot up, the sleeping bag falling off her as she sat in the dark tent. The hairs along her arms stood at attention, goosebumps rippling along her skin. She held her breath, listening. The white noise had ceased and was replaced by gusts of wind whipping throughout the trees.

Marisol's eyes were glued to the sides of the tent. She waited for the wind to brush up against it, to shake the fabric and wake everyone up. The rustling of the leaves outside grew louder, yet the tent remained motionless. A chill washed over her as the branches clacked against one another. Distant creaks and groans of bending and swaying trees echoed around them. She swung her hand to the side and shoved against David's back.

"What? What's wrong?" he mumbled, flipping over to face her as he rubbed his fingers against his eyes.

"Something's happening outside," she whispered.

David sat up as a yawn escaped his mouth. He leaned over Marisol and reached for the zipper to the door.

"Well, don't go out there!" she hissed at him, slapping his hand away.

"How am I supp—"

"Shhhhh! Just listen."

"It's...windy?"

"Ugh!" Marisol grunted as she spun her head toward him and glared. "It's *more* than that."

"What the hell is going on?" Ben groaned, rolling onto his back. "Why are you two arguing at whatever godforsaken time it is?"

"Fine!" she snipped. "You two go back to bed and ignore all of the strange noises."

"You won't let me go outside," David whined. "What do you want us to do?"

Marisol bit down on her bottom lip, her leg bouncing up and down. "Just forget it."

"Tell me," David insisted, getting impatient. "What can I do? I can bring Ben and we can go check."

"I don't need either of you to check things for me. I'm a fully capable woman."

David sighed. "I'm just trying to help."

"Then go back to bed. It's probably nothing. And if it *is* something, I can handle it."

"*You* woke *me* you know," he said, glancing from Marisol to Ben who gave him a small shrug in response. "But okay. If you need me..."

"I won't."

"Fine." He shook his head. David shuffled into his sleeping bag and settled back down next to Ben. He leaned his head to the side and against Ben's shoulder as he closed his eyes.

"Sorry I woke you," Marisol added softly, looking over to him. She listened to the leaves continuing to flutter in the branches above the tent. After a while, the wind dissipated, and the clattering of tree limbs faded in response, giving way to the chorus of insects. The undertone of white noise returned, encompassing her in a resonating hum of buzzes and chirps. She laid down and tugged the sleeping bag up to her chin. Her eyes searched once more for the seams of the tent, now clear in her vision. She followed them, tracing invisible lines between them until her eyes drooped closed and plunged her back into darkness.

"I don't understand," Ben said, his mouth hanging open. He stood outside the tent, hair disheveled and wearing only his sweatpants. A cleared path loomed before him. The trees were parted, as if they stepped aside to present an unhindered way forward through the wilds of the rainforest. "This wasn't here yesterday."

"This is exactly what happened last time," Marisol said, standing next to him with her hands planted on her hips. "We woke up and bam! A way out, like we had spent hours clearing it ourselves."

"What's in that direction?" David asked from Ben's other side.

"Only one way to find out," he answered. "It's not often we're given an easy way through, especially since we're not using our tools."

Marisol crossed her arms. "And we're assuming it's a safer path because it *looks* safer?"

"It's either that or going through those thorn covered palms," Ben said.

"So let's get dressed, pack up, and go. I don't think we should linger here too long." David stared at the trees for a moment longer before he turned and ducked back into the tent.

"We need to find some water soon," Ben said, following him. He pulled off his sweats and replaced them with khaki pants before throwing on a long-sleeved safari shirt.

David looked up at him as he pulled on his still-wet pants. "I know. I've been out since yesterday morning."

"Why didn't you say anything?"

"Didn't want to cause a thing. I'll have to try to sweat less, I guess."

Ben smiled. "Good luck with that. You should drink what's left of mine, though. I don't need you fainting out there."

"I'll be okay, for now. Maybe this new path will lead us to some water."

"Are you boys done yet?" Marisol called from outside.

Ben poked his head out from the tent and looked up at her. "How many times do I have to tell you that you don't have to wait for us?"

"I always figure you two might want a little one-on-one time together," she said, wiggling her eyebrows up and down.

"Well, it is getting *very* hot and steamy in here. We're talking sweat, water, potentially dying from dehydration. Super intimate stuff."

Marisol pushed past him and into the tent. "Alright, smartass."

"Be careful," he said as she brushed up against him. "Might not be able to take all the heat in there." Ben laughed as Marisol shoved him from behind, making him fall out of the tent and into the dirt.

Marisol stood at the entrance to the path. She closed her eyes and took a deep breath, steadying herself, uncertain of why she was so nervous.

David touched her arm from behind. "You don't have to take the lead, you know."

"It's fine. It's my turn anyway."

"Your turn or not, you don't have to. I can go first."

Marisol turned to face him. "It's not about being first." Her hands trembled at her sides. "I don't have a good feeling about this."

"What do you mean?"

"I can't shake this feeling that this isn't the right way."

"We don't have to go this way." A look of concern moved over David's face. "What do you want to do?"

"I can't say I want to go the other way either. I'm sure it's nothing. I can tough it out. Just nerves."

"You sure?"

Marisol nodded and turned back toward the opening. "As soon as Ben hurries his ass up!" she shouted as she straightened her shoulders and held her head up.

"Sorry!" Ben called, jogging across the clearing while zipping up his pants as he stopped next to David. "Nervous bladder."

"The last thing I want to hear is that *you're* nervous," Marisol said, her back to him.

"Then forget I said it," Ben said, shrugging at David. "I have one hundred percent confidence in this."

"Little late on that, but I'll take it." Marisol swallowed as she stepped over the threshold and into the cleared path.

As they walked, Ben ran his hands along the curvature of the wood, investigating how the bushes and tree limbs conformed to the trail before them. The trunks towered above their heads, the branches creating a domed canopy which blocked out most of the sunlight. David glanced up as the leaves fluttered around them. Ben reached behind to his backpack and grabbed at his machete as a gust of wind rushed over them from behind, whipping at their clothes. The branches rattled together, the knocking and scraping filling their ears.

Marisol pushed her foot into the soft mud, but David's hand shot out, grabbing at her arm to stop her in place. "Don't," he said, pulling her in closer. She faced him, but his eyes were already elsewhere, scanning the trees.

Ben spun around to face the entrance to the trail, his hair falling around his face as the wind slowed to a light breeze. He blinked several times, trying to focus his vision, before bringing his hands to his face and rubbing at his eyelids. Still not believing his eyes, he squinted, his stomach knotting and twisting at the sight before him. The air caught in his lungs while he froze in place, watching the last bit of bright light from the clearing disappear as a thicket of branches fused together, sealing them inside.

"Ben! Don't!" David yelled, tugging at Ben's arm.

Ben yanked his arm away and swung his machete down, the blade chipping away at the thick branches before them. Sweat dripped down the side of his temple as he raised his arm again, ready to swing. David jumped in front of him, his hands covering his face as he braced for impact.

"What are you doing? Move!" Ben growled, reaching to grab at David with his left hand.

"No!" David stood up straighter, holding his hands in fists at his side.

"This isn't a fucking game," Ben said through his teeth.

"You don't think I know that?" David swallowed, hearing the dryness from his mouth in his voice. He stared into Ben's eyes and steeled himself. "I've been through this. You haven't."

"Oh really? So, you've got this then? You're an expert? You said yourself you don't know what you're doing."

David winced at his words as they sliced at him. He stepped toward him. "I know you're scared," he said, his voice wavering. "But this isn't the way. And you know that." David stood his ground, keeping his eyes locked on Ben, hoping he wouldn't notice him shaking.

"David's right," Marisol said, her voice soft from behind Ben.

"Please," David pressed, his eyes welling up. "I trust you, but-but this..." He turned to face the knotted limbs at his back and ran a hand along the machete marks on the bark. He looked back to Ben, his fingers still tracing the grooves in the wood. "This is too dangerous."

"I'm willing to risk it. We can find another way out once we get to the other side. Now move. Please."

"We can just follow the path. It's the safest way."

Ben looked over his shoulder at the cleared trail. "We don't know where it's leading us."

"We don't know where this would lead us either," David replied, waving his arm at the branches. "You've trusted me so far."

"Well, I haven't seen anything like this until now."

"Exactly. But I have." David looked to Marisol before moving his eyes back to Ben. "I know I'm not like you. I may not know how to rough it, but I do know that this doesn't feel right."

"And maybe it's not. But can you at least let me try?"

"Okay," Marisol said, stepping up next to David. "But only a few minutes and then we're heading the other direction. We can't afford to waste time, not when things like this are happening."

David looked down at her, glaring. "Marisol, I—"

"There's no use arguing," she interrupted. "Both of you are too headstrong anyway."

"I'm not headstrong, I just—"

"Give him five to hack and slash these branches and save the day," she said, motioning to Ben. "And then when that doesn't work, we can keep going." Marisol crossed her arms and popped her hip out, her eyes panning between David and Ben. "Okay?"

"Okay," Ben and David grumbled in unison.

Marisol tugged on David's sleeve, inching him away from Ben and back down the path. David glared at her as he held his hands up in question.

"We would have been there all day," she said, flinching at the sharp sound of Ben's machete resuming its assault on the branches.

"I don't like it."

"Me either, but for as long as he's been out here, he really hasn't run into this."

"After Dr. Morrow…"

"I know." Marisol glanced back to Ben. "He wasn't there, though, David. I think if he saw Dr. Morrow just *vanish* like we did, he'd think a little differently. But you can't force him. And we're sticking together, right?"

David nodded his head, his gaze focused on the dull silver blade in Ben's hand as it chopped back down and bounced off the wood. "I hope she didn't just vanish," he mumbled to himself. Ben let out a loud and angry grunt, making David jump, before stomping back over to where they stood. "No dice?" David asked, concealing a grin as Ben stopped in front of him.

Ben shook his head as he sucked on his lower lip. He kept his eyes to the ground and tucked his machete back into its sheath on his backpack. "Lead the way then."

Marisol eyed David, offering a small shrug and roll of her eyes, before heading away from the now inaccessible campsite.

Ben walked silently behind David, his feet kicking up the damp leaves matting the ground. David slowed, squeezing in next to him on the narrow pathway.

"I wasn't trying to—"

"Me either," Ben interrupted. "I'm sorry I yelled at you."

"I'm sorry I was difficult." David looked up out of the corner of his eye, seeing Ben continuing to walk with his head down next to him. "We okay?"

"...yeah." He nodded.

David continued to stare, trying to read his face. He knew there was more. If Ben were anything like him, he would expect him to be quiet when things weren't okay. *Just say something to him*, he thought. David opened his mouth as his foot caught on a root. Ben's face blurred as he fell forward, his ankle twisting where it snagged under the root. He hit the ground with a heavy thud, the air forced out of his lungs as the gear on his backpack rode up and over the top of his head.

"Oh shit!" Ben gasped, collapsing to his knees beside him. He pulled the weight of the backpack off David's head and ran his hand through his hair. "You alright?"

David gulped air back into his lungs before rolling and pushing up to a seated position. He looked down, seeing his sock covered foot. He wiggled his toes as he ground his teeth together, trying not to wince at the deep throbbing emanating from his ankle. "I lost my shoe," he said, dazed and still staring at his foot.

Marisol stepped over him and crouched down, pulling his sneaker out from a large root that had formed into a low arch where it erupted from the ground. "Got it! Let me help." She squatted in front of him while undoing the laces. Reaching out, she grabbed David's foot and lifted it toward the shoe in her opposite hand.

David inhaled sharply and pulled his foot back, holding it in the air a few inches above the ground. His eyes darted up to her, and he wondered if he looked as worried as she did. "I can do it," he said quickly, holding his hand out for his shoe.

"Let me take a look," Ben said, grazing David's lower leg as he gently rolled his sock down his ankle.

"Really, it's fine. I just twisted it. We should keep going."

"If you sprained it or fractured it, you shouldn't be walking on it. That is, *if* you can walk on it."

David pushed his hand away. "I can walk on it. *I'm fine.*"

Ben shook his head in frustration. "You're ridiculously stubborn, you know that?" He stood and held his hand out. David grasped it in return.

David grimaced as he stood and placed weight on his ankle. He raised his eyes to Ben's and was met with a stony-glare and the faint twitch of an eyebrow. David picked at his lip with his teeth. "All I need to do is walk it off."

Ben held on to David's arm, steadying him. "You're going to get yourself hur—" He paused, squinting down the trail behind them. "What *is* that?"

A series of sharp snaps reverberated throughout the trees from both ends of the trail. David whipped his head to the side, looking past Marisol. His eyes widened as he watched branches splintering and falling at the far end of the path ahead of them and moving toward them. Marisol shrieked as a loud crack sounded off above their heads.

David spun around as a falling branch collapsed onto Ben. His grip slipped from David's arm as he crumpled to the ground. David dove forward, his feet digging into the damp earth as he shoved the branch off him. He fell to his knees, his hands cupping either side of Ben's head. His eyes were closed, and a small river of blood ran from his temple and trickled down his cheek.

"Is he breathing?" Marisol asked, her voice shaking, as she sank to her knees next to David.

"His chest is moving. I...I think he's unconscious." David

threw his backpack to the ground, ripped the zipper open, and shoved his shaking hand inside. He growled in frustration as his hands searched blindly inside the bag. With a shaky huff, he yanked his hand out and slammed it onto the backpack. "I can't find the fucking first aid kit." His hands moved back to Ben, gingerly running his hands over his hair.

Marisol quietly slid David's bag over and rummaged through it before pulling out the red plastic kit. She fumbled with the snaps, trying to get it open. She stopped and looked up as David tore at one of his shirt seams, ripping the fabric into pieces. He grabbed a water bottle off the bag and tipped it over Ben's temple. The blood on his face smeared and rinsed away before rising back up and dribbling down his face, mixing with the remaining water. David held the torn piece of cloth to the wound. The light brown fabric turned dark as the mixture of blood and water absorbed into the fibers, staining them a dark red.

"Ben," David urged, nudging his shoulder with his other hand. "Ben, wake up."

Marisol leaned over Ben and brushed the hair off his face before tapping her fingers against his cheeks. Her eyebrows knitted together as she held her breath, stealing a glance at David who remained hovering over him, applying pressure to the gash on his head. David held his breath alongside her, his eyes never leaving Ben's face.

"David, I—" She paused, light movement catching her attention. "Ben! Hey, buddy...you with us?" Marisol ran her hands along his face, stroking his cheeks as he stirred.

"Thank God," David exhaled, his words barely audible. His entire body trembled, and his heart raced so quickly he thought it must be skipping beats. "Ben, can you hear me?"

"Yeah," Ben mumbled. His eyelids fluttered open as he blinked up at David. He let out a soft breath before closing his eyes again.

"Hey, hey, hey," David said, pressing his hand against Ben's chest and shaking him awake. He cradled his face in his hand, running his thumb along his cheekbone. "Marisol," he said softly, without looking away, "can you set up the tent? We're not going anywhere for a bit. We can at least get him out of the dirt. Ben, can you see me okay?"

Ben let out a slight groan in response, his head moving with the slightest nod. "I'm dizzy," he muttered, pressing his head into David's palm. "Can you help me sit up?"

"Of course," David whispered. He wrapped his arm behind Ben's back and lifted him up to face him.

Ben lurched forward as he sat up and vomited. He remained hunched as David held him up by his shoulders, his body slack against his hands.

"I'm sorry," Ben creaked, looking up at the vomit splashed across David's shirt.

"No, no it's okay. It was already ruined." David leaned down, looking into his eyes. "Are you okay? Do you still feel sick?"

Ben gave a weak shake of his head while raising a hand to his mouth to wipe his lips. His eyelids drooped as he stifled a small moan.

Marisol walked over to David and crouched down behind him, leaning in to talk into his ear. "Throwing up after a head injury isn't good, David."

He stabilized Ben, having him put pressure on his bleeding temple, before scooting back and standing up. Carefully pulling off his soiled shirt, he crumpled it and tossed it to the side of the trail. Taking a deep breath, he turned to Marisol, then quickly glanced to Ben who was hunched over and leaning his elbows on his knees, his head hanging between them.

David forced his attention back to Marisol and whispered under his breath, "Like how not good?"

"I don't know. All I know is that it's not just a simple knock. At the very least, it's a sign of a concussion. I had to know all of that when Mateo played soccer. Dizziness, vomiting, confusion...I don't remember the rest."

"What do you do for that? Isn't one of the things not letting them fall asleep…or is that a myth? I knew he shouldn't have tried forcing our way out of here. Do you think I made it worse by moving him? Should I lay him back down? Is he going to be okay? I-I don't know what to do…" David ran his hands over his face, his heart starting to pound harder in his chest.

"David, slow down. Let's get him cleaned up, check his head, and go from there, okay?" Marisol nodded in sync with David before taking his hands in hers and giving them a squeeze. She set her eyes onto his. "I'm sure he'll be fine."

"We don't even have ice," David said, meeting her eyes, but looking through her.

"David…" She squeezed his hands tighter, redirecting his attention. "He's going to be fine."

27

David and Marisol watched intently as Ben took a sip from his water bottle. Ben narrowed his eyes at them, his chest heaving with a long sigh as he secured the lid on the bottle and placed it on the ground next to him.

"You guys don't have to keep staring at me," he said, raising his eyebrows. He brought a hand to the side of his head and closed his eyes.

"What's wrong? Are you okay?" David asked, the words pouring out of his mouth like a spilt drink.

"David…" Ben warned behind clenched teeth. He opened his eyes, seeing David already readying himself for action.

David sat back, lowering his eyes. "Sorry."

"Stop apologizing. And stop worrying…if just for five minutes, please."

"You *have* been kind of hovering over him for the last hour or two," Marisol said.

"I'm sor—" David snapped his mouth shut and let a sharp, frustrated breath out through his nose. "I can't help but worry."

"I know." Ben took another deep breath. "It's just that my head is killing me and the last thing I want is to keep explaining that I'm gonna be okay. That I *am* okay."

"But you definitely have a concussion."

"People get concussions all the time. I'm thinking clearly, I'm not disoriented...I have a migraine from hell and am exhausted, but nothing to worry about."

"Well," Marisol said, jumping in. "It's well past lunch. Surely some food can ease the moodiness a little bit, huh? Where do we stand on eating? I can offer us some fairly squished plantains from Ben's backpack."

David stared at the two of them as he ground his molars. "You're okay planning a meal, but no one here wants to talk about what happened?"

"If you want me to take blame for it, I will. I think I paid my price, though, without having to listen to it all over again." Ben closed his eyes once more, leaning his forehead into his hands, ranting to the floor of the tent. "I'm sorry I freaked and tried to cut through everything. And I'm sorry we had to stop early, and that I fucked up all of our progress for the day. That's on me." He sat up briefly before scooting down and onto his sleeping bag. "And I probably won't eat. I'm still queasy, but you two should help yourselves. I'm closing my eyes for a bit."

Marisol dug into Ben's backpack and pulled out a couple of unripe plantains. She offered a sympathetic smile as she handed them to David. "Relax," she whispered, her eyes moving over Ben, whose chest was already settling into a quiet rhythm. "We're here for the night anyway."

Marisol stretched her legs, pressing her toes against the bottom of her sleeping bag as a yawn escaped her lips. She rolled to her side and propped herself up on an elbow, finding David sitting up next to her. She reached out a hand and gently touched his back. He startled, his head turning to look down at her.

"Morning," he mumbled.

She raised her eyebrows as she took him in. His eyes were half-closed, and his voice was grainy and harsh. She sat up and leaned around him. Ben was still asleep, David's sleeping bag draped over him like a blanket. Marisol looked back to David, her face scrunching in worry.

"Did you not go to bed?" she asked, half-whispering.

David shook his head in slow motion. "I didn't feel comfortable without anyone watching him overnight. Just in case, you know?"

"We could have switched off. How are you still awake?"

His shoulders raised slightly and dropped back down. He grumbled something inaudible in response.

"Okay, well, I'm up now. Lie down and get some sleep."

"That'll only slow down the day." David's voice dragged, barely stopping between words. "Ben'll probably be up soon anyway."

"At least go stretch your back or legs or something. You know it's just as bad to go without sleep as it is for Ben to be walking around with a concussion."

"It's one night." David uncrossed his legs and crawled over to the tent flap, unzipping it. He tripped forward as he tried to stand, his foot collapsing under his weight.

"Oh my God, David!" Marisol leaned over and ran her fingertips against his ankle. The skin was taut and puffy. A deep purple splashed across the outside of the ankle and spread down to the top of his foot. "This is from yesterday?"

David winced as he moved his toes, curling and uncurling them several times. "I didn't realize it was that swollen."

"Can you put any weight on it?" Ben asked, his voice groggy as he pushed himself up on his elbows and stared at David's foot.

"He tried, but—"

"It's not that bad," David interjected. "I didn't mean to wake you up. How are you feeling? You've got a pretty nasty bruise yourself." He pointed to his temple, mirroring Ben's injury.

Ben chuckled, lightly prodding the scabbed gash on his temple. "Guess we've both seen better days, huh? Head still hurts like crazy, but no worse for wear."

"Then we should get going." David bent to grab his bag. He

fished out a pair of socks and slid them on, careful to be gentle while pulling it over his swollen foot.

"And you think you're going to get a shoe on that?" Marisol scoffed. "That foot is twice the size of your other one."

"We can't stay here. We need to keep going. If I have to walk without the laces, then so be it. As long as Ben is okay to go, we're going."

"We still need to find some water," Ben said.

"That too."

"Can I at least pack all this shit up while you two stubborn men take it easy?" asked Marisol.

David's eyes shifted to Ben, who grinned and gave a small laugh. "I will happily concede this time. Shall we then, David?" He squeezed past him and crouched outside of the weather guard above the door. He held his hand out to David and leaned in, pressing his lips against David's ear. "I know you can't stand up," he whispered. "Let me help you."

David clasped his hand in Ben's as he pulled, lifting him up from the floor, and helping him stand balancing on one foot. He led him hopping down the path and behind a pile of fallen branches.

"Okay," Ben said, positioning David up against a tree trunk. He got on his knees and slid David's sock off. "Let's see how bad you were lying."

"I can walk on it," he insisted, flinching as the sock rolled off his foot.

"Sure you can. People manage to work through broken bones all the time." He looked up at David. His hands wrapped around the lower half of David's calf. "Doesn't mean you should. Now...this is going to hurt." Ben slid his hands down and palpated the swollen part of his ankle.

David squeezed his eyes shut and pounded his fist against the trunk behind him. His jaw tensed as he tried not to pull away. "Fuck, that hurts."

"Told you." Ben shrugged, not taking his eyes or hands off David's ankle. He held the heel of his foot in the palm of his hand while his other hand gripped around his toes. Guiding the end of David's foot, Ben tested the joint, rotating it back and forth. "I don't think it's broken." He released David's foot and stood back up. "It'll suck to walk on, but I'll be there with you to help."

"*I* should be the one helping *you*."

"We can help each other. Besides, don't think I didn't catch you saying you were up all night keeping vigil by my bedside."

"I wasn't…you know what? I won't make an excuse for being worried about you."

Ben smiled as he leaned in and kissed David's cheek. "Good. Because I think that was sweet."

Dim light permeated the jungle as the canopy overhead became thick and cluttered. Overlapping branches of dark leaves blotted out the bright blue of the sky and cast dark shadows on the ground with only small trickles of sunlight filtering between the gaps. They could hear the occasional macaw and hawk above the trees, but all they could see were more leaves.

"Dammit," David cursed as he stumbled over his feet, catching himself on a nearby tree trunk.

"Do we need to stop?" Ben asked, arching an eyebrow at him.

"No. We're already behind."

"You know we're not on a schedule, right?" Marisol said, turning to face him. "The agreement was slow and steady, remember?"

"And careful," Ben added.

"We're doing all of those things now," David said.

"You're being—"

"Stubborn. I know," David snipped. "It's not even my ankle, it's the fact it's dark and wet and all we've done is walk for days on end…and for what?"

"We're making progress," Ben said, stepping around to face

him. "We've already come a lot further than I thought we would. Your idea was solid, and it's working."

David pointed ahead. "Is it?"

A stretch of dense jungle crept into the once-clear trail they had been traveling on. Giant palms with sharp thorns along the stems branched in every direction, obscuring the bottom of the trees. Large, hanging ferns clung to the limbs and trunks, adding another shade of green to the bright palm fronds and dark ficus leaves dominating the landscape.

"We're out of trail," David continued. "What if this was all about getting us more turned around?"

"We won't know unless we keep going." Marisol walked forward and pried at the palm fronds, peeling them back. "Whoa!" She ripped her hand away as the frond curled forward, grazing her skin before she stepped back and out of reach.

David rolled his eyes as he let out a frustrated breath. "What is it now?"

"It...*moved*." Marisol ran behind them and to a nearby tree, reaching up to the lowest limb and bending it down toward her.

"Hey! Stop!" David said, limping up behind her. "Snapping branches off is the same as using the machete. What are you even doing?"

"I need something that I can poke around with."

"Find something on the ground then. We need to stop being so careless."

"You think I was careless?" said Ben from down the trail.

"No, that's not...I-I—" David sighed, dropping his chin to his chest. "I just think we need to be more careful."

"We're being as careful as we can." Marisol snapped the branch off the tree and strode past David. She stepped up to the palm fronds and ran the end of the branch against them.

"Whoa," Ben gasped, stepping beside Marisol.

"That's what I said."

They watched as the frond leaves curled toward it like fingertips grasping for purchase. Marisol pulled the branch back, feeling resistance from where the frond leaves had wrapped around it. As she tugged, the palm fronds on either side leaned forward, their leaves stretching and closing onto the exposed branch. Like a chain reaction, the palm fronds surrounding them swayed and reached one-by-one, searching for the instigator. Marisol released her grip and watched as the branch slowly became encompassed by the palm fronds. The three of them stood in silence, staring at the plants before them. As the branch vanished completely into the thicket, the palms returned to their stillness, unmoving and unassuming amongst the other foliage.

"Well…" David said, trailing off mid-sentence, unable to find the words to use.

"Yeah," Ben breathed in response.

"Well shit." Marisol broke into a fit of laughter.

David and Ben raised their eyebrows at each other before looking down to Marisol as she giggled to herself, still staring at the palm fronds.

"*Mimosa pudica*," she said, stifling her laugh.

David raised his eyes to Ben and shrugged, shaking his head in question. "Should we know what that means?"

Marisol turned to David and snorted, throwing her hands on her hips. "I thought you took a million botany classes, Mr. I've Read Every Book On Campus? You don't remember the touch-me-not plant? Dr. Hammond has them hanging all over her office and would bring one to every lab."

"Oh! The sensitive plant!" Ben exclaimed.

"I would think out of all the plants, David would remember that one," Marisol said, biting back a smile.

"Because I'm *sensitive*?" David mocked, mimicking her voice. "Hilarious. But yeah, I do remember that one now. The leaves and petioles react to ionization and touch, and then close up around themselves."

"Kinda like that?" Marisol asked, pointing behind her to the now still fronds.

David started to offer a retort, but stopped, his mouth hanging open in pause.

Marisol stepped back and moved her eyes up and down,

looking him over. "Wow. I can literally see all of those thoughts happening at the same time."

"Shut up. I guess I don't....I guess what I'm—"

"You want to know how it's happening in a regular old palm frond?" Ben finished for him. "What did you call it, Marisol? The mimosa plant? Isn't it the only one that does that?"

"*Mimosa pudica*. And it's induced nyctinasty; when seismonastic movements cause the leaves to close, it forces the plant's sleep cycle. It's not the only species that has rapid plant movement, but it's one of the most interesting in terms of how it works. It relies on ion movements through protein channels. Other species, like white mulberry, for instance, catapult pollen at half the speed of sound. But most rapid plant movement is triggered for defense or propagation. We still don't know *why* the *Mimosa pudica* is different. And to top all of that...no, I've never heard of it or seen it in palm species."

"My guess is that it's like any of these other instances. It's almost like cross-evolution, right? These normal plant species are taking on properties of other plants," Ben said.

"Or," Marisol said, holding her finger in the air, "these are variants of the 'normal species,' and have genetic differences that we wouldn't know of. Or it's rapid evolution. Or we're wildly hallucinating all of this because we're tired and dehydrated and Lord knows there's a million volatile properties in tropical flora which we've been exposed to for weeks."

"Quite the set of options we have," David said, a smile breaking across his lips. "I don't think we'll know. At least not with what we have. The biggest question is—"

"What do we do now?"

"Exactly."

"I want to propose a theory," Ben said, inhaling. "If we piggyback onto David's previous theory of the rainforest protecting itself from us and also factor in Marisol's idea of it keeping us in here to starve us out, wouldn't it make sense that it would want to keep us away from resources? Close us off from the things we need to thrive?"

"I suppose it's possible," David replied. "What exactly are you suggesting?"

"That if that *is* the case, we need to push through the most dangerous parts to get out. I know we want to be conservative with clear-cutting, but I don't think this is going to work if we keep trying to find the paths of least resistance."

"Even after what happened with you before?" David asked.

"Trust me, this headache won't let me forget it, but if we're really going for this..."

"Then we really need to go for it," said Marisol with a curt nod. "I'm game. David?"

David looked past them and to the patch of palm fronds. He turned his head, seeing both of them staring at him, waiting. He sucked on his bottom lip as he slowly nodded his head. "But we should hold hands or tether ourselves together or something. The last thing we want to do is get separated...again."

"I agree." Ben held his hand out to Marisol. "I can go first."

Marisol grasped his hand, trying to steady the nervous tremors rippling throughout her body. David's palm pressed against hers when she held out her opposite hand, his fingers firmly gripping the back of hers.

"Just don't let go back there," Ben said, looking over his shoulder. His eyes flicked up to meet David's before he turned around, parted the palm fronds, and stepped through.

28

"Oh, come on!" David whined, tugging at the threads of his shirt as they slowly unraveled from his sleeve after pushing through the palms.

Marisol rolled her eyes. "It's just a shirt."

"If you haven't noticed, I'm down to like this one and one other one." David brought the threads to his mouth and ripped them against his teeth, leaving the severed pieces snagged onto the spikes of the palm fronds. He inched away as the leaves curled down, brushing against the loose threads. Pausing, he looked over his arms and legs. "Anyone else get scratched to hell?"

"Nothing too bad," Ben answered, looking up at David from where he sat cross-legged on the ground. He rested his head in the palms of his hands as his fingers rubbed at his temples.

David plopped on the ground next to him. "You hanging in there?"

"Yeah, I'll be fine. A little dizzy still, but a lot of that is probably lack of water."

"Hey guys!" Marisol's voice echoed from behind the line of trees to their right.

David hopped up, putting most of his weight on his good foot. He pulled Ben up with both hands before following

Marisol's voice through the woods. The ficus trees towered above them, the branching canopy far beyond their reach. They weaved between enormous, buttressed roots which draped from the trunk of the tree as if forming labyrinthian walls snaking along the jungle floor. David could just make out the top of Marisol's head from behind them.

"It's almost prehistoric," David whispered to himself.

"These trees have to be at least a few hundred years old," Ben said to him, running his hand along the rounded edge of the root. "I mean, the trunks themselves are bigger than a bus."

David stared off, mumbling under his breath. "It's crazy to think of something living that long."

"Have you ever been to the redwoods back home?"

David shook his head as his eyes moved over the bark, mentally cataloguing the colors and textures.

"Well, I get the same feeling when I'm there and surrounded by those magnificent trees. Makes you feel insignificant and yet important because you're a part of something so much bigger." Ben stopped and grabbed David's hand, smiling at him. "It doesn't have to be depressing."

"I didn't say it was." He found Ben's face and returned the smile. "I'm just deep in thought."

"You should live out here more often…and less in there," Ben said, tapping David's head with a finger. "And go visit the redwoods."

"Maybe we could go together?"

Ben's smile widened. "Maybe."

They stepped out of the shadows of the looming trees and into the open air. Marisol stood a few feet ahead of them. Leaf litter covered the soft dirt as small ferns fought their way up and into the sunlight. They stood, side-by-side, as they looked out over an expanse of bright, blue water. The sun shimmered off the lake, adding glints of gold and white to the serene surface.

"You see that, right?" David asked. "Like…there's water there?"

"There is definitely water there," Marisol beamed. Rushing

forward, she tossed her backpack to the ground and kicked off her shoes. Then, with a quick flourish, she peeled her socks off and shoved them into her sneakers before walking to the edge of the water and submerging her feet.

"You were right," David smiled, looking over to Ben. "I wouldn't have tried to go the way you suggested. We would've missed this entirely."

"Lucky guess out of desperation," Ben chuckled, watching Marisol at the water's edge.

"Bullshit." He tugged at Ben's arm to turn him around.

Ben faced him and smiled, lifting his hands to David's waist and pulling him closer. "Seems we make a good team."

"I think so." David met Ben's gaze as he felt his fingers hook into the belt loops of his pants. He blushed, averting his eyes. "Um..."

"We can always go check out those trees again. Give Marisol some privacy?" The corner of Ben's mouth raised in a sly grin.

David cleared his throat and took a step back, letting Ben's hands fall back. "As tempting as that sounds, and it is *really* tempting..." David hesitated, looking down at his tattered clothes and mud-splattered skin. "I am honestly beyond disgusting. Not that you haven't seen me in some pretty bad states, but I think almost a week of sweat and dirt, and well, everything else is probably not the biggest turn on."

Ben laughed. "Yeah. We are a little rank."

"A *little*?" David dramatically looked Ben up and down.

"Okay, okay, I get it. Raincheck?"

"Like you'd have to ask." David bit down on his lower lip before limping around Ben, dodging his hands as they playfully reached back out for him.

"Tease!" Ben half-yelled, half-laughed after him.

David dropped his backpack by Marisol's and sat down in the damp leaf litter before carefully prying off his shoes.

"How is it?" Marisol asked from the shoreline, leaving the water to come sit next to him.

"Pretty fucking swollen," he answered, pulling off the sock. "And apparently crazy bruised."

"Yikes." She grimaced as she looked down at his foot. "Does it hurt?"

David stared at Marisol and raised his eyebrows.

"Right. Obviously." She stood up and pulled off her shirt and pants, laying them on her backpack and up off the ground. She extended her hand down to him. "Do you need help?"

David grabbed her hand and stood, holding his foot up off the ground before gently lowering it to stand. He undressed to his underwear with Marisol helping to slide his pant leg over his foot. She crossed her arms and yanked her sports bra off, covering her breasts with one hand while sliding her underwear off.

"You know the rules," she warned, wagging a finger at David.

"I won't look if you won't."

"Are you skinny dipping?" Marisol teased, nudging him with an elbow.

"There is no way I'll feel even remotely clean if I keep wearing these."

"I get that. Between you and Ben, our tent is so nasty."

"Oh, like *you're* not sweaty and gross?"

"I'm a lady," she said, sticking her nose in the air. "I've never sweat a day in my life."

"I must have had you confused with some other chick staying in our tent."

"*Lady.*"

"Lady," David corrected. "Now go get in the water so I can take these off."

"You both look like crap," Marisol said, standing over David and Ben as they lay on their backs inside of the tent, towels wrapped around their waists.

"You're not all sunshine and rainbows yourself," Ben said without opening his eyes.

"Between David's busted ankle and the giant bruises on your head and shoulder…"

Ben lifted his head up to look at the green and yellow splotches stretched over the crook of his neck. "My shoulder looks much better thank you very much." He ran his hand along the skin, before laying back down and closing his eyes.

"I can't argue my case," said David, his eyes closed. "I'm just glad we decided to spend the night instead of trying to squeeze all the water purification and cleaning clothes—"

"And bodies!"

David shook his head. "Thanks, Ben. And bodies, all in one day. I can't even explain how good it feels to not be so grimy— even if it's just for a night."

"It certainly smells better in here," Marisol mused.

"Don't start on that lady shit again," David said with a chuckle. "I don't want to do anything but lay here the rest of the night."

"Well, not to burst that bubble, but we need to catch some fish," Ben said. "Take advantage of the lake before it gets dark."

"I'd be happy to skip dinner if it means I don't have to move."

Ben sat up and stared at David, his fingers tapping on the sleeping bag below them.

"What?"

"You really think I'm going to let you not eat?"

"Nope. I think you'll force me to eat, which means I don't need to fish, because you'll catch enough for the both of us."

"I'd let him starve after that one," Marisol said.

Ben slapped the back of his hand against David's side, making him flinch, before leaning over him and grabbing his backpack. "Oh, that's definitely on the table…"

Walking along the shoreline, David stared out at the lake as hundreds of small bats flitted throughout the air, snatching at bugs hovering over the dark water. He brought the meat of a roasted fish to his mouth and took a bite, tossing the bones to the water's edge. After letting out a satisfied sigh, he lowered himself to the ground and leaned back on his elbows. His eyes drifted to the sky and the thousands of stars dotting the deep indigo canvas. David tried to pick out the constellations in his head, connecting invisible lines in his mind to create the images he remembered from grade school.

"You have to admit, a view like this is almost worth all the pain and hassle," Ben said, coming over to sit next to him.

"Almost." David smiled, turning his head to face him. He glanced around Ben to their tent and supplies, scrunching his eyebrows. "Where'd Marisol get off to?"

"She said she was going to hang in the tent a bit. She seemed a little down, but she didn't want to talk to me about it."

David licked his dry lips, keeping his eyes on the tent. "It was all out of nowhere? She didn't say anything?"

"I mean, I was talking about my family an—"

"Ah," David said over him. "Makes sense."

Ben frowned, looking back to the tent. "Was it me?"

"No. She misses her dad and brothers a lot. She's been really homesick since we got here."

"Now I feel like a jerk."

"Don't. You didn't know." David bent forward and started to get up, avoiding putting pressure on his foot.

"Here." Ben hooked his hands under David's arms and lifted him up. "We going to go cheer her up?"

David laughed, meeting his eyes. "I was thinking more of sitting with her so she's not alone. But you're more than welcome to try." David hobbled over to the tent, crouched, and stuck his head inside. "Mind if we come in?"

Marisol raised her eyes from the picture frame sitting in her lap and gave a small shake of her head.

Ben ducked into the tent after David and squished himself against the wall. "I'm sorry if I—"

"Please don't apologize." Marisol held her hands up, stopping him. "I wasn't trying to be dramatic."

"Missing your family isn't dramatic," said Ben. "It's normal." He held out his hand. "May I?" Marisol handed him the picture frame. He sat back, looking it over. "That's a great family picture. Only girl in the family?"

Marisol smiled sadly. "Yep. Me and my brothers and my dad. My mom passed away when I was little."

"I'm sorry." Ben passed the frame back. "I can't imagine losing my mom. I'm the youngest of three with two older sisters. I miss them a lot. One of the downsides to not being back home."

David looked over to him. "I thought you said you don't miss it?"

"Well, most of the time I don't. But, if we're being honest, I feel like I'm missing a lot. Both of my sisters are married and have kids. I've got two nieces and a nephew, and my oldest sister, Beth, is due next month for another. I miss that kind of family time, I guess. I don't miss my mom pressuring me to settle down and start a family, though." Ben let out a small laugh.

"Luckily, I haven't had to deal with that from my dad. He's been really supportive," Marisol said. "He practically begged me to go start my own life in California."

"He may change his tune after he hears about all of this. Time to settle down and stop exploring once you get lost out in the rainforest."

Marisol laughed and looked down at the photo in her hands. "My brothers may flip out more than him. They're insanely protective."

Marisol froze as a metallic clang pierced the white noise of the jungle.

"Did we leave our cooking stuff outside?" Ben whispered, leaning his ear against the fabric.

Before anyone could answer, a sharp hiss reverberated from the outside of the tent, followed by several splashes from the lakeshore. David's face went pale, and his eyes trained on the door of the tent as another scrape of metal cut through the night. Marisol pushed herself into David and wrapped herself around his arm, her fingers digging into his skin.

David shifted uncomfortably, flinching as more breathy hisses boomed around them. "What the hell is that? It sounded like a cat but a hundred times bigger."

"That's not a cat," Marisol warned, looking at the walls of the tent. "I've heard this before. Alligators make that noise."

David pressed back against Marisol. "Alligators...like plural?"

Ben jumped toward him as a dark shape pushed against the fabric next to him. They watched the outline of bumps and grooves press along the vinyl as it dragged across the tent. The slow movement and friction against the material sent shivers down their spines. David cringed, his skin tingling at the sound. They held their breath, collectively waiting. Marisol threw her hands over her mouth to stifle a scream as something smacked against her back through the tent.

"Caiman," Ben whispered, his voice almost completely silent. He ran a shaky hand over his face. "I can't believe we left all our stuff out there."

Dark silhouettes moved along the fabric on either side of them, large and exaggerated in the lantern light. Ben held a finger up to his mouth. Another loud hiss erupted beside him and he jerked, almost diving into David's lap.

"What do we do?" David mouthed. His heart rattled in his chest as Marisol's hands dug tighter into his arm. He looked into Ben's eyes and noticed the peaceful blue which normally gave him comfort was obscured by his enlarged, black pupils.

"Lay low. Don't move," Ben mouthed back.

They huddled together in silence as they listened to the

caiman clamoring over their supplies. Spurts of hissing and growling on either side of the tent continued for what felt like hours. Marisol slowly inched in front of David after she was smacked again in the back, this time making her lose her grip on him as she was knocked forward. They released their grips on each other after a while when they heard soft splashes from the nearby lake, followed by the sounds of the caiman slowly dissipating. Once the area quieted for a time, Ben took a breath and crawled forward, reaching for the zipper to the door.

David gasped as his hand shot out and grabbed the back of Ben's arm. "What are you doing?"

"I'm just taking a quick look. I need to make sure our stuff is okay."

"Forget our stuff," Marisol said, her voice shaking. "Don't open the door. It can wait until morning. Let's just settle in. It's..." She looked down at her watch. "Jesus. It's already one a.m."

Ben let out a small sigh as he sat back up. "Until morning then." He slid David's backpack over and pulled out the first aid kit. He unsnapped the lid and rummaged through it.

"Here," David said, turning on a flashlight and shining it into the plastic box. "What are you looking for?"

"I wanted to wrap your ankle to help with the swelling."

"You don't have to do that."

"I know. But it'll help. You should also prop it up." Ben turned and grabbed his backpack, stacking it on top of David's. "There."

"That's going to be super comfortable," David said, sarcastically.

"Shut up and let me fix you. Besides, if we have to make a run for it tonight, you're going to be the slowest and most likely to get eaten. And I can't help you then."

Marisol snorted as she scooted away from David and straightened out her sleeping bag. "I like that he doesn't put up with your bullshit."

Ben flashed David a toothy smile before holding up a roll of bandages. "Found it. This'll only take a minute."

David glanced over to Marisol while Ben wrapped the bandage around his foot. "You're just fine going to bed? My adrenaline is still through the roof."

"I'm fine as long as they're not going to attack us through the tent. They were probably just investigating."

"It didn't sound like investigating."

"I thought you were an animal expert?" Marisol joked, her back turned to him as she laid in her sleeping bag.

"Animal expert?" Ben asked, arching an eyebrow.

"Oh, he didn't tell you he was going to be a zoologist?"

David groaned and shifted his gaze to Ben, shaking his head in resignation. "I wasn't going to be a zoologist."

"Yes, you were!" Marisol insisted, sitting up and lightly shoving his shoulder. "It's not something to be embarrassed about, you know."

"You never stop, do you?" David turned his attention away from Marisol and back to Ben. "I almost pursued that PhD instead of the ESPM program."

Ben wrinkled his nose. "ESPM?"

"Environmental Science, Policy, and Management, with emphasis on organisms and environment—mainly invasive species and their effects." David narrowed his eyes at Marisol. "Doesn't mean I was going to be a zoologist. And I'm sorry if my animal knowledge didn't prepare me for being surrounded by caiman in the middle of the rainforest."

"Touchy topic then?" asked Ben.

"Only when I'm bugging him about it," Marisol answered for him.

"Well, your wrap is done at least. And not to rub salt in the wound, but I agree with Marisol. As scary as that was, I think their curiosity is sated. I've never been quite that close to them before."

"Scary?" David scoffed. "More like fucking terrifying."

"One more thing to add to your little notebook?" Marisol asked, smirking at David.

A small grin played on Ben's lips. "What little notebook?"

"Enough questions," David said, rolling his eyes. "You wanted to go to bed, so let's go to bed…and hope none of us are dinner by morning."

"It's already morning. We'd be breakfast," Marisol corrected. "I just…I…goodnight."

29

Ben ran his hand along the trunk of a rubber tree lining the edge of the path. They had been trekking throughout most of the morning, happy to move on from the lake after a restless night. After filling their water containers, they wasted no time heading back into the jungle. As they walked, the landscape morphed from bright bromeliads into sharp and spiny trunks and limbs. David inched around the large, spiky bamboo clumps, the twinge of phantom pain from his back keeping him wary. Their shoes squished into the mud, their steps loud from the suction of their shoes pulling from the soaked earth. Ben had stopped when he saw the rubber tree; it was the first time they had slowed all morning. His fingers brushed against a faded red square painted onto the trunk.

"This is a marker," Ben said, his hand still lingering over the square. He slowly turned, his eyes wide, looking toward them. A smile broke across his lips. "We're not far. Maybe a couple of miles. I know this grid."

"You're serious," David said, glancing between Ben and the red square on the tree. He blinked, not believing the words.

"Dead serious. The grids near the lodge are marked and recorded on a map." Ben dropped to his knees, ripping his backpack off and swinging it in front of him. His hands plunged into the body of the bag, digging frantically. "Please, please, please work," he whispered, as he extracted a small, silver object gripped in his hand. He flipped it over into his palm, watching the needle waver.

"I've tried using a compass before. All it did was point me in a circle," Marisol said, crouching down beside him. "You think it's going to start working now?"

"It has to." Ben's eyes focused on the red needle as it bobbed back and forth. "If we head the wrong way, we'll end up heading in the opposite direction. If we head the right way…"

"Then we're out," David exhaled.

The needle swung back and forth, swaying as they held their breath, the silence between them punctuated only by the birds chirping in nearby branches. Ben tensed his jaw as the red line of the needle settled on the large "N" on the face of the compass. A slow, steady breath seeped out from between his lips as his lungs deflated. He glanced to his side, seeing Marisol waiting to meet his gaze. Turning his head up to David, he locked eyes with him, David's face worried and expectant.

"I can get us home," he near-whispered, breaking into a wide smile. His eyes moved between them, the corners beginning to water. "I can get us home."

Ben wove through the trees, increasing their pace as they moved forward. He had found another red square, this time painted onto an algae-covered, wooden stake pounded into the dirt. A crack of thunder rumbled through the sky, its dark blanket blotted out of sight by the canopy. Raindrops pounded the branches, the slapping of water against the leaves taking over the normal, lively buzz of the rainforest. Trickles of rain dripped onto them from gaps in the leaves above, seeping into their clothes and soaking their skin. The forest exploded with light as another loud crash of thunder shook the ground underfoot.

"We should find a place to stop!" David yelled over the storm.

"But we're so close!" Ben bellowed back over Marisol's head.

Another snap over the sky caused David to jump, and his hands flew up to cling to the straps of his backpack. He whipped his head to the right, watching the trees and shrubs beside him as lightning illuminated the branches. David focused, the heavy rain drowning out most of his other senses. He stared at the limbs as they lit up from another flash, the quick burst of light giving them the guise of fingers moving and reaching in the dim light.

He squinted after the flash subsided, staring at the shadows moving beyond the trees. Goosebumps rose on his skin and a wave of chills tingled down his spine. With his feet frozen to the ground, his heartbeat thumped in his ears, mixing and mingling with the chaotic rhythm of the rain beating against the canopy. He watched as the branches clawed and grasped at the open spaces between them, moving closer together with each shimmering flash of light.

"David! Keep up!" Marisol yelled to him.

He tore his view from the trees and to Marisol, who stood several yards away. Her hair was plastered in wet ringlets around her face, the strands having come loose from her ponytail in the onslaught of rain. She raised her hand, waving for him to catch up. He stole another glance to his side before skirting around the prickly trees and over to where she stood.

"You good?" she asked, her voice raised above the rain.

David nodded, the rainwater dripping down his face from his drenched hair. "Thought I saw someth—" He paused, watching Marisol's eyes slide past him and widen in terror. "Wh-what?"

Marisol raised a shaky finger and pointed behind him. The pit of his stomach ached, turning over on itself as he tried to muster up the courage to turn around. He swallowed, steeling himself. When he turned, David's heart skipped and the air caught in his lungs as his body went cold.

The thorny roots of the walking palms and scraggly branches of the surrounding shrubs were closing in on themselves as if the jungle were stitching itself together to close an open wound. The clear spaces they had passed through moments before were now occupied by twisting vines which draped from the canopy, seemingly pulling the two sides of the path together. The spines from nearby trees interlocked and leaned toward them, creating a barbed blockade, closing out the little light that had been present. David watched, rooted to the spot, as the path sealed itself shut and moved closer to where they stood.

Water streamed down his face as branches twisted and cracked above him, opening a path to the deluge from the sky above. David's body pulsed to the pounding of his heartbeat, the heavy thumps echoing in his ears. Marisol was screaming, but her voice was distant and muffled as if he were submerged in water trying to listen to people talking on the shore.

"David!"

David blinked and looked down to see Ben's hand gripping his arm, twisting him around and yanking him backward.

"David!" Ben said, inches from his face. "We have to move!"

David looked at him, trying to focus on what he was saying. His gaze wandered past Ben and to the trees ahead. The path was closing. Vines spiraled around the trunks and along the ground, weaving into the exposed roots and working their way back up into the branches overhead. Marisol bounced on her feet a few feet away, anxiously looking between them and the way forward. The forest behind her swayed, the trees, ferns, and shrubs morphing and forcing them down into the little space they had left.

Ben reached down and squeezed his hands. "David! Hey! I need you to snap out of it!"

David's eyes moved back to Ben, feeling him squeeze tighter against his hands, his nails to digging into the skin. He breathed in, his lungs straining against the air as he struggled to fill his chest and catch his breath.

"David," Ben repeated, reaching up to his face and making him look into his eyes.

"Yeah." He blinked several times, bringing his eyes into focus. "Okay." He nodded, still gasping for air between breaths.

"Guys! Come on!" Marisol yelled as she slipped between two trees at the end of the trail.

Ben shoved David forward as they ran to catch up. David tumbled to his knees as his ankle gave out underneath him. Without stopping, Ben yanked him up by his arm and dragged him to his feet.

"Go on," David said, pushing Ben toward the trees. "I'm okay. Keep an eye on Marisol."

"You should go fir—"

"There's no time to argue. Just go!"

Ben squeezed David's arm and turned, tilting his body to the side as he shimmied between the set of trees after Marisol. David followed, sucking in his stomach and squishing between the ever-shrinking gaps in the trees. He looked back once more, terror seizing him as the jungle moved before his eyes.

He remembered Dr. Morrow talking about how formidable this ecosystem was, how it was the perfect setting for a horror movie, how it was oppressive and dark and pointy. David watched as the palms, with their long, thorn-covered roots, stretched across the trail, the vines attached to them snapping and falling away like strands of loose hair.

This is scarier than any movie, he thought before he forced himself to break away and slide between the trees, trying to block those images from his mind.

He emerged from the trees to see Ben and Marisol already several feet ahead. David's eyes darted around him, the branches from every tree bending and swaying in a breeze that he couldn't feel. The sounds of snapping twigs behind him made his skin crawl and heart quicken.

"We should almost be there," Ben panted, a mixture of sweat and rainwater soaking him from head to foot.

Tears streamed down Marisol's cheeks as she looked behind them. "It's still coming!"

Cracks and groans echoed around them as the jungle rearranged itself, closing off both new and old paths. The ripping of roots lifting and tearing from the soggy earth continued from behind them.

"We need to keep moving," David said. The hair on his arms and the back of his neck stood on end, each noise sending a shiver along his skin.

Ben wiped the compass off on his shirt and turned, trying to find the right direction. Mid-turn, he tossed it into his pocket and unhooked the machete from his backpack.

"What are you doing?" Marisol snapped, tugging at his shirt.

"We don't have a choice!" Ben swung the blade down, chopping away at the vines and branches. He reached forward, throwing the debris to the side and gritting his teeth as he watched more take its place. He brought the machete down again, clearing the way forward.

Marisol shrieked from behind him and fell to her knees, catching herself with her hands. "David!"

David lunged forward and grabbed her arms to pull her to her feet. She slipped out of his grip and back down to the ground as he tried to catch her, his muddied hands leaving streaks on her arms.

"It's got my leg!" Marisol turned onto her back and sat up, reaching down to her left leg. A dark red vine crept out of the bushes to the right and tangled around her. The thick tendrils twisted around her ankle and calf and weaseled into her pant leg. She ripped at it, trying to slide it off.

"Don't move!" Ben said, stopping and crouching down beside her. "Remember, you need to be still."

"I'm trying," she sobbed, her body shaking as she sat crouched in the mud. Marisol laid her leg flat on the ground and sat back. Immediately, the vine went taut and wrenched her leg forward, dragging her through the mud and toward the trees. She cried out, digging her hands into the soft mud to stop herself from being pulled deeper into the jungle. A deep groove trailed in the mud behind her as she kicked, trying to loosen the vine.

David dove into the mud and grabbed her hand, but her body pulled tight between his grip and the vine as it continued to tighten around her leg. He could feel the tension in her muscles as he drew her closer to him.

"Cut the fucking vine!" David grunted, trying to keep his grip on her. He dug his feet into the mud on either side of her for leverage.

Ben bent down and swung his machete, slicing it through the vine and watching it fall away. Marisol scooted backward, her hands and feet frantically slipping through the mud as she slid back on her butt. She twisted, throwing herself against David's chest and curling up in the mud between his legs.

David wrapped his arms around her and held her tight as she sobbed into him. He began to loosen his grip to bring them to their feet, but Marisol clenched her fists against his shirt, stopping him. Before he could blink, her hands tore at his back as she was yanked away once more. David reached for her, but barely grazed her fingertips by the time he reacted. He slipped in the mud, crawling after her as he watched her getting pulled toward the thorny trunks ahead. Marisol's leg lifted up, suspended by another vine twirled around her leg. David's mouth dropped as he saw it jerk her up and away from the ground as her hands clawed behind her to gain purchase. He dove forward and grabbed at her hand, gripping her wrist, and pulled against the vine, bringing her closer to the ground. Marisol scratched at his arms, trying to pull herself back.

He lifted his head to look at Ben, who stood over them, frozen and still holding his machete. His wet and muddy hair fell around his face and over his wide and panicked eyes.

"Ben! Fucking do something!"

Ben blinked and looked down to the machete in his hands.

"Cut it again!"

Ben swung forward, slicing the blade through the vine as it lodged into the tree behind it. Marisol splashed into the mud as she dropped the remaining inches back onto the ground. She forced her way back against David, pressing herself into him. David's grip tightened around her as her body heaved into his, the sobs wracking her body.

"We need to move fast," David said, his eyes wandering to the blade in Ben's hand.

Ben shook his head, his shoulders sinking in defeat. "It's not going to work." He looked behind David and to the direction from which they had come.

David turned his head, following Ben's gaze. Thick curtains of vines draped around the trees, the tips buried into the dirt and out of sight. Large spines erupted through them, pressing forward and closing in. The pops of broken and shifting branches grew in intensity as they looked on.

"We're going to be stuck here," Marisol cried, raising her head from David's chest.

"No," David said sternly, his forehead creasing with determination. "No. No we're not. Get up." Thick mud caked his clothes as he brought himself to his feet. He reached around and unsheathed his machete from his backpack. His eyes met Ben's. "We cut through…your call on where. When there's enough cut away to squeeze in," he turned to Marisol, "you go through and don't stop going. Don't wait for us."

"But—"

"There's no time. Take off your backpack."

"But my stu—"

"I promise I won't let anything happen to it. You need to be as small and as fast as possible." David's eyes settled on Ben as he walked up to the bushes and raised his machete. "Ready when you are."

The rough edges of the bark scraped along Marisol's skin, burning and tingling as she clawed her way through the bushes. She kept her head down, propelling herself forward with her hands in front of her. The sharp twigs sliced at her hands as she snapped them and pushed them out of the way. She wasn't sure how long she had been running, or at least quickly fumbling through the dense wood. Roots pressed at the soles of her shoes as she pressed on, not taking the time to slow or look back. Her muscles burned and she groaned, wondering if she was even still going the right direction. With a grunt, she snapped off branches in front of her and tumbled forward onto her knees, hitting the dirt with a soft thud. A light breeze passed over her. Her skin tingled and itched, the scratches from the branches leaving red marks along her face and neck. She glanced to her arms and saw the fabric of her shirt torn in several places. Marisol raised her head, a sharp gasp escaping her lips. She stumbled to her feet and looked at the open space before her. A large sign stood but ten feet away.

TAMSHIYACU-TAHUAYO RESERVE D5 ENTRANCE

"What are you waiting for?" David panted as he sliced his machete through the thin twigs. He looked behind them; the vines carpeted the ground, stopping mere inches from where they stood. The thorns broke through the ferns and bushes and pressed at their backs, tugging at David's clothes when he stepped back. "Go!"

Ben turned his head to the side, locking eyes with him. "You'll be right behind me? Promise?"

"Promise. Now go!"

Ben threw his machete to the ground and plunged forward into the trees. He could hear David's blade ricocheting off the branches as they folded back in on themselves, repairing the gash they had opened. Pausing, he glanced back, but saw nothing but the jungle closing in behind him. Ben tucked his head to his chest, leaned his shoulder forward, and pushed through the foliage. The branches snagged in his hair and tore at his clothes, like greedy hands trying to halt his escape. Squeezing his eyes shut, he pressed onward, tensing as sharp thorns stabbed at his skin. Small pools of blood spread through the cotton fabric of his shirt, already soaked with water and sweat. He twisted to try and look behind him but flinched as the limbs tugged and ripped out his hair, leaving the dark strands dangling in their grip.

Frustrated, he stopped to untangle himself, pulling at the twigs sticking into him and blocking his way. Ben glanced down at his watch and tried to remember if he had even looked at the time before diving in. Peering over his shoulder, he hoped to see or hear David following behind him, yet there was still nothing. Nothing but leaves and limbs and worry. Ben swallowed, resigning with the gut feeling that he had to keep moving, so he tucked his head back to his chest and continued on.

He ground his teeth as the branches continued their assault on him. Without warning, something warm and wet wrapped around his arm. Ben yelped and whipped his head around, getting more tangled the more he struggled. The plants sliced at him as he flailed, and he screamed out, ripping his arm back instinctively as he pictured his last run in with the vines. His arm jerked forward, the warm grip tight and unrelenting. He contorted as best he could and tried to tear his arm away, to push himself back into the trees and away from this new onslaught.

"It's me! Stop fighting!" a familiar voice cut through his panic.

He stopped and opened his eyes, slowly turning toward the voice, his breath ragged in his chest. Marisol stared back at him through the trees, her hand still wrapped tightly around his arm. Ben let her at him as she reached in with another hand and began snapping the branches back, clearing his way. He fell to his knees as he stared up at her. Fresh scrapes covered her face, the blood around them already clotted and dried.

Marisol crouched in front of him, her eyes mirroring his own panic. "Is David behind you?"

Leaves whipped against David's face as he tore his backpack off and threw it on the ground alongside his machete. His knees sank into the mud as he leaned forward, rummaging through the contents of the three backpacks laid out on the ground before him. Untying the sleeping bag from Marisol's backpack, he slid it behind him, pressing it into the spines which loomed closer with each passing minute. Next, he dragged Ben's bag in front of him, digging through the mess of clothes and jars of random concoctions.

"Found you," David whispered, as he pulled out Ben's copy of *Tarzan of the Apes*, shoved it into Marisol's bag, and zipped it closed.

A soft breeze blew from the trees in front of him. David glanced up. The opening where Ben and Marisol had entered fused shut once more, the branches weaving into one another and obscuring the way through. He swore under his breath, turning to his backpack and detaching the sleeping bag from the top. David swung the bag onto his back, securing it in place before picking up Marisol's and strapping it on backwards, the body of the backpack resting against his chest. His hand searched through the mud, eventually grasping the handle of his machete. He stood, careful not to brush up against the spines, and faced the path ahead.

With a few swings of the blade, David dove in, grimacing as the branches lashed against his face. He felt blood dripping down his cheeks as he attempted to shield his face with his forearm. Moving forward with his machete in front of him, he carefully cut away the encroaching plants. Some vines cut away easily, but he couldn't gain enough purchase to make much of a path through the thicker limbs. After trying a few different angles, David stopped, hesitating as his eyes moved to his sides. His heart thumped in his chest as he watched the red vines creep through the branches, winding through the gaps and heading toward him. He scanned the area, holding his breath, his lungs screaming for air. There was no clear direction. The jungle had stitched itself back together one last time.

David let out a long, shaky breath. He bit down on his lower lip, his eyes watering, as he ran through his options. A small tickle on his ankle caught his attention, and he twisted himself around to look. A weak groan escaped him as he shook his head and closed his eyes, a few tears falling down his cheeks and stinging his open cuts. His eyes opened to see the tips of the vines inching around the top of his shoe, the rootlets creeping up and over the heel and into the opening of his pant leg.

Just move forward. Don't give up. You can think your way out of this.

David twisted back around, facing forward. He took another breath—steadier this time—while the beating of his heart pounded in his veins.

"I'm not a threat!" he cried, closing his eyes. "I won't do any more damage. I-I-I'm sorry we disturbed you." Tears streamed down his cheeks as the vine crept higher up his leg. "I swear, we didn't know—if that's even what this is. I don't even know who I'm talking to, but please. I'm not trying to do any harm. I...I just want to go home."

The jungle squeezed tighter against him, the plants grabbing at his clothes and tangling his hair. David swallowed as he let the sensations run over his body. His ankle throbbed and his head ached. He had tried everything. David sucked in a quick breath as thorns pricked into his skin and pierced through his clothes. More vines continued to creep through the limbs to tickle his face, probe around his hands and feet.

"I'm sorry," he whispered.

David held his breath as the vines slowly wrapped around him. He listened to the sounds of the leaves moving against each other and the vines crawling along the woody stems. He let his mind drift to Ben and Marisol, hoping they weren't left to the same fate, ensnared somewhere in the layers of greenery and thorns. David imagined Marisol shouting his name after he sent her in first. A rat in a maze.

"David!"

His eyes shot open. *Am I imagining it?* He waited, his breath pumping out in shallow bursts.

"David!"

"Marisol!" he yelled out, his voice cracking. David strained against the tendrils and pushed himself against the thorny twigs, ignoring them piercing into his skin.

"David! We're coming!"

The straps on his backpack pressed against his shoulders as he leaned forward. He squinted into the branches and saw Marisol's silhouette against the sun.

"Marisol! I'm stuck!"

He flinched as a machete blade chipped away at the limbs in front of him. Marisol's hand stuck through the branches, reaching out palm open and waiting for his hand in return. David stretched forward, his fingertips barely brushing hers. The vines tugged against his backpack and he gasped, unable to reach her. Another breeze whooshed around him and he was pulled back as the rainforest tried to reclaim him. He pushed with the balls of his feet, growling through his teeth as he willed his ankle to take the pressure. His shoes slipped in the mud and his foot gave way. He slid further back into the jungle, the opening ahead getting smaller as he watched Marisol reach in after him.

David stared into Marisol's eyes as she peered at him through the branches. His heart hurt at the fear he saw glossing over her pupils.

"It's going to be okay," he said, not breaking eye contact. David wasn't sure if he managed to say it out loud or if he had just thought it. He reached up, slipping her backpack off his chest, and pushed it toward her. A weight tugged on the other side of the bag in response.

"Good idea! Just hang on!" she shouted to him.

David let go of the backpack, letting it slip out of his fingers. "Your picture is in there…from your dad."

"What? No!"

"And Ben's book," he continued, trying not to listen to the panic in her voice while suppressing his own.

"We're getting you out, David," Marisol cried.

He dropped his machete to the ground and brought his hands up to his face and then around to the back of his head. His body scraped against the limbs as the vines pulled against his backpack, dragging him away from Marisol's voice. The trees closed around him, her silhouette becoming another shadow amongst the limbs. He tugged at the straps, slipping them off as he fell to his knees, the thorns from the branches below him slicing into his shins and kneecaps.

As he knelt on the ground, the familiar cool, rubbery sensation of the vines danced along the back of his neck. David closed his eyes and focused on his breathing. He began to name the things around him.

Vine, mud, spikes, bark, leaves...

David inhaled through his nose and held it for a minute before releasing it through his mouth.

Rain, sweat, roots, thorns...

He repeated the same breathing and cataloguing over and over again until he lost count of how many times he had taken a breath. Warm tears trickled down his face, burning the cuts along his skin.

He opened his eyes. Marisol's voice floated through the air, though he couldn't tell what she was saying. He lifted a shaky hand to the back of his neck. His fingers brushed against the plants as they slid off and away from him. Turning slowly, he watched them sway as they dangled from an overhead branch. He staggered to his feet and spun around, ignoring the stinging of the branches against his skin.

"Thank you," David whispered, his mind racing. "I don't know what I did, but thank you." He blinked, waiting to see the shadows lurking and moving between the branches, returning for him if he moved. With a steadying breath, he lifted his foot and crept forward.

He snuck through the trees, careful to avoid any bending or

breaking of the limbs. His legs wobbled from nerves as he stepped around the roots. He removed his shirt after a couple of feet as it continually snagged against the twigs, threatening to snap them off. The ends of the branches scraped his arms and chest, leaving dark red marks streaked along his pale skin. As he stuck his leg through another layer, a set of hands reached through the trees and wrapped around his torso.

Before he could react, he was yanked through the last of the foliage and into Ben's arms. Another set of arms pressed against him as Marisol joined in, hugging him tightly. They were talking to him, but their words were muted and distant. David could feel the vibrations of their voices tingling along his skin.

He stood there a moment, caught up in the sensation of flesh on flesh. He had so recently thought he would never feel anything other than the cold, menacing grip of plants against his skin. David lifted his head and turned toward the tree line, waiting for one last assailing vine or limb or curse to come breaking through and drag him away.

"What is it?" asked Ben.

"Nothing," he said, turning to face them. "Literally nothing."

30

"No, Papa, I'm fine." Marisol leaned her elbows on the large wooden table, a cellphone tucked between her ear and shoulder. Her feet kicked at the legs of the chair as she shifted in her seat. "The next flight is in a couple weeks, I think." She looked out through the mesh screen of the stilted hut and down into the trees. "Yes, I promise," she sighed into the phone. "I love you too, Papa." Marisol placed the phone on the table and rested her head in her hands. She stared down at the scratches on the table, the small grooves blurring as tears filled her eyes.

"You alright?" David walked up behind her and rested his bandaged hand on her shoulder.

"Mmhmm," Marisol hummed, raising her head and wiping her eyes. "It's just hard. I want to tell him everything, but he'll just freak out."

"So, did you decide to stay with him for a bit before heading back home?"

"I think I will. The layover goes to Miami anyway, so it's just cancelling the second leg. What about you? What did you tell your parents?"

"I haven't called them." He pulled a chair over, collapsing into it and leaning against the table next to her.

"What? David! After everyth—"

He held his hands up and let out a breathy laugh. "I *will*… maybe." He ran his fingers along the resin covered-table. "It's probably just easier to wait until I'm back home. No need to waste someone's data and take up the Wi-Fi for that. Those phone calls have to be a fortune."

"I'm sure they're worried sick about you."

"And I'm sure they don't even remember I'm out of the country. Besides, I'm just happy to be right here." David tapped his pointer finger against the table before motioning to the window. "And not out there."

"Except we have to have this whole debriefing thing. I don't know how to even begin to explain…"

"Well, Ben's been talking to them for the last hour since we got back. Hopefully, he's got most of it covered, although I know he's wanting to call his family, too. I feel bad they kind of ushered him away."

"Makes sense since they actually know him. I feel like everyone just keeps staring at us."

"Because they *are* staring at us," David chuckled. He shook his head, running his fingertips over his oily scalp. "I wish they had let us clean up first before sequestering us in here."

"No kidding." Marisol looked down at her arms, mud and blood still smeared across them. Several small adhesive bandages plastered her skin, covering her various scrapes and cuts. "At least we got patched up?"

"At the very least."

"I mean, after Dr. Morrow…" Marisol started, her gaze drifting to the expanse of jungle outside the window. "I don't blame them for being wary."

"Do you think she's still out there?" David asked, lowering his voice to a near-whisper, as if it were too painful to say out loud.

"I don't know." Marisol turned her head to look at David. "I hope so."

"Me too."

Marisol sat up and straightened her posture as the heavy

wooden door to their right swung open, banging against the timber wall and rattling the hut. She stole a quick glance to David before redirecting her attention.

"Were you able to reach your families?" Claudio asked from the doorway, nodding to the phone on the table.

"Yes, thank you," David answered quickly as he stood up, pushing his chair back under the table.

"If you're both ready…" Claudio waved his arm in front of him, motioning through the door.

Marisol stood and touched the small of David's back, pushing him. He limped forward and crossed the room, passing Claudio and stepping onto the raised walkway of the lodge. Marisol followed, speeding up to walk next to him. They walked past the main cabin and toward the staff buildings. David paused, looking back to Claudio.

"The last one on the right," Claudio said. "The door's propped open."

David made his way to the open door, stepped inside, and was met with a host of familiar faces. Paul stood at the far wall, rapidly flipping through pages of a textbook expertly balanced in his hand. Nelly and Andy sat together on a table along the wall, talking quietly between themselves. David's attention moved to Ben, seated in a wooden chair in the corner; he jumped to his feet once David entered the room. A small smile flashed across his face as he crossed the room to meet him.

"Hey," Ben whispered, close to his face. "I'm sorry I got pulled away. They just want to hear it from you guys, too. I think they want to make sure I didn't go completely batshit crazy." He gently ran his hands down David's arms, stopping at the cotton bandages wrapped around his hand. He raised David's hand in his, inspecting the handiwork as he flipped it over and ran his fingers along David's palm. He frowned, letting out a big sigh. "I can re-do these when we're done. How's your ankl—" Ben dropped David's hand and grimaced as Claudio cleared his throat from beyond the doorway. "Sorry!" Ben stepped to the side, offering David his chair.

David's stomach knotted as he walked further inside. He stepped next to the chair, offering it to Marisol, who threw herself into it, crossed her arms along her stomach, and shrunk in on herself. Claudio stepped in behind them and leaned against the door frame.

"So," he began. His fingers tapped against his shorts as he shifted his weight on his feet. "I'm sure during this time that you've become acquainted with Ben here, you've found he's not the irrational or illogical type."

David looked out of the corner of his eyes to Ben before redirecting them back to Claudio. He swallowed, nodding in agreement.

"But this all does seem a bit fantastical."

"I swear it's not," David blurted out. "I didn't believe it until I saw it. I can guarantee whatever he said to you is the truth. I can't explain it."

"He says that you *have* explained it."

David spun his head around to Ben, his eyebrows raised in question. "What?" he mouthed as his face slackened in worry.

"You kinda did," Ben said, face scrunching in apology.

David stared back at Claudio, his mouth hanging half-open. "I don't know about that. I, uh...I mean..." David swallowed and licked his lips, his mouth going bone-dry.

"You think it's something about the research?" Paul asked from behind him, snapping his book shut. "Or at least, something to that effect? About exploring beyond our mapped grid?"

David turned around to look at him. "In a way," he said, his voice raspy and dry. He swallowed again. "I think we're...*invasive*? If you will? Like, we were causing it to happen because we were clear-cutting for research stations and taking samples. And maybe those species have different defense mechanisms we haven't yet discovered or studied...and we're going into places where people haven't gone before, and maybe that means we're threatening its survival or ecosystem or it's trying to st—"

Ben touched David's arm, cutting him off.

"Sorry," David said, taking a breath.

"And I'm sure you have plenty of experiences to make you think this?" Paul pressed.

"I think we do."

"We can get to all of that later, Paul," Claudio said, stepping forward. "The one thing Ben couldn't tell us about was Julia."

David tucked his head down, looking at Marisol. She still sat half-balled up in the chair.

"We don't know what happened," David said quietly, raising his head and making eye contact with Claudio. "We woke up at the second site, and she was just…"

"Gone," Marisol finished for him. "We tried to look for her. That was when we got a hold of you here. We did try." Marisol raised a hand to her eyes and wiped away the tears beginning to build up.

David rested his hand on her shoulder, running his thumb along the back of her neck. "I found her SAT phone and one of her bags, but that was it. There was no…*anything* to show where she may have gone."

"Do you have reason to suspect she had enough supplies with her to continue to sustain herself out in the grid?"

David lightly squeezed Marisol's shoulder as he took a deep breath, contemplating his next words. "I think…I think if anyone was going to be able to do it, it would be her." He spun, looking around at everyone in the room. "I-I don't think she's…" David cleared his throat.

"I agree," Marisol said, standing up from the chair. "She's really tough, and she knows what she's doing. I don't know what the next steps would be, but Ben was surviving out there just fine for, like, a month."

"And she taught me everything I know," Ben added.

"Very well." Claudio nodded, studying the three of them. "Why don't we discuss next steps once you're all recuperated?

An additional few hours isn't going to change anything right now. Let's get you set up in some rooms. We just had a new group of guests arrive yesterday, so we're a little short on space."

"David and I can share a room," Ben offered.

David stiffened and eyed Ben out of the corner of his eyes. Ben glanced back and cocked his head to the side, the look on his face a silent question at his response.

"Alright," Claudio said, turning to Marisol. "If you'll follow me, I'll show you to your cabin. Ben, I know you said David needed some clothes. Feel free to take some from here while I get your cabin set up. All of your stored things are in Paul's cabin."

"Thanks, Claudio." Ben smiled. He waited as everyone left the room then turned to David as Paul made his way out and shut the door behind him. "What? Should I not have offered? You can stay with Marisol. I didn't mean to insin—"

"No, not at all," David interjected. "Sorry. I just…I guess I'm not used to…" He shrugged, letting out a sigh. "I'm happy you offered." The corner of his lip raised in a half-attempt at a smile.

"You seem thrilled." Ben arched an eyebrow at him. "Don't look at me like that. I get it. You're worried what they're all thinking or what they're going to say or not say. Don't be."

"Like it's that easy…"

"It is." Ben crossed to the dresser and opened the top drawer, pulling out various shirts and throwing them on the bed. "It doesn't matter. I've been out here with all of them for over a year. They know me, and they've never treated me any different. Because I'm not different." He walked over to David and stretched a shirt out by the shoulders, holding it up against David's chest. He looked down and met his eyes. "And neither are you. Okay? Now try this on and make sure it fits. Actually don't, you're all muddy; it'll be fine. Take this one, and I'll snag a few more."

David draped the shirt over his arm as he watched Ben rifle through the next set of drawers, pulling out gym shorts and khaki pants. He stared down at his feet, wanting to say something to break the tension, but as usual, couldn't find the words.

"Earth to David," Ben said, as he snapped his fingers. "What size pants?" He stood, hand propped on his hip as he tapped his foot on the wooden floor.

"Um…34."

Ben went back to sifting through the drawer. "Look, if you're more comfortable bunking with Marisol, that's more than fine. I mean, my feelings may be a little hurt since we just spent weeks sharing a sleeping bag, but—"

"No. I guess I'm still not used to just being me sometimes, especially around other people. I didn't mean to get weird. And I'd much rather share a bed than a sleeping bag."

"God, I can't wait to sleep in a bed!" Ben exclaimed, tilting his head back. "So, do you think you could try to stop over-thinking for just a little bit then? For me?"

A small smile passed over David's face. "I will…work on it."

"Promise?"

"Promise." David's gaze moved to the door, his smile dropping. "Do you think they're going to go looking for her?"

"Probably. But they went looking for me, too. Not that that means anything really."

"…yeah."

"Hey," Ben said, coming over and wrapping his hands around David's waist. "Let's get showered and settled, and then we'll regroup." He removed his hands and bundled up the small pile of clothes in his arms. "And I'm definitely going to need to double check all of your cuts and stuff. Marisol, too. Not that I don't trust whoever bandaged you up, but you don't need another infection."

"I *definitely* don't want that."

"Me either." He shook his head and wrinkled his face in disgust. "No offense, but that was insanely gross. Satisfying to fix, but gross."

"Yeah, I'm sorry you had to do that."

"No apologies necessary. You were cute, all passed out and feverish."

"I'm sure," David snorted as he opened the door and stepped out onto the walkway. "Which cabin is ours?"

Marisol sat waiting at a long, wooden table in the main cabin. Her backpack sat on the table off to the side as she stabbed small pieces of fruit with a fork from the plate in front of her. The lodge visitors shuffled around the various tables, gathering food from a large buffet on the far side of the room. Most of them sat in small groups, talking excitedly to themselves over heaping plates of fish, bread, and rice. Marisol listened in on the group nearest to her as they discussed their morning hike.

"Hey," David said, plopping down into the chair next to her. He peered over at her plate. "How can you be picky when this is the first real food we've had in weeks?"

"How can you be in the mood to eat? My appetite is out the window," she grumbled without looking up from her plate.

David leaned back in his chair and shrugged. "I always have an appetite." He glanced over at the buffet table as he sat forward, resting his hands on the table. "I'm gonna go get a plate before it's all gone." David pushed his chair back and edged around the perimeter of the room toward the food, avoiding all the tables where people were seated.

"Think he'll have the foresight to bring me a plate?" Ben asked, pulling a chair out across from Marisol and taking a seat.

She smiled up at him. "I think that may be asking a lot."

Ben returned the smile and leaned his head to the side, looking her over. "What's up?" His eyebrows pinched together in concern. "Besides the obvious...obviously."

"A lot of the obvious. I'm worried about having to answer questions, anxious to put all this behind me. I don't even know what to do from here, just pretend Dr. Morrow isn't out there missing or hurt or..."

Ben reached his hand across the table and laid it over hers. "You were right earlier, you know. I was out there a long time, even without all that crazy shit...on my own. Julia is tough. She's capable. If she's even half as tough and capable as you, she's probably fine. It's just a matter of finding her."

Marisol sighed and offered him a forced smile. Ben gripped her hand a little tighter before leaning back in his chair and sliding his hands through his hair.

"Felt good to take an actual shower with soap, didn't it?" he said, changing the topic.

Marisol giggled, touching her hairline. "My hair has never been more thankful for shampoo." She watched Ben fiddle with the waves falling around his face. Her gaze drifted behind him but quickly moved back to catch his eyes. She lifted her eyebrows and a small smile played on her lips as David approached him from behind.

"Some dinner for you," David said, placing an overflowing plate in front of Ben. He sat his equally full plate next to Ben's as he slipped into the chair beside him.

"Wow," Ben mouthed to Marisol, smiling, as he nudged his head in David's direction. "Thank you." He gave David's thigh a light squeeze under the table before grabbing a roll from his plate and ripping it in half. "Speaking of getting cleaned up," Ben said, his mouth half-full of bread. "Look at this handsome, clean-shaven face!"

David suppressed a smile as his hand moved up to his face, running his fingers along his cheek and chin. His hand lingered a moment before going back to his silverware as he scooped up a spoonful of mashed yucca.

"Well, since I didn't get to see you earlier really, I wanted to give you this back." Marisol reached into her backpack and pulled out *Tarzan of the Apes*, sliding the book across the table to Ben.

"Oh man. Thank you. With everything going on, I...well, thank you."

Marisol's eyes wandered to David. His head was down as he meticulously scraped the remnants of food off his plate with a

369

fork. She redirected her gaze when he looked up, catching a glimpse of her staring.

"What?" he asked, looking around him. "Was I chewing with my mouth open or something?"

"No," she started, licking her lips and nibbling on the inside of her cheek. "It's just...well, when I went through my bag..." She went quiet, her eyes moving away from David's. "Your, uh, your book wasn't in there. I don't know what happened, but—"

"No. You're right." David nodded, looking down at the table before raising his eyes to meet Marisol's. "I left it."

"What?!" exclaimed Ben, spinning in his chair to face David. "What do you mean you left it?"

David swallowed and took a breath, setting his fork down. "It was in my backpack. I could have probably saved it...but as everything was going through my head and I thought 'this is it,' you know, I just...I thought about how Marisol looked at her photo of her and her dad and her brothers and how you looked at that," he said, waving his hand toward Ben's book on the table, "and how much those pieces of little memories meant something to you. I-I thought of how upset either of you would be if you lost those things. And before I knew it, I was just letting my bag go, book and all. And I didn't care, you know?" David held his breath as his eyes danced between Ben and Marisol, waiting for either of them to speak. "It was always my dad's collectible. Not mine. It wasn't worth the fight to keep when I would rather have fought to get back to you guys."

Marisol jumped up, shoving her chair back. The sound of the wood scraping against the floor sliced through the room. She moved around the table and behind David, leaning down and wrapping her arms around his chest. Marisol rested her chin on his shoulder, holding him tight. Ben leaned over from his chair and hooked his arm around David's, taking his hand in his.

"You guys are going to make me cry," David said, swallowing away the lump quickly rising in his throat. "I don't want to be known as the group crier."

Marisol hugged him tighter. "Aww, we're a group?"

"I mean, you're a bit like a third wheel, but…"

"Hey!" Marisol let go, giving David a slight swat on the back of his shoulder. "That's not nice. For that, you're definitely known as the group crier. Officially."

Ben smirked as he leaned in and pecked David on the cheek. "It's at least a well-deserved title."

"I'm sorry to interrupt." Paul's voice flooded over them from the opposite side of the table. He sat in Marisol's chair, pulling it back toward the table. "If you don't mind, I think we should talk a bit about what you said earlier."

31

The room quieted as the remaining guests and guides trickled out of the building and back outside. Paul sat across from David, Ben, and Marisol, scribbling in a notebook laid out in front of him.

"And you're not sure where exactly you were on the grid? Even with the GPS features on the SAT phones?"

"We told you, they stopped functioning. We lost all use after we contacted Claudio for help," Marisol said. "We received one really garbled call and then nothing."

"I know we had to be at least a few miles out from the second camp," Ben added. "But my compass eventually stopped working, too. And then after a little bit, I couldn't even get back without walking in circles...even with leaving trail markers."

Paul reached down beside him into his bag and brought up a large roll of paper. He spread it out between them, displaying an aerial view of the reserve and the mapped trail sectors.

"This is like the one Dr. Morrow had," David said, leaning forward. "But hers was much smaller than this."

Paul pointed a finger down at a square northeast of the overhead view of the lodge. "This is where Julia's second camp was. Can you show me where you think you went after she went missing?"

Ben leaned forward, shoulder to shoulder with David. "Well, this is our third site." He tapped his finger a few squares away and looked to David. "If that helps any."

"I mean…" David shook his head.

"I don't think we passed through Site C at all before we ended up at Ben's fourth camp," Marisol said. "But as far as *how* we got there? I doubt we'll ever know. We kind of just stumbled our way through."

"Right," said Paul. "Down the path that 'suddenly appeared' overnight?"

"You don't have to believe us," David said, sitting back from the table. "And we've told you everything. It's not like we're hiding information."

"David," Ben turned, whispering to him. He placed a hand on David's arm. "He's just trying to help."

"It doesn't feel like it. All it's doing is making the two of us feel super shitty that we didn't map or pay attention to the compass or whatever."

"We feel bad enough as it is," Marisol added, facing Ben. She turned to look at Paul. "I *wish* we knew what direction we took. If I had to guess, I'd say whichever was the shortest route, because we weren't walking for more than a couple of days."

"You have my apologies for making you feel that way. I should have been clearer about my intentions," Paul said, sitting back in his chair. "My goal is to gather all of your information and map out a search pattern branching from the second campsite. If I knew the direction you took, I would be able to eliminate it from the first sweep."

David sighed and leaned back over the map. "Sorry." He lifted his eyes to Paul. "I want to help, but if we give you a direction and we don't know for sure, isn't that just as harmful?"

Paul offered a sympathetic smile and rolled the map back up. "You're right. And I'm sorry I pushed so much. You two have been very helpful. Hopefully, we can start a search this week once a couple more staff come in from Iquitos. As for you three, your flights are scheduled for two weeks from now. Claudio wanted me to let you know that you're welcome to stay here and take a boat back to the city then, or you can go back this week and secure lodging there. We don't need an answer now."

"I should be in the search party," said Ben.

"It's a liability, Ben. We're using staff."

"I am staff. At least some of the time. Just reinstate me now as a guide, and I can help."

Paul shook his head and shoved the map back into his bag. "You can stay as a guest and help with the other visitors until your flight, but we're not going to take you back out."

"Give me a good reason. I know my way around as much as anyone here. I can handle it."

"I don't doubt that you can, but it's not your place right now. If you want to help, you can help around here to free up some responsibilities while we dip into the staff pool. I know it's not what you want to hear," he said, standing up from the table, "but we can't have you going back out after all of this. It's not a scientific mission. That said, I know how much you care, but you need to take a step back and let us do it methodically. Okay?"

Ben bit down on his lip, annoyed. "Yeah, I get it. Okay. And I will help...around here. I've always earned my keep."

"And it's always been appreciated."

"You were really going to go back out there? Just like that?" Marisol said as they walked toward their cabins. The slats of wood creaked under their feet as they strolled along the walkway.

"Is it bad that I want to find her?"

"I think it's bad that *you* want to be the one to find her. You're not responsible you know," David said, breaking his gaze from the bright black and yellow birds flitting to and from the railings beside them.

"She was in a rush to find me..."

"We're not getting into this again, okay? It's out of our hands.

The bigger question is, what are *we* doing?" Marisol waved her hand back and forth between them.

"Well, you're going to stay here, right?" Ben stopped and turned toward David. "Why stay in the city?"

David cocked his head. "Um…hot water? Restaurants? Air conditioning?" His heart panged as Ben broke his eye contact and continued to meander down the walkway, leaving David standing alone. "Wait up. I wasn't trying to be an asshole. I guess I hadn't thought about it." He grabbed Ben's arm, slowing him and spinning him around. "We'll talk about it?"

"Sure," Ben said, offering a small smile.

Marisol looked toward the river as they resumed their walk. "I was thinking of staying. I don't have the money to stay in the city, and we have everything we need here. It's just another two weeks."

"See? Marisol is staying."

"Fine," David groaned dramatically, tossing his arms at his side. "Count me in."

"Perfect. That means tomorrow, you and I can go out on a boat and catch fish for everyone for dinner," Ben said without missing a beat.

"…wait, what?"

A soft breeze blew over Marisol as she laid in a large woven hammock. A sizeable book rested on her stomach. Marisol stared out of the screened walls, the green of the jungle below blurry in her vision. Between the gentle sway of the hammock and the slow-moving overhead fans easing the humidity, it was easy for her to relax and allow herself to zone out. She didn't notice as the heavy wooden door to the hammock room clacked against the doorframe.

"Morning," Ben said, sliding into the hammock hanging next to hers.

"Jesus! You scared the shit out of me."

"Sorry. I wasn't trying to sneak up on you or anything. What're you reading?"

"Just an encyclopedia they had in the main area. I was flipping through it at breakfast. Speaking of, I didn't see you guys."

"Oh, I overslept by a longshot." Ben chuckled to himself as he kicked off the floor, swinging his hammock. "Managed to snag some leftovers from the kitchen, though."

"And your grumpier half?"

"He's not grumpy! And he's still sleeping."

"I thought you two were going fishing."

"Well, we still are, whenever he eventually gets up. I figured it was our first night in an actual bed and without general fear of, you know, *everything*. He's allowed to sleep."

"I was up all night. I couldn't stop running things back in my head. I was kind of hoping I would find some peace in here and take a nap."

Ben draped his foot over the side of the hammock, dragging it on the floor to stop the swaying. "And here I am, busting in here to bother you. I can go."

"No, it's okay. Can I ask you a question?"

"Of course." Ben sat up in the hammock to face her.

"Say the people here go out to find Dr. Morrow and run it as usual, clear-cutting, blazing trails, all that jazz."

"Okay?"

"Do you think it's closer? I mean, we were basically still seeing those defenses up until we got out. I know the section we came out of is a bit away from here, but I guess I'm worried about people hiking and triggering it. I'm starting to question everything, you know? Like should we be stopping them?"

"Mmmhmm." Ben nodded as he ran a hand along the back of his neck. "I think that's a valid question. I think they believed us, so they know to keep an eye out for the things we mentioned. And to be honest, most of the trails here are well-blazed already. I didn't run into issues when I traveled along my regular trails, right? Maybe it's like what David said and it was the major clear-cutting into those more unexplored areas."

"I hope so. I'm just ready to go home."

"I'm sure your family will be happy to see you."

"What about yours?"

"My family is excited to see me even if it's only been a week. They're a little much."

Marisol smiled. "That sounds great, though. It's cool you all are so tight."

"The tightest," he said, returning the smile. "Anyway, I'll let you get some rest. I may stomp around outside our cabin and see if David rolls out of bed."

"Worst case, you can run in and yell 'the plants are back!' and see what happens."

Ben snorted, stifling a loud laugh. "I think he would legitimately kill me. Hell, if he pulled that with me…"

"Not to mention he'd be stuck to you like glue afterwards. He'd never leave the bed again."

"Starting to sound like a better idea by the minute then." Ben winked and got up from the hammock, walking to the door. "Hope you get some sleep."

Ben's footsteps faded as the door slammed back onto the frame. Marisol closed her eyes and listened to the slight grind of the fan above her and let her mind drift away.

Ben stood behind the long, wooden buffet table and smiled at the line of guests waiting for the food to be placed. David sat at a distant table with Marisol, watching the groups of people mingle with one another.

"Attention everyone!" Ben announced. "I would like to take a minute to let you know we have a *very* special meal prepared tonight by this *very* lovely gentleman in the back." Ben waved his arm in front of him, gesturing to the tables at the back of the room.

"Oh my God," David mumbled, his eyes widening. He slid down in his chair and held a hand up over his face.

"What is he doing?" Marisol gasped, a giant smile breaking out over her face as she glanced at David next to her.

"A few of you had the chance to meet David over the past few days. Well, he caught almost all the catfish you will be having tonight! Make sure to thank him when you see him around. He fished his butt off today. I am not generally one to be out-fished, but I'll concede this time. He also prepared a delicious twist on banana bread for dessert. So, everyone give it up for David and what I'm sure will be a wonderful meal after a day of exploration!"

David's heart sped in his chest as applause broke out from the far side of the room. He clasped his now shaking hands tighter to his reddening face as he shrunk down into his chair.

"Look at you!" Marisol said, punching his arm.

"I'm pretty sure I'm gonna puke."

"Oh, you're fine!" Marisol shoved his leg. "No one is even paying attention anymore. They're all just hungry and getting food."

"Don't be so shy!" Ben's voice boomed over the thumping in David's ears. "You should be proud."

David grumbled against his hands. "Can't I be proud in private?"

"Not today. I'm proud of you, and I want everyone to know. That banana bread is legit."

David dragged his hands off his beet-red face. "I told you I could cook."

"And you actually caught all that catfish?" Marisol asked.

"I did," David laughed. "I don't know how, but...yeah."

Ben leaned down and kissed him. "I snagged a total catch."

"Can't imagine any of this will be useful once we leave," David replied.

Marisol smiled at him. "Banana bread is *always* useful."

David laid back in a wooden slat lounge chair, looking over the river from the deck of the main hall. He watched Ben crouching at the bank as a pair of visiting researchers descended the wooden ramps and stairs to meet him. Ben waved them over, pointing out a swarm of butterflies congregating on the shoreline.

"What are you smiling about?" Marisol asked as she dropped into the chair next to him.

"What? Nothing."

Marisol followed David's line of sight and looked back to him, a playful smile crossing her face. "Admiring your beau?"

"Shut up," David said through a wide smile.

"I think it's sweet."

"You think everything is sweet."

Marisol laughed. "Not everything."

"He really is good at this—showing people all this stuff. He just lights up."

"You're so into him."

"Did you hear that they crossed out two more sections of the reserve today?" David asked, ignoring her.

Marisol's smile dropped. "I did. They still have no clue where she is."

"I heard they found a notebook."

"Really?"

"It was wet and ruined. But it has to be hers, right? It's a lead at the very least."

"Enough to search the areas around there?"

David shrugged. "I think so. I was going to ask Ben if he could find out more."

"Are you trying to ask him telepathically by staring at him or…"

"You know you're the worst, right?"

"You love me."

David huffed in response, trying to hide his smile.

"You do." Marisol leaned back in the chair and reached over to take his hand in hers. "You can't deny it."

32

David sat cross-legged in the dirt, staring at the wooden sign marking the small trail leading into the jungle before him. He absentmindedly slapped at a mosquito on his calf, scrunching his face up at the smear of blood left behind. After wiping the remnants of the squashed bug onto the leg of his shorts, he tilted his head back, hearing the soft crunching of footsteps behind him.

"Whatcha doing all the way out here?" Ben asked as he walked up behind David and leaned his hands on his shoulders.

He kept his head tilted back, staring into Ben's blue eyes peering down at him. "Thinking."

"That's a surprise," Ben chuckled, lowering himself down to sit next to him.

David leaned over and rested his head on Ben's shoulder. "I don't know. We've been so wrapped up in everything here that we haven't even talked about what's going to happen when we go back home." David shook his head. "I don't know."

Ben wrapped his arm around David and pulled him in closer. "What's going on?"

David let out a heavy sigh and closed his eyes. "I don't want to go back to what I had—what I *didn't* have. As awful and traumatizing as this trip was, I wouldn't have Marisol as a friend, and I wouldn't have met you. These last couple weeks...I haven't been happier."

Ben tightened his grip around him, running his thumb back and forth over his hip. He looked down at his arm as a few small raindrops splattered onto his skin.

"Please don't tell me it's starting to rain," David groaned, burying his face into Ben's chest. "This is so nice."

"We can always just go curl up in bed in our room. It's almost dinner anyway. I know it's not the same without the mosquitos and the dirt and—"

"Okay, smartass." David shoved him away as he pushed himself to his feet. He looked up to the sky to see waves of dark clouds rolling over the treetops. He reached a hand down to Ben and pulled him to his feet, wrapping his arms around him. David pressed his forehead into Ben's. "I'm glad I met you."

"Me too," Ben smiled, leaning against David's forehead in return. "As sweet as this is, we're going to get drenched if we don't move."

"Why can't you just carry an umbrella?"

Ben let out a soft laugh before pulling himself away. "Race you to the room?" He nudged David's shoulder and took off running back toward the lodge.

"You *know* I don't win those!" David called after him. He kicked the wet leaves at his feet before trudging after him, the rain pelting his skin as he followed.

David rolled off Ben, grabbing the sheets around their feet and pulling them up over himself as Marisol burst into their cabin. The door slammed shut behind her, shaking the furniture.

"Marisol! What the f—"

"Guys!" She rushed to the foot of the bed and climbed on top. "They found her!"

Ben shot up, his eyes widening. "What! Like now?"

"Last night, I guess. Claudio just told me at breakfast, which you two missed *again* today by the way." Marisol vibrated with excitement as she bounced her legs against the bed. "I left my food and ran straight here."

"Where? Is she here? Is she okay? Do they need help?" David's questions spilled out in a string, one after the other.

"He wouldn't tell me much. They got back early this morning before sunrise and left on one of the boats as soon as they got back."

"To Iquitos?" asked Ben.

Marisol shrugged, shaking her head. She paused, looking between the two of them, and stifled a laugh. "Oh, shit. I'm totally interrupting." She adjusted and made herself more comfortable on the end of the bed. "Makes sense about breakfast then."

Ben laughed, sitting up against the headboard. "It's alright. I think that news is way more than interruption worthy."

"If they boated her back, it has to be for medical treatment," David said, talking to himself. His eyes focused on the soft wrinkles of the sheet covering his lap. "Who went with her?"

"Paul and a couple of the other guides. Onelys went with them, I think, and Javier." Marisol laid on her side at the foot of the bed. "You're doing it again, though—thinking so hard to yourself that you're weirding everyone else out."

David raised his eyes to Marisol's and arched an eyebrow.

"Well you are!" Marisol rolled her eyes. "Claudio said not to worry and that it's all under control. We're still on schedule for our ride back to the city."

Ben shifted on the bed, pulling his legs up to his chest under the covers.

"We should find out what happened," David said, looking to Ben.

"We can definitely ask. I'll see if I can't pull Claudio aside, away from the guests."

David glanced back to Marisol, eyebrows raised. "Anything else?"

"Wow," she said, throwing up her hands and feigning insult. "Bearer of good news gets kicked right on out."

"We need to get dressed."

"Like we all didn't share a tent together for a week and change," Marisol scoffed. "I guess I'll just wait for you outside. Unless you're going back to…" She waved her hand over the bed, winking at Ben.

"We'll be right out," Ben said, making a face they'd come to know as the 'stop messing with David' look. Marisol strutted back outside, the door swinging shut behind her. Ben adjusted under the covers and picked at his nails as they sat in silence for a moment. He chewed on his lip and took a shaky breath. "Hey, speaking of the city…I was hoping to talk to you about that."

"We're only going to be there less than a day," David said over his shoulder as he slipped on his underwear and a pair of shorts.

"No, I know, but—"

"Can we get into it later? Marisol's waiting and—"

"Yeah," Ben cut him off. "Later's fine."

"I'd be lying if I said I wasn't getting ridiculously spoiled with these," Marisol said as she swayed back and forth in a woven hammock.

"They are really comfortable," David said from the hammock next to hers. "Can you believe we leave tomorrow?"

"I'm going to miss it a lot, I think. Don't get me wrong, I'm already packed, but I'm definitely going to miss it."

David stared up at the rafters as his hammock swung lightly. "Same."

Light tapping of raindrops on the roof of the hammock room created a soft pitter-patter that filled the empty space. David breathed in, taking in the smell of the fresh rain. He closed his eyes, listening to the steady droplets on the wooden roof. His heart constricted in his chest as he turned his head toward Marisol, his vision obscured by the fabric of the hammock.

"So, um...so, do you think we'll still be friends?" He squeezed his eyes shut, instantly regretting asking the question out loud.

"What?" Marisol's legs swung over the side of the hammock facing him as she sat up and looked down at him curled up in his hammock. "I didn't think you were capable of asking such a stupid question."

David opened his eyes and looked up at her, his body still squished into the smallest possible mass in the center of the hammock.

"Of course we'll still be friends. Why wouldn't we be?"

"Well, you're going back to your friends and your life and..." He shrugged, directing his eyes back to the roof. "I guess I don't know where I'd fit, if at all."

"You will fit just fine. And Ben, too. Have you guys decided what you're doing? You're more than welcome to stay with one of my brothers or my dad in Miami before heading back to Cali. Ben doesn't really have anything outside of what he has here."

David groaned, wrapped his arms around his waist and curled up tighter. "I know. He wanted to talk tonight, which is great and all, but we don't have to know right out the gates, do we?"

"*You're* the planner!"

"Ugh, I know!" David said, sitting up and throwing his head into his hands. "I want to know all the plans and intentions and he's so...so..."

"Spontaneous?"

"Yes! And I don't get that!" He shook his head and started to laugh.

"That's why he's good for you."

"Maybe." David lifted his head up from his hands. "Or maybe he'll just drive me back to my meds."

Marisol laughed and laid back in her hammock. "You'll be

fine. I am sad that we're leaving without being able to see Dr. Morrow."

"Me too. At least she's getting taken care of. Supposedly the hospital in Lima is pretty great. I talked to her briefly on the phone yesterday. They said she may be cleared in the next couple of weeks. Think she's headed straight back to Berkeley, to be with family."

"I don't blame her. I can't stop thinking about how that could have been us. Lost, dehydrated, no food…just wandering and hoping."

"That *was* us."

"Well, yeah, but you know what I mean. *Lost* lost. Truly lost. We at least had Ben's trails and camp. Though, I guess she was lucky she made it as close to the lodge as she did. We had to have gone the complete opposite direction when we split. I still don't know how they found her; it couldn't have been easy out there alone with no supplies and no help."

"But she's like you. She's a fighter. Tough."

Marisol smiled and sat back up to face David.

"From what Claudio said, it sounded like every time she tried to forge a new way out, it just closed back up…but she never gave up. At least she didn't have to deal with any of that vine shit, only mixed-up trails. There's some solace in knowing that she knows she's not crazy—that we experienced the same thing. Granted, we experienced it tenfold. But, we at least had each other. Imagine still wandering around out there, never finding our way out."

"Trust me, I imagined it plenty."

"To new beginnings."

David snorted and looked around the empty room. "Are you, like, giving a toast? With what?"

"Here!" Marisol grabbed their water bottles from the floor underneath their hammocks and handed David his. "To new beginnings."

David held up his water bottle, a grin crossing his face. "To new beginnings."

David perched on the end of the bed, his left leg tucked under him. Ben stood in the doorway, running his foot back and forth across the planks on the floor, waiting to go inside. David kicked off his shoes and looked up. Smiling, he tapped the edge of the bed next to him.

"Come join me," he said. "I literally can't stop thinking about all of the things I want to do with you back home. We can bring in food from my favorite restaurant, curl up and watch a movie —God I miss movies. I have so much space in my apartment. You can have an office to work in and write articles for journals and papers. Of course, whatever you want to do, too. I'm sure there's so much you miss."

"I was, um…" Ben continued to toe the floorboards. "I, uh…I was…I was hoping I could talk to you about that."

David's smile dropped as his heart fell into his stomach. "That's…that's not what I was expecting to hear."

Ben crossed the room and sat on the bed opposite him. He hesitated, staring at the space between them. "I…I'm not going to go," he said, the words barely escaping his mouth.

David's heart pounded in his ears. "What do you mean you're not going to go?" A million thoughts raced in his head, making him dizzy.

"Hear me out. Please." Ben reached forward and grabbed David's hands. "I want to start a project here. Research what happened…*why* it happened."

David stared blankly ahead. His insides felt suddenly hollow, his thoughts echoing inside him like a cave. "We've been here for two weeks waiting to go home. When were you going to tell me this? When did you even make that decision?"

Ben swallowed hard as he looked into David's eyes. Disappointment spread across David's face, and his shoulders slouched, his whole body sinking. Ben's mouth stayed half-parted, as if his lips were the last defense in stopping his words from shooting out. When he spoke, his voice was strained and tight. "I don't know. I didn't know how to talk to you about it. I didn't want you to hate me. And honestly, I thought…I thought maybe you would ask. That maybe you would want to stay. I know Marisol wants to move on, but I thought maybe, after everything, you'd want to stay…with *me*." Tears built up at the corners of his eyes and fell down his face.

"Ben, I *can't* stay." David's bottom lip quivered. "I have my PhD to finish an-and I just can't."

Ben wiped at his eyes. "No, I get it."

"Can't you come back? Like, come home with me, and then after a while, you can come back. *We* can come back."

Ben slid his hands away and thumbed the sheets on the bed. "Everything we saw…that was all new, not just to us, but to *everyone*. We could be the first ones to study it. This place is a research center, above all else. They logged everything we said when we came back. If it's not us, they'll just fly someone else in and assign them a post. Some person would be brought in to try and study it, study what *we* discovered. It should be *us*. Hell, it should be *you*.

"We could pioneer a whole new kind of research—hands-off, non-intrusive. We could change everything, invent a whole new way of conducting in-situ botanical studies. Imagine the possibilities. We would reinvent the field. You and me. People like us wait our whole lives wishing and waiting for an opportunity like this. It's groundbreaking, David. If we go, they'll give it to someone else, and we'll miss out on the discoveries of a lifetime. I want you to stay and do this with me. Our names, our research, *your* hypothesis and theories. It should be the two of us."

David curled his arms up around himself and watched as his tears fell onto his arms, rolling away and onto the mattress.

"I-I didn't want this to go this way. I-I lov—"

"Don't do that!" David snapped. He whipped his head up and narrowed his eyes onto Ben. "Don't even fucking say that."

"I'm not saying it to try and get you to stay. I just…" Ben moved closer and grabbed David's arm. "I would regret it if I never said it. It wasn't supposed to be with all of this attached."

"Well, it is attached, Ben. The boat's coming first thing in the morning."

"I know." Ben hesitated, licking his lips. "It's bringing a bunch of supplies I ordered for another trek out."

David stared at him, numb and frozen, like all the oxygen had been sucked out of the room. He couldn't tell if his heart was pulsing with anger or sadness or a mixture of the two.

"There's enough for the two of us. I...I ordered enough for us both to go."

"I don't understand why you didn't say anything to me. You were lying to me this whole time."

"No," Ben said, his voice shaking. "I tried...a bunch. I was fucking terrified to talk to you."

"Why?"

"Because I fucking love you. I know you don't want me to put that on you, and I'm sorry about that, but I can't not tell you. You don't have to say it back. But...you make me *so* happy, and I've never felt this way with anyone, and I didn't want to lose that. I don't want to lose *you*. Things have been crazy, I know, but I have fallen so freaking hard for you. So, I love you, okay? And I know it's probably too little too late and that I probably messed this all up."

David sniffled, running the back of his hand under his nose. His heart was in a vice, constricted and barely beating. "I love you, too."

"So stay."

"I can't." David stood up and walked toward the door. He wiped at his eyes, trying to stop the flow of the tears still pouring down his face.

Ben jumped up after him. "David, wait."

"I'll stay with Marisol tonight. It'll just be easier that way."

"Don't do that. David, please, just please don't do that. I'm sorry. I-I—" Ben broke down crying, holding his hands over his face.

David moved to him and wrapped his arms around him. Ben

hugged him back, leaning his head down into the nook of his neck and sobbed.

"I *am* sorry," he mumbled into David's shirt.

"I know you are…but the last thing I want to do is to say goodbye. I can't. So, can we just have tonight, at least what we can, and not say goodbye?"

Ben nodded into David's shoulder as they stood in the middle of the room, holding each other. "Okay."

Marisol passed through the main cabin, taking one last mental photograph. David sat in one of the chairs outside, staring off at the river and the staff unloading the covered speedboat before they packed it up to head back to Iquitos. She plopped down on the ground next to his feet, kicking off her shoes. He quietly wiped a tear from his eye with the side of his hand. She glanced up at him and placed a hand on his knee.

"Hey, what's wrong? I thought you'd be thrilled to get back home."

"Ben's staying," he half-whispered.

Marisol gasped, her mouth agape, as she moved to sit in front of him. "What? What do you mean he's staying?"

"He wants to start a new research project, focusing on everything out here. So, the stuff they're unloading? It's supplies he ordered to go back out."

"Where is he? I'm going to kill him."

A pained laugh escaped his lips. "Don't do that."

"Was he just not going to tell you?"

"I don't know what to do, Marisol." David leaned his head back against the chair. "He told me he loved me."

"He did? Wow," Marisol breathed. "What did you say?"

"I said it back."

"You did? David, I…I'm so sorry. Who says that to someone and then breaks up with them?"

"Break up? No." David shook his head, his eyes watching the

puffy clouds float across the sky. "He wants me to stay. The supplies are all ordered. He wants me to pioneer this study with him, be innovators in the field. Have it be *ours*. Put *our* names on it."

"Oh..." Marisol sat back and breathed a sigh of relief. "Then why are you sitting here?"

"Why am I sitting here?"

She shook her head in frustration. "Yes, David. Why? Why aren't you staying? You should stay."

"What? I can't do that." David pressed his fingers against his closed eyelids as a low groan slipped between his lips. "I've spent almost the last ten years studying and working for...for..."

"For what? It's already done. This was the last thing you needed for credits. Your dissertation is already written. You basically already have your PhD without needing to do anything else. And what are you going to do when you get your doctorate anyway? Or are you going to go for another degree and then another until you find something that inspires you? What's your plan?"

"I...I don't know! Not this! I don't know how many times I have to say it. I'm the last person that should be out here. You know that."

Marisol straightened and folded her arms across her chest. "Actually, I don't know that. You practically *spoke* to the jungle, David. You saved all of us, for real. That was all you. These past two weeks out here? You've been thriving. You can't deny that; you've practically said as much. You haven't stopped smiling, and you've been so happy—like really, *truly* happy. Why are you even questioning it? I think out of everyone, you'd be the one to be the most at home out here...*Tarzan*." Marisol smiled, meeting David's eyes as he looked up from his hands. She reached out and squeezed his knee. "You said you've learned from being out here that the best things come from something scary. Like I've told you before, follow your gut. Hell, screw your gut. Follow your heart."

David stared at her, the ambient sounds of the nearby birds

and lapping water encompassing them. He slowly nodded to himself, letting his eyes drift past Marisol and to the river and tree line in the distance. He put his hand over hers, still gripping his knee, and smiled. Marisol moved her other hand on top of his, her fingers patting against the back of his hand.

"I don't know what I would have done without you. Thank you for being such an amazing friend," he said as he stood up and wiped the remaining tears from his eyes.

Marisol stood and embraced him, hugging him almost too tightly. "You too," she whispered. "And that's not going to change, you know. No matter where we are or what we're doing."

"It better not." David took her hands and squeezed them, then took a deep breath and held it, waiting.

Marisol squeezed his hands in return before pushing them away. "Well, go on."

"I'm going to miss you."

Marisol smiled, shoving David toward the screen door. "Seriously. Get out." She watched as he stepped through and disappeared into the main hall.

David jogged to their cabin, ignoring Claudio calling out to him about missing the boat. The elevated walkway shook as he ran and rounded the corner to their room. He swung the door open and saw the space cleared out. Ben's backpack was gone. He checked the dresser, pulling each drawer out. Empty. His heart sank.

I'm too late. I told him I didn't want to say goodbye. Why did I say that?

He sprinted down the walkway, his shoes slapping against the wooden slats. One of the guides leaned up against the railing, knocking mud from the bottom of his boots.

"Have you seen Ben?" David asked, breathless.

"A while ago. He said he was going to take a shower before inventorying his new supply delivery and heading out. Why? Something wrong with the shipment? Is everything okay?"

"Yes," David said, grinning. "Everything is perfect." He ran down the wooden path and cut left, bursting through the door to the men's bathroom. David rushed toward the sound of running water and stopped abruptly before a curtained stall. Without pausing to catch his breath, he threw open the mildew-stained plastic sheet.

"David! What're you—"

David lunged forward and pressed his lips against Ben's, pressing him into the back wall of the shower. He wrapped his hands around the back of Ben's head as his clothes stuck to him, the cold river water pouring over them from the shower head. David's hands gripped harder, not wanting to let go. Ben pushed back, kissing him deeper in response. David gently, almost painfully, peeled his lips away and looked up into Ben's eyes. He smiled slowly.

"So…when do we leave?"

ACKNOWLEDGMENTS

I have so many people to thank, and hardly know where to begin. This passion project started from the desire to re-experience my first trip to the Peruvian Amazon back in 2010. I had the pleasure of booking my travel through a company called Amazonia Expeditions, which took me into the Tamshiyacu-Tahuayo Reserve and submersed me in a world I could only dream of. It was the beauty of the nature and culture there that inspired this story. I think I wrote some brief descriptions shortly after my visit in 2010 and expanded to the first few original pages in 2016. It was around that time my husband, William, discovered my then-titled "story.doc," and encouraged me to write. He traveled with me back to Peru with the same company again in 2017. This time, I brought my laptop and sat looking out over the rainforest and put everything I saw to paper, not knowing what I wanted to write or where the story would go. I didn't even have a plot. I let the idea slip away and left it to gather digital dust until January of 2020. With the urging of my husband, I attended a writer's conference, I joined the "writing community" on Twitter, and made connections with the indie publishing crowd. Nine months later, I not only had a complete novel, but a novel that was so much a part of me in so many ways. Writing this story helped me discover a lot about myself, and I hope you were able to find some part of yourself in the pages as well. But writing doesn't occur in a vacuum. I would not have been able to come near accomplishing this without the help of friends and family.

William, thank you for being the push that kicked this whole thing off. There is no doubt that I would have never discovered this passion without you. Thank you for always believing in me, challenging me, and pushing me to be my best. You believe in me more than I could ever believe in myself and for that, I will always be grateful. I love you so very much.

Mom and Dad, thank you for being encouraging and supportive while I attempted this crazy idea. Mom, thank you for constantly hounding me for more chapters every single week —you definitely kept me on task. Dad, thank you for both the writing resources and words of wisdom. I'm very fortunate to have you both rooting for me on this journey. I'll make sure you get #1 fan mugs to add to your collection.

Wesley, my universe, thank you for being young enough to take naps so Mommy could write this. It won't pay for you to go to college, but maybe it'll be a fun humble brag in school.

Travis, thank you for being an endless source of positive words, encouragement, and love at all hours of the day and night. Without you, I don't know if I would have had the confidence to keep going when things felt impossible. Thank you for being one of my biggest cheerleaders as well as the most amazing and supportive friend. I don't know how I lucked out with you, but you're definitely stuck with me now...can't imagine this journey without you there.

My Midtown Glitter Gals, thank you for being insanely supportive, for keeping it real, and for being a source of inspiration and a shoulder to cry on. You all are a force to be reckoned with, and the fiercest and most formidable women in the world. I will never cease to be amazed at how lucky I am to have met you all. Your never-ending light, love, and unbridled enthusiasm are unmatched and beyond appreciated. Thank you for reading my story in advance and offering me feedback. And lastly, I'm forever grateful to you for bringing so much joy and friendship into my life.

A huge thank you to my fellow authors who have helped me along the way, either by offering critique, encouragement, or from leading by example. P.J. Stanley, thank you for constantly supporting me, for being my alpha reader, for feeding my ego, and for introducing me to the world of self-publishing. To Rory Michaelson, for the wonderful advice and constructive conversations of this whacky industry, the constant encouragement, and for consistently setting the bar higher than I could ever reach with your top-tier writing (the constant laughs and smiles don't hurt either). Thank you for being an awesome friend. Blake R. Wolfe, thank you for showing me that throwing your heart on the page can make all the difference, and for being one of the most driven workers I've ever met. To my remaining writing group members, Astrid Knight, Taiylor Wallace, and Zach Harris, thank you for the hype, constructive criticism, endless support, and for keeping me forever under the influence of imposter syndrome while reading your work. And last, but certainly not least, to Anthony Nerada for being an endless light and absolute lovely human and friend, and Dalton Valette, for not only the positivity and support, but for also being one of the kindest people out there. Now that you're finished with Untouched, please check out these authors' current and future novels and short stories. They are all so talented and deserve the world.

Big thanks to the faculty at University of California Berkeley Plant and Microbial Biology department, especially Dr. Devin Coleman-Derr, who gave me permission to use his ongoing research on abiotic stress response and plant growth promoting microbial communities. Marisol wouldn't have been the same without your work.

To my beta readers, thank you for taking the time out of your lives to read my rough draft. Your feedback helped me shape Untouched into the book it is today, and I am truly thankful for you.

I would be remiss without thanking Amazonia Expeditions, the ecotourism company I used on my trips to the Amazon, of which this entire story was based. Paul Beaver, thank you for creating an environmentally and socially ethical, unique, and one-of-a-kind company that allows people like me to experience a world that very few have touched. Thank you for sitting on the phone with me and talking me through the logistics of camping, the ecosystems present in the reserve, and for sharing your passion about the rainforest and its inhabitants. Thank you to my guides: Josias (2010), Andy (2017), and Claudio (2017), for not only sharing your knowledge, but your enthusiasm for nature and wildlife. I learned so much from you and hope to run into you again one day. I hope you don't mind the use of your names, but I wanted a way to immortalize my adventure while giving credit to the inspiration. Finally, a large thank you to every staff member working in both the Amazon Research Center as well as the Tahuayo Lodge. You are all some of the hardest workers I've come across and you do so much to keep everything in perfect shape. Thank you.

Finally, thank you to the readers and for anyone that gave Untouched a chance. It means the world to me that you've picked up my little adventure. I hope it brought you something, even if just a small escape for the duration of these pages. If you enjoyed it (or even if you didn't), please take the time to leave a review. Every review helps create more visibility and allows me a chance to take feedback, improve, and hopefully share more stories with you in the future. Truly, thank you. Your support is invaluable.

ABOUT THE AUTHOR

Jayme Bean is an independent author who enjoys writing stories that speak both to the wonders of the world and the highs and lows of the human condition. Inspired by her travels around the world and her career as a zookeeper, she writes using her experiences, which lend a unique viewpoint to her stories. Jayme calls the sunny state of Florida home and shares her life with her husband, son, and four cats. Feel free to stop in and catch up with Jayme on social media and follow her future work on Goodreads and JaymeBeanAuthor.com.